THE OPEN DOOR

CHARLEMAYNE REEVES

The Chronicles of Caelium Series:

The Timekeeper's Tale
The Silver Strand
The Open Door

CAELIUM
GROVE OF EIKS
NORTH FOREST
WEST MOUNTAINS
TIMEKEEPER'S COURT
WALL OF MIST
COURT OF MOUNTAIN FAIRIES
SELKIE ISLES
COURT OF MERROWS

THE CHASM
HAIMA MOUNTAINS
TRAVELLER'S PASS
THE PLAIN
COURT OF WARRIORS
MEALITA
SOUTHERN SEA

This I know:
True love is the Source of all things.

CHAPTER 1

BEN

Benjamin frowned as he bent to eye level with the wooden beams of his latest project. The right corner slat just wasn't fitting the way he wanted. It was slightly off-center. He scanned the slat for the umpteenth time, then shook his head, frustration creasing his brow. He couldn't see anything amiss. Sighing, he moved his eyes back over the wooden bars. He'd been working on this project for weeks now. The Castle Ball was fast approaching, and if he didn't find the problem soon, his gift wasn't going to be ready in time.

At last, he spied it. There was a tiny bend in the wood at the edge of the longer beam where it slid in place with the crossbar. "Ah, there you are," he whispered. Grinning, he pulled it free.

He moved to the lathe, working to smooth the bend into submission. He had done the same maneuver more times today than he could count. The muscles in his back and arms ached with fatigue. They strained with his effort, and a line of sweat ran through his brow towards his right eye. He paused to swipe it with the back of his sleeve.

A few more passes, and he held up the beam again. The bend looked smooth, but looks could be deceiving. He'd been fooled before. This time, though, the beam fit just right. To Ben's relief, it slid right into place. He blew out a breath, slipping a wooden peg through the slot.

"Finally," he breathed.

He tapped the peg gently with his mallet, then he stepped back and admired the new piece. For all his smoothing and re-smoothing, Ben was satisfied. It looked great. All it needed now was a nice stain, then the crib would be ready for its tiny, new occupant.

Exhausted, Ben collapsed into a worn leather chair in the corner and lay his head back against the seat. He had converted the back room at the Timekeeper's Court into his workshop after the fall of the Court of Orm. Peace had blanketed the land in sleepy silence for several cycles now, and Benjamin enjoyed the quiet solace of his West Mountains home and the workshop where he spent many of his afternoons. Sunlight streamed through the open window, and dust motes floated peacefully in its rays towards the wood shavings littering the floor. His well-used lathe sat atop them in the center of the room, along with the new piece and several stacks of wood of various shapes and sizes. Pots of stain and paint sat on shelving along the walls, and his tools hung from pegs and sat in boxes beneath them on the floor.

A narrow cot perched in the corner. Rumpled blankets were strewn across it. He slept there often when he had worked well past dinner, and he was too exhausted to climb the steps to his room. Last night had been one of those nights. So had a lot of others recently. Benjamin had been working endlessly on the new piece. He was trying to have it ready before the Castle Ball, but with all the other responsibilities of his role as steward of the Timekeeper's Court, the extra work had exhausted him. Even though his woodworking added to his load, he enjoyed the silence of the shop. Working with his hands eased his burdens somehow.

He sighed as he ran a hand through his too-long hair. The thick golden strands curled on their ends and reached well past the pointed tips of his ears. He was going to need a haircut soon. He scratched absently at the edge of his jaw, where a thick patch of stubble was growing over his chin. That, and a shave. It was probably best if he did it before tonight's dinner, too. That was, if he could manage to drag his tired frame up the steps to his room.

The muscles in his temples ached, and he gazed longingly at the cot in the corner. Just a short rest before dinner; that was all he needed. He closed his eyes, too tired to move from his seat.

He was just drifting off when a loud rap sounded on the window in front of him. A small smile formed on his lips at the sound. He already knew who it was. He sighed, opening one eye to a slit and gazing groggily through the glass pane at the far end of the room.

Reina's wavy, red hair fanned out from her face like a wide halo. Her hands were cupped to the full-length glass, and her bright green eyes peered in at him through the pane. Her bare forearms were stained with dirt, and the knees of her linen pants were muddy from working in the garden. She was always there after training. It was her special place, just like the workshop was Ben's.

"Get up, sleepyhead!" she shouted. Her voice sounded muffled through the windowpane. "It's almost time for dinner!"

Benjamin closed his eye. Pretending to ignore her, he threw an arm over his face, settling further into the chair as he tried to hide his grin. He knew the action would irritate her, and irritating Reina was one of his favorite things to do. She was his best friend, after all, and irritating her came with the territory. He pressed his lips together, stifling a laugh as her growl of annoyance sounded through the glass. She waited a moment more. Ben didn't move.

"Ben! Seriously! Don't make me come in there!"

Ben dropped his arm, chuckling as he gazed through the window at her. Reina smirked. "Very funny." She made a rolling gesture with her hand, as if to say, *get a move on*. Her look was enough to make him know she meant business.

Ben held up his hands. "Alright, alright, no need to get huffy," he teased.

Slowly, Benjamin pulled himself to stand. He made an exaggerated display of moving at a creeping pace as he stretched his arms, yawning. He ruffled his hands through his messy hair, making it stand on end as he eyed the cot in the corner. "Maybe just a short nap before dinner?" He slid his eyes to Reina, watching her warning glare intensify. Her green eyes smoldered, and he flashed her another grin, holding up his hands. "Alright. I'm coming."

Reina narrowed her eyes. "You better be," she said quietly. Then she disappeared from the glass.

Ben turned back to the workshop, another chuckle rumbling in his chest. A pile of wood was stacked on the floor at his feet. He didn't see the end of one long beam sticking out in his path. A jolt of sharp pain shot up from his foot as his pinky toe turned at a wrong angle.

"Ah!" Ben hopped to the cot on his good foot, pressing his mouth together as his toe throbbed. He sat, tucking his knee to his chest and holding his foot in his palms. He pressed his hurt toe with his fingers, glad Reina hadn't seen it. He knew what she would say. "Serves you right for not covering those feet! Who works without shoes anyway, Ben?" Ben smirked at her imaginary words. Reina was always on him about wearing shoes.

Silently, he scanned the room. The floor and the workbench were littered with supplies, wood chips, and shavings. He should really pick up before dinner, but it was already so late. He thought of Reina's sharp green eyes peering through the window. She wouldn't stand for him being late again. Especially not after last time. Ben had barely made it to dinner before dessert and coffee were served. He'd come barefoot and still dressed in his work clothes. Reina had been furious.

He grinned. Her face was almost worth repeating his infraction, but he wouldn't irritate her further. Not tonight, anyway. Besides, he was too tired to do it right now. Tacking on a cleanup of the workshop to the end of his day was just too much.

So many of his responsibilities felt like that lately—too much. Most days, he felt stretched beyond his own capacity. It wasn't really the workload of stewarding the Timekeeper's Court. It was the mental strain–the toll it took on Ben's mind. He constantly worried that he wasn't doing enough. What if another day like the battle with the Court of Orm came on his watch? Would they all be ready?

Johann and Henri had helped him with the fleet of griffins for several cycles, and they mostly had it in hand. But other things weren't so easy to delegate—like the Mortal Timekeepers. Most of them were well-acclimated to life in Caelium after leaving their Mortal homes to battle the Court of Orm with the King's army. Some had elected to leave Caelium after Orm's defeat and return through the gate, but the ones who had stayed still needed training and skills practice. They needed to stay sharp. Who knew when they would need to stand and fight again?

Ben had to admit–he still felt inadequate to the task. It was terrifying, in the beginning, to think that it was mostly up to him to train the Timekeepers. He wasn't even a Timekeeper in his own right, so how could he train those who were? As a mountain fairy, he had no special skills. He couldn't control the elements like the Timekeepers could, and he had never trained anyone outside of the griffins' stable yard.

It was Arto and Lina who had convinced him. For some reason, they believed in him. The Master Timekeeper to the King and his mate, the Princess, had seen something in him he still could not see in himself. Arto had said he had a "leadership quality that people responded to," or something like that. Ben didn't quite believe him, but according to Master Arto, this quality was what made him the *obvious choice* for stewarding the Mortal Timekeepers and the Timekeeper's Court after Arto left to live with his Royal wife in Leyth Castle.

It probably had something to do with his heritage. Ben had, at one time, been the heir to the Court of Mountain Fairies. But that was before. Before Orm stole the throne from King Ard-Mathan, and before his parents, and nearly everyone he knew, had been killed and his court destroyed by the giants and the fires of the drake. Now, the Court of Mountain Fairies lay as a pile of rubble in a valley further south. Ben's heart still ached with the memory. His true home was gone forever.

After their court was destroyed, Ben and the few others who had survived had taken up residence at the Timekeeper's Court with Benjamin's grandmother Ita, where they'd lived for many cycles. But his grandmother had been killed in an attack by the Court of Orm—the last of his family was gone.

Since her death, the Timekeeper's Court had felt even less like home. Of course, Ben was grateful that Master Arto had opened his court to them, but Ben had to admit that he spent most of his days there feeling overwhelmed and out of place.

When Ben had first come to the Timekeeper's Court, Master Arto had placed him in charge of the griffins. Ben had gladly spent his days in the stable yard with Johann and Henri, two fae friends from home, and he had come to love caring for the large, flying animals that lived there. When Arto was home, he had personally seen that Ben was taught the Histories and was well-trained for combat. His lessons had served him well in the battle with the Court of Orm, and now, he felt well-equipped to pass on those skills to the Timekeepers. Teaching combat wasn't the problem. Thanks to Arto, Ben could teach those skills in his sleep. But the Timekeepers had special skills of their own, and Ben was at a loss when it came to their powers. *That* was the problem.

Each Timekeeper had developed a gifting since passing through the gate into Caelium. Ben was hopeless when it came to that side of their training. He was mystified by their abilities to manipulate Water, Earth, Air, and Fire. Thankfully, he had Reina. Almost immediately, she had taken the helm on that side of the training. Ben didn't know what he would do without her.

Reina was a Timekeeper herself and a natural leader. The

group responded well to her. Ben did, too. In fact, she had helped him understand the Timekeepers' abilities as best he could without performing the skills himself. Because of her, he'd learned to incorporate their skills into their daily training. He, in turn, had taught Reina to fly on a griffin's back and had helped her with the more physical battle maneuvers. He also taught her the Histories and incorporated the same lessons into the Timekeepers' training.

Reina was often bored with the Histories, and she would grumble and squirm in her seat in the library alcove when he brought out the large book—a copy lent to him by Princess Lina herself. Ben ignored her, no matter how much she protested. The Histories were a necessity. Often, he found himself repeating Arto's words. "You must understand Caelium's past in order to prepare for its future."

Ben understood that wisdom, but after Orm's defeat, he hoped they'd never need to fight again. So far, they hadn't, but evil would always lurk in the deep, dark corners of the realm. So, Ben vowed to keep his corner of the West Mountains ready. And, despite her protests at the Histories lessons, Reina was helping him to do just that.

Reina was like Ben's right hand. In many ways, he felt as if she had always been with him. They were so close that Ben sometimes wondered if they could read each other's minds. The two of them were a *great pair*. At least, that's what Amelie always said. Ben knew she was hinting at more than friendship, but he shrugged off her words every time she said them. He and Reina were best friends. Nothing more. Why couldn't everyone just accept that fact?

It was funny. Before Reina had come through the gate, he had always been more of a solitary creature. He preferred to spend his days in the stables with the griffins. Master Arto had somehow sensed his need to be alone when he'd first come to the Timekeeper's Court, and Ben would always be grateful that he was allowed those early cycles after his parents' death and the destruction of his court to grieve with only the griffins to see. But now? Now, he'd hardly make it through the morning before he would be off in search of Reina.

Most people made him feel self-conscious, and he felt drained if he was around anyone for too long. Every day after Timekeeper training, he would retreat to his workshop or hop on the back of a griffin and take to the skies, craving the restorative solitude of the open air. His favorite spot was just south of the Timekeeper's Court, where he would hide out beneath the falls of a wide pool, finally able to release his breath. But Reina didn't make him feel that way at all. He didn't feel drained after being with her, even if he was with her for the whole day. Not even a little bit.

Wearily, he stepped into the hall and shut the door of his workshop. He moved through the winding halls of the estate, ignoring the ache of his limbs as he trudged up the entry hall steps to the second floor. At the top, he turned right. Ben nearly always went barefoot, and he savored the feeling of the plush carpet of the upper hall beneath his tired feet. Once behind his door, he flopped onto his mattress and stared up at the ceiling. Green vines curled across the exposed beams. They had just begun to bloom, and the delicate white Moonflowers gave the room a heady scent. He inhaled, struggling to lift his heavy eyelids. If he wasn't careful, he would be lulled to sleep under their thick canopy.

Sighing, he hauled himself upright and scratched his head, causing a wood shaving to fall from his hair to his lap. He watched it as it tumbled onto his work pants, then flicked it to the floor with his thumb. Its tip was tinged dark with wood stain. Slowly, he stood and lifted his arms in a stretch, his shirt crinkling with the movement. It was stiff with dried sweat. He sniffed the crook of his arm. "Ech." There was no doubt about it. He would have to bathe before dinner. If he showed up like this, Reina's angry face would be nearly as red as her hair.

He chuckled, imagining her temper flaring out of control at his appearance and her fingers igniting with flames. Her fiery temper matched her curly locks, that was for sure. And both certainly went well with her Fire skill. He could see the pointed look in her green eyes now, glaring at him across the table, struggling to keep her heating fingers in check. It was a tempting idea, but he thought better of his prank and lifted the stiff shirt over his head as he padded to the bathing room. It was her special night, after all. He couldn't tease her too much.

The hot water had made him feel better. It had infused him with energy and loosened his tired muscles. His arms and shoulders barely ached as he pulled a clean dinner shirt over his head. He moved to the mirror, checking his appearance. The gold of his curls was tinged dark with water and the stubble still grew on the square turn of his jaw, but at least he was clean. "Good enough," he muttered. He tucked the tail of his shirt into his good slacks, grinning at the dark leather on his feet. He'd even worn shoes for the occasion. Reina couldn't balk at such an effort, even if he was going to be a *tiny* bit late.

Mountain fairies almost never wore shoes, and Ben was no different. It was the one holdover from his former life that he refused to relinquish. His grandmother, Ita, had always worn them, but then again, she'd been…domesticated.

Her days at Leyth Castle and the Timekeeper's Court had seen to that. Besides, she had been the realm's healer. Shoes were a necessity if you were going to travel all over the realm. Ben grinned at the memory, his heart giving a squeeze. He still missed her more than words could say.

Benjamin had never seen Johann or Henri wear shoes. Granted, his friends spent more time in the stable yard with the griffins than they did with anyone else, and shoes weren't a requirement for riding griffins.

Unlike her constant pestering of Ben, Reina had never mentioned Johann or Henri's lack of footwear. At first, Ben had balked when she insisted that he wear shoes to dinner. But still, she had insisted. She said it was only proper that the steward of the Timekeeper's Court wore them. Ben didn't understand why she thought it was 'proper,' but he guessed it had something to do with her being from the Mortal Realm. Rules were different there, or so he guessed.

Eventually, like most things she asked, he'd given in. Ben had pretended he hadn't seen her small smile when he showed up to dinner that first night with shoes on. But of course, he had noticed. He noticed everything about Reina.

He grinned as he flipped down his collar, smoothing its edge. If he didn't have time to shave, at least his shirt could look presentable. After all, tonight was Reina's eighteenth birthday. Marking her Mortal birthdays had given Ben great enjoyment since she'd passed through the gate. He always made time to carve her some trinket or another to add to her collection, and this Mortal year had been no different. He grinned as he imagined the look on her face when she opened his gift. He was pretty sure she was going to love it.

A towering load of lumber from the Eiks in the North Forest had appeared at his door two weeks prior, with a note from Willow, the dryad leader. At the center of the forest was the Grove of Eiks, the messengers of the Four Winds, where Willow and the other dryads made their home. Their wood was sacred.

Dear Benjamin,

A gift for your Reina, on her eighteenth birthday, from the Four Winds.

Or perhaps…it is a gift for them all.

–Willow

Benjamin had frowned down at Willow's scripted scrawl. He hadn't known what she meant by "a gift for them all." In fact, he was surprised she had sent such a gift in the first place. The note accompanying it still puzzled him, but even so, he had used a small piece of the beautiful, stripped wood from a fallen Eik to craft Reina a gift of his own.

Grinning, Ben stopped at his desk to scrawl his own quick note. Swiftly, he rifled through the stack of parchments until he found a clean scrap. Then he dipped his quill, hurrying to write his words. When he finished, he folded the note into fourths and carefully tucked it into his pocket for later. Then he swiped Reina's small gift from the shelf above the desk and headed towards the dining hall.

He thought about Reina as he moved down the steps. In the past, she'd been excited for her birthday dinner. She'd spent days planning the menu and talked endlessly to Ben of flower choices and her own attire. He frowned. This year, she didn't seem to be looking forward to it. She and Amelie had planned for the event as they normally did, but according to Amelie, Reina had allowed her to make most of the choices. Reina barely talked about the dinner, and when she did, Ben thought there was something…*off* in her voice. Even when she had babbled on about flower choices with him, there was a sadness in her eyes that he didn't quite understand.

Reina loved flowers. The courtyard gardens where Benjamin's grandmother had often worked were a testament to that fact. The central space of the Timekeeper's Court was overflowing with hanging vines, tall green plants, and heaps upon heaps of flowers from all across the realm. Every possible bloom from the four corners of Caelium had been propagated in the West Mountain dirt. There were tall Larkspurs from the North Forest, squat Water Thistles from beneath the Southern Sea, wild Mountain Aster from their own West Mountains, Desert Lilies from the East, Night-blooming Jasmine, Primrose, Evening Stars from the Selkie Isles, and so many more. Reina had spent every afternoon that Ben could remember on her hands and knees, turning over soil and clipping away wilted buds until the courtyard was nothing short of artistic beauty in living display.

It was twilight when Ben stepped into the entry hall, the heady scent of Reina's blooms lifting to his nose as he rounded the stairs. In front of him, the doors to the back courtyard were flung open, and gauzy curtains billowed inward from their high frames. The petals of the towering Evening Stars Reina had planted along the walkway lit the path to the pavilion in a calming blue glow. Their bell-shaped blossoms swayed gently in the warm evening breeze.

Ben scanned the entry hall. When no one appeared, he tucked himself beneath the stairs, hiding between two tall columns to wait for Reina. The narrow space beneath the stairs was one of his and Reina's secret spots. They always met here before dinner to have a moment alone before going in to the dining hall with the rest of the group.

Tonight, though, Ben had another motive. He wanted to give her his gift without the prying eyes of Johann and Henri. He knew the two of them would poke fun at him for it anyway, but at least he could have a moment alone with her while she opened it.

His two friends always seemed to get a good laugh from joking about his and Reina's close friendship. Benjamin had no idea why. He and Reina were just that—close friends. Amelie was no better. He remembered her grey eyes twinkling over a note he had written to Reina earlier in the week. He certainly didn't want to be pinned under her knowing grey gaze while he gave Reina her gift at the dinner table. So, he would do it here. All three of them would be with the others in the dining hall by now. He would be safe to give Reina her present, tucked beneath the stairs and out of sight.

In a moment, he heard Reina's familiar footfalls descending the steps. He narrowed his eyes. Another set of footfalls matched her pace. Ben's heart sank. *Blast.* There was someone with her.

He grimaced, tucking himself further beneath the stairs as Amelie's eager voice carried to his ears. She was ticking off the boxes for Reina's dinner tonight. Amelie's long, golden hair swished as she and Reina came around the corner, and Ben stood stock still in his hiding place, waiting for the two to pass him. Reina pretended not to notice him, but he knew she would circle back once Amelie was gone.

At last, he heard Amelie's heels clacking away from him against the marble hallway. He heard Reina give her some excuse about a forgotten scarf, then he heard her soft flats padding towards him. In a moment, she slipped in beside him, smiling sheepishly. "Hi," she whispered.

Ben didn't answer. He couldn't. Not when she looked like… like *that*. He scanned her slowly from head to foot, hoping his thoughts didn't read on his face. She looked unbelievable. He wasn't used to it, and for some reason it was making him nervous. His heart skipped as she readjusted her position, brushing his arm in their narrow hiding place.

Ben cleared his throat too loudly. "Hi," he answered. His voice reverberated off the stone of the entry hall, and he nervously stepped backward, forgetting to tuck himself into their hiding place. He was nearly standing out in the hall.

Reina jerked his arm, pulling him back in beside her. "Shh, Ben! Someone will hear," she hissed. She searched his face, her green eyes glittering in the dim light. Ben stared down at her blankly, and she frowned. "What's wrong with you? Why are you staring at me like that?"

Ben opened his mouth, then closed it again. He didn't know how to answer. Instead, he let his eyes drift. Reina's long red curls were pinned back from her face. Tiny coils trickled down beside her cheeks, and the tip of her thick locks curved down her back. Her floor-length dress was deep blue and strapless, and she wore dangling, blue sea glass earrings–a gift his friend Kai had sent from his mate–Lady Elysia in the Court of the Sea. Delicate sandal straps peeked out from the hem of her dress. They were sewn together with silver thread. Amelie's handiwork, no doubt. He swallowed, lifting his eyes again to her face.

She frowned up at him, then glanced down at her dress, smoothing her hands across her midsection.

"Is there something on my dress?" She swished her skirt left and right, looking for an imaginary stain.

Ben shook his head. "N-no," he stammered. "You look…" He gestured weakly with his hand. "You look fine."

Reina's face relaxed, and Ben smiled what he hoped was a normal smile, then reached into the pocket of his shirt, producing the note. He held it out to her, and she took it, smiling softly. "For later?" she whispered.

Ben wet his lips. "Y-yes. Later," he stammered. Apparently, he was still having trouble speaking. His head felt all muddled. But how could that be helped when Reina looked like…well, like *that*.

Reina swiped a long curl behind her neck as she studied the folded parchment, and his eyes flew to the spot, transfixed. Ben ground his teeth, gripping his fists into tight balls as he fought to ignore the sudden flurry of feeling. What was wrong with him? This was Reina he was talking to. Usually, he said what he wanted. Jokes, teasing. But right now, the curve of her neck was distracting him. He blinked at it, frowning. His throat felt sort of dry, and he pulled on the edge of his collar, clearing his throat.

Reina flicked her green eyes up to him at the sound. They crinkled at the edges with her smile, and his heart did a little flip. He dropped his eyes to her mouth, and suddenly, there was a tinny sound in his ears. He could see her lips moving, but he couldn't hear the sound. His head felt fuzzy, and he braced an arm on the wall in front of him, leaning towards her instinctively. He was so focused on her moving mouth that it startled him when Reina nudged his shoulder. She arched one brow. "Ben? Did you hear me?"

Ben tore his eyes from her lips, dropping his arm as he stood abruptly upright. He had heard her that time. "Um, yes." He shook his head. "I mean, what did you say?"

Reina grinned again, and he flicked his eyes back to her mouth. She had put something on her lips to make them slightly darker. They shimmered in the soft light. "Intoxicating," he whispered.

Reina frowned. "What did you say?"

Benjamin tugged on his collar. *Intoxicating?* He shook his head. "Um, nothing. I just...I think I need to eat. My head feels a little fuzzy."

He brushed his forehead lightly as Reina studied him curiously. He ignored her stare until she looked back at the parchment, and he finally released his breath. What in the name of the realm was wrong with him? Wasn't she the same girl he'd chased through the valley on a griffin's back yesterday?

He had come to see her in the garden, to pass a note. As usual, she'd been digging in a dirt patch. This was a particularly muddy patch right beside a small stream. When she'd turned, she'd lobbed a fat mound of mud right at his face. *Thwack!* It had hit him square in the jaw. "Ha! Take that!" she had shouted. She had jumped up and ran, cackling as Ben scooped up a mound of mud, taking off after her. He'd chased her all the way to the stable yard, where she'd mounted the closest griffin. He'd swung astride Jade, chasing her into the sky. Ben had followed her in the air all across the valley until he'd finally controlled his laughter enough to whistle low, signaling both griffins to return to the earth.

When they touched the ground, Reina had taken off again at a run, but he'd tackled her and held her still beneath him while he smooshed the mound of mud into her cheek. His hand had been so slick that it had slid across her teeth, swiping them with gritty, dark brown sludge. "Ha! Take *that*!" he had shouted. But Reina had not been amused. She sat silent beneath him with mud on her teeth, her shoulders heaving. Peals of laughter had rolled out of Ben's chest.

Suddenly, she'd let out a battle cry, scrambling from beneath his hold to pin him to the ground. Then she wiped her muddy cheek all over his face. He had let her. He hadn't wanted to stop her. Not even a little bit. Besides, he was laughing too hard to fight her off. His laughter had only succeeded in making her angrier. She'd growled loudly as her cheeks flamed red, and then she had stalked away from him, fingers flaming.

He grinned at the memory and let his eyes drift to the freckled spot on her cheek where the dark mud had been. Her skin was luminous in the evening lantern light. It looked soft. Ben wanted to brush it with his fingers. He started to reach to do just that, but he stopped himself, sticking his hand in his pocket instead. He glanced up, hoping she couldn't read his thoughts in his expression. If she could, she'd probably laugh in his face. He gripped her gift tightly in his other palm. What was he thinking?

Reina raised her slim brow. She pointed to the small package in Ben's hand, the one he was holding in a death grip. "Is that for me?" she said quietly.

Ben's eyes flicked to her mouth. *Blast.* He hadn't heard her again. "What did you say?"

Reina rolled her eyes and swiped the small package from his palm. "Never mind." She lifted the package to her ear and shook it gently, then frowned over at him. "What's with you tonight, anyway? You seem…distracted."

Ben didn't answer her immediately. The candlelight from the entry hall was striking her hair in such an interesting way. It was distracting. There were tiny threads of gold in it that he hadn't noticed before. It made her look like her hair was on fire. The muscle in his jaw flexed lightly, and he stuffed his other hand into his pocket, leaning casually against the wall. He shrugged, forcing himself to look back at her face.

"It's nothing. Just got a lot going on."

Reina pressed her lips together, but she didn't question him further. Instead, she flicked her eyes back to her present and began ripping the paper off it. She stopped mid-rip and grinned.

"May I?" she asked.

Ben grinned, relieved to have something to focus on besides Reina. "Of course. Be my guest," he teased.

Reina pulled the rest of the paper away, revealing a small wooden box. Its top was carved to resemble a pair of wings. She grinned down at them, brushing her fingers over the carved feathers. "Lovely," she murmured.

Ben smiled at her profile. "Griffin's wings," he said lightly. He studied her face, watching delight skitter across her features. "Look inside."

Reina lifted the lid. There, a satin strip of cloth cradled a small wooden bracelet. Reina gasped. She held it to the light, examining the details. Two delicate strands of wooden leaves were strung together with a small wire, and in the center, a perfect, star-shaped Mountain Aster hovered between the strands. Ben had fitted its petals with small, lavender gems—Reina's favorite color.

CHAPTER 2
REINA

She smiled up at Ben through her lashes, watching his lips break into a wide grin. His voice was gravel. "Do you like it?" he murmured. Reina's chest flushed at the sound, and she dropped her eyes to watch the bracelet's gems glitter in the candlelight. She turned it left and right, causing the light to refract in tiny prisms inside the lavender petals. The bracelet was truly beautiful. She could tell Ben had put his whole heart into it.

And it had all been for her.

Reina swallowed against a sudden lump forming in her throat. She had known this was going to be hard, but Ben was making it even harder. How could she face what was coming? How could she bear to tell him what she had to do? Blinking against her watery gaze, she pretended to clear her throat, pasting a wide smile on her lips. She wouldn't focus on that now. After all, she and Ben still had this moment, and Reina was going to make the most of it.

She could feel Ben watching her intently as she struggled to calm her swirling thoughts. She forced her focus on the glimmering gems, watching them dance in the soft light. It was mesmerizing.

Something in Reina's chest tugged as she studied Ben's gift—something deep and profound. There was something about the bracelet, some elusive meaning that she couldn't quite place. She searched her thoughts, coming up empty. But it was no wonder. Ben's stare would make reasoning evade anyone's mind. She pushed her questions down. "It's lovely, Ben. Truly." she murmured.

"Want me to put it on you?" he asked.

Reina nodded, and he held out his rough, stained hand. She laid the delicate bracelet into it, and her palm brushed his warm fingers with the motion. She pulled away too fast, causing her cheeks to flush in the low light. He flicked his eyes to her face, but she didn't lift her own. Instead, she kept her eyes on the bracelet, hoping Ben wouldn't notice her quick movement or pinking cheeks. He might tease her if he did, and she didn't think she could handle that. Not right now.

Thankfully, he didn't appear to notice her embarrassment. He grasped her forearm wordlessly in his rough hand and turned her wrist so her hand was palm up. Then he wound the small strands of the bracelet around it. "It's a symbol of love," he said quietly. Reina's eyes shot to his face, and he shrugged lightly, clearing his throat. "I, I mean, well, um, the friendship kind of love." He didn't look up, and Reina watched curiously as some unreadable emotion passed over his features. Ben sniffed. "Bracelets are common gifts where I come from. But still, I thought you might like it." He lingered at her wrist a moment more, working to fasten the clasp.

Reina studied his face quietly as he worked. Several days of dark stubble grew along his chin, and his hair was shaggier than she'd seen it in a while. The dark strands were tinged gold at the tips from hours in the sun, and they curled up on the edges, framing his face. The ends were still wet, and while she watched, a drop of water from a strand above his pointed ear landed on his collar. He was still working with the metal clasp, and he squinted his golden eyes and clenched his jaw, like he often did in deep concentration. She giggled, and he lifted his eyes to her face.

"What?" he asked, flashing her a sideways grin. He had finally succeeded in fastening the clasp, and he dropped his hands from her wrist. He braced one against the wall, and the other he shoved into his pocket.

Reina shook her head. "Nothing," she said teasingly. He studied her intently, and she swallowed hard. She was blushing again for some reason. She could feel the heat pinking on her cheeks.

Wanting to break the tension, she reached up to tug on the curled hair above his ear, letting her arm partially hide her blushed face. "Nothing except you need a haircut." She let her eyes float to his jaw. "And a shave."

Ben rolled his eyes. "I'll have you know I took extra care to be presentable this evening." He held out a foot, gesturing to his shoe. "See?"

Reina raised her brows. She laughed out loud at his booted toe, and then clamped a hand over her mouth and peeked out from beneath the stairs. Too loud. Luckily, no one had heard. She spun back to him and nodded approvingly. "Very nice," she whispered.

Ben bowed from his waist. "Thank you, oh, Birthday Queen." Reina giggled, and Ben tapped his head with one finger. "As for the hair...you can cut it this time." He shook his head, making his eyes wide in exaggeration. "I'm not letting Amelie anywhere near it." He ran a hand through his damp locks and paused at the pointed tip of his ear. "She nearly took off my ear before."

Ben mocked a blade clipping the tip of his ear, yelping silently before sliding down the wall in mock agony. Reina doubled over in silent laughter, covering her mouth.

"Come on, Ben," she whispered between giggles. "I'm breaking my own rules. We're late for dinner, and on my birthday, too." She tugged his arm, and Ben hauled himself to his feet.

Reina remembered something just as she stepped into the hall. She spun back around the edge of the staircase, nearly bumping Ben in the chest. He pulled up short, his eyes going wide. Reina grinned up at him sheepishly. "I forgot my manners," she whispered. "I meant to say thank you. So, thank you for my gift, Ben," she whispered, her face suddenly growing serious.

Light danced in her green eyes as Ben smiled down at her. "You're welcome," he murmured. "Happy Birthday, Reina."

CHAPTER 3
REINA

Reina had just found her seat in the dining hall when Amelie's cornsilk hair swished into view. Her friend plopped into the chair beside her, frowning down at Reina's neck. "Where's your scarf?"

Reina pressed her lips together. "It's ah, well, I…forgot it again. Let me go get it."

She moved to stand, but Amelie hauled her back into her seat, giggling. "I *know* there wasn't a forgotten scarf, Rei. Now, let me see!" Her grey eyes sparkled as she hauled Reina's wrist towards her face. "I figured you and Ben were off hiding somewhere, and I spotted the bracelet from the doorway." She turned Reina's wrist left and right, causing the gems to sparkle. "It's gorgeous," Amelie whispered. She wiggled her eyebrows at Reina mischievously. "Too gorgeous for a *best friend* birthday gift, if you ask me."

Reina rolled her eyes. "Not now, Am, okay? The others will hear." She flicked her eyes around the table, then looked back to Amelie. "Besides, Ben *is* my best friend. There's nothing more to it." She sniffed and lifted her napkin, spreading it primly onto her lap. "Best friends are perfectly entitled to give each other gifts."

Amelie grinned, folding her arms. "If you say so," she said quietly.

The last of the Mortal Timekeepers filed into the dining hall just as Johann and Henri took their seats across from Amelie. Benjamin appeared at the door, and Reina watched as Johann jabbed Henri in the ribs. He whispered something in Henri's ear, and both chuckled under their breath, following Ben with their eyes as he moved to his seat. Ben ignored them, flicking his eyes to Reina at the end of the table and giving her a quiet smile. Reina grinned back at him, then dropped her eyes.

Amelie watched their exchange with raised brows, then turned to give Reina a flat stare. "What?" Reina asked innocently.

Amelie grinned. "Nothing. It's nothing," she said in a sing-song voice. "Just...quite the greeting."

Reina frowned at her, then flicked a quick gaze to Johann and Henri. Thankfully, they hadn't heard her. "Amelie, seriously. Knock it off, okay? It's my eighteenth birthday. It's hard enough as it is."

Amelie gave her a knowing look. She twisted her mouth.

"You're right." She nodded solemnly, moving to grab Reina's hand. "I mean, I *know* you've been worried about your birthday. But you're here in Caelium now. Not Monrovia. The Monrovian throne is fine without you sitting on it. Your sister has it well in hand, I'm sure, and you shouldn't feel guilty that you're here and not there." She squeezed Reina's palm lightly, leaning towards her.

"I'm sorry I'm pushing you, Rei," she said, her voice low. "It's just…you two make such a great pair." She slid her eyes in Benjamin's direction. "And he's not bad to look at, right?"

Reina gave her a warning stare, and Amelie raised her hands in mock surrender. "Okay, okay. Just friends. I get it." She crinkled her nose. "Sort of." She sat upright, pretending to straighten her cutlery, then leaned towards Reina's ear. "I'm just saying, it might be good for you to admit to yourself that there's more there than just friendship," she whispered.

Reina ground her teeth. She didn't need this right now. Not with everything else she was dealing with. Amelie didn't understand. She just didn't understand her and Ben's relationship. They were strictly friends. That was all. Nothing more. But Amelie was relentless. Reina knew if she didn't concede to her, she would never stop. She wouldn't have a moment's peace for the whole evening. And her peace was slim as it was.

She flicked her eyes to Johann and Henri. They were busy stuffing rolls from the heaping baskets at the center of the table into their mouths. Reina grabbed a warm roll and began to spread golden butter across it. "Amelie, will it make you be quiet if I agree to…explore the bounds of mine and Ben's relationship?" Reina whispered.

Amelie's grey eyes sparkled. She grinned, obviously delighted. She nodded emphatically. "As long as you promise."

Reina nodded. "I promise."

Amelie pretended to lock her mouth with an imaginary key. "Good. Then, I'll be so silent, you won't even know I'm here." She flicked her sparkling grey eyes to Ben, then turned back to Reina. Amelie's face was suddenly solemn. "Just this one last thing, and then silence. I promise you. But I just have to say it. You owe this much to yourself, Rei, before you make a decision. Okay? You owe it to yourself and to Ben to find out if friendship *is* really all that is there, like you both constantly claim."

Reina took a small bite of her roll. She chewed it slowly, then swallowed, lifting her cup. She let her eyes drift to Ben over the rim of her glass. She wouldn't tell Amelie yet, but her decision was already made. She would just pretend to consider her relationship with Ben as anything more than it was. But she knew the truth. Despite Amelie's insistence, there was nothing else there to explore. Besides, she had vows to keep. She set down her glass and wiped the corner of her mouth with her napkin. Ben would do just fine here without her.

Ben was grinning widely at the girl to his left. Her short dark hair was hiding the side of her face. She giggled as she curved it behind her pointed ear and leaned closer to him, batting her long lashes. *Vic.* Reina watched as Ben leaned towards her, and she whispered something into his ear. It must have been funny, because Ben laughed his hearty laugh—the one he used when Reina said something truly hilarious. Vic giggled, letting her hand rest lightly on his shoulder. Then she lifted a fat berry and popped it into her mouth. Ben sipped at his drink, and she held another berry out to him in her fingertips. Ben eyed the berry over his glass. Then he scooted back and opened his mouth. Vic grinned at him before tossing the berry, landing it straight on his tongue. Ben pumped an arm over his head, and Reina could hear Vic's tinkling laugh from her seat. Her heart sank a little, and she lowered her glass, swallowing her tea around her tightened throat. Maybe Ben would be more than fine without her. Especially if he had Vic.

Vic was the newest resident of the Timekeeper's Court. One afternoon, she'd simply appeared in the courtyard. She claimed she had lived alone in the mountain caves after the Court of Mountain Fairies was destroyed, but somehow, Reina was suspicious of that story. Still, Vic's scraggly appearance didn't prove otherwise. She had been mud-spattered and thin, and Amelie had immediately ordered her sent to a room for a hot bath, fresh clothes, and a tray. Within days, she'd become a favorite with everyone. Everyone except Reina.

Despite everyone's positivity, Reina couldn't stand her. There was something about Vic that was…off. Reina had mentioned her feelings to Ben, but he'd shrugged her off. Ben was like that—too prone to give people the benefit of the doubt. Still, something Reina had said must have made an impact because up until now, he'd kept his distance.

Reina gripped her napkin below the table as Vic whispered something else in Ben's ear. He threw his head back, and Reina's stomach tightened at another of his hearty laughs. It seemed Vic had won him over, too.

Reina forced her eyes away, but the sound of Ben and Vic's laughter rang in her ears. She felt sick—like she might vomit. Quickly, she lifted her glass. She took a long sip, trying to ignore Amelie's pointed gaze.

Nothing was wrong with her. At least, not anything like Amelie was thinking. She was just upset about her birthday and all the things it required of her. She put her glass down, forcing her mind off Ben and Vic as she began to fill her plate.

Admittedly, she wasn't used to hearing Ben use that laugh with anyone but her. It stung a little. But that was normal, wasn't it? To want your best friend's attentions all to yourself on your birthday? Reina lifted her chin. She thought so.

Amelie continued to cast furtive glances in her direction, but Reina ignored her, until, at last, Amelie looked away. Only then did Reina release her breath, safe from Amelie's sharp gaze. She didn't hazard a look at Ben again, but from the edge of her eye, she could see Vic's dark head close to his seat, letting her hand rest on his forearm.

Reina's stomach burned as she swallowed a bite of potatoes.

She wished he would talk with someone else. Or that he and Johann would switch seats. Then Ben could talk with Henri. That would be much better.

She picked at her plate, unable to really enjoy anything, until she finally put down her fork. Amelie eyed her still hand dubiously, but Reina didn't acknowledge her. She told herself it was the announcement she was about to make that was making her feel sick. That was all it was. It had nothing at all to do with Vic, or Ben, or Vic *and* Ben. They could do what they liked. Why should she care? Things were about to change anyway, so what was the difference?

Reina picked at the edge of her napkin, thinking. She had come through the gate to Caelium in her fifteenth Mortal year. Here, her Mortal kingdom of Monrovia seemed a distant memory. It was blurred at the edges—its image disconnected and hazy. The faces of her sister and Lord Malcom were smudged, like an oil painting viewed up close. The fact that she had ever called Monrovia home felt like a dream. Still, that didn't change anything. Reina had a throne to fill—the Monrovian throne.

As heir, the Monrovian people depended on her. It was long past time for her to go home, especially now that her eighteenth birthday had come. In fact, she should've been attending her own coronation ceremony this very evening. She had already stayed far longer than she had meant to. Cecelia and Lord Malcom had been left to attend to matters while she was away, but now, it was time to go home. The kingdom was her responsibility and hers alone.

Reina let her eyes drift across the table, her heart squeezing. She was going to miss everyone so much. She grinned at Johann and Henri, who, as usual, were shoveling food into their mouths at breakneck speed. The faces of many of the other Mortal Time-keepers who had followed her through the gate sat around them, chatting animatedly. She purposely avoided Vic and Ben at the table's other end. And Amelie, who was eyeing Reina's full plate with worry creasing her delicate features.

It was funny. She had once felt like she'd never get used to life in Caelium, but now, it felt more like home than Monrovia did. These people were her family, and they needed her, too. Maybe even as much as those in Monrovia did. Her heart was divided. In more ways than one.

Silently, she let her eyes slip to Ben. He was sipping from his glass, but his eyes caught hers above the rim. He frowned at her troubled expression and set down his drink. Then he braced his hands on the edge of the table. Reina could tell that he was close to pushing back his chair and heading in her direction. That would cause a firestorm, and it was the last thing she wanted—especially tonight. She worked to pull her face into a pleasant mask and shook her head slightly, but Reina knew Ben wasn't fooled. He could always read her, right from the beginning.

Since she'd led the charge through the Main Gate, Reina and Ben had been inseparable. They were as opposite as two beings could be. He was quiet, gentle, and reserved, while she was loud, fiery, and forward. He had a cool head, and she always seemed to let her temper get the best of her. But despite their differences, almost immediately, they had become the best of friends. She'd spent nearly every waking moment in Caelium with him.

At first, she hadn't known anything about the realm or her own identity as a Timekeeper, but Ben's passion for the Histories had taught her everything she needed to know. She'd quickly learned to master her Fire skill, and in turn, she had assisted Ben with the Mortal Timekeepers' special skills training. Depending on their personality and the Mortal region in which they were raised, some Timekeepers, like herself, had a Fire ability, while others had the ability to manipulate the Air, the Earth, or Water.

Master Arto and Princess Lina could master Fire, too, and Reina had spent her early days mimicking their skill until she was able to will her fingertips to flame. Sometimes, her skill still flared when she didn't mean for it to, like when her feelings got out of control. But she was working on it.

Tending the garden seemed to help, especially if she did it every day. She had always loved to make things grow, and she even had a garden in the courtyard of the Monrovian palace. Though, it was nothing like the one she had here.

Here in Caelium, like the mysterious appearance of her Fire skill, her ability to cultivate plants had taken on a magical quality, and the beauty in the courtyard was proof. While Ben was in his workshop, she spent every afternoon turning over soil, pruning, and planting new seeds. As a result, the garden was full to bursting.

Lavender Mountain Aster had quickly become her favorite. Rows and rows of their fluted clusters dotted the open spaces of the garden like purple stars. At night, their petals produced an intoxicating fragrance. It made Reina drowsy, and she had even fallen asleep in the flower bed once. Ben had somehow known where she would be, and she had woken up with one of his messages tucked under her fingertips. Her heart squeezed at the memory, and she touched the glittering petals on her wrist gingerly. That was the first time he had left her a message.

Reina's eyes darted around the table as Ben scooted back in his chair. She widened her gaze at him pointedly, but he ignored her. Now, he was moving towards her. She wished he wouldn't. Her eyes were already pricking with memories, and she didn't want to cry right here in front of everyone.

Someone was bringing a cake out of the kitchens. There were candles on top, and their bright flames blurred together in her watery gaze as they sat it in front of her. Reina blinked down at it. The top of the cake looked like it was on fire. Reina gripped her glass and gulped past the lump in her throat as Ben knelt beside her chair. Everyone's eyes were on her.

Ben gripped her forearm lightly with his warm, rough fingers. "Reina?"

She didn't meet his gaze. Instead, she stared down at his hand.

The tips of his first two fingers were stained dark with wood stain, and she gazed at them intently, willing herself not to cry.

Amelie's chair scooted back quickly. It scraped the floor in a screech, drawing everyone's eyes. Amelie waved at the faces around the table. "Um, hi, everyone," she said cheerfully. She swiftly lifted her glass of tea, holding it high as she grinned around the table. "Thank you all for coming to this joyous occasion. Now, join me in raising a glass to our dear Reina, on the occasion of her eighteenth Mortal birthday."

The table lifted their glasses, and Amelie turned. Reina's smile wobbled, and she blinked up at Amelie, hoping her friend could read the thanks in her gaze for the diversion. "To Reina," said Amelie.

Ben lifted Reina's glass. "To Reina," he repeated with the rest of the table. Reina peeked over at him. He smiled at her gently. "Now, blow out your candles," he said quietly.

Reina turned to the cake. It was slightly lop-sided but looked absolutely delicious. Thick white frosting covered three layers, and eighteen oversized candles were crowded on top of it. One was already sliding off on the left. She braced her arms on the table and sucked in a deep breath, blowing out the flames in one try. Johann and Henri hooted while the rest of the table erupted into cheers.

Reina grinned shakily as she sliced the first piece, laying it gently on a small plate. Then Amelie took over while Johann moved to refill tea glasses and Henri served up dark, hot cocoa from the canister on the cart by the back of the room. Everyone was distracted, chatting and enjoying their sweet treats, as she pushed the plate towards Ben.

Still kneeling beside her, he glanced over at the plate. "Thanks," he murmured. He swiped a fork and took a bite, then peered up at Reina. She was trying to hold her lips in a convincing smile, but Ben's golden eyes were peering too deeply. He chewed slowly, then swallowed. "It's good," he said quietly, gesturing to the cake. "Why don't you try some? It's your cake after all."

Reina bit the inside of her lip as she slid her eyes to the cake. She shook her head silently. Under the table, she twisted her napkin between her fingers. Ben set down the fork. His warm hand stilled her fingers as he scooted her chair out slightly to face him. He frowned up at her. "Reina, tell me," he murmured. "What's wrong?"

The lump threatened her throat, and she flicked her eyes to her lap. Beneath her bodice, Ben's folded message tickled the skin where she had stashed it earlier. She scratched over the fabric, twisting nervously in her seat. "I…I don't want to tell you," she whispered.

Ben's brows pulled together heavily over his eyes. "Why?" he whispered. "We've never had secrets." He waited, and when Reina didn't answer he dipped his head to look in her eyes. "Tell me."

Reina flicked her gaze around the room. No one was looking at them, long having grown used to seeing her and Ben side by side. "Not now, okay?" she whispered. "Later. Meet me in the library. I promise I'll tell you then."

She shot him a fake smile, but Ben still didn't look satisfied. To placate him, she swiped the fork and took a large bite of her cake, chewing appreciatively. Her eyes widened. It *was* good. "Mmm." She nodded to Ben and pointed to the cake with her fork, flashing another fake smile. "Delicious," she said, her voice muffled.

She knew he could see right through her façade, but he didn't press her, somehow knowing she would break down in front of everyone if he pushed her any further. Instead, he slipped her a small smile. He stood behind her, pushing her chair back in. Then he knelt over the back of it and whispered into her ear. "Later," he murmured.

Reina shivered, his breath tickling the back of her neck and sending little chills across her arms. She nodded silently, watching him make his way towards Henri and the cocoa table in the corner.

Amelie's hair swished as she dropped herself back into the seat beside her. She placed a mug of cocoa in front of Reina as she studied Ben's back curiously. "What was that about?" she asked quietly. She took a sip from her own mug and eyed Reina above the rim, waiting.

Reina shrugged. "Nothing important," she said casually.

"What's not important?" Johann's booming voice asked, folding his large frame into the seat across from Amelie. He hadn't bothered to change from the barn, and his long blond hair had a couple pieces of straw stuck in one side. He stuffed a large bite of cake into his mouth, chewing loudly, then slurped from his mug.

Amelie eyed him in disgust. "Johann, please," she said flatly. "How many times must I tell you to chew with your mouth closed?"

Johann rolled his eyes. "Yes, Mother," he teased. He made a big display of fluffing his napkin in his lap and taking a teeny bite of cake, which he chewed exaggeratedly with his mouth pinched tightly together. The contrast of Johann's muscular body against the dainty napkin and tiny bite made Amelie grin at him despite herself. Reina giggled at them both as Amelie shook her head.

Henri scooted into the seat beside Johann. His smaller frame took up considerably less space. Henri's dark eyes studied Reina's wrist quietly as he took a sip of cocoa. "Is that a Lavender Mountain Aster you have there, Reina?" he asked, his mouth twisting slightly.

Reina looked down at her wrist and smiled. "Yes."

Henri nodded, leaning forward to get a closer look. His eyes twinkled. "A gift from our fearless leader, perhaps?" he asked, grinning.

Reina nodded. "Yes." She frowned. "Why?"

Henri and Johann shared a loaded look, and Reina flicked her eyes back and forth between them. "What?" she asked them flatly. Henri shrugged as Johann went back to shoveling cake into his mouth. Reina eyed them. She was getting annoyed. "*What*, Henri?" she insisted. The corner of Henri's lip lifted almost imperceptibly, and Reina's temper flared. She could tell she was the butt of some private joke. Her fingers began to warm. "It's my favorite flower,

Henri," she snapped. "I don't see what the problem is."

Henri remained cool. He shrugged one shoulder lightly. "Alright," he said placidly. "If you insist." He stirred his cocoa gingerly with a spoon, something he never did. The tapping sound it made inside the mug made Reina furious. She clenched her jaw, folding her arms as she struggled to keep her fingertips cool.

"If you have something to say, Henri, just say it," she said flatly.

Amelie folded her arms and stared daggers across the table at Henri. "Yeah, spit it out, Henri," she said, mirroring Reina's irritation.

Henri shared a glance with Johann, then met Reina's gaze. His eyes were sparkling, like he had a secret joke. He dropped his eyes to the bracelet.

"It's a lovely gift, Reina. Truly. I can see why it's your favorite flower. It's just…an interesting choice is all." His smug grin was about to make Reina explode. Despite her efforts, she could feel the tips of her fingers growing hot. What did he mean, *an interesting choice?*

Johann's face was turning red. He looked as if he were about to burst with laughter. Reina stared at his blue eyes pointedly, but he didn't meet her gaze. Instead, he raised his mug. Reina gripped her napkin tightly under the table. She inhaled slowly, focusing as she forced her fingers to cool. Henri wiped his lips primly with his napkin. "You know, in the Court of Mountain Fairies…"

The sound of a chair scraping the floor and a heavy hand hitting the table cut him off. Reina started in her seat, and all eyes turned towards Ben as the table fell silent. His large palms were gripping the table's edge so hard Reina thought it might break. He glared hotly in Henri's direction.

Reina blinked at him in surprise. She had never seen Ben so angry. His usually serene face was pulled into a terrifying expression. His eyes glowed like hot, golden coals and the muscle in the corner of his jaw flexed menacingly. Vic was pale in her seat to his right. She stared at her lap and didn't move as Ben glared. Henri stared back at him in shock. His dark eyes were wide circles, and his mouth was slack.

"*Enough*, Henri," Benjamin said in a low voice. He squeezed the table tighter, and the muscles in his forearms rippled.

Henri swallowed silently. "I–I'm sorry, Ben. Truly. It was just a bit of fun."

Ben held Henri's gaze a moment more, then he stared down hard at the table. He sighed deeply. "It's fine, Henri. Just...no more, okay?"

Henri nodded mutely as Ben released the table. He stood with his hands on his hips, staring at the floor. The dining hall was silent. Everyone was still staring at him. He sighed again and shuffled his feet, running a hand through his hair. "Sorry, everyone," he said, raising a palm. "Everyone just...just get back to the party, okay?"

With that, Ben moved back to the cocoa in the corner. Reina watched as he filled and downed two glasses. The room resumed their chatter as he wiped his chin with the back of his sleeve. Then, he left the room, shutting the heavy wooden doors quietly behind him.

"Go," Amelie said softly. Reina turned, and Amelie smiled at her encouragingly. "Go to him. You can start your…evaluation. He obviously feels more than he's saying if he's willing to defend you like he just did." Reina glanced at the door, then she turned back to Amelie. She nodded mutely, and Amelie squeezed her hand under the table. "I'll see you tomorrow, okay?"

Reina nodded. "Okay."

Reina knew where he would be. The library was one of their places, like under the stairs. Many nights they stayed hidden behind high shelves, whispering until long after all the others had fallen asleep. Before they knew it, the pink light of morning would come streaming through the windows, and they'd reluctantly creep to their beds before anyone could notice. Reina's chest tightened at the memories of those nights. It grieved her that this might be one of the last ones.

She padded quietly over the marble floor, the light of Caelium's dual moons casting its silver streams through the tall windows. The entry hall was empty as she crept past, making her way to the far end of the front left corridor. There, the library doors were cracked slightly, and the lantern flame was lit on the wall by the door. Reina smiled up at it. The lantern was their signal that one was waiting for the other inside.

She lifted it as she pulled the door open. Normally, a little thrill of excitement swirled in her belly at the prospect of meeting Ben in one of their secret spots. But tonight, her heart was heavy with her news. She'd wrestled with the decision for weeks, never mentioning it to him. Only Amelie knew anything about it.

Ben had said that they had no secrets. And for the most part, that was true. They told each other everything. But there was one secret she hadn't told him. At least, not yet.

The thought of telling him made her stomach twist. She could already see the way he would look at her. Her decision would crush him, just like it was crushing her. Even the thought of *telling* him was crushing her. But there was nothing for it. She had to tell him she was leaving Caelium.

And she had to tell him tonight.

CHAPTER 4
REINA

The library was silent except for the distant sound of falling water. Reina shut the door quietly behind her and turned the lock. Though no one ever had, she certainly didn't want anyone intruding on their conversation tonight. She blinked past the dim light of her lantern, following the golden light of the sconces lining the lowest bookshelves. Above her, the warm, night air floated gently through the tree branches of the large oak that marked the center of the room. Shelves rose around her, three stories high. They surrounded the tree with its thick canopy of leaves, rising out of the moss-covered flooring. A trickling stream flowed from between the shelves to the right. It wove gently through the soft floor before disappearing beneath the exposed tree roots in the room's center. Reina followed the stream, stepping on to flat stones placed at intervals in the moss.

As usual, Ben was waiting for her in the hidden alcove. He was facing the slick grey rock of the mountainside that served as the library's back wall. A waterfall flowed from high in the rock, tumbling over the stone to a pool beneath. Ben had rolled his dark pants to the knees, and his legs dangled in the water.

Reina grinned at his boots, which he'd tossed in a jumbled heap to his left. She knew he hated them. Ben only wore them when she pestered him about it, and his gesture in wearing them tonight hadn't gone unnoticed—a little extra gift for her birthday.

Her steps were quiet on the mossy floor. Ben didn't hear her until she was nearly beside him. As she knelt to remove her shoes, he half turned, watching her intently as she tucked her dress to her knees and let her bare legs dangle beside his in the cool water. She wriggled her toes in the gentle current, letting her head fall back in a sigh. The water felt heavenly.

Ben lifted his legs out of the pool and turned to face her with his arms wrapped around his knees. He rested his square chin on top of them, and though she wasn't looking, Reina could feel him peering intently at the side of her head. For a moment, she pretended not to notice, but then he nudged her shoulder with his knee, and she flicked her eyes to his face. He grinned at her, his golden eyes shimmering in the lantern light. Reina smiled back at him but quickly dropped her eyes. She bit the inside of her cheek, watching her toes swirl in the water. The look on Ben's face was too much. It was too kind, too…*Ben.*

She peeked up at him, and his smile widened. Still watching her. She wished he would look away. His staring was making her nervous. Normally, she didn't care if he gawked. She would make some jab at him, and he would laugh, and that would be the end of it. But tonight, it was bothering her.

A warm flush spread to her cheeks. It probably had something to do with what Amelie had said about exploring their friendship for something *more*. Reina sighed. Even though she knew there was nothing more to it than friendship, Amelie's words were nagging at her. Her usually sharp thoughts felt muddled. And that was the last thing she needed. Especially now.

Reina pushed Amelie's suggestions to the side. She didn't want to waste what precious little time she had left with Ben worried about something silly like whether there was more to them than friends. She already knew the answer anyway. It was friendship between her and Ben, and nothing more. If Amelie couldn't understand that, then that was fine. At least she and Ben did.

Satisfied, Reina pulled her feet from the pool and faced Ben, tucking her knees in the same way he had done. Still, she didn't look at him. She let her fingers trail near the edge of the pool, watching as the water swirled in little lines behind them. She knew she was delaying the inevitable, but she couldn't help it. She didn't want things to change between them. And she knew as soon as she told him, they were going to.

Ben sighed loudly, and Reina grinned at the sound, flicking her eyes up to study his face. He had that look he sometimes got when he was going to tease her. His golden eyes glittered mischievously, and he was wearing a lopsided grin. Reina giggled at his expression. The tightness in her chest eased a bit with the familiarity of it, and she relaxed back onto one palm. "Come on, out with it, then," she said, flicking water playfully at his knees.

Ben tapped his fingers against his forearm. He wiggled his dark brows in her direction. Reina swatted at his leg, smiling wide. "Stop it, Ben. What is it? Tell me!"

Ben leaned back onto his palms and let his head loll on one shoulder. "Ahh, just basking in being the life of the party tonight," he teased.

Reina laughed out loud, then pinned him under an arch stare. "What do you mean the *life* of the party? From where I was sitting, you looked more like the *death* of it." She scrambled onto her knees, mimicking Ben's hard stare at Henri, gripping the edge of the pool like he had the table. A chunk of moss crumbled off in her palm, and she held it aloft, growling.

Ben laughed out loud, and Reina joined in, holding her midsection as he mocked his own angry face and growled back at her.

Ben sighed, relaxing back as he shook his head. "That'll teach him to tease you on your birthday," he said, grinning.

Reina chuckled again. "I've never seen you even a *little* bit angry." She shook her head, her eyes widening. "It was shocking. I mean, I was scared for my own safety, really. And I *know* Henri was, too."

Ben smiled broadly. "Good."

Reina tapped a finger on the flat stone beneath her. She narrowed her eyes, thinking. "What was Henri talking about anyway? And why did you get so mad about it?"

She slid her gaze to him, watching as Ben dropped his eyes. He shrugged lightly. "It's nothing, really. He just made me mad. I…I didn't like the way he was talking to you." He lifted his gaze, studying her face intently as he let her absorb the words, and the uncomfortable sensation in Reina's chest returned. Swiftly, she flicked her eyes away, tucking a lock of hair behind her ear. *Why* was him looking at her making her so nervous?

Ben flattened his mouth into a line. "Henri was making you upset. And you've already been worried about this birthday for some reason." He paused, waiting, but Reina didn't meet his gaze. Instead of answering, she smoothed the fabric of her skirt. But she knew what he was talking about. She was delaying the inevitable again, but her time was almost up.

Ben bumped her leg with his foot. "There's something you're not telling me, Rei," he said quietly, "and I want you to tell me what it is."

Reina swallowed uncomfortably. Her heart was speeding up. It thumped quickly against the inside of her bodice. She suddenly felt like she was going to be sick again. She cleared her throat, and Ben sat up, peering closely at her profile. "Tell me," he prodded lightly.

Unbidden, tears formed at the edges of her vision, and she bit her bottom lip, willing them not to fall. Ben scooted closer. "Rei? What is it? What's wrong?"

A small curl above her ear had slipped out of place. Ben tucked it back carefully, the rough skin of his fingers brushing the top of her ear. She shivered, and he frowned. "Are you cold?" he asked quietly.

The concern in his voice was too much, and her gaze blurred as an errant tear slipped onto her right cheek. She swiped it quickly with the back of her arm. "I'm f-fine," she whispered shakily. She was going to miss him more than she could explain.

Ben tucked his large hand under her chin, forcing her face towards his own as another tear slid down her cheek. He wiped it with his thumb. "Look at me, Rei," he whispered. She obeyed, but the kindness in his eyes nearly took her under. She couldn't hurt him. She didn't want to.

He frowned lightly, concern creasing his features. "Now, something is obviously bothering you, and I want to know what it is. You know you can tell me anything, right?"

He released her chin and stuffed a hand into his pocket, producing a small, square handkerchief. He held it out to her, and Reina took it, blotting her cheeks with the edge. She hesitated, gathering words. It was going to kill him. Her leaving would kill him, just like it was killing her.

"It's my birthday, is all," she said quietly. Ben studied her in silence, giving her space to go on. He was so patient. It was one of the qualities Reina loved about him the most. She wished she was more like that. She swallowed and continued. "My eighteenth. It's a big one, you know?" She met his gaze briefly, and he nodded encouragingly, though she knew he didn't really know what she meant. She hadn't told him very much about her Mortal home or her place there. He knew little stories—snippets, really—but nothing beyond that. That was the way she had wanted it. Because to tell him anything would be to tell it all. And she could barely stand the thought of it.

She took a breath, gathering herself.

"In Monrovia, the eighteenth birthday is special. For a variety of reasons. One reason is because it's when a girl comes of age. This means she is free to make her own choices, out from under the protection of those who raised her." She paused. "In my case, that was my grandmother, Nan."

Ben nodded again, grinning. Reina smiled. Stories of Nan were one of the few things she *had* told him—one of the things that was safe. "Go on," he said quietly. Reina nodded, hesitating slightly as she gazed out over the water.

"In Monrovia, the eighteenth birthday is special for another reason. It's the age that most women wed." She slid her eyes in Ben's direction, watching as his face blanched slightly. He recovered quickly but not before she had seen it.

He flashed her a small grin. "Alright," he said quietly. His voice sounded tight in Reina's ears. He ran a hand through his hair as Reina pressed her lips together. She had to say this next part quickly, or she would never get it out.

"For a person who is part of the royal family, like me, the eighteenth birthday also marks another milestone. It's the date which the ascending ruler takes the throne." She paused, studying Ben's face quietly, watching as realization dawned.

He blinked rapidly, then slipped his eyes to her. "So, that means what? You're a Queen?"

Reina smiled softly. She was trying her best to keep her composure, but her heart was racing out of her chest. She nodded. "I'm supposed to be at my coronation ceremony right now. Then, yes, I would become Queen of Monrovia." She paused again, unsure how to say the next words, watching as Ben templed his hands beneath his chin, thinking.

Reina took a deep breath. The next part was the hardest. She hurried to release her words, her voice sounding high and tight in her own ears. "After my coronation ceremony, I would go to bed. And the next day…" She sped on, letting the words slip rapidly off her tongue. "I would marry my betrothed."

Ben's face spun to her quickly. He blinked in confusion. "You're betrothed?" He moved his eyes rapidly over her features, searching her face for answers.

Reina's stomach was tied in knots. She nodded mechanically, hating the desperate look on Ben's face. "Monrovian rulers' mates are chosen in infancy. For me, the mate chosen was Lord Malcom." She waited, allowing her words to sink in. She was betrothed. Somewhere, on the other side of the gate in the Mortal realm, her future husband was waiting for her.

Slowly, Ben turned to face the waterfall. He was blinking rapidly again. Reina could tell he was trying to assimilate the mountain of information she had given him, to decipher what she could mean by telling him all that she had. He leaned back onto his palms, and Reina watched as the confusing play of emotions moved across his features.

She knew she wasn't being quite fair—not forthright enough. She needed to spell it out for him, to say what she really needed to say. Ben deserved to hear it, but even so, the thought of spelling it out made her physically ache with pain.

"Who's managing the kingdom in your absence?" Ben asked her quietly.

Reina mimicked his posture. She sat back onto her palms, staring at the waterfall. "My sister, Cecilia. With Lord Malcom's help, of course." She smiled at the thought of Cecilia sitting on Monrovia's great, gilded throne. It was an amazing thought, but it wasn't fair that she leave her sister alone there any longer. The throne wasn't Cecilia's place. It wasn't her burden; it was her own. Cecilia wasn't able to bear it.

She shook her head. "But she's only there until…"

Ben swung his head to her, and silently, Reina lifted her eyes to him. His own eyes were full of horror. He ran them rapidly over her features, searching for the truth. She could see he had put the pieces together. He knew now. He knew she was leaving.

He dropped his gaze, scrambling to his feet. Reina scurried up behind him, hurrying to explain. "Ben, I…" But he spun away from her, moving to the opposite edge of the pool with his hands on his hips. Reina followed, reaching desperately towards his back. She touched his shoulder lightly. "Ben, please. Let me explain."

Ben let his head fall back, then he turned to face her, folding his arms. He was using the fake smile he used when he was upset or disappointed. It was the one he used when he didn't want the other person to know what he was really thinking. He flicked his eyes to her.

"So, when do you leave?" he said cheerfully. Too cheerfully.

Reina didn't answer. She studied his expression carefully until he finally looked down at his feet. The tiny muscle in his jaw flexed and relaxed repeatedly.

She sighed, stepping towards him to place a hand gently on his forearm. "Ben, you know this isn't easy for me. It's what's been wrong with me these past few weeks, leading up to my birthday. Why I've been so upset."

Ben pulled back slightly, leaving Reina's hand suspended in the air. She folded it around herself as he put his own hands behind his head. He stared up at the open ceiling, where the leaves of the large oak tree partially obscured the night sky. "You didn't answer my question," he said quietly.

He lowered his face to peer down at her, and Reina shuffled her bare feet on the moss floor. It tickled the tips of her toes, and she resisted the urge to reach down and scratch them. She bit her lip. "I've already stayed here too long, Ben. I should've never put Cecilia in the position she's in. It's not her burden to bear. She's not…able to do the job. And as much as it pains me, it's not fair to her that I stay." she said softly. She lowered her voice even further, flicking her eyes to the ground. "And it's not fair to Lord Malcom either."

Ben still had his hands braced behind his head. He swallowed hard, and the sharp angle of his throat bobbed up and down. He dropped his arms and stuffed his hands into his pockets. His voice was low and gruff. "I see," he said quietly. Reina almost couldn't hear him.

Silently, he flicked his eyes to her wrist, where the gems of her bracelet gleamed in the lantern light. An expression of pain passed his gaze, but he stuffed it down quickly. Then he lifted his eyes to her face. He took a step towards her. "And what about us?" he said gruffly.

Reina's heart tripped over itself. She tucked her fingers over the bracelet. Its gems felt cool against her palm. "Us?" she asked softly.

Ben took another step towards her. He was so close, she could feel the heat from his skin. He nodded, peering down at her as he held her gaze. "Us." He lifted one hand, gesturing broadly to the library. "I mean…" He shrugged lightly. "What about everybody here at the Timekeeper's Court?"

Relief washed over Reina's back. He meant *us* as in everyone. For a moment, she thought he'd been talking about the two of them—himself and her. She was glad he hadn't been. She wasn't sure she even knew how to answer that.

Quickly, she nodded, hoping her nervous expression from a moment ago hadn't given her away. She stepped back slightly, putting a little distance between them. His closeness was making her head spin. "Of course." She nodded emphatically. "Of course, I will miss you all terribly…"

Ben was nodding, too. He was smiling his fake smile, but Reina could tell that he was hurting. There was a sharp corner to his eyes that gave him away. It made her stomach hurt even more than it already did. She moved closer, grasping his forearm as she studied his face. He was staring defeatedly at the air between them, not fully meeting her gaze.

"So, that's it, then?" he said, his voice gravel.

Reina swallowed. She dropped her hand, nodding silently. "That's it. I—I have to go," she whispered.

He looked away, nodding at the waterfall. And when he turned back to her, his expression had changed. Suddenly, he was back to his old, cheerful self. He put his hands on his hips and grinned down at her. "So, how many days until you leave?" he asked brightly.

Reina blinked up at him. The rapid change in his emotions was making her head spin. She swallowed, stuffing her own feelings down. "Um, well, I…As soon as I can, I guess," she said quietly. Her brow creased as she studied the lightness of his features. Had she been mistaken at his disappointment from a moment ago? Did her leaving not bother him at all?

His grin softened thoughtfully. "Could you give it two weeks?" he asked her, sitting to put on his boots. "There's still a few things I need your help with."

Reina studied his profile curiously. It was perfectly serene—like she hadn't just crashed their whole world in around them.

The sudden change in him left her reeling. A moment ago, she was sure he was devastated. But now, he didn't seem to care that soon, he would never see her again. In fact, he seemed completely at ease with the news. And he had only asked her to stay a little longer to what—*help him out*? The thought made her chest ache.

She sat stiffly beside him as he deftly laced his boots, fumbling to tie her own strappy sandals. The straps felt thick in her fingers, and she struggled with shaking hands as Ben hopped to his feet.

Ben waited patiently until she finally succeeded, then stuck out a hand. Reina took it as he pulled her to her feet. He beamed down at her. "Happy Birthday, Reina," he said quietly. She didn't answer, and he tucked his hands back into his pockets, peering up at the moons between the tree branches. He cleared his throat. "Ah, it's getting late. Lots going on tomorrow." He began backing away. "Don't forget my note, okay?" Then he turned and jogged through the shelves and out of sight.

Reina blinked as his back disappeared between the high bookshelves. In a moment, she heard the library doors shut soundly behind him, and she sank weakly to her knees by the pool, dumbfounded.

She had thought he would be completely devastated that she was leaving him, but he barely seemed to care that she would soon be off to rule Monrovia with Lord Malcom as her new husband. She frowned down at her bracelet, thinking back to when he had given it to her beneath the entry hall steps. The way he had looked at her had made her heart soar—like she was special, like she was important. Reina bit her cheek, her throat tightening around a lump. Obviously, she had misread the situation.

Sure, Ben enjoyed her company. No one would argue that they were good friends. But to him, she was just like the rest. Johann, Henri, Amelie…Vic. Reina swallowed hard. Maybe Ben even met with Vic in secret hiding places. Maybe he passed her special notes when no one else was looking, too.

Vic. Reina hugged her knees tightly to her chest, resting her chin on top. She thought of Vic's pert face and petite frame. Ben had seemed happy enough in her company at dinner tonight. Reina bit her lip. He probably thought she was beautiful, with her dark eyes and honey skin. And she *was* beautiful. At least, Reina thought so. Anyway, Vic was certainly a stark contrast to her own fiery red curls and pale complexion. She flicked her eyes to her bare forearm. It looked almost translucent in the lantern light.

She slid her eyes back to the waterfall, silently chiding herself. She was jealous, and she had no right to be. What did she care if Ben thought Vic was beautiful? Ben was free to think anyone was beautiful that he wanted. It wasn't like she had her own claim on him or anything. Just because he was her best friend in the world—this side of the gate or otherwise—didn't give her the right to dictate his preferences. And besides, she was going to marry someone once she went back through the gate. So, why did she feel jealous?

Reina chewed on her lip, thinking. Ben would probably pursue a relationship with Vic once she was gone. Reina could definitely see that happening. And why not? Vic was a mountain fairy and so was he. Why shouldn't he pursue her? She would ask Amelie what she thought about it, though she was almost certain her friend would deny Ben's interest in Vic. For some reason, Amelie was dead set on the idea that she and Ben were meant for each other. Johann and Henri seemed to derive joy from the idea as well, even if it was just to have a little fun at her and Ben's expense.

Even with all the boys' badgering, she and Ben had always maintained that they were friends—nothing more. It was probably best that he had asked her to stay an additional two weeks, so she could prove that fact to everyone. Amelie would likely insist that she use the extra days to explore the relationship. And she would do it, if for no other reason than to prove it to her friend, herself, and everyone else that there was nothing more between them. She would help Ben with whatever it was that he needed her help with, and then she would go back through the gate, ready to move on with her life. She would take the Monrovian throne and marry Lord Malcom, and Ben would be free to do whatever he wished.

Satisfied, or at least, partially so, Reina stood. She smoothed the front of her dress, and the paper from Ben's note crinkled against her skin inside her bodice. After all she'd faced this evening, she'd almost forgotten it. She pulled it free.

Rei,

Meet me at our picnic spot tomorrow? I'll be waiting.

Ben

Reina's heart sank as she brushed her fingers across Ben's quiet lettering. It might be one of the last messages he ever gave her. Carefully, she refolded the message and tucked it back inside her dress. Then she left the library and climbed the front hall stairs to her room.

She loved their picnic spot. It was one of her favorite places in the West Mountains. Normally, she would think nothing of flying there to meet him and enjoying lunch. Maybe even a swim. But tonight, the idea of being alone with him again made her nervous. After the strange way he'd reacted to her news, she felt awkward about being around him. She wasn't sure she would know what to say once they were alone again.

She shut the door to her rooms behind her and sat heavily onto her mattress. Ben might not have been bothered by her decision, but Reina had to admit to herself that she was. Even though she knew she had no choice in the matter, it still upset her to have to leave Caelium. Not to mention Ben, Amelie, and all the others. She knew her destiny lay with Monrovia and Lord Malcom, but that didn't make things easier. In fact, she felt as if this might be the hardest thing she would ever have to do in her entire life.

Exhausted, she flopped back on the soft coverlet and draped one arm over her eyes. After she was gone, she knew Ben would move past it all with ease. He had proven that with his reaction to her news tonight.

But Reina didn't think she ever would. She would never truly be able to move on. The world on this side of the gate had marked her heart forever. And if she was being honest with herself, so had he.

CHAPTER 5

BEN

Ben's hands were shaking as he pushed his bedroom door shut behind him. He leaned his forehead against it, his mind swirling with Reina's words. Just moments ago, he'd been in the library. She had told him all of it: She was a Queen, she was leaving, and she was betrothed to someone called Lord Malcom from her Mortal kingdom of Monrovia.

The news had set Ben's mind on fire. He fumbled through the flames, searching for clarity against the searing pain of his burning thoughts. Tears threatened, and he clenched his fists, swallowing hard against the lump forming in his throat. Reina was leaving him. In two weeks, she would be gone. It didn't seem real. He couldn't believe it.

Ben could tell it had been hard for her to tell him. Her already fair skin had been even more pale than usual, and her brows had done that little pinched thing they did when she was truly upset. When she'd told him, his hearing had gone, and a tinny buzzing sound had replaced her voice in his ears. He wasn't sure what his face had done, but he was sure it wasn't good. It probably hadn't looked like what he'd intended—the face of a supportive, happy best friend.

He'd really tried to be happy for her. Truly. But his own emotions had swirled out of control, just like they had in the dining hall with Henri. They seemed to keep doing that where Reina was concerned.

Exhausted, Ben flopped himself across his mattress. He blinked up at the ceiling, imagining the hurt he'd seen in Reina's eyes when he had finally succeeded in masking his true feelings. He could tell he'd confused her with his rapid change in emotion, and he cursed himself for making her feel worse than she already did. It hadn't been on purpose. It was just that he wasn't exactly sure how to handle this.

The strength of his feelings had startled him. He'd been devastated. Jealous, even, of some man he didn't even know—some Mortal called Lord Malcom. It was crazy how out of control he had felt. He'd barely been able to stop himself from pulling her into his arms and begging her to stay. But that would have been *truly* insane behavior. And besides, what good would it have done?

It made sense now why Reina had been so upset about this birthday. When Ben thought about it, it was clear she'd been trying to tell him for weeks. Little things she had said made sense to him now, and looking back, he could see how every conversation they had shared had been tinged with her grief. In her own way, she had been trying to prepare him for what was coming. So, why was he so upset now that she'd actually told him?

Ben tucked his hands behind his head. It wasn't like Reina had always been in Caelium. She was already fifteen Mortal years old when she had come through the gate. Only three Mortal years had passed since her coming, but to Ben, it felt like she'd always been with him.

The passage of Time in Caelium didn't function like its counterpart in the Mortal realm. What seemed like a short season in Mortal years could stretch on much longer here. The cycles passed so slowly that one might forget to keep track if they weren't paying attention. And Ben hadn't been. He had been so focused on stewarding the Timekeeper's Court and all the responsibilities that fell on his shoulders, that he had to admit, he had taken Reina for granted. It just seemed to him like she'd always been here. Like she'd never leave. Even when a few Mortal Timekeepers passed back through the gate after their victory in battle with the Court of Orm, he had never dreamed Reina would go. She was too much a part of his world to make that possible.

Ben remembered when she'd first come to the Timekeeper's Court. From the start, it had been clear that she was a leader. The other Mortal Timekeepers hung on her every word, and she naturally developed her Fire skill with ease, soon helping the others to hone their own skills with confidence. She had fallen into her new life easily, and she'd helped him acclimate to his role as steward of the Timekeeper's Court in the process. He could see now that she was well-equipped to rule—a Queen, even then.

Instinctively, Ben had known that her commanding presence signaled her destiny as a ruler. But it had never occurred to him that she might leave, that there might be a seat of power for her to occupy in another realm. And it had certainly never occurred to him that there might be a Mortal man who would stand beside her in that role.

The thought made Ben's stomach turn, and he rolled onto his side, clutching his middle. He knew he held no claim on her. He had no right to be feeling the way he was feeling. She wasn't *his*. At least, not in any romantic sense. Reina was his best friend. Everyone knew that. And he had thought that was all it was. But the way he was feeling made him wonder.

Ben frowned. If he was being honest with himself, it wasn't just how he'd felt tonight. It was how Reina made him feel every day. Reina understood him completely. And Ben would miss that. As strange as it sounded, it was probably what he would miss the most—being truly known by someone else. It was the first time in his life he had experienced it. Nineteen cycles in Caelium, nineteen revolutions of the Rotha-Am, and he had never felt truly seen or understood until Reina had come through the gate.

He wondered if she felt the same. Did whoever this *Lord Malcom* was make her feel that way? Could she tell him anything and everything? Could he read her thoughts with just one look? Could she read his? Ben wondered. It seemed almost impossible to him to have two people like that in your life.

As much as that thought pained him, Ben knew he would have to let her go. If she felt her destiny was to rule the kingdom of Monrovia with Lord Malcom by her side, then he wouldn't stop her. He would support her decision the best he could. In fact, he would do his best to ensure she never knew his pain. It was what a best friend should do. And that's what Ben was to her. He was a best friend.

It would be tough, and Ben wasn't at all sure he could do it. Reina would still be here for another two weeks. In Caelium, that was a long while. It would be hard to convince her she had his support for that long.

Ben didn't even know why he'd asked her to stay. The words had just come out of him. He had thought she would want to get on with her plans as soon as possible. But amazingly, she agreed to stay.

He would have to be careful with his emotions if he was going to convince her of his support. There couldn't be any repeats of what had happened in the library. No, Reina needed to believe that he was all in for her leaving. And that would need to start when he saw her tomorrow.

By now, she'd probably read his note. It was nothing special—just a picnic invitation. Nothing they hadn't done a thousand times before. But somehow, this time felt different.

Ben wasn't sure what he would say to her once they were alone. He was afraid if he said too much, his words would somehow betray him. Or what if she read his true feelings on his face? She might see that he really wanted her to stay, and he couldn't allow that. It was selfish, and his selfishness was the last thing she needed right now.

Wearily, Ben stripped off his shirt and climbed beneath the covers. He was exhausted, and with Reina's news, he couldn't think straight. Maybe if he slept on it, he'd feel more solid about his decision to support her transition back into her old life in the morning. As it was, he wasn't sure how he was going to do it. Every trace of his body screamed for him to get up out of bed, to go to her. To beg her to stay.

He tossed and turned half the night before he sat up, balling the covers into his fists and staring hard at the door. Just a few quick steps down the hallway, and he'd be at her room. He would knock softly, and she would answer, like she'd done so many times before. Or maybe he could slip a message under her door.

Silently, he eyed his desk. Messages had never failed him. It would be easy. Yes, a note would be good, and maybe their picnic tomorrow would be easier to bear once he had told her the truth.

"*Grrrr.*" Ben flopped back down onto the mattress. He wouldn't do it. It wouldn't be right. He pressed his eyes with his fingertips and blew out a breath. There was nothing for it. He would just have to endure Reina's leaving the best he could, all the while making her believe he was okay with it.

He folded his arms across his chest and stared up at the ceiling, repeating reassurances to himself. He'd had done hard things before, hadn't he? Yes. And this was no different. He'd lost people—his parents, his grandmother, his friends. He'd even lost his home in the Court of Mountain Fairies. Losing Reina would be no different. Easier, in some ways, than losing the others. He'd known the others longer, so, surely that would make it easier. Wouldn't it?

Despite what the others might think—Johann, Henri, Amelie—the loss of her wouldn't devastate him. He was sure they would insist it would, but they were wrong. It wouldn't. He would be just fine.

If Reina had to go, then who was he to say otherwise? *Nobody*, that's who. Just a friend—someone with whom she had passed her days in Caelium. But that was over now. Or at least, it would be in two weeks. After that, he would never see her again. He would have to be okay with that. And he would be, even if he didn't feel like it right now.

Ben squeezed his eyes shut. Despite his efforts, despair threatened to close in around him at the thought of Reina stepping through the gate. He swallowed hard against the lump forming in his throat. He was fooling himself.

There was no way he would survive without her.

CHAPTER 6

BEN

Ben yawned as he squinted through his window at the lightening sky. He'd been up half the night waiting for sunrise. What little he had slept had been a constant dream. It was one he was still trying to sort through. The sun was just beginning to send its pink-tinged light over the mountain peaks. In a moment, she would appear in the gardens below.

It was Reina's custom to rise with the sun. Most mornings, she headed straight for the courtyard gardens. She said she liked those quiet moments to herself. The ones before the estate buzzed with activity, before everyone was up and moving about. She said the silence helped her to think.

Almost always, she wore one of Ben's old work shirts and a pair of his worn slacks to work in the dirt. The baggy shirt was permanently smeared with grass stains, and her knees were a solid patch of ground-in dirt. The pants were far too big for her, the thick fabric sagging around her shoes. She'd walked on the hem so often that her boots had chopped it to pieces, the strips of fabric fraying around her heels.

A small movement below caught his eye, and his heart skipped. Ben waited in silence, watching as Reina's fiery hair appeared from the great room doors below. He grinned. Her wild hair was piled in a bun on top of her head, framed by a cream-colored cloth that was tied around her head in a wide band. She had a mug of steaming tea in one hand and her bag of gardening tools in the other. Ben studied her back as she moved to her favorite corner of the garden, the one with the most Mountain Aster. She plopped her bag onto the path and disappeared beneath the overhang of a large Wisteria.

Ben had installed her a little bench there last cycle. He knew she would be sitting on it while sipping her steaming tea, waiting for the sun to make its grand appearance.

Normally, Ben would have left her in peace. Even though she was a social creature, he knew she craved her quiet solitude as much as he. He tapped his fingers on the windowsill, studying the pastel Wisteria blooms gently swaying in the breeze. He should really leave her alone. They were meeting at their picnic spot at mid-morning, anyway. But his dream still curled its long fingers around the edges of his mind. He wanted to see her. He had to.

Quietly, he made his way down the stairs and into the entry hall. He paused at the base of the steps and listened, checking the house for the sounds of early risers. Dull, morning light illuminated the corridors, but the house was silent as he crept through the great room and out the back doors.

He grinned as he stepped into the garden. His bare feet made no noise as they squished silently into the dirt path. This was the perfect opportunity for one of his favorite activities—sneaking up on her. Reina would never hear him coming. Just as she was about to take another sip from her mug, he would hop into view, and she would shriek, sloshing her tea onto the dirt.

Ben chuckled low to himself. He could just see her green eyes flashing with rage. Her fingers were sure to blaze to flame, and if he was lucky, he might even have to duck a fireball thrown from her fingertips.

It was perfect. She would spend all morning thinking of a retaliation. He would have to be on his guard.

Ben crept closer to the Wisteria, intent on his plan. From beneath the low limbs, he could see the ragged hem of her pants jiggling up and down above her boot. She set down her mug on the edge of the bench beside her, just as a slight breeze parted the blooming branches of the Wisteria. Instantly, Ben's excitement died. Reina was crying.

He shifted upright, and the quick movement caught Reina's

eye. She locked his gaze, then spun away, hurriedly swiping at her cheeks. Her hip caught the mug as she spun, knocking it from the bench. Ben lunged, but it smacked hard against the stones lining the path before he could reach it.

Ben studied the broken pottery, which now lay in two pieces. Swiftly, he knelt to pick them up, listening as Reina sucked in a shaky breath. Carefully, he turned the sharp pieces of the mug over in his hands. It was her favorite. Another one of his gifts—white clay with little circles of flowers etched on the outside.

Reina sniffed, glancing back over her shoulder. "Is it broken?" she asked. Her voice was too cheerful. Ben knew she was trying to cover for her crying. He glanced up at her. Her eyes were puffy, but she flashed a tight grin, then swiftly looked away before he could smile back at her. Ben frowned. She was upset with him.

He looked down at the mug. The handle had broken off, and the jagged edge of what remained of it stuck menacingly out from the side. "Ah, it's nothing a little work in the shop won't fix."

Reina swiped her cheek as she stood, reaching for the mug. "I'll do it," she said quickly. "No need for you to waste your day. I know you've other things you need to be doing." She grabbed for the pieces in his palms.

Ben couldn't get his words out fast enough. "Reina, be careful! It's…" But it was too late. She hissed, drawing her left hand away as a trickle of blood ran down her thumb. "The edge is sharp," Ben muttered.

Reina sucked on her thumb, then pulled the wound back to examine it, frowning. Her face flamed hot. "Yes, Ben, I can see that," she snapped. She half turned, wringing her thumb.

Ben set the pieces down onto the bench. "Let me see it," he said softly. He reached for her palm, but Reina tucked it to her chest, shielding it protectively.

"It's fine," she said tightly. "Really. I can take care of it. Just…" She fluttered her opposite hand. "You can just go do…whatever it is you were headed to do before, okay?" She brushed past him, jogging swiftly back up the path into the house.

Ben frowned after her as she turned left inside the great room. He was confused. He didn't understand why she was so upset with him. Was it something he said last night? Maybe how he had behaved? He needed to find out—to make amends before things got worse. To make sure she was okay.

He started after her, moving quietly into the great room before rounding the corner to the kitchens. Reina was standing by the long counter on the far side of the room. She was rummaging through the cabinetry, probably looking for some clean cloth to wrap her finger. Ben knew just where it was, but it was too high for her to reach. Quietly, he moved behind her, opening the cabinet to her right. Then he reached to the highest shelf, where a neat stack of cloth was stored.

Reina froze as his arm reached above her head. She cradled her hurt thumb against her chest, not moving as Ben reached for a clear jar storing dried Tamarisk blooms next to the cloth. His arm brushed her shoulder with the movement, and Reina stiffened, sidestepping towards the basin.

Ben frowned at the side of her head as he tore a neat strip of cloth off with his teeth. Reina never acted this way. She was always easy and light around him—full of fun when she wasn't pestering him about one thing or another. At least, she had been until last night.

He held out his palm, and Reina dropped her own into it mechanically. She didn't look at him, keeping her eyes on her thumb and her mouth flattened into a thin line. A red heat was flushing up the sides of her neck as he sprinkled crushed Tamarisk blossoms onto her wound.

Ben watched her reaction curiously, then dropped his eyes to her wrist. The lavender gems of her bracelet glittered up at him like a beacon. He swallowed, pushing the swirl of emotions the bracelet caused down deep. Silently, he flicked his eyes back to her face. He studied her expression as he wound the cloth strip around her thumb. He wanted to ask her why she'd been crying, but her face was so shuttered he decided to leave it for later.

He held her hand for longer than was necessary, wishing she would tug it away with some smart comment like, *Can I have my hand back now, Benjamin, or do you plan to keep it all day?* But she didn't.

Unbidden, the details of last night's dream sprang into his

mind, and he had the strange urge to rub his thumb in small circles over the soft, pale skin on the inside of Reina's wrist. He stared down at it, resisting, and instead flicked his eyes back to her face. That was no better. A small, red curl had escaped her head wrap. He studied it, wishing he could wind it around his fingers. Maybe he would even release the rest of her hair from its bonds. Then he could lace all his fingers through it.

Reina met his gaze, and Ben dropped his eyes. Heat rose in his chest. *Where did that come from?* This was Reina he was thinking about. The woman he'd spent nearly every day with since she had come through the gate. Now, he was daydreaming about lacing his fingers through her hair? About rubbing her wrist? Crazy talk.

He stared blankly down at her bandaged thumb until Reina finally tugged her hand out of his grasp. "Thank you," she muttered. She tucked her hand back against her chest, swallowing tightly.

Ben didn't say anything. His thoughts were still swirling. And the way his thoughts were going, it was entirely possible that he might be going insane.

He wanted to tell Reina about his dream, but he didn't know how she might react. Things had happened in his dream world that she might think were…well…insane. So, he decided against telling her for now. It was better to stay quiet about it, at least until he could sort out how *he* felt about it.

He jerked his thumb over his shoulder. "I, um, I'm gonna take your mug to the workshop, okay?" he stuttered.

Reina bit the inside of her cheek. She nodded. "M'kay," she said quietly.

Ben backed away. "Okay. I'll, uh, I'll see you later." He didn't wait for her to respond before he spun away.

He finally let out his breath when he reached the garden. The sun was just peeking over the mountain top as he padded back to the bench under the Wisteria. Silently, he tucked himself beneath the low branches and sank onto the seat. He braced his elbows on his knees and laced his fingers into the front of his hair, his heart thumping against his chest. "What is *wrong* with me?" he muttered.

Between Reina's news and his dream, he felt like he was going crazy. And maybe he was. Since when couldn't he tell Reina exactly what he was thinking? And why had he suddenly been so interested in her wrist and her hair? His mind felt muddled, and his feelings swirled like a whirlwind inside his chest. It took him several moments of hiding under the Wisteria until his mind quieted. Then he picked up the pieces of Reina's mug and headed to his workshop.

He set the broken mug on the workbench as he rummaged through the shelving, searching for something to bind the pieces. Soon, he found what he was looking for. He grabbed the small canister and moved back to the workbench. Then he swiped the binder on the handle and pressed the cup tightly against it. He held the new binding together with a leather strap, then he set the mug by the window to dry in the warm sunlight.

Ben collapsed into his chair and propped his feet on the table, letting his head rest against the top of the seat. He had decided to hide out in here until breakfast was ready, so as not to risk another encounter with Reina. Ben didn't think he could trust himself to be alone with her right now.

Exhausted, he closed his eyes, but visions from last night's dream wouldn't let him rest. Images of Reina played rapidly behind his eyes, until finally, he gave up. He sighed, running a palm through his hair as he sat upright.

There was absolutely no way he could be alone with Reina again. Not after what he'd nearly done this morning. He'd been dangerously close to losing control with her, and he couldn't imagine her reaction if he had given in to his impulses. Ben shook his head. *Crazy.*

He rested his forearms on his knees, staring out the window. He'd have to make up some excuse to skip out on their picnic. Reina wouldn't mind. He was sure of it. That much was obvious from her cool behavior towards him this morning. He snagged a piece of parchment from the corner of the table and bent to scrawl a quick note, bowing out of his and Reina's plans. Then he folded it into quarters and left it on the table for later.

He flopped back down in his seat, determined to relax. But all he could think about was Reina. Her leaving, her stiff behavior towards him, her upset feelings. It was no use. He was buzzing inside. There was no way he could relax.

Sighing, he hauled himself from the chair. He moved to the window, gazing out at the rising sun. He tapped his foot restlessly as the golden rays shone through the pane. Ben closed his eyes, thinking. What he needed was a good project. Something to occupy his hands. Something to occupy his thoughts.

He turned back to the room, searching. The crib sat finished at the side of the room, a clean linen sheet draped across it. But there, in the corner beside it, Willow's towering pile of lumber sat in a tall heap. Except for the small piece he had cut to craft Reina's bracelet, it was still unused.

Another image from his dream sprang into his mind at the sight of it, and suddenly, Ben knew what he was going to do. In fact, the idea was perfect. It would be a detailed project, one that would take him well over the two weeks until Reina left to finish. It would be intricate and detailed. Absorbing. But that was what he needed right now—a project that would completely consume him, one that would make him forget what he was about to lose.

He crouched down by the large pile of lumber and ran his fingers along the smooth lines of the wood. It would keep his hands busy, that was for certain. Then maybe he wouldn't be thinking about touching Reina's wrist or hair with them. Too, it would keep him away from the Timekeeper's Court. Reina would be out of his sight, and hopefully, out of his mind. At least, that's what he hoped.

True, he would miss most of Reina's last days in Caelium, but that was probably for the best. She was going to be gone soon, anyway. He would have to get used to being without her.

Ben stood, propping his hands on his hips. It was decided. He would start the project as soon as possible. The others would just have to handle the responsibilities at the Timekeeper's Court without him. Besides, he was pretty sure Amelie and Reina could handle the household and the Timekeeper training alone. Henri and Johann had been taking care of the griffins by themselves for quite a while now, too. Everything would be fine.

It would have to be. He was going to the Court of Mountain Fairies. Today. It was the right decision. He was sure of it.

It was for the best—for the both of them.

CHAPTER 7

BEN

Ben swiftly slipped the message under Reina's door, then he jogged down the stairs and out the front door. He didn't slow until he was well away from the house. After their awkward exchange this morning, he didn't want to risk facing Reina again. Or anyone else, for that matter. His feelings were too raw. He wasn't sure how many people knew about Reina leaving, and he couldn't trust how he would react if someone asked him about it. Certainly, he didn't want a repeat of his explosion with Henri at the dinner table last night.

At the far right of the estate, the stable was nestled at the base of the sheer grey mountain. Thankfully, Ben managed to remain unseen as he slipped inside. He'd already decided he would take Cyrus. Cyrus was the fastest and highest-flying griffin in the fleet, and he was somewhat of a favorite of Ben's. Cyrus had been the first griffin Ben had ever flown.

Technically, Cyrus belonged to Princess Lina. He had been a gift to her from Master Arto. But the princess had insisted on keeping Cyrus stabled at the Timekeeper's Court, and she encouraged Ben to ride him whenever he could. Ben was glad. He loved riding Cyrus.

He moved through the cool darkness of the stable hall, stopping frequently to stroke the feathered necks of the griffins that nudged his shoulder as he passed. Cyrus's stall was on the left end. He had already heard Ben, and the griffin's large head was sticking out of the stall, his beak bobbing up and down as he chirped impatiently. Ben could hear his large talons scraping the inside of the stall door. "Shh, Cyrus. We have to be quiet," Ben whispered. Cyrus studied him intently with his large eye and was quiet as Ben gently tucked a bridle over his head and opened the stall door.

Within moments, Ben and Cyrus were soaring high above the valley. Ben tugged gently on the reins, guiding Cyrus south over the mountain tops. The griffin glided smoothly, pumping his large wings in the mid-morning air. The sun's rays warmed Ben's skin, and he savored the fresh air and the free feeling of flying high above the trees. Ben did some of his best thinking on the back of a griffin. There was something about gliding high above the landscape that freed his mind and settled his body. It always helped him to gain perspective.

His tension from the morning relaxed as Cyrus soared, and Ben allowed his mind to drift. He closed his eyes, lifting his hands from the reins and holding them out at his sides. He balanced on Cyrus's furry back, his hair blowing back in the warm breeze. For a moment, it felt as if he were the one flying, and exhilaration filled his chest. But too soon, his dream from the night before floated to the front of his head. His body reacted to it instantly, and this time, it wasn't because of Reina.

Ben bobbled on his seat, and he quickly returned his hands to the reins, his heart leaping into his throat as his eyes snapped open. The earth tunneled below him, and he quickly righted himself, gripping Cyrus's flanks with his legs. Once he had his seat, he closed his eyes again, working to calm the hammering in his chest.

Parts of his dream had been terrifying. Terrifying and true. Some of it had been memories—horrifying things that Ben had worked hard to forget. The images wreaked havoc behind his eyes, events from his childhood too terrible to mention. He couldn't stop a cold sweat from breaking out on the back of his neck, and he tensed up on the reins, causing Cyrus to squawk in disapproval.

Ben knew the griffin could feel his tension. Cyrus pumped his feathered wings erratically, and Ben patted his furry back, whispering low. "Sorry, boy," he said soothingly. Ben tried to relax as Cyrus's flight became smooth, but it was no use. Inside, his feelings were in a firestorm. He gripped the reins with white knuckles as visions from the night played over and over in his head, and reality blurred with memory in a terrifying display.

Ben stood alone on the hillside. Soot tinged his nostrils, and a heavy cloud of dark smoke hung low over the scene. He gazed in desperate horror into the valley below, where his home, the Court of Mountain Fairies, was being destroyed before his eyes.

Screams of the fallen rang loudly in his ears. Ben wanted to run to them—to help in some way, but his feet were glued to the earth. And when he opened his mouth to scream, no sound emerged. He stood frozen, forced to watch helplessly as the court of his ancestors was burned to the ground by the fiery breath of the drake—the great dragon that served the Court of Orm. Giants smashed boulders into the walls and crushed fae women and children beneath their heavy feet, while fae traitors from within stormed and pillaged, carrying spoils and prisoners away.

Ben fell to his knees, tears gathering in his gaze. Horrifying screams lifted to his ears, and when he could stand it no longer, he turned away, weeping bitterly.

But that's when the parade started.

Countless, lifeless, half-charred bodies stood in a long line to Ben's right. He lifted his eyes, swiping his cheeks as they flooded past him in a steady stream. They were all crying, making Ben cry again, too.

The bodies were passing a small object between themselves, holding it to their faces. Ben squinted at the object, watching as a young woman lifted it to her cheek. A clear tear ran into the object—a small glass jar, already half full. They were putting their tears into the little glass jar, he realized.

The process continued until the last figure stopped in front of him—a small girl. She held the jar to her cheek, collecting the damp streams into it. Then, she handed the jar to Ben. Ben gazed silently down at the glittering liquid, then, slowly, he brought the edge of the jar to his face. The small girl smiled as she watched his tear roll past the jar's lip.

Ben pulled the jar away, holding it at eye level. He examined the liquid swirling inside of it. So many tears, so much loss. It was almost more than he could bear. He didn't know why he did what he had done next. But for some reason, he had turned his wrist. He poured the jar's precious contents onto the charred earth.

It seemed a waste. All that grief poured out on the ground. And for what? What was the point of it?

He stared in silence as the tears gathered themselves into a small pool at his feet. Then, slowly, they began to trail down the hillside towards the rubble of the ruined court in the valley below. Ben watched with interest as the tiny rivulet continued its path, a thin, jagged line, until all at once, a loud rumble began.

Ben braced himself as the ground began to shake. Then, suddenly, the earth separated before his eyes, a large crack forming beneath the stream of tears. Ben jumped backward as a rushing gush of water flowed up from an underground cistern. It met with the tears, and he stood slack, watching in amazement as the roaring water flowed to meet the ransacked North Wall. The dark blue water flowed around the tumbled stone, wrapping the corners of buildings, filling empty spaces, and picking up fallen stones and debris in its path. It continued to flow until it filled the entire valley, and all the fires set by the enemy were quenched.

Briefly, the valley looked like a small lake. Despite the reality of his memories, somewhere deep in the back of Ben's mind, he knew this was a dream. But it looked so real. The surface of the water glittered brightly in the sunlight, and it seemed almost impossible to Ben that he had just witnessed the destruction of the court moments ago.

Soon, the water began to dissipate. It flowed on from the valley, a rippling river between two distant mountains, until all the water had drained into the Southern Sea. Once again, the valley was dry. All that was left were the remnants of the walls and the shells of a few buildings—the palace where Ben's family and a few others had lived. Everything else was gone.

Ben stared blankly at the scene. He was at a loss. What now? What am I supposed to do? *he thought. He stood limply on the hillside, staring as a mixture of fear and grief gripped him, threatening to pull him down. Everything he had ever known was gone. Orm had taken it all.*

Slowly, gently, a familiar female voice lifted to his ears. Ben blinked, searching the valley below him for the sound. At once, his eyes landed on his home inside the tumbled North Wall. Someone was inside. He could hear her. Curious, he headed that way.

He entered the court through what once had been the doors. The frame was destroyed, but a few foundational stones still remained. A tiny flower had sprouted at the base of them. Ben raised his brows as he peered down at it. He was amazed that such a delicate flower could have survived the fires and subsequent flooding he had just witnessed. Yet, here it was, smiling up at him. The five-pointed petals swayed softly in the breeze, and on impulse, Ben bent to pluck it. He twisted the stem between his fingers, watching the flower twirl. It was a Lavender Mountain Aster.

Cyrus tucked his wings as he touched down on the hillside. He shook his feathered neck as he scratched up the dirt and immediately bent to nibble at the ground. Ben slid from his back, surveying the dismal scene. His former home, the Court of Mountain Fairies, lay below him in the valley. Or what was left of it. The court was in shambles. The ground below was dry and scorched, the walls were almost completely demolished, and what buildings were left standing were half blown to bits, empty shells of their former selves.

Ben sat heavily on the charred ground. He hadn't been back here in so long. In truth, he had avoided it. It was just too painful to visit. He pressed at his left chest, his Amloga Flame, his connection with the Source, aching with memories. They swirled in his head, the real horrors of the court's destruction mixing with the events of his dream world.

Ben frowned. His dream—he still didn't know what to make of it.

Ben took one last, long look at the kitchen of his former home before he turned to walk back through the great hall. To his amazement, the palace was in great shape. In fact, despite the destruction of the court, it looked exactly as he remembered it. The high ceiling with its templed beams soared over his head, while long, handwoven tapestries depicting the Histories of the Mountain Fairies hung on the whitewashed walls at his sides. The deep stain of the wide-plank, wooden floors looked untouched by fire, and a gentle breeze blew through the wide windows to his right. Ben turned to look at them. Somehow, they were unbroken. The glass panes glittered in the sunlight, flung open on their frames, their gauzy curtains billowing inward towards the high-backed chairs that had once served as his parents' thrones.

At the front of the hall, he pulled the large doors wide. He gazed longingly back at the throne seats behind him, imagining at any moment that his parents would appear. But they didn't, and the seats remained empty.

He moved to step outside, but just as he did, his bare toes thumped into something hard. He pulled back, wincing as sharp pain shot through his foot. Ben blinked in surprise at the blocked doorway, where Willow's lumber lay in a towering pile. He scanned the large heap of wood, wondering how it had come to be at his door. It was so high that it reached well above his head. Willow's note about it being a gift for Reina and for "them all" was still attached conveniently at his eye-level.

Ben swiped the note, scanning its words as an idea wisped through his head. He knew exactly what he was going to do with the gift. If Willow's lumber had materialized in his doorway, then surely, his tools were somewhere close, too. Ben grinned as he jogged back through the palace, searching each room. Sure enough, he found them, tucked neatly into the corner of the back study. Everything he needed was there.

Soon, he had hauled the lumber to the ransacked doors of the court and set up a makeshift workspace. He worked there, cutting and shaping Willow's gift, until the sun was dipping below the horizon and his shirt was drenched in sweat.

At last, Ben stepped back, satisfied with his progress. He wiped his brow with his sleeve and sat heavily on a nearby stone that had once been part of the North Wall. After working all day, his throat felt like sand, and his stomach grumbled. Ben swallowed, pressing his middle. He needed to find something to eat and drink somewhere. Somewhere being the operative word. He stood, scanning the valley. He just didn't know where that somewhere might be. There was nothing around him but silence.

Just moments later, he heard the sound of a rickety cart hobbling down the cobblestone street behind him. Ben raised his brows. He knew that sound. There was no one else it could be. Ben spun, watching the towering cart rolling down the cobblestones towards him. It was Jubal with his baker's cart. Ben grinned. He hadn't seen the old satyr in many cycles, not since before the court was destroyed.

A large burlap cover was tied over Jubal's cart, shading his goods. Ben could smell the fresh baked bread hiding beneath it. It made his stomach twist and his mouth water. Jubal's shaggy legs and chipped hooves were visible from behind the cart's rickety wheels, and Ben could hear him playing the breathy notes of his flute, which he always wore around his neck, with his free hand. On the cart's right side, a large, clay water jug sloshed with the cart's movements. Ben eyed the water jug greedily. He hoped Jubal would give him a drink.

Jubal stopped his cart just in front of Ben's newly crafted door. Ben had raised it at its old place where the crumbled walls of the North met the West. Now, the singular door stood as one-half of the towering entrance of the once lively Court of Mountain Fairies. Jubal stuck his head around the side of his cart, surveying Ben's work with his shrewd gaze. Then he moved closer, pulling the hood of his cloak off his head to reveal the two twisted horns that curled back behind his ears. Jubal grinned, showing his long teeth, then he squinted at Ben with his watery blue eyes.

"Benjamin, it's good to see you, my boy," he croaked. "I was wondering how long it would take you to come." He eyed Ben's sweat-soaked shirt, then he reached to lift the clay cup that hung by the water jug, filling it with cool, clean water. He handed it to Ben, then he turned to lift the corner of the burlap. He lifted a large, round roll, tearing a generous piece. Then he passed it to Ben in his gnarled fingers. "Eat, drink, and be merry, young Ben," the old satyr said cheerfully.

Ben smiled around a mouthful of bread. He recognized Jubal's words. It was what they used to say in the Court of Mountain Fairies when they sat down to eat after a hard day's work. Ben chuckled at the fond memory before he downed the rest of his cup and pulled another large bite from the roll.

"Thank you, Jubal."

Jubal nodded as he leaned his shoulder wearily against the side of his cart, wincing. He grinned at Ben, gesturing to his weathered frame. "Old bones," he said, patting his furry thigh. "They don't hold out like they used to."

Ben smiled. "What are you doing here, Jubal? I thought you lived in the caves now. At least, that's what Ma Ita told me."

Jubal nodded. "I did, for an age, after the destruction. But the Court of Mountain Fairies has always been my home. A little fire from the drake couldn't keep me away forever." He gestured to the shell of a building behind them. Inside, various pots and jugs, a small table, and a bedroll were visible from the street. "So, I moved back in."

Ben studied Jubal's makeshift dwelling. He frowned. "Why?" he asked.

Jubal folded his arms. For a moment, he gazed into the distance. Then he peered back at Ben, grinning. "Well, someone's got to feed you while you work. Speaking of 'old bones,' carry mine with you when our home is restored, will you?"

Ben frowned over at him. He didn't quite catch the old satyr's meaning, but still, he nodded respectfully.

Jubal nodded once in return. "Good. Now, I'll be going." He flipped the burlap back over the top of his cart and moved to the rear, picking up the handles. Then he began rolling the rickety cart back down the street. He called over his shoulder before he rolled the cart out of sight. "I'll see you soon, Benjamin!"

Ben patted Cyrus's flank as he studied the ramshackle court. Despite the destruction, Ben half expected to see Jubal's baker's cart rolling down the scorched street behind the crumbling walls. But, of course, the old satyr was nowhere to be found. The court lay in dejected silence.

Silently, he scanned what was left of the North Wall until his gaze landed on the tumbling foundation of the court doors. His eyes widened. Amid the broken stone and charred wood, something green had sprouted from the dry, charred earth. Quickly, he moved down the hillside to get a closer look.

There, at the left edge of the foundation, grew a solitary Mountain Aster. Its lavender petals smiled up at him, swaying gently on the breeze. Just like in his dream. Ben bent to pluck it, twirling it in his fingers.

He turned to head back up the hillside, wanting to put it in his pack on Cyrus's flank, but he recoiled as he took his first step. His toe had bumped against something hard. It throbbed as he stepped back, blinking at the towering pile of lumber in amazement. It was Willow's gift—the same one that should have still lain in his workshop at the Timekeeper's Court.

Ben chuckled to himself. It wasn't lost on him that this was the *third* time he had bumped his bare toes on a pile of wood. Granted, once had been in his dream last night, but still. If Reina knew, she would absolutely say, "I told you so." And she had told him. Thousands of times. Ben shook his head. Apparently, her admonishments about his bare feet had been right. He was even hurting his toes in his dreams now.

He folded his arms, thoughtfully surveying the strange appearance of Willow's gift. Of course, he already knew what he was going to do with it. In fact, he didn't know why he hadn't thought to haul the wood here himself.

It wasn't going to be easy. He knew that. Just being back in the old court was hard for him. But even so, the project was ideal. Hopefully, it would keep his thoughts of Reina at bay, and it would put some physical distance between the two of them before she had to go.

Ben couldn't think of anything better. He couldn't trust himself to be around her for long, so this was the perfect solution. He reached into the bag stashed on Cyrus's side and retrieved a piece of parchment and a quill. Then he knelt to scrawl a quick note. He wouldn't be going back to the Timekeeper's Court anytime soon.

When he was finished, he rolled the parchment and tucked it safely beneath Cyrus's bridle, then patted the griffin's flank and whistled low, signaling him to fly home to the Timekeeper's Court.

He watched as Cyrus disappeared in the sky, then he spun to

face the ruined doors. There was just one thing left to do before he got started.

He was going to see Jubal.

CHAPTER 8

REINA

melie pushed from her stomach to her feet in one fluid motion. "Up!" she shouted. The Mortal Timekeepers groaned across the training ground in the far end of the courtyard, struggling up from their stomachs into a crouch. It was only the tenth time they had done it in a row.

Reina ground her teeth, hopping to her feet. She brushed a sweaty lock of hair out of her eyes, flicking her gaze across the group. Judging by the grimaces and the amount of sweat they were all producing, it had been a bad idea for her to let Amelie lead the morning exercises.

"Down!" Amelie shouted.

Reina collapsed onto her stomach, arms and legs quivering. Yep, she *definitely* regretted her decision to let Amelie lead.

Normally, Ben led the group in a light, physical warm-up in the courtyard beyond the gardens. After, while the Timekeepers recovered, he would lead a discussion of the Histories. Then Reina took over for special skills training.

But not today.

Today, Ben had slipped a note under her door after he had bandaged her thumb. His hurried scrawl had cancelled their plans for a picnic at the waterfall. He had said he would be gone for most of the day. Reina bit her lip. Despite their awkward exchange in the kitchens this morning, she couldn't deny she was disappointed. It was the first time he had ever cancelled their plans like that.

Reina guessed she understood why he had cancelled. Sort of. After their exchange in the kitchens, it was probably best that they had a little distance. Still, she had been looking forward to their time together at their picnic spot. The waterfall was one of her favorite places in the known worlds.

At last, Amelie clapped her hands. "Okay, that's enough for today. Thanks, guys!" she said cheerfully. Only a slight sheen of sweat lit Amelie's forehead. She barely looked winded.

Reina slid her eyes to the group. Several Timekeepers had collapsed onto their rumps, chests heaving, and some of them were even lying flat on their backs. Reina rolled to her own back. She stared up at the sky, catching her breath and making a mental note not to let Amelie run the session again.

"Reina, your turn!" Amelie's voice was chipper. Reina snuck her a look. Amazingly, Amelie looked better than she had before they had started exercising. Reina didn't know how she did it. Amelie sighed happily, her hands braced on her hips. "Light exercise in the morning feels great, doesn't it?" she said, grinning.

Reina rolled to sit with a groan. She tucked her arms around her knees. "Yep. Feels great," she said, wincing.

Reina sighed, scanning the courtyard. She didn't feel much like special skills training today. Ben's message swirled in her head, and she couldn't focus. Anyway, she'd be gone in two weeks. They would all have to learn to manage without her soon.

She drummed her fingers on her leg, thinking. Maybe she'd give the Timekeepers a little independence, let them practice on their own. She stood, dusting the dirt from the front of her shirt. "Fires, by me. Earths, to the back. Winds, to the right," she called loudly. "Waters, to the library. Practice manipulating the waterfall in the alcove. Try to start and stop the stream."

Slowly, everyone struggled to their feet. Reina wondered how much special skills training they would actually get done after that morning exercise session. They looked as exhausted as she felt. The Timekeepers moved slowly into their positions as Reina stretched her arms above her head, wincing. Her sides and shoulders were already getting stiff.

Amelie dabbed the glistening skin on the back of her neck with a cloth, eyeing Reina curiously. "Not leading training today?"

Reina shook her head. "Not today," she muttered.

Beyond them, the Winds lifted their arms, stirring a large vortex in the middle of their small circle. To their left, the Fires lit a bundle of sticks at their feet into a high blaze. Then they split the flame into parts, balancing it on the tips of their fingers. The Earths were further back, near the sheer mountain side. They always trained at a far distance, just in case. Reina watched as one of them raised a fist. The others followed suit, and when the group lowered their arms, a jagged rift opened in the ground beneath them. Reina could feel the earth shake from where she stood. She shrugged. "They're all nearly experts in their special skills, anyway."

Amelie stepped in front of Reina's face. Her delicate features were pulled into a worried frown. "Reina, what's wrong? I know you. Something's up."

Reina twisted her lips. She flicked her eyes around the courtyard anxiously. "I don't want to tell you here," she whispered. "Someone might hear."

Suddenly, Amelie gripped her hand. Reina frowned. "Am, what are you—?"

"Come on," Amelie said quietly. "We need to talk."

Amelie tugged Reina away from the group, towards the gardens near the great room doors. Reina followed behind as Amelie slipped quietly beneath the heavy boughs of the Wisteria, safely out of earshot.

Amelie pulled her down on the narrow bench. Ben's bench. Reina flicked her eyes to the smooth wood. He had made it for her last cycle, after he had discovered that she liked to sit beneath the Wisteria, hidden from view. Reina's heart squeezed at the memory.

Amelie put a slender hand on Reina's forearm. Her blonde brows were curled into an anxious frown. "Okay, nobody can hear us under here. So, tell me."

Amelie's grey gaze peered worriedly as Reina bit her lip. Unbidden tears were already forming in her bright green eyes. "I've made a decision," she said quietly. She took a deep breath. "I'm leaving, Amelie."

Reina lifted her gaze, watching Amelie stare at her blankly. Amelie blinked in confusion. "To meet Ben? Is that what this is about—you and Ben? Did something happen between you two in the library last night?"

Reina swallowed against the lump in her throat. "Sort of," she said softly.

Amelie nodded, but Reina knew she didn't understand what she was trying to say. Even though Amelie knew Reina had been wrestling with the decision to leave Caelium for weeks, she could tell that her friend wasn't grasping her meaning right now. Reina sighed, picking at the wood on the edge of the bench beneath her. It was killing her to have to make Amelie upset. She had already had to do it with Ben, and she hated the idea of doing it again. "He's upset with me," she muttered. "Ben, I mean."

Amelie frowned. "Why? What happened?"

Reina scrubbed her boot in a soft patch of dirt. She watched as the soil turned up over the toe, stalling for time. "Because…" she hesitated. "Because I'm leaving soon," she said quietly. She lifted her eyes, hating the look of hurt on Amelie's face. The look of realization was dawning in her grey eyes.

"I'm leaving Caelium."

CHAPTER 9

BEN

Ben swiped the sweat from the back of his neck, breathing hard. The sun was beaming down on him, and his shirt was tacked to his back with sweat. If he remembered the path he had taken with his grandmother Ita correctly, Jubal's cave was only a short distance north of the court. She had visited the old satyr sometimes, and once, Ben had gone with her.

His breath was coming hard and fast. He should have easily made the hike, but his body was exhausted. Ben felt as if he really *had* hauled Willow's wood from the palace and rebuilt the court's ruined doors like he had in his dream last night.

In reality, all he had done today was haul Willow's towering lumber pile inside the court's tumbled walls. The simple task had drained him, even though it had been physically easy.

But it wasn't the physical labor of the task that exhausted him. Ben knew that. It was the memories. The emotional strain of being home again, of seeing the valley in ruins and remembering the people he had once loved there and had lost. The harsh reality of coming face to face with his home after so many cycles, of seeing the destruction of the Court of Orm in sharp relief was almost more than he could bear. That feeling was only multiplied by the enormity of the task that lay before him, the one his dream had sparked, the one the appearance of Willow's gift in the valley of the Court of Mountain Fairies had solidified.

No, the physical labor was a relief from it all. A release. It was his emotions about the past and his future without Reina that were the problem. But that was why he was here, wasn't it? To help him move on? To put some distance between himself and Reina, and hopefully, to help him forget her once she went back through the gate to Monrovia?

Of course, so far, it wasn't working very well. Thoughts of Reina still dominated his mind. There was what had happened in the kitchens this morning, but also, there was his dream—the rest of it.

Ben sighed heavily. He couldn't think about that right now. He didn't want to. In fact, he'd do anything to keep from thinking about it. Mostly because his dream had brought the reality of her loss to the forefront of his mind. He knew now that when she went back through the gate, it would be more than he could bear. The loss of her was going to crush him.

Besides, he didn't know what to make of Dream Reina—the one who had wrapped her arms around him in the kitchen of the palace, the one who had pressed her lips to his own. Ben shook his head, trying to clear his thoughts. No, he couldn't think about that. He wouldn't. It was better to keep busy. It was better to throw himself into this project and try and forget—better for him and for her.

His project was what he was coming to talk with Jubal about. His dream had inspired him, and on his way to the valley, Ben had made another decision. The doors were a large project, yes, but Ben had decided that the project wasn't quite large enough. If he was going to forget Reina, he would need something bigger. Something enormous. Something like rebuilding an entire court.

Of course, Ben had no idea how he was going to accomplish that. But he was sure of one thing: It would keep his mind as busy as his hands. And for a long time, too. That was what he needed right now. It was either that or allow his pain to pull him under.

The Court of Mountain Fairies had not only been the fairies' home. It had once been home to the satyrs, too. But the satyrs' entire lineage had been destroyed in the raid by the Court of Orm. That is, all of them but Jubal.

When the drake had come, and with it, the giants and the lyncaths—the terrifying wolf beasts of Orm's making—the gentle satyrs hadn't had a hope of escape. Their beautiful section of the city, the Northwest Corner, had been completely demolished, and with it, all of their kind. All except Jubal. The old mountain satyr was the only one left.

After his loss, Jubal had taken up residence in the caves in the foothills just north of the court. Ben was ashamed to admit he hadn't been to see Jubal in a long while—too long, in fact. He hadn't been since well before his grandmother Ita had died.

Ben's father and mother had been rulers of the court before the blaze, and Jubal had always been loyal to them. Ben knew he should have made more of an effort to see him, but the memories were just too hard. So, he had avoided Jubal just like he had avoided his home.

Ben pulled in a deep breath as he crested the hill near Jubal's cavern. He could hear Jubal's small flute, and the fresh smell of baking bread wafted from the cave's opening. It had been a long time since he had sampled Jubal's bread in his waking hours, but the memory of its sweet taste from his dream set Ben's mouth to watering.

Jubal had always been a baker. Ben could remember him rolling his rickety cart up and down the cobblestone streets of the Mountain Court, selling fresh bread and baked goods and playing his flute as he went. Everything he made was delicious, and some of his goods even had healing properties. In fact, it had been Jubal who had taught Ben's grandmother, Ita, to make the Tamarisk cakes when she had become the realm's healer in her youth.

Jubal had always been wise, and he'd always had a special connection to the Source. Long ago, he had been Ben's parents' trusted advisor. His gift for interpreting dreams had made him a valuable wealth of knowledge to the leaders. Often, Ben's parents had called on him for wise council, and to Ben's knowledge, he had never steered them wrong. Ben was hoping Jubal might do the same for him now.

That is, if he could convince Jubal to help him. As it was, Ben wasn't sure he would be able to. He wasn't sure what state he would find the old satyr in. Ben had only ever known Jubal as a jovial soul, but he had heard that the satyr had since turned to bitterness. Over the cycles, the loss of his family and home had made his heart turn hard.

Since the fall of the court, Jubal often travelled to Meallta to sell the baked goods from his cart in the streets. But that had all ended when Jubal was set upon by thieves several cycles ago. They broke his cart, and that had been the final affront to Jubal's high spirits. With the loss of his livelihood, along with everything else he had ever known, Jubal's heart was broken beyond repair. He hadn't left his cave since.

Ben stepped over Jubal's threshold, blinking in the dim light of the cave's opening. Jubal had his back to him, pulling a fresh loaf from a makeshift oven at the back of the oblong room. He hobbled backward on his hooves as he balanced the loaf on his wooden tray. Jubal looked older and weaker than Ben remembered. His grey hair was shaggier, and his dark horns were chipped and worn where they curved around his ears.

Ben didn't want to startle him. He cleared his throat softly. "Jubal?" he said quietly.

He hadn't succeeded. Jubal jumped, toppling the loaf of bread from the wooden tray. He reached to catch it but quickly jerked his hand away from the steaming loaf as it fell to the cave floor.

"Grrah!" Jubal shouted. He wrung his hand where he'd fumbled the hot bread, stomping a hoofed foot as he glared in Ben's direction. Jubal's shaggy brow frowned above his watery blue eyes. "What do you want?" he growled.

Ben blinked in surprise. Jubal had never spoken to him harshly. He tucked a hand to his chest, dipping his chin. "It's me, Jubal. Benjamin, remember?"

Jubal bent his gnarled hand to swipe the ruined loaf from the ground. He tossed it into the fire. "Yes, I know who you are," he spat. "So? What do you want?"

Ben twisted his mouth, stepping further into the room. "I, um, I came to see you because I…well, I need your advice."

Jubal glared across the fire at him. His mouth was pulled into a flat line. He studied Ben's frame with narrowed eyes for a long moment, and Ben was sure he was about to toss him out on his ear. But to Ben's surprise, Jubal gestured silently to two makeshift stools by the open fire.

Ben moved towards the nearest one quickly, while Jubal turned to slice large pieces of an iced cake on a stone shelf behind him. He handed Ben a slice on a crude clay plate along with a dipper of water in a small cup. Then he settled onto the stool across from him with his own slice. He eyed Ben as he took a large bite.

"Ita's grandson, yes?" he said in a gruff voice.

Ben gave a muffled "Mhm" around a bite of cake, nodding. He swallowed and swiftly scooped up another mouthful. It was delicious. He hadn't realized how hungry he had been. He ate it with a sip of water, then swiped his mouth with the back of his hand.

Jubal nodded once. "And how is Ita?"

Ben paused another bite in midair, then set it back onto his plate. He should've realized that Jubal wouldn't know. He swallowed another sip of water, remembering.

"She, ah, she was killed." He dropped his eyes. "By a lyncath, just before the fall of the Court of Orm," Ben said softly.

Jubal set his plate weakly on his lap. Quietly, he turned his head to peer out over the valley. His face was a mask of pain. "So much destruction," he said gruffly. "So much death."

Ben followed his gaze. Images from his dream played behind his eyes, and quickly, he turned his head. He flicked his eyes back to Jubal's aged profile, searching. "That's actually what I want to talk to you about."

Jubal turned, peering back at him. "Death and destruction?" He looked down at the fire and shook his head, his scraggly grey beard wiggling below his face with the movement. "I have no wish to talk with you of death and destruction," he said gruffly. "I have no wish but to forget."

Ben shook his head. He cleared his throat. "Well, that's not exactly what I meant. I meant, well, I want to talk to you about a dream I had recently. One you were a part of."

Jubal looked up at Ben quietly with his watery blue eyes. Ben waited. He didn't want to push the old satyr too hard. But Jubal had always been interested in dreams. Ben hoped he still was.

"Go on," Jubal said flatly. Ben nodded once, then began.

"It's sort of complicated, and there was a lot going on, but in my dream, I rebuilt the doors to the Court of Mountain Fairies. Some other things happened, too, but that's not important right now."

Jubal gazed quietly into the fire. Then he raised his eyes. "How do you know?" Jubal asked gruffly.

Ben blinked. "How do I know?"

Jubal jerked his chin. "How do you know that the other things aren't important?"

Ben studied the fire for a moment. He wasn't sure that they weren't important. He just knew that he didn't want to talk about the other part of his dream right now—the part with Reina. In fact, he couldn't even bear to think about it.

"I, um, I guess I *don't* know." He shrugged one shoulder. "Maybe they are. But what I really wanted to talk to you about is rebuilding the doors."

Jubal pulled thoughtfully on the tufted hairs at his chin.

Ben continued, letting his words tumble out. "It's a big project. It will probably take several weeks. And after that I'm going to rebuild the entire court." He shrugged. "I mean, I know it sounds crazy, but…"

Jubal interrupted him.

"Are you asking me what I think, or are you telling me what you're going to do?" he asked sharply.

Ben pressed his lips together. Jubal really was as gruff and bitter as Ben had expected. It was a sharp contrast from the Jubal he had once known, but even so, Ben wouldn't be deterred. He'd met too many terrible beasts in his lifetime to let a little gruffness from an old satyr scare him away.

He lifted his chin. "I'm asking what you think," he said openly. "About the dream and about me actually going through with it."

For a long while, Jubal stared into the fire, pulling gently on his scraggly grey beard. Then he stood. He hobbled to the edge of the cave, bracing one gnarled hand on the rock face and peered out into the desolate valley below. A heaviness seemed to rest on Jubal's shoulders as he surveyed the dismal scene, sagging under the weight of what Ben knew were so many dark memories. He stood there longer than Ben would have expected, and once, he even thought he'd heard Jubal sniff.

Quietly, Ben set his half-eaten cake by the fire and moved to Jubal's side. The satyr sniffed again, swiping his eyes with the back of his hand as Ben appeared beside him. Ben pretended not to notice. He stared out silently into the valley below, never turning to Jubal's face.

Finally, Jubal spoke. His voice was shakier than it had been before. "Why would you wish to do this, Benjamin?" he murmured. "Why stir up trouble for us all? When Marcus and the others hear, it won't go well for you. You can be sure of that. And it won't go well for anyone who helps you either."

Ben nodded. He had considered that. He narrowed his eyes, continuing to stare out at the ruined court. "True," he said simply. "But I will deal with Marcus if it comes to it. Besides, I'm ready to go home, aren't you?" He cut his eyes to Jubal, whose lips were set in a determined line. His narrowed blue eyes were fixed on the right corner of the tumbled North Wall, where his home had once stood.

His voice hitched with his next words. "I'm not sure it will *be* a home without them." He paused, and Ben nodded. He knew Jubal was talking about the family and friends they had lost. Jubal met his gaze, then looked away. "But yes, I suppose I'd like that."

Ben grinned quietly at the side of Jubal's face, then he faced the valley again.

"So, does this mean you think my dream is from the Source? And that you'll help me?"

Jubal twisted his mouth. He adjusted his posture on his chipped hooves. He stood a little straighter. "Depends on what I'd be doing," he quipped. "I'm busy, as you can see." He gestured to the quiet room behind him.

Ben nodded, grinning. "Of course, I don't want to disrupt your work here, but…Well, in my dream, you fed me. Bread from your baker's cart. And you gave me water. I was exhausted, and you came at just the right moment."

Jubal considered Ben's questions and words a moment more before he finally answered. His words were slow and deliberate, and even though there was still a hint of irritation in his voice, Ben could tell that he was enjoying their conversation. He was sure it felt good for Jubal to stretch his skills in dream interpretation since they had so long been out of use.

Jubal lifted his chin, peering sidelong at Ben. "In my humble experience, Benjamin, it seems clear that such a dream, one which was sent to the heir of the Court of Mountain Fairies, one with a directive to rebuild the doors, and beyond that, one that has sparked a desire to rebuild the court of his heritage is, without much doubt, from the Source. But such a special task might require that one receive a sign in the waking hours that it is his duty to follow through with it. So, I ask you, have you received such a sign?"

Ben didn't even have to think about it. The answer came to him directly—Willow's gift from the Eiks. And the towering pile of lumber's miraculous appearance at the ruined courts doors was further proof. What other sign did he need??

The Lavender Mountain Aster that he'd plucked from the doors' foundation this morning. The one that exactly matched the flower in his dream—the one that matched Reina's bracelet—

sprang into his thoughts also, but he didn't dwell on it for long. Instead, he pushed it to the side. Best to keep his thoughts off that for now.

Jubal raised one crooked finger in Ben's direction. "Might I ask, in this dream of yours, what was the condition of the rest of the court? And was there anyone else present?"

Ben hesitated. He wasn't ready to tell Jubal about Reina's appearance in his dream. He didn't want to think about it. He shifted his feet, crossing his arms. "It, ah…the palace was restored. The kitchens and great hall were exactly as I remember them. But the rest of the court still lay in ruins."

Ben said no more. Jubal peered questioningly at the side of his face. "Anything else?" he pressed.

Ben wet his lips. He didn't meet Jubal's piercing gaze. "Um, well, I guess there was something else." He shifted uncomfortably. "There was Reina. She was there," he muttered.

Jubal nodded. He folded his gnarled hands at his waist. "And who is this Reina?"

Ben cleared his throat. "She's…ah…she's my best friend," he answered quietly.

Jubal lifted his chin. "And she was in the palace?" he asked. Ben nodded. He could feel Jubal's eyes boring into the side of his head. "And what was she doing there in this dream?"

Ben shifted. He cleared his throat. "She was in the kitchen. Baking a cake."

Ben could hear humming from outside the palace doors. He grinned. That was what Reina always did when she was intent on her work in the garden. The sound propelled him forward, and he tucked himself inside the great hall just in time to see her long red hair rounding the corner towards the kitchens.

Ben stepped over the threshold in awe. Inside, the palace was immaculate. It was just like he remembered. Thick tapestries hung on the sandstone walls, and a wide oak floor lay beneath heavy upholstered chairs near the left windows, while polished wooden steps with a decorative iron railing led up to the second and third floors on his right. The windows were flung open, and a light breeze billowed inward on the gauzy curtains. High above, exposed beams templed themselves towards the solid roof.

Ben could still hear Reina's humming. The sound was captivating, and he followed it towards the back of the house. He rounded the corner beneath the stairs, pausing at the door of the kitchen on his left. Quietly, he leaned against the doorframe to watch Reina work.

Her back was to him, and her long red hair was pulled out of her face. It cascaded down her back in a long stream. She was wearing a pale green dress, one Ben hadn't seen before. He scanned it to the hem, trailing to her bare feet. Ben raised his brows in surprise. Reina wasn't wearing any shoes.

He shifted his weight, and the wood flooring creaked, causing Reina to peer backward over her shoulder. She grinned broadly. Her smile was one Ben had never seen her use. The beauty of it nearly took his breath away. "Hi," she said happily. "Come see what I'm making."

Ben moved towards her, stopping short to peer over her shoulder. Flour caked her bare arms to the elbows. Whatever she was baking, the batter smelled delicious.

Ben moved a little closer. He bent towards her neck, inhaling. Reina's scent mixed with that of the batter lifting to his nose. "It's a cake for my birthday," she said, smiling. "I'm turning nineteen this year, you know."

She lifted the bowl to pour the batter into a round pan, but her hand slipped. The bowl started to drop, and Ben lunged towards it, catching it on his palm before it smashed into her workspace. Ben blew out a breath, and Reina giggled.

His arm was wrapped around her, and she was pressed as close as if Ben had been riding behind her on Cyrus. She turned her face towards him, grinning. "Nice save," she said lightly. She tipped her chin, and Ben studied her face. His heart ticked up a beat at her nearness. She was flirting.

Reina giggled again as she spun towards him and wrapped her flour-y arms around his neck. Ben was still holding the bowl aloft. He had it in a death grip as he stared down at her in awe. Silently, she reached behind her back and pried the bowl from his hand. Ben blinked down at her, mind swirling, as she tucked his arm tightly around her waist. "Reina, what—"

She put a batter-caked finger to his lips. "Shhh, Ben."

That's when he noticed them—the bracelets on the counter behind her. The lavender gems gleamed in the soft light. One of them he recognized as the one he had given her for her eighteenth birthday, and the other, an almost identical copy, lay on the countertop next to it.

Ben flicked his eyes from the bracelets to Reina's face and back again. He was trying to make sense of the situation. Two bracelets? He knew what that meant. He studied her face carefully, searching for answers. She smiled up at him sweetly. They had to be hers, didn't they?

They had to be, but Ben had only ever made her the one. The other looked almost exactly like it. The clasp was slightly different, but still—almost an exact copy. He slid his eyes to it, studying its glittering lavender gems. Had he made her another and forgotten about it? No. No, he hadn't. He was certain of that.

Ben's thoughts swirled. If the new bracelet was hers also, and if Reina wore one on each wrist, well, then that could only mean one thing. Reina had a mate. Ben searched his mind, his brow creased in confusion. And if he had given them to her, then he was the mate. The realization caused a rapid fire of flutters to skip across Ben's chest, and he moved his eyes back to her face, searching for the answers. He hadn't given her a second bracelet, though, had he?

Reina gave him a feline grin.

"Is that for me?" she asked.

Ben was distracted by his study of her expression. He was still trying to sort out whether she had taken the bond. And even more, whether she had taken the bond with him. "Hmm?" Ben's shirt was rolled to the elbows, and Reina trailed her fingertips lightly down his forearm to his palm. Ben stiffened, and she pursed her lips.

"The flower, silly. Is it mine?"

Ben looked down at the Mountain Aster in his hand. He had forgotten he had plucked it from the base of the doors. He nodded mutely, and Reina slipped it from his palm. His arm was blazing where her fingers had touched, and for a moment, he wondered if she had actually set his skin on fire.

Reina leaned back against the countertop and brough the flower lazily to her nose. She lowered her long lashes, inhaling, then lifted her gaze. Ben studied her eyes, silently captivated by the contrast of the lavender petals to their green hue. "Thank you, my love," she whispered.

My love? Ben's mind swirled as Reina tucked her face into his neck. She rested her nose against his collarbone, her soft breath warming his skin. Ben swallowed convulsively. Silently, he wrapped his free arm around her back. The feel and scent of her was overpowering, and the strong urge to wrap his fingers into her hair hit him like a wave. He lifted his hand, but before he could do it, Reina lifted her face. All he managed to grasp was one long curl.

Ben watched the curl pull between his fingers with her movement. Somewhere, in the back of his mind, it occurred to him again that this was a dream. But he pushed the thought away. Reina grinned, and he smiled down at her. This felt so natural, so real. "Happy Birthday, Reina," he said gruffly.

She melted into him, then, and Ben cradled her head in his palm.

Her face was so close, and Ben realized to his amazement that he was going to kiss her. Reina, his best friend in the known worlds. He was going to kiss Reina. Strangely, it felt like the most natural thing he had ever done. He lowered his head, closing the distance.

A tiny bit of batter was stuck to his lips from her finger, and the sweet taste of it melded with her lips as he covered them with his own. A thousand sparks exploded in Ben's chest with her touch, and he pulled her closer, holding her as tightly as his own body would allow.

He wanted to stay like this forever. He wanted to stay here, in this dream with Reina, in his home at the Court of Mountain Fairies forever.

At last, Reina pulled away. Her breathing was heavy, and so was Ben's. She rested her forehead in the crook of his neck. "Stay," she whispered. "Stay here with me."

And Ben would have. There was nothing he wanted more. But before he could answer, the moment was gone.

Despite her words, Reina pushed away from his chest. She backed to the end of the counter, and Ben watched, confused, as she swiped her arm over the free air. A large gate opened beneath her palm, its oblong surface wavered and shimmered in the morning light. Realization dawned on Ben, then, and his heart sank in horror. He reached for her, desperately. "Reina, no. Please!"

He had almost forgotten. It's Reina who wouldn't stay. It was she who was leaving, not him.

Ben funneled through his head, searching for pretty words to keep her on his side of the known worlds. But no pretty words would come.

Instead, his voice came out plain, pleading, and desperate. He held out his hands. "Please, Reina. Don't go." His voice cracked, but Reina's face was blank, shuttered and dark.

She held Ben's gaze until the last moment. "I'm sorry, Ben," she whispered. Then without another word, she turned and stepped through.

The gate snapped shut behind her, and Ben collapsed against the counter. "Reina, no," he wheezed. His throat was closing in on itself, and a great, gaping hole was forming in his chest. Tears filled his eyes, and he gripped the spot over his Amloga Flame, just to the left of his heart. The pain of it was like fire searing through his shirt, and he slid to the floor with a groan.

He felt like he was dying. There was no way he would survive this. He was going to die without her. Ben closed his eyes as memories of past losses flooded into his head. They had all hurt, but none had ever been as painful as this.

Ben wasn't sure how long he had been sitting on the floor. But when he stood, golden sunlight streamed sideways through the kitchen windows. Reina's bracelets still lay on the countertop across from him. Their glittering gems glared up at him like a dark omen. On impulse, Ben swiped the newer one and put it into his pocket.

"And that's all I remember," Ben muttered.

Jubal grunted in response. He turned back to stare out at the scorched court walls. "So, she's a baker," he said quietly. "Hmm, I would like to meet this Reina. Why did you not bring her with you?"

He turned to face Ben again, his blue eyes piercing as he waited for an answer. Ben dropped his gaze, staring hard at his feet. "Because she's leaving," he said quietly.

"Leaving?" Jubal asked. Ben nodded. "And where is she going?"

Ben bit the inside of his cheek. He lifted his eyes to Jubal's face. "She's going home. In two weeks, she'll go back through the gate to Monrovia."

CHAPTER 10

REINA

Amelie blinked at Reina in shock. "You're leaving?" Her voice was garbled, and her eyes were already filling with tears. "When? I mean… I mean I thought you hadn't decided yet."

Reina swallowed against the lump in her own throat. She crossed her arms. "In two weeks," she whispered. "I plan to tell the others tonight at dinner. I don't want to do it without Ben here." She shielded her eyes with her palm and peered up at the sky, scanning for any sign of Cyrus. "Surely he'll be back by then," she said absently.

Just then, Reina heard Cyrus's unmistakable call. She spun, just catching a glimpse of the griffin's back legs from her perch beneath the low Wisteria as he touched down outside the arch in the courtyard wall. Quickly, she strode across the yard towards him, her heart hopeful. Maybe Ben had changed his mind about cancelling their lunch plans. Maybe he'd come to get her, after all.

"I'll be right back," she called to Amelie over her shoulder.

Cyrus was waiting for her outside, pawing at the dirt with his sharp talons. He unearthed a fat worm and quickly scooped up the treat with his large beak. Reina studied his back, and her heart sank. Ben wasn't on it.

Disappointed, she trudged towards Cyrus and lifted his bridle limply in her hand. The griffin studied her quietly with his large, dark eye, then cooed, tucking his beak into the crook of her neck.

Reina closed her eyes and rested her head against the side of Cyrus's feathery neck. Her disappointment at Ben's absence was stronger than she wanted to admit. Tears stung her eyes, and she ran her hand absently against the opposite side of Cyrus's neck, stroking his downy feathers. If she felt this bad about a cancelled picnic plan, how was she supposed to survive never seeing him again once she went back through the gate?

Reina hugged Cyrus's large head, her fingers brushing over something tucked beneath the other side of his bridle. Her eyes popped open. Ben had left her a message.

Gently, she unwound herself from Cyrus's feathery embrace and rounded his other side. There, tucked beneath the bridle was a small, rolled parchment. Swiftly, she pulled the message free, her heart pounding.

It was strange for Cyrus to show up alone. Where was Ben? Her mind spun, as a fearful thought creeped into her head. What if he was lying hurt somewhere? Or what if something worse had happened?

Hurriedly, she scanned his words. Ben's handwriting was even messier than usual. It was obvious that he'd been in a hurry. She searched his scrawled letters, bracing for the worst. But then the anxiety of the moment dissolved. Instead, her heart flamed with anger. And, too, it pricked with hurt. Ben wasn't coming back until the night before the Castle Ball. He would be gone for two whole weeks—the exact amount of time he had asked her to stay.

Tears blurred the edges of Ben's script, and Reina crumpled the note in her palm. She sniffed, ignoring the ache in her heart. So what if Ben wasn't coming back until the night of the Castle Ball? Why should he? He was free to do whatever he wanted, wasn't he? Clearly, the Court of Mountain Fairies, which is where he mentioned he would be staying, needed his attention more than she did. Plus, it was good for them to have some distance, especially after their stiff exchange in the kitchen this morning.

What she didn't understand was why Ben had asked her to stay if he was going to be gone the whole time. Why did it matter if she was here or not? Why ask her to stay at all?

Reina didn't bother to lead Cyrus to the stables. The griffin knew the way, and Reina knew he wouldn't be long about heading there for his lunch of dried berries and oats. Besides, Johann and

Henri would be there, and she couldn't stand to face the two of them right now.

She swiped her eyes with the back of her sleeve as she marched back through the courtyard, not making eye contact with anyone as she hurried to escape into the house. Luckily, Amelie was busy helping the Winds whip individual funnels of swirling air on their palms. Her back was to Reina, and Reina didn't glance her way as she passed. She held her breath as she ran to stop her sobs, not releasing it until she was safely behind her own room's doors. Then she crumpled onto the floor in a heap and let the tears fall.

When her tears were finally spent, she let her head rest against the heavy oak door. She had to admit it—she was devastated by Ben's absence. Now that he was staying at the Court of Mountain Fairies, she would only get one more night with him before she went back to Monrovia—the night of the Castle Ball. She let that thought sink in. It made her stomach hurt, and she wrapped her arms around her middle, trying to hold herself together.

But maybe his absence was for the best. Things had been strained between them since their exchange in the library, and they had only gotten worse when he'd found her in the kitchens this morning. She frowned, thinking of the funny way he had held her bandaged thumb, how he had studied her hair, how he'd dropped his eyes and stepped stiffly away. It was odd. She couldn't understand it.

Absently, she touched her bandaged finger, then she unwound the wrap and pressed lightly at the skin beneath it. The flesh there was smooth, already healed. She let her hand drop to her lap.

Ben was her best friend. She wanted to keep him that way. If their strained interactions of late were any indication, then maybe the only way to do that was from a distance.

That didn't mean his note didn't hurt. It did. The thought that he wanted to be away from her, to be separated from her during her last days in Caelium stung. She didn't think there was any way around that.

She studied the bracelet on her wrist thoughtfully. At least their separation would be good practice for when she was truly gone. She would have to get used to being away from him, because soon, she would be truly away. A whole other realm away, in fact.

She bit her lip, her heart sinking with her heavy thoughts. It was a sad fact, but it was true. Soon, she would step through the gate, and then she would never see Ben or the others or Caelium, ever again.

Reina sighed, steeling herself for what was to come. If she could manage to get past some of the sting now, maybe it wouldn't hurt so much when she actually had to go.

At least, that's what she hoped.

CHAPTER 11

BEN

Ben paused, chest heaving as he peered up through the broken panes of the glass ceiling. Above him, the silver light of Caelium's dual moons shone brightly in on his head. He had worked until well past midnight, but that wasn't unusual. Most nights, he stayed in his makeshift workspace in the atrium behind the palace long past his usual bedtime.

Despite once being a dining hall, it made a good workspace. The long table was perfect for a workbench and while several of the high, slanted windows of its roof were shattered, plenty of natural light shone through, and the wall sconces still held the snubs of old candles that he used when the daylight ran out.

It was in the atrium that he had found his tools. To Ben's amazement, they had appeared in the same way Willow's gift had. He had found them gathered in the back right corner, waiting for him.

He stood at the long table in the oval room's center, smoothing the edges of an intricate carving on the upper panel of one door. His dark golden hair hung in limp strands against his forehead, and a line of sweat ran through his eyebrow. It dropped into his left eye, and Ben wiped it with his shirttail.

He dusted his design, then studied it in the candlelight. Though he'd been working almost continuously, he was still amazed that the doors were nearly complete. It had only been one week. Tomorrow morning, he would fix the large panels together and put the doors in their place in the North Wall. Then…

Well, he didn't know what he would do then.

Ben's muscles ached with overuse, and he snuffed out each candle in turn before heading to his bedroom. He'd taken up residence in the large one at the back of the house, just past the atrium. It had never been occupied, even when his family had lived here all those cycles ago. Instead, it had functioned as a small library. Ben had always liked it. It was quiet. Private. He'd often come in here as a boy when he'd needed an escape.

He shut the bedroom door behind him, leaning his back wearily against it. Empty bookshelves stared back at him from the far wall of the nearly empty room. In fact, all that remained inside was a threadbare rug, a small, rickety wooden table, and a chaise that had seen better days. He collapsed onto its overstuffed seat and stretched his toes out past the edge. He stared down at them, wiggling their bare tips in the free air. If he stayed much longer, he'd have to do something about a bed.

He pulled the blanket he'd found in the back of a forgotten closet up under his chin. It smelled slightly damp, but it was warm. Ben didn't care about the smell. He knew he didn't smell much better. His shirt had been soaked through with sweat several times in the past few days. He sat up, pulling the sweat-stiffened fabric over his head. His skin felt sticky as he peeled it away. Tomorrow, he would have to take a swim. It was that or have his shirt permanently adhered to his frame with sweat.

He collapsed back on the chaise, closing his eyes. It felt good to lie down. Now that he had, he realized just how tired he was. He snuggled deeper under the blanket and turned onto his side, wincing as something sharp dug into his thigh. His eyes popped open. Frowning, he flipped to his back and thrust his hand into his pocket.

His fingertips had found the offending object. Ben ran them over the sharp edges of the bracelet's gems. He remembered tucking it into his pocket in his dream, but, somehow, it had made it into his pocket for real. Instantly, his mind was transported back to his dream world, and he was once more in the kitchen, with Reina. He let himself go this time, closing his eyes.

Reina was so close. Ben could smell the cake batter clinging to her hair. The bracelet in his pocket lay behind her on the countertop, and the one he had given her on her eighteenth birthday was beside it. Reina wrapped her arms around him, and he wound his fingers into her hair. He wanted to stay here, to hold her forever, but he knew it wouldn't last.

And he was right.

Soon, she stepped away. Behind her, an open gate shimmered in the soft light. Ben wanted to scream as he watched her step through it. Then the gate closed, and she was gone.

Ben's eyes welled in the darkness. He clutched the bracelet tightly inside his pocket before he pulled it free and tossed it carelessly on the small wooden table behind him. His throat closed around a lump, and he swallowed hard, pulling the blue blanket up over his head as hot, heavy tears slipped past his eyelids. They rolled off his cheek, falling on the overstuffed cushion beneath him.

He swiped hard at his eyes. It was exhaustion. That was what was making him emotional. At least, that's what he told himself. He stuffed his feelings down deep, crossing his arms across his chest to stop the ache.

But sadness overwhelmed him in the quiet bedroom, and soon, he was crying again. It wasn't just Reina. It was everything—

everything that had happened here. Grief washed over him in heavy waves, and he pressed the place to the left of his heart, where his Amloga burned with so many memories.

Finally, mercifully, he fell asleep. He floated there in quiet relief, and his mind became a blank slate. But a blank slate swiftly fills, and soon, she came to him. *Reina.* They were at the waterfall, and she was pulling her long hair into a high knot on top of her head, a bracelet decorating each wrist.

Cool water dripped from the tips of Ben's hair and ran off his chin. He swiped a palm over his damp head from where he perched, watching her. She grinned up at him from the ground, and his stomach did a little flip. Then she turned and dove into the deep pool, surfacing just behind the waterfall.

Ben grinned at the hazy outline of her red hair hinting behind the waterfall's stream. He stood, diving from the high, flat rock to chase after her. He dropped through the open air, cutting a perfect arc and savoring the fresh, tingling feeling as the cool water sluiced past his shoulders.

He surfaced behind the fall, expecting Reina to be there, but when he came up, she was gone. Sudden fear gripped him. It was happening again. Reina had left him.

Ben searched the area frantically, calling her name over and over. He even swam to the base of the pool, running his hands along the stony bottom in desperation. But Reina was nowhere to be found.

His heart thumped rapidly in his ears as he climbed back to his perch on the flat rock. From there, he could just see the wisp of an open gate before it dissolved out of sight. Ben dropped to his knees, his heart squeezing as he bent to pick up a small object on the stone in front of him. It was Reina's second bracelet—the new one. She had left it there. She had given it back to him.

Ben studied the lavender petals glistening in his palm, his heart breaking wide open. He was too late. Reina was gone.

The next morning, Ben woke in a foul mood. He sat up in a huff and ran a frustrated hand through his hair. He was sick of these dreams. They did nothing but torture and confuse him with cryptic messages and dark displays of his future torment. What good were they? Why did he keep having them?

Dejectedly, he eyed the bracelet on the table beside him. He thought about destroying it, taking his mallet to its gems. Maybe that would keep Reina out of his dreams at night. But then he decided against it. Grumbling, he swiped it and dropped it into his pocket.

By the time he got to the North Wall, the smell of fresh bread and hot tea was wafting from Jubal's cave. Ben's stomach growled, but he didn't bother to hike the cliffs to Jubal's like he usually did. Instead, he set right to work.

By midmorning, he had fixed the foundation and was ready to

raise the doors. He didn't notice Jubal hobbling down the hillside as he struggled to fit one of the large doors onto its hinges.

Jubal eyed the single door, then studied Ben's sweat-soaked shirt.

"Take a break, Benjamin. Come sit. Eat," Jubal said gruffly. Ben peered up at the raised door and the other one waiting on the ground, his muscles quivering. His breath was coming in short bursts, and his mouth was as dry as the cracked earth.

Jubal settled onto a large, tumbled down stone from the ruined wall. Then he set a warm, flat loaf of bread and a clay cup of steaming tea on the smaller stone in front of him. He gestured to the stone opposite him. "Come. It will be cold if you wait much longer."

Ben nodded. he could use a break—a short one. "Thanks."

He moved to the opposite stone and sat heavily, then downed his tea in one gulp. Jubal refilled it from a large pitcher as Ben broke the loaf of bread in half. He stuck a large piece into his mouth and chewed. It had a warm, nutty flavor.

Jubal waited patiently as Ben drank two more cups of tea and finished the loaf, then he stood and moved towards the raised door. It was three times as tall as Ben and twice as wide. Jubal examined the door carefully, his gnarled fingers resting on his hips. "Impressive work, Benjamin. Possibly even better than the originals."

Ben came to stand beside him. "Thank you," he said quietly.

Jubal studied the flowers sprouting around the base of the door's foundation. "And these Mountain Aster. Weren't here yesterday, were they?" Jubal shook his head. "Haven't seen anything bloom here in ages. Not since…before."

Ben nodded. He scraped at the dry, cracked dirt with his foot. He remembered. The valley at the Court of Mountain Fairies had once been lush and green. Aster had clustered around the doors in large clumps, spreading up onto the hillside beyond. Ben eyed the new flowers silently. Several were in full bloom and green shoots of new plants were sprouting up all around them.

Jubal said no more as Ben set to work, loading the second door with ropes. Jubal came beside him, and together, they raised the second door, dropping large pegs into its hinges and hammering them into place.

Ben had left holes in the center of each door, where he planned to fit two iron rings. He wished he still had the old ones, but he was sure they were long gone by now.

Ben studied the open holes intently, and when he turned, Jubal was holding out the very rings from his memory. Ben blinked down at them in surprise. They looked just the same. He took them from Jubal's crooked fingers in awe, turning them over and over in his palm. They were just like he remembered. The center of each ring was fitted with a delicate pair of translucent, glass wings, the symbol of the Court of Mountain Fairies. Ben couldn't believe the wings had survived.

"Where did you find them?" he said in amazement.

Jubal eyed the glittering wings proudly. "They were amidst the rubble…after the drake. They were wedged in a pile of stone, so not much damage was done."

Jubal watched silently as Ben worked to fix the rings into place. Today, the old satyr had a wooden staff, and he leaned on it heavily, playing breathy notes on his flute as Ben moved before and behind the large doors.

Ben fixed the second ring into place then shut both doors firmly behind him. He tested the old rings with a sharp pull, swinging each door open and closed several times. He grinned. They worked perfectly. He left the right door open a crack, then he stepped back and tucked a hand into his pocket, surveying his work. The doors looked fantastic. In fact, Ben thought they were probably the best work he had ever done.

In the top of each door, he had carved a pair of fairy wings. They looked just like the ones he remembered—just like the glittering glass ones on the iron rings. Two wide blades with a smaller set of blades below. Under each of them, a circle of Mountain Aster blooms was carved in a winding circle. Below the left one, a glass bottle, like the one from his dream. It was tipped on its side, and all the glistening tears inside it were tumbling out in a winding stream on the right door's side.

The sun was high, and Ben was getting warmer by the moment. His already sweat-stiffened shirt was tacking to his shoulders again. The coarse fabric itched. His hair hung limply over his brow, and generally, he felt dust and grime had gathered into every crevice of his body. He was looking forward to heading to the waterfall.

"Yes. Even better than the originals," Jubal said, scanning the doors. "And the Source obviously agrees." He gestured to the ground near the doors' foundation, where Lavender Mountain Aster now miraculously grew in thick clusters. Shoots of tender new plants had begun to sprout down the wall, and a green carpet of new grasses tickled Ben's bare feet. Thin, green vines wound themselves up the stone columns beside the doors' hinges, and tiny, white buds of sweet Jasmine were already beginning to bloom on them.

Ben grinned over at Jubal. "Obviously," he joked. Jubal laughed, and Ben laughed at the hearty sound he remembered. The old satyr had softened before his very eyes in the last week. He was nearly back to the Jubal Ben once knew.

Jubal leaned against his staff. "Well, now that the doors are complete, might I hear more about what occupied the rest of this dream? Or rather, *who* occupied it?"

Ben's eyes shot up in surprise, but Jubal eyed him steadily. Despite the heat, Ben could feel the prickles of another heat coming to flare on his chest. Jubal had always had that uncanny way of reading people, but Ben still wondered how he had known there was more to say. He sat down heavily on the stone across from Jubal and sighed, while Jubal poured him a strong cup of tea. It was tepid now, but Ben didn't mind. He took a long sip, draining the cup.

He studied the tea leaves coating the cup's base, trying to decide where to begin. There was so much to say about Reina and what she meant to him. He decided to start with the basics, and he relayed again the happenings of his dream, how Reina had appeared in his old home's kitchen, how she was making a cake for a birthday that had yet to come, how there were two bracelets on the counter behind her.

He talked about how she had put her arms around him, and then, with a tight throat, he told Jubal how she had opened a gate and stepped through. Jubal sat silent, listening as Ben went on to tell him about how close he was with Reina in the waking hours. He talked about how she was the closest person to him in the world, how she was his best friend, how he'd given her a single bracelet for her birthday, as a token of his friendship, and how later, he'd found the new bracelet from his dream in his pocket when he was awake. Then he talked about Monrovia, and how she was betrothed to Lord Malcom, how she was set to take the throne, how she would leave in a week, after the Castle Ball.

Jubal tugged on his scruffy beard as he listened gravely to Ben's long speech. He studied Ben with a knowing gaze in his watery blue eyes, nodding at the appropriate intervals. When Ben stopped speaking, more from the fact that his throat was closing around a large lump than the fact that he was finished, Jubal sat with him in silence as he gathered his emotions. Then he spoke, softly but with deep feeling.

"How could you have told me that this is not important, Benjamin? These moments with Reina in your dream are anything *but* unimportant. In fact, they carry equal urgency and equal weight with your work on the doors. Just as you had a sign in the waking hours about your commission to complete the doors, so you have also had a sign regarding your tender moments with Reina. The bracelet appearing in your pocket speaks to the desires of the Source, just as the appearance of Willow's lumber did."

Ben leaned forward and braced his elbows on his knees, gripping his tea cup tightly in his palms. What Jubal said made sense. And if he was understanding him correctly, then it was important that Reina stay with him. It was the will of the Source.

Ben frowned. But how could he compete with her plans to return to Monrovia? She had a whole life there: a throne, her sister. Lord Malcom.

Ben eyed the ruins around him. He had no kingdom to give her, and certainly no throne. As for her betrothed, he was certain she had never thought of him in that way, just as he hadn't allowed himself to think of her that way. Until now.

Jubal continued. "Ask yourself, Benjamin, what is the *true* desire of your heart concerning Reina? Is it that she would go back to Monrovia, to claim her crown and her betrothed, never to be seen by you again?" Jubal gestured to the ruined court around him. "Or is it that she would stay here, with you?"

Ben blinked at Jubal in surprise. He pointed to the nearest

section of the North Wall, which tumbled out around them like pebbles washed out in the mouth of a stream. "Here? You mean, *here* here? You think she should stay *here* with me?" Jubal didn't answer. He eyed Ben evenly with a quiet smile.

Ben laughed incredulously. He stood, pacing rapidly back and forth. He couldn't believe what Jubal was insinuating. The old satyr watched him patiently as Ben stopped in front of him, gesturing to the wall. "*Look* at this place, Jubal! It's a complete disaster. You saw how hard the work was for me to just fix the doors, and now, you're acting as if the entire court was restored, and I could just… just ask Reina to stay"—he gestured wildly at the ruins—"*here* in complete and total destruction, while her own Mortal court of Monrovia wastes away with no leader, and her betrothed wonders why she doesn't appear." He shook his head, folding his arms. "It's ridiculous! I mean, I know I said I was going to rebuild the court, but truly, I don't even know if I *can* rebuild it. The doors alone were hard enough. I would need the entire *realm* to help me do it." He scoffed, staring at the tumbled stones of the North Wall. "There's no way I can just…just ask Reina to stay here. No way."

Jubal didn't answer, and Ben hung his head. He swiped his bare toes across the new grass beneath them.

"There's nothing for her here, Jubal," he muttered. "I have nothing to give her."

Jubal watched Ben carefully, all the while continuing to tug on his beard. He leaned heavily on his staff and moved his watery eyes slowly over the ruins of the Court of Mountain Fairies. A slow smile came over his face as he pointed to the Northwest Corner, where the satyrs had once dwelled. The charred edges of the broken buildings were almost more than Ben could stand to see. He remembered the satyrs' screams, and the smell of death that had permeated the West Mountains, long after the Orm's foul beasts had gone.

"I remember when my children danced in the streets at the Festival of Light. Do you remember it, Ben?" Jubal grinned broadly, and a low chuckle rumbled in his throat. He cut his eyes to Ben. "You danced with them, too, if I recall."

A muscle feathered in Ben's jaw, and he nodded. He remembered. The Festival of Light was a celebration of love. Strings of tiny lanterns had crisscrossed above the streets, mirroring the sparkling stars. At the end of the night, everyone had taken one. Each had whispered words to their lantern's light—words that were meant for their one true love. Then, together, they released them to the skies, their words rising with the lanterns' light to the Source. Ben remembered the sky had been full of the paper lanterns, lifting up on the breeze. He smiled at the memory.

Jubal chuckled low, his eyes distant. "Yes. I would wager you will dance at the Festival of Light again." Ben peered at Jubal's profile. It was a beautiful thought, but those words were a fantasy. He nodded, deciding to let the old satyr have his moment. The serene, joyful look on Jubal's face as he studied the ruined court was too precious to break. It was the first time Ben had seen him fully in his old form, since before the court was destroyed.

Jubal raised one crooked finger at the newly finished doors. "And remember to take these old bones with you when you do. I always did like the Festival." He chuckled again as he hobbled forward on his staff, moving to start back up the hillside. "It will be nice to sleep at home again!" he called over his shoulder.

Ben nodded, raising his hand in a weak wave. He was beginning to think the Jubal was losing it. He peered at the Northwest Corner, where Jubal's old home lay in a tumbled heap. He was crazy if he thought he would ever sleep there again. Ben frowned. Surely Jubal didn't think that was possible.

The sun was beaming down, and sweat was beginning to roll down Ben's back. The waterfall was only a short hike away, and he could already feel the cool water of the pool sluicing across his skin. He started in that direction, his mind full of his own thoughts and dreams, Jubal's words, and despite his best efforts, Reina.

CHAPTER 12

REINA

Reina was too hot. The midday sun was beaming through her window, and she thrust off the covers in a huff. She sighed, trying to relax. But now, the sun was shining in her eyes. Grumbling, she flung her forearm across them as she angrily flopped onto her side. Everyone was against her—even the sun. She couldn't even mope in peace in her own room.

It was almost time for lunch, but Reina had already decided she wasn't going down. She didn't want to face anyone. She just couldn't right now. They would all have questions. Questions she wasn't ready to answer. Besides, she hated to cry in front of anyone, and she was sure that as soon as she locked eyes with Amelie's questioning grey gaze, she would burst into tears.

The only time she had been around anyone in the last week was during morning exercise and special skills training. She had avoided eye contact with them all, and right after, she always retreated to her rooms to hide.

Her stomach growled, and Reina tamped her hand across it, grimacing. This morning, Amelie had led another torturous exercise session, and Reina was starving. Despite her best efforts, Reina hadn't been able to keep Amelie from leading them. Every. Single. Morning for the past week.

Silently, she twisted her lips, eyeing the door. She needed food. Just a quick trip to the kitchens, then she could come back.

She flopped onto her back. No, it was best she stay up in her room. Someone would see her for sure, and she would get roped into some mindless conversation. No, she just couldn't do it.

Reina could hear the group still practicing in the courtyard below. It was time for battle tactics, Ben's specialty. Amelie was leading today. Reina could hear her voice shouting loudly. Metal clanged against metal, and soon, curiosity got the best of Reina. She moved to the window to watch.

Amelie's blonde hair swished as she demonstrated a swift thrust with a sword. She handed the weapon back to Diego, watching as the dark-haired Timekeeper mimicked her movements. Reina smiled. Amelie was doing a good job. A great job, even. Her training as a guard in her Mortal home was showing through. But even so, Amelie wasn't Ben.

Ben. Where was he today? What was he doing? Was he thinking about her, too?

Reina turned away from the window and folded her arms, gazing about her room. Despite its large size and high ceiling, it suddenly felt too small. In fact, Reina didn't think she could bear to stay inside for one more moment.

She moved to the armoire, stuffing a change of clothes into her pack. She slung it across her shoulder, then she hurried down the steps and out the front door. She was careful to move silently as she passed the archway of the circular courtyard. Thankfully, Amelie's back was to her, and the others were engaged in a series of complicated battle movements, so she slipped right past them without notice.

No one stirred as she stepped inside the stables. Reina tucked herself past the doors, then froze as Henri's lithe frame skittered past the far doorway. He and Johann were beyond in the stable yard. Henri had just tossed a lump of mud at Johann's back, hitting him squarely between his shoulders. Johann yelped, then he bent to pick up his own handful of mud, tossing it at Henri. Henri ducked, the mud landing on the ground, just as Reina slipped behind a half wall.

Brushes, bridles, and buckets hung on hooks in front of her. A tall pile of fresh hay was just behind her, and its sweet fragrance folded to her nose, mixing with the thick scent of the animals and dirt. She crouched low, watching their backs from the wall's corner as Johann's booming voice carried easily through the stalls.

"You know she's got a thing for me, right?"

Henri choked on his laugh. He stabbed at another tall pile of hay just inside the doorway and tossed it onto the ground in front of him. "*Sure*, Johann. Whatever you say."

Johann's eyes widened. "I mean it, Henri!" He stepped in front of the doors, and his large frame blocked out most of the sunlight. He put a hand to his chest. "Look, do you think I don't know when a woman is interested?"

Reina clamped a hand over her mouth as Johann held up his palm, counting with his wide fingers.

"She watches my every move, she corrects me constantly, and she acts as if she is disgusted with everything I do. It's a dead giveaway! Amelie is in love with me!"

Reina stifled a giggle. Johann spun at the sound, and she ducked behind the half wall, knocking two buckets off their hooks. They clattered to the floor as she tumbled backward, falling into the pile of hay.

"Oof!"

A tuft of hay was tickling her nose, and she blew it upward as Johann's large face and Henri's slim one appeared above her head. Henri's lips were pulled back over his teeth, and his bow was pulled taut against his cheek, an arrow aimed squarely at Reina's throat. She lifted her arm, and Henri's face relaxed. He rolled his eyes, while Johann blushed bright crimson.

Reina rolled to stand, brushing bits of hay from her sleeves and plucking them from her mass of curls. She lifted a bridle casually from the shelf nearest her, readjusting her pack as if nothing was amiss. She brushed past them, hoping they wouldn't ask her any questions about where she was going or why.

Henri narrowed his shrewd eyes and opened his mouth as she passed, but she spoke before he could get a word in. She cast a backwards glance at Johann as she tugged open the second to last stall. "Amelie, huh?" she called over her shoulder.

Johann froze, staring at her, agape. His face was past red now. It was turning purple. Henri closed his mouth, staring sideways at him. Johann didn't answer. Instead, he turned away, moving stiffly out the back doors. Henri shot her a grin before he trotted after him, his laughter and Johann's shouts echoing back to her ears.

"Just shut up about it, Henri, before I belt you!" Johann shouted. She heard Henri's guffaw, which quickly cut off. Reina heard a thud, which she assumed was Johann knocking him to the dirt.

"Hey!" Henri shouted. "Get back here!"

Johann's booming laugh reached her ears as he and Henri trailed away.

Reina giggled as she turned back to the open stall. *Good.* She had gotten rid of the two of them easily enough. And no questions, either.

She stroked the large griffin in front of her before slipping the bridle over her feathery head. The griffin stared at her with her large green eye.

"Hi, girl," Reina murmured. Jade laid her beak into the crook of Reina's neck, cooing softly. "Want to go out for a while?" Jade lifted her head and pawed at the fresh hay beneath her talons in excitement. Reina giggled. "I'll take that as a 'yes.'"

She led Jade out the far stable door and into the yard, then she braced herself on her furry back and swung astride. She was glad she had worn her gardening clothes. They were perfect for riding. She whistled low and patted the griffin's rump twice. Jade kicked up dirt and hay behind her as she lunged across the yard and lifted into the sky on her dappled wings.

Takeoff was only second to landing in Reina's book—second worst, that is. There was nothing more frightening than the feeling of rising off the ground, lifting high into the sky with nothing surrounding her but the open air. But griffins were the fastest form of travel in the West Mountains, and she didn't have much choice. Soon, she had done just that, heading south to the waterfall.

The irony of her choice to visit there did not escape her. While it was true that she wanted to go for a swim, she knew she could've easily done that in the lake in front of the estate. She told herself she was going to the waterfall to be alone, to give herself the solitude to work through her feelings without interruption. But deep down, she knew she was really going there to feel close to Ben.

Reina was still disappointed that he had cancelled their picnic, and she had been thinking of going by herself all week. She'd even stopped by the kitchens on her way out, managing to snag a few treats from the island when no one was looking.

Who needed Ben? She could have her own picnic.

Reina gripped Jade's feathers tightly as she dipped towards the earth. She touched down in a small grove of evergreens just north of the waterfall. Immediately, the griffin began pawing at the earth, searching for a snack. Reina slid off her seat and patted Jade's feathery neck. "I'll be back in a little while," she said softly, but Jade ignored her. She was too busy lifting a fat worm into her mouth.

It was just a short hike through the wood to the waterfall, and Reina took her time, enjoying the quiet closeness of the path. The trees bent towards her, their needled branches creating a canopy of green. Dappled patches of sunlight shone through their arms, splotching the dirt. Reina made a game of avoiding the bright cracks, skipping from one patch of shade to the other. Birds chirped merrily over her head, and tiny forest creatures skittered in the undergrowth.

Surrounded by green, Reina felt more at peace than she had in a long while. She forgot her troubles as she skipped through the patches of shade. But the feeling didn't last.

She slowed her movement as a strange emotion bloomed inside her chest. Frowning, she pressed her hand to the left of her heart, a heavy ache spreading beneath her fingers. It was something like she had felt when she had first come to Caelium, and she realized with surprise that she was homesick. But this time, she was homesick for the place she hadn't left yet.

The waterfall was roaring up ahead. Soon, the trees would open, and she would be standing in a secluded oasis tucked between two sheer, grey cliffs. She tucked her homesickness away, anticipation replacing it as she hurried to the edge of the wood.

To her left, the towering waterfall rushed over the cliff from a river flowing higher in the rock. It tumbled headlong over grey stone, which had been weathered glistening and smooth by so much rushing water. At the base of the stone, the falling water met with a pool, an oval of smooth, clear liquid, save for the foaming white froth where the fall came to meet it.

Reina knew that the water seeped through the colorful pebbles at the pool's base. Ben had told her that it drained into the underground rivers that crisscrossed unseen beneath the West Mountains. That river system connected all corners of the realm in a twisting path below the surface of the ground.

Even the library at the Timekeeper's Court met with the underground river system, or so Ben had said. He'd told her that she could follow the stream that ran behind the waterfall in the alcove, and eventually, she would meet the river. She'd taken his word for it, but she wasn't about to put it to the test. There were too many dark creatures lurking in the deep places of Caelium, and Reina didn't wish to meet them unless she was forced.

She dropped her bag onto a large, flat rock and quickly stripped her worn slacks and linen work shirt, leaving them in a heap at her feet. Then she lifted one of Ben's thin, light blue overshirts from her pack. She tucked it over her head, smoothing its rumpled front. It was oversized on her small frame and reached halfway to her knees.

Reina remembered the day he gave it to her. It was the first time they had gone to the waterfall. She hadn't brought a change of clothes, and he had stripped his shirt and handed it to her. She had worn it over and over again, but the fabric still faintly held his scent—sunshine and wood shavings.

She tried not to think about Ben's bare chest as she dove under. Resurfacing, she flipped onto her back, floating with her ears submerged. The blue sky was mirrored in the pool beneath her, and she let herself relax, enjoying the muffled sound of rushing water. She inhaled deeply, swishing her arms above her head. She imagined her arms looked like Jade's dappled wings, and she closed her eyes, pretending she was lifting up on the soft breeze.

Presently, a thought drifted into her head, and she turned to peer at the waterfall. A little gap was hidden behind the falling water, and she and Ben sometimes left messages for each other tucked in the rocks there. She wondered if there were any there now. Curious, she swam over to find out.

As she dipped her head, the memory of Ben's hands holding on to her back and guiding her towards the pool's edge slipped into her mind. It had been the same day he loaned her the shirt. She hadn't known how to swim, hadn't needed to, before she came to Caelium. Ben had thought that unacceptable, dangerous, even, for a Timekeeper. So, he gave her lessons.

Every day that week, they had come to the waterfall for a picnic, and after, he had patiently guided her across the pool, showing her how to part the water with her hands and kick her feet in just the right rhythm to keep herself afloat. She had watched in awe as he dove from the smooth stone, his golden hair glinting above his bare torso as he cut a perfect arc into the water.

Ben had been a good teacher, and soon, she'd been swimming on her own. She thought back to that day, realizing she had been a little disappointed when his large hands didn't have to rest on her waist anymore to guide her across the water.

Reina pushed the memory away as she lifted out beside the waterfall. Its cool spray splashed her gently on the side of her face, and she tucked her arms over her chest as she stepped into the narrow space behind the falling water. It was cool there. Water dripped from her hem and ran in little rivulets down her bare legs, and she shivered in Ben's wet shirt despite the day's heat.

Silently, she searched each crevice in the slick rocks, looking for little rolls of forgotten parchment. She had almost given up, when a small patch of cream paper above the left side of her head caught her eye. She grinned as she pulled the note free and unwound the tiny roll of paper. Ben's lettering was at the top, and her reply was written beneath it. She wondered if he'd ever read it. Probably not. He would have taken it, like he did the others, if he had.

His script was a hurried mess, as usual.

The Castle Ball is next Quarter. Arto asked me to bring someone. Any interest?

The first time she had read it, Reina's heart had thrilled at the invitation. She had fumbled through her bag for a quill, which she had learned to keep with her for just such occasions. It had occurred to her that Ben might ask someone to accompany him to the ball, and she had secretly worried that it might be Vic. But he'd asked her instead. She was secretly glad about that, too.

Only if I get to fly Cyrus, she had responded.

Ben hardly ever let her fly Cyrus. He knew Reina was a nervous flyer. And Cyrus was temperamental as it was, preferring Ben and Princess Lina over anyone else. But he was the fastest griffin in the fleet, so naturally, Reina wanted to fly him, if only to prove to herself that she could.

Her stomach flipped as she reread the note, but she quickly subdued it. Ben's invitation to her was nothing out of the ordinary. He had only asked her out of convenience. Certainly nothing to get excited about.

Ben needed to deliver the crib he had made as a gift for the new Royal baby, and Reina was the obvious choice to help him do that. She'd helped him out with the last one, when he had delivered a commission bound for the Court of Merrows to a large, glass-topped chariot floating on the Southern Sea. She was sure that was the reason he had invited her to go with him. He just needed her help. It was nothing more than that.

Reina froze as the outline of a familiar figure moved beyond the waterfall. *Ben.* What was he doing here?

Worriedly, she glanced down at her soaked shirt. There was no way she could get back to her dry clothes without being seen. The light blue fabric was opaque, but still, she blushed at the thought of Ben seeing her in it.

She made herself as still as possible, peering out at him from her hiding spot as he shed his shirt. He stepped onto the flat stone where she had jumped from moments ago, tossing his shirt to the side.

He hesitated, then flicked his eyes below, scanning the water. Reina backed further against the cool stones of the rock wall behind her. She knew he had spied her pack and her clothes. She pressed herself as flat as possible, shivering as rivulets of cool water trailed down her back. She didn't make a sound, but Ben had already guessed where she was. "Drat," she whispered.

He dove a perfect arc, then pulled long strokes across the smooth water in her direction. Reina's heart leapt into her chest as he stepped out of the water. This would be the first time she had seen him in over a week, the first time she had been alone with him since their awkward exchange in the kitchens.

Ben was obscured by the falling water, and she followed the fuzzy outline of his frame warily until he came into clear view. Water dripped from the ends of his shaggy hair, which was now more burnished than gold. The drops landed on his tanned skin, making little, winding lines down his chest.

Reina only stared until he nodded in her direction. "Reina," he said quietly.

Hearing her name on his lips suddenly made her self-conscious, and she wrapped her arms across her chest, his message crinkling in her right palm. She sniffed. "Ben."

He flicked his eyes to the parchment. "For me?" he asked, stepping towards her.

He was close—close enough that Reina could see his wet lashes clinging to one another. They created a dark frame around his golden eyes. When she didn't answer, Ben shot her a sideways grin, making her stomach do a flip. She nodded mutely, holding out the roll of damp paper.

Ben took it, his rough fingers brushing her own. Reina pulled her hand back swiftly as little shockwaves traveled up her arm. Ben unfolded the paper, quickly scanning his invitation and her term of acceptance. He chuckled, peering up at her. "So that's a 'yes' then? I mean, provided I let you fly Cyrus?" He tapped her arm with the paper playfully. "I guess I can live with that," he said teasingly.

Reina lifted her chin. She was suddenly fuming, and she pulled her hands into fists, stilling the flames in her fingers. Ben was acting as if everything was perfectly normal between them. As if he hadn't just avoided her for an entire week. As if he didn't care that he had wasted half the time she had left in Caelium—half the time she had left with him. She glared at his jovial expression. Apparently, he didn't care.

Ben's smile faltered at the look on her face. "What?" he asked warily. Reina didn't answer. Instead, she spun away. She couldn't take it anymore. He was unbelievable.

Ben followed her to the pool's edge. "Reina? What's wrong with you?" She didn't wait to hear more. Instead, she lifted her arms and dove under.

Reina smiled to herself as she shot across the water. Her dive had been a perfect arc. It was probably even better than Ben's.

She kicked hard, making distance, until finally, she ran out of air. She was satisfied to see she was almost at the pool's other side, and she pulled herself towards the bank as Ben splashed in behind her.

Reina didn't bother to hide as she lifted out of the water. She didn't care if Ben saw her in her wet shirt or not. She was too mad to care.

Her left fingers were already in flames, and she clenched her fist to still the heat as she marched to her dry clothes. She fumbled with her slacks. They slipped out of her hands, which only succeeded in making her angrier. Hot tears sprang into her eyes as she bent to pick them up again, and she swiped at her cheeks furiously.

Ben's soft footfalls sounded behind her as she studied the slacks through her watery gaze. With all her wracked emotion, it was amazing she hadn't singed the fabric. She waited, not turning, but Ben didn't move. Reina ground her teeth. It was obvious she needed to change. So why wasn't he turning away?

She gave an exaggerated exhale, but still, he didn't budge. She could feel the heat from his chest radiating onto the back of her head. Reina crossed her arms, suddenly conscious of her wet clothes. Ben's nearness was making her nervous.

Ben put a hand lightly on her shoulder. Reina shrugged it off, stepping away. He waited a moment. "What's wrong?" he asked quietly. Reina didn't answer. "Rei, tell me," he pressed.

That was it. Reina had had enough. He knew *very well* what was wrong, and if he didn't, well, he didn't deserve to hear it from her, did he? She spun towards him, leveling him with a flat stare. Her long hair was dripping down the front of her shirt, and she tossed a wet lock of curls behind her shoulder, shrugging lightly. "It's nothing, Ben," she said nonchalantly. She struggled to pull her face into a calm mask, but she knew she hadn't succeeded. Ben was never fooled. The fact that he could read her thoughts irritated her now more than ever.

Reina swirled one finger in the air. She couldn't keep the anger from her voice. "Could you turn around, please?" she snapped. Ben didn't move. He just blinked down at her with his sharp eyes. His burnished hair was parted over his left ear, the pointed tip of which flared towards the back of his head.

Despite herself, Reina had a sudden urge to span her fingers across it, to trace the outline of a shape so different from her own. It would be easy—so easy—to reach out her hand, but instead, she shrugged the thought away, angrier than ever that she had had such an impulse. She held Ben's gaze for as long as she could, but as usual, it felt as if he was peering into her soul.

Finally, she dropped her eyes. "I need to change," she muttered. Ben stared down at her for a moment longer, but Reina kept her gaze trained on the ground between their feet. She shuffled her weight, acutely aware of his half-clad figure dripping water on the stone in front of her.

At last, he turned away, and she released the breath she hadn't known she'd been holding. Ben swiped his shirt from the stone and moved to the edge of the pool, where he doused the sweat-stiffened fabric. He faced away from her, scrubbing at the shirt with a flat rock, hopelessly attempting to get out the stains.

Reina eyed him from her perch. His shirt would need a good washing when they went home. But that wouldn't be her problem for much longer. In fact, the Timekeeper's Court wouldn't even *be* her home soon. Her heart squeezed at the thought, and she pushed it away as she lifted Ben's wet shirt over her head and slipped back into her dry clothes.

Soaked in the warm sun, the heat of the dry fabric felt good against her cool skin. She squeezed the last of the dripping water out her hair and twisted it into a high knot as Ben wrung out his shirt. He stood and tossed it over his head, still facing away from her. Then he planted his hands on his hips and gazed out across the water.

Reina studied his back. She was so angry with him. So hurt by him leaving her alone, hurt that he didn't care she was leaving soon.

But somehow, she already missed him, too. "Done," she said quietly.

Ben turned, his expression patient as his agile feet scaled the rocks towards her. It irritated Reina to no end. How could he be so calm when she felt like she was going to explode? She lifted her pack with one arm, slinging it across her back harder than was necessary. Then she folded her arms, looking away from him as her fingers cooled.

He stopped on the stone a few feet away from her. "Rei," he said quietly, his voice a patient question.

She bit the inside of her lip. "Ben," she mocked. He chuckled under his breath, stepping closer.

Ben folded his arms the same way she had done, cocking his head to one side. "I want to show you something," he said softly.

Reina didn't answer. What could he possibly want to show her?

He dipped his head towards her profile. "Do you want to see it?" he said, prodding.

His composure was infuriating. Reina's chest flared, and she clenched her fists, warring with the flames that wanted free. She huffed in irritation. "Not really," she snapped.

Ben frowned down at her. He studied his feet for a moment and adjusted his weight, then raised his eyes. "And why not?" he asked patiently.

Reina felt like she was going to explode. Was he really going to make her say it? She chewed the inside of her cheek. "Just trying to create some distance. You know, like you've been doing?"

She tapped her foot, and Ben stared at it, absorbing her words. He peered up at her, obviously confused. "What do you mean?"

Reina dropped her arms as she spun to face him. "You know very well what I mean!" she shouted. "I'm leaving. Right after the Castle Ball, Ben!" Her throat tightened, and she swallowed past it, struggling to speak. "We only have a few more days to be"—she flailed her arms—"to be together before I go." She sighed, fighting for control of her wavering voice. "I understand that you're upset with me, but did you have to stay away the whole time? I…" Reina shook her head. She couldn't say more. She was going to cry if she did. Already, a tear was escaping down her cheek, and she swiped at it furiously, turning away to hide it.

Ben gave her shoulder a gentle tug, turning her to face him. He pulled her close, and despite herself, Reina collapsed against his chest. Ben folded her tightly into his arms, and she wrapped her own around his low back, resting her forehead on the little dip between his ribs. He smelled of sunshine, and swimming, and sweat, and wood shavings—much better than her swimming shirt—and as he rested his chin on top of her head, Reina thought she had never felt safer in her entire life. What little shield she'd held against the sting of her leaving collapsed as Ben ran one hand down her back.

He nuzzled the top of her head. "Come with me," he whispered.

Little shivers tingled down past Reina's ears. She nodded against his shirt, and he moved his hands to her arms, slowly unwinding them from his back. Then he laced her fingers with his, the warmth of his palm resting solidly against her own.

Reina was still hurt. And she was still angry, but still, she allowed herself to be led along. It was quite against her nature, but Ben's quiet, gentle way often had that effect on her. So, she went with him. And as she padded along behind him, the thought occurred to her that she would follow him anywhere.

CHAPTER 13

BEN

Reina had left Jade at the edge of the woods, and Ben was glad of it. He had been dreading the walk back to the valley. He was exhausted.

Jade cooed low as he approached, studying him curiously with a large eye. Ben patted her neck as she ruffled her wings. No doubt she could sense his swirling emotions. They were bouncing around inside of him like a school of tiny fish rushing from a net in a stream.

Jade rested her large beak against his upper arm, cooing again. Ben grinned. Griffins had always understood him better than most. "I'm okay, alright? Don't make a fuss in front of her," he whispered. Jade blinked her large eye slowly, then stood to attention. Ben smiled. "Good girl."

Reina had just finished stuffing her pack into the saddle bag on Jade's other side. Without a word, she braced both her arms on the griffin's furry back and gracefully swung astride. Ben smiled up at her, and she shot him a smirk.

"You can fly, but I prefer to sit in front, okay?"

Ben nodded. He tried not to let his emotions play across his face. He was totally fine with that. More than fine, in fact. "Sure. Absolutely."

He wouldn't have had it any other way. The thought of holding Reina close in his arms, even for a while, was all he wanted.

Reina focused her gaze over the top of Jade's feathered head. "Good," she said decidedly. "Then let's go. I can't stay out all day. I've got work to do at home."

Ben moved to Jade's back, pressing his lips together to stifle his grin. The way Reina said *home* made his heart leap. To him, home was wherever she was, and right now, that was the Time-keeper's Court. He studied the back of Reina's head thoughtfully as he jumped astride behind her. He wondered if she felt the same.

Reina handed him the reins, and Ben scooted forward until his thighs brushed the backs of Reina's legs. He wrapped one arm securely around her slim waist, then he whistled low. Jade leapt forward at his call, and he tightened his grip on Reina as they leapt into the air.

Reina tucked her hands over his forearm, her grip revealing

the bit of trepidation about flying she refused to let anyone but him see. He smiled as Jade swooped, and Reina's fingers pressed harder into his skin. He had always been able to see through her tough exterior. Even Reina knew he could. Ben could tell that his keen awareness of her feelings sometimes irritated her, but he simply couldn't help it. For him, Reina was like the sun. He was drawn to her fiery heat and burning light, and he noticed every nuance of change in her expression and posture, even when he could tell she didn't want him to.

A few reddish-gold strands of her fiery hair had escaped from above her ear. They tickled Ben's cheek in the wind. When they were finally cruising smoothly, he let go of Reina's waist to capture them.

His fingers brushed her skin with the motion, and she stiffened. Ben paused, waiting. Then, slowly, he let his fingertips graze her hairline. The strands of hair were forgotten, but still, he pretended to be tucking them back in place, lingering longer than was necessary. He wondered if she had noticed.

Reina didn't stop him as he trailed the skin beneath her ear. She relaxed against his chest, letting her head rest on his shoulder. Ben froze, blinking down at her. So, she had noticed.

Lightly, he continued, trailing down the side of her neck. Reina shivered, and Ben was sure he was going to burst into flames. He pressed his lips together. If he didn't stop, he was going to something truly crazy—something like kissing her. Slowly, he pulled his hand away.

Reina sprang up like a coiled spring. She scooted forward, giving more than enough space between them to ensure their bodies couldn't touch. Then, she tucked the stray hairs firmly behind her ear on her own.

Ben watched her reaction, frowning. He wouldn't have touched her again, but she was gripping Jade's feathers so tightly he was afraid she was going to pull them out. Carefully, he scooted forward. He wrapped his forearm loosely across her stomach, being careful only to touch her where necessary. He didn't want to make her uncomfortable again.

Touching her certainly hadn't felt uncomfortable to him. In fact, it had been more than comfortable. When she leaned into him moments ago, he had felt his world catch fire. She hadn't stopped him when he ran his fingertips over her skin, so he thought she felt the same. Ben slid his eyes to Reina's hands. Obviously not. Judging by her white-knuckled grip on Jade's feathers and the stiff way she was sitting in his arms, it was clear he was mistaken.

Ben squared his jaw. If that was the way she felt about it, then he certainly wouldn't do it again. Besides, touching Reina did strange things to him. It made his insides all fluttery. Made him think strange thoughts. He'd very nearly kissed her a moment ago, and that was the last thing either of them needed. Reina would be gone soon, off to marry Lord Malcom and rule Monrovia as Queen. Kissing her would be a disaster.

Jade's talons scraped up dirt as they landed on the hillside above the Court of Mountain Fairies. Ben slid down first, then held a hand up to Reina. She ignored it, sliding wordlessly off the griffin's back on her own. Ben frowned at the back of her head as she pulled her hair free. He dropped his palm, stuffing it deep into his pocket as she rewound her fiery curls into a high knot. Apparently, she couldn't even stand to touch his hand now.

Inside his pocket, his fingers found the other bracelet—the one from his dream. Ben brushed the cool gems of the Mountain Aster, his thoughts straying to Reina's smooth skin beneath his fingertips. He watched as she spun to face him, tucking stray hairs behind her ears.

She twisted her lips, chewing the inside of her cheek as she avoided his gaze. Ben cleared his throat. Her skin was forgotten. Now, it was her mouth that had his attention. She pressed her lips together as she stared into the valley beyond him, and all Ben could think about was pressing them with his own.

He startled out of his reverie as Reina brushed past him. He turned to watch her move down the hillside, headed for the doors. Ben led Jade to shade beneath a cluster of small trees, then he followed after her.

Reina stood in front of the doors, her head lifted to study the designs Ben had carved on their high frames. Since this morning, countless clusters of Mountain Aster had sprouted around the foundation. Reina stood among the five-pointed flowers, their blooms reaching as high as her knees. They trailed out in trickling fingers to the hillside above, like intricate constellations of tiny, lavender stars.

The doors dwarfed Reina in size, and now that Ben could see them in comparison to her small body, he realized just how large his project had been. It was amazing to him that he had been able to complete them in just one week.

He stopped beside Reina's shoulder, but she didn't turn. She folded her arms. "Quite the accomplishment, Benjamin," she said quietly.

Ben grinned. Reina only used his full name when she was truly impressed with something. "Thanks."

She twisted her mouth. "I assume this is what you've been doing all this time?"

Ben nodded. "Yes."

Reina cocked her head, following the carved tears flowing from the bottle near the doors' base. "Impressive."

Ben slid his gaze to her. He could tell by her tone that there was more she had to say. She pressed her lips together thought-fully. "Though, I have to admit I was less than impressed to have our picnic cancelled." She sighed. "And to be without you for a whole week." She turned, her eyes questioning as she studied Ben's face. "Especially since I'll be gone soon."

Ben watched her as she held his gaze. Her eyes were full of questions he wasn't sure how to answer. And there was a hint of something else in them that he couldn't name. Grief? Longing?

Whatever it was, it made the left of his chest ache. Without thinking, he reached for her hand, giving it a squeeze.

Reina dropped her eyes. "I'm sorry, Reina. Truly." He shook his head. "I didn't *want* to be away from you. Of course, I didn't. I just...I just got so absorbed with the work here..." He gestured to the ruins, shaking his head. "Anyway, I'm sorry."

Reina gave his hand a small squeeze before she dropped his palm. Then she folded her arms protectively over herself as she studied the doors. She nodded appreciatively at his designs.

"They really are some of your best work, Ben." She frowned slightly, flicking her eyes to him. "But what made you decide to fix them in the first place?" She gestured to the court ruins. "I mean, it seems kind of pointless with the rest of the court lying in ruins." Ben pressed his lips, and she held out a hand. "No offense, of course. I just...I'm just trying to understand."

Ben studied the doors quietly. He wasn't exactly sure how to answer Reina's question. He didn't know how to without giving too much of his dream away. "I um...I had a gift, from Willow," he said softly.

Reina frowned. "The dryad?"

Ben nodded. "Yes. She sent wood from a fallen Eik. It had a note." He flicked his eyes to her wrist. "The lumber is what I crafted your bracelet from. And the doors, too." He shuffled his feet nervously. "And then...and then I had a dream." He swallowed, then cleared his throat. "Jubal was there." He dropped his eyes. "And you."

Reina turned to face him, clearly interested. She peered at him intently. "Jubal?"

Ben nodded. "The mountain satyr—Jubal Hightree. He used to be the baker here, among other things." Ben smiled. "He fed me while I worked. Kept me company." He flicked his eyes to Reina. "Jubal used to interpret dreams for my parents."

Despite the many times he had recited the Histories for her, Ben had never told her how he was, at one time, heir to the Court of Mountain Fairies. She had always just known him as Benjamin: The Griffin Keeper, and then, later, as Benjamin: Master of the Timekeeper's Court.

Ben watched her carefully as he said the next part. "My parents were the rulers here, in the Court of Mountain Fairies."

Reina nodded slowly. Her face was pulled into a relaxed mask, but Ben could tell she was pretending. The information had surprised her. He wondered if she felt as shocked as he had when she told him she was set to be Queen of Monrovia.

She slid her eyes back to the doors, absorbing his words. "So, what happened in this dream?" she asked softly. Ben shrugged. His heart was pounding, but he feigned nonchalance. "Well, in the dream I went home." He gestured to the crumbling wall of the palace nearest them, which had once made one side of the great hall. Its edges were charred, and there was a large hole in the side of it where the window used to be. "The palace was just as I remember it. It was completely restored."

He paused, the muscle in his jaw flexing. Reina lifted her brow. "And then what?"

Ben cleared his throat. He didn't quite know how much of the next part he should say. "You were there, in the kitchen," he said slowly. "You were making a cake."

He waited, watching Reina blink rapidly. He hoped she wouldn't make him say more. She turned away, her expression shrouded as she scanned the palace wall. "And where is this kitchen? I'd like to see it," she said quietly.

Ben nodded. He couldn't see any harm in that. "Sure. Follow me."

Ben picked his way through the rubble that had once been the palace steps with Reina close on his heels. After stumbling over several loose stones, he finally made it to the front doors—or what was left of them. Their dark wooden frame was charred black from the drake's fiery breath, and the right door hung limply from the top hinge. Ben gave it a hard tug, and it pulled free. Then he tossed the ruined wood to the side and stepped through.

Reina gingerly stepped over the threshold behind him. She blinked into the dim light, allowing her eyes to adjust to the great hall's interior. Ben stepped to the far end of the hall and leaned against the wall, surveying her reaction. It felt strange to have her in his old home—a little too close to his dream. Only this time, it was for real.

Quietly, Reina padded onto the threadbare rug in the room's center. Besides a set of lopsided curtains hanging on what once had been the window frame to her left, it was the only piece of decoration left in the hall, save a broken rocking chair in the far corner. It had once been housed on the second floor, but now there was a large hole in the ceiling above Ben's head, where the chair had fallen through an upstairs bedroom floor.

Ben watched her as she spun in a circle, studying the room's high beams, then she moved to the rocker, gently pressing the top of it. The old chair tottered back and forth with a faint creak, then stilled again. Reina folded her arms.

"It's got good bones," she said, staring up at the rafters. Her voice reverberated off the empty sandstone walls. Ben nodded. He followed her gaze to the ceiling, where a small starling gazed down at them from its nest in the crook where the rafter met the wall. "Apparently, she thinks so, too," Reina said, giggling. Ben smiled up at the little bird, watching it start at Reina's musical laughter. It fluttered its wings and zipped out the large hole in the wall to its right.

Reina turned her gaze to him, still grinning. "Well, is this all there is?" she teased, holding her hands out to the empty room. She strode past him then, jabbing his stomach gently with her elbow as she passed. He grunted, shielding his midsection protectively as her giggle echoed past him in the hallway.

He thought she was going to stop in the kitchen. Ben eyed her warily as she paused in the doorway, but she kept moving. She slipped past the hall to the atrium, towards the back bedroom where Ben had been sleeping. Ben followed her, leaning against the doorframe as she moved inside.

He watched as she explored the bare bookshelves. Then she stepped behind the chaise, fanning her fingers across its worn fabric. She eyed Ben's threadbare blanket lying in a rumpled heap near the foot, and she raised a brow. "Your bed, I take it?" she said, teasing.

Ben smiled as she hopped over the edge of the seat, stretching herself luxuriously across the overstuffed cushions. She snuggled under the worn blanket, feigning sleep. He chuckled, crossing his arms. "For now."

Reina gave the thick upholstery a heavy pat, causing a cloud of dust to puff past her fingers. She coughed as she sat upright, waving her hands to clear the air. "Not bad," she said, half-choking. "I mean, I could do without the dust."

She stood, giggling as she moved towards the door. Ben stepped back, careful not to touch her as she slipped past him into the narrow hall. He watched as she moved away, trailing her fingers down the wall, willing her not to stop at the kitchen.

His heart skipped when she reached the door. She peered inside curiously, and Ben prayed to the Source she wouldn't go in. It would be too much for him to see her there—too close to his dream.

Reina's red hair disappeared past the doorway, and his stomach clenched. His feet felt like stones as he dragged himself to follow her. He didn't go inside. Instead, he leaned against the frame, watching her.

Ben tried to appear casual, but his muscles were wound in a tight knot. He could hear his heartbeat thrumming loudly in his own ears. It wouldn't have surprised him if Reina could hear it.

He watched her as she moved lithely around the island. Her green eyes missed nothing as she took in the room. Of course, it looked nothing like the bustling kitchen it once had been. The countertops were layered in dust, and some of the cabinet doors had come off, exposing chipped cups and plates inside of them. No fire burned in the large hearth in the right wall, and the large iron pot above it hung haphazardly on its trivet.

Reina stopped near the large basin behind the island, spinning towards him. She braced her arms on the counter behind her and leveled him with a teasing grin. "So, about this dream."

Ben's heart tripped over itself. He swallowed tightly. "What about it?" He hoped his tone sounded bored, but he truly doubted it.

Reina smirked. "*Tell* me about it. You said I was in it, didn't you? So, where was I when I was baking this cake?" She raised a brow. "You said I was in the kitchen, right?" She flicked her eyes around the room, then pointed to a spot near her feet. "Was I here?"

Ben studied her silently. His mind was spinning in a thousand different directions. He wanted to explain, but he wasn't sure he knew how. In fact, he was certain he didn't know how. So, perhaps it was better if he just showed her.

His chest felt like it was on fire just looking at her, and he was sure if he showed her what had happened in his dream, he would burst into flames. Ben wondered if Reina felt something similar before her fingers ignited. She studied him curiously, and Ben only hesitated a moment before his feet took over. Then he was walking towards her.

He saw her expression change as he moved past the island. She frowned slightly, a small, blanched look of panic draining her features. "Ben?" But he didn't answer. His movements were determined, never breaking his gaze.

Ben knew he was scaring her. He could tell by the look on her face. He could only imagine what his own face looked like—a jumbled mix of nervousness and longing, he was sure. But he couldn't help himself. The sight of her standing there brought the memory of her lips on his own, and there was nothing that could have stopped him from being close to her in that moment.

He stopped one step from her, his chest heaving. His hands were shaking as he braced one on each side of her, his fingers grazing hers where she gripped the counter. She didn't move, didn't pull away from his touch like he was worried she would.

"What are you doing?" she whispered. Her green eyes searched his own, and Ben grappled for command of his swirling thoughts. He needed to explain, to help her understand.

He hadn't understood himself until this very moment, right here in the kitchen, right here with Reina penned between his arms, looking for all the known worlds like the mate he had known in his dream.

Ben dipped his head to her ear, grazing her cheek with his jaw. "You were exactly here," he whispered. Reina shivered, and he moved his head backward to investigate her face.

Heat was rising in her cheeks, and the green of her eyes shimmered in the low light. "A-and what was I…what was I doing?" she whispered.

Ben hadn't often heard her stumble on her words, and the thought that he was the cause of it thrilled him. He rocked his head slightly from side to side. "Several things," he said softly, grinning.

Her full lips parted, and he resisted the urge to tip her chin. He adjusted his weight, allowing the fingers of one hand to cover the top of her own. He rubbed his thumb in a little circle over the back of it as he spoke. "For one, you were baking."

Reina visibly relaxed, the tension of the moment momentarily broken by his joke. She rolled her eyes. "I know that, silly. I mean, *why* was I here?"

Ben hesitated. That was the crux of the issue, wasn't it? He wasn't sure how she would feel about the rest of the dream—why she was here, or what that meant, or the fact that they had kissed. He knew how he wanted her to feel, of course. For the first time, he felt that truth as certainly as he had ever felt anything in his life.

The bracelet burned in its hiding place in his pocket, and for a moment, he considered showing it to her. But then he thought better of it. That might be too much. She might not like the fact that he'd dreamed they were mates. He sighed, the tiny muscle in his jaw flexing as he studied his bare feet.

"Ben? What is it?" she prodded.

Ben met her gaze. He wet his lips. "I, um, I don't know how to tell you. It's kind of hard to explain." He dropped his eyes again.

Reina moved her small hand beneath his chin, forcing him to look at her. "Tell me," she whispered. "I want to know."

Ben blinked down at her large green eyes. He studied the line of freckles that marched across her nose to fan out onto her cheek. Her skin looked soft, and he traced the line of it to her chin. He paused on her lips. "I could probably show you better than I can tell you," he said gruffly.

Reina gave a small nod. "Okay, then show me," she whispered.

Slowly, Ben lifted one arm to curl it around her back. He lowered his face towards her own, and when she parted her lips, he knew it was an invitation. He pulled her to him as one of her hands lifted to wrap in the hair at his ear. Then he met her lips.

It was a kiss unlike any other he had experienced. Sweet, smoldering heat radiated down his back, fanning out to his limbs. His body was on fire, consumed by the moment. Consumed by Reina. His dream didn't hold a candle to the fire of this moment. And there was nothing he could've done that would have prepared him for the onslaught of emotions that caved in on him.

Right then and there, he knew. He was holding his mate—his one true love. And as they deepened their kiss, a niggling thought wormed its way into the back of his mind.

Soon, Reina would leave him. And Ben was sure now.
He would never survive it.

CHAPTER 14

BEN

A clattering crash sounded from the front great hall, causing Reina to start. Ben pulled back to listen, frowning. Reina's eyes were muddled, and her breathing was coming as fast as his own. He held a finger to his lips. "Quiet, okay?" he said softly.

He had pulled her hair down from its knot moments ago, and she smoothed it back towards the nape of her neck as she frowned up at him. "Ben?" she said softly, reading the worry in his gaze.

Ben stepped away, quietly opening the kitchen drawers. A forgotten blade was stashed in the back of one. He pulled it free, then stalked towards the kitchen door with Reina on his heels.

In the great hall, a small, cloaked heap was lying in the front doorway, and above it, a set of battered horns. "Jubal!" Ben shouted. He moved towards the old satyr's crumpled body and knelt beside him, cradling his head in his lap.

Ben eyes searched for an injury. Jubal was holding his midsection, and a small pool of dark blood was gathering on the dusty wood floor beneath it. It was rapidly spreading outward. Ben flicked his gaze to Reina as she sank to the floor beside him, gesturing to the blood. Wordlessly, he handed her the blade, and she began ripping strips of fabric off one sleeve to press on top of Jubal's hands.

Jubal opened one eye and peered up at him. "What happened?" Ben asked him.

Jubal swallowed convulsively. His lips were pale, and his mouth was very dry. "Marcus. It was Marcus and the banded mountain fairies."

All the color drained from Ben's face. A cold fear coursed through his chest, laced with tangled, dark memories. "Where?" he said flatly.

"At the doors," Jubal croaked. "They burned them to ash. When I tried to stop them, one of his men stabbed me with his blade. Ran me straight through." He stopped, pulling in a ragged breath, then turned his eyes to Reina. She was pressing heavily on the satyr's stomach. "A little less pressure, ah, Reina? I presume?"

Reina blinked down at him, clearly surprised he knew her name. She cut her eyes to Ben.

Jubal coughed weakly. "There's no use anyway. I'm as good as gone. And a relief it will be for me to go." He sighed and closed his eyes. "Ah, it will be so good to see them all again."

He grabbed Ben's hand with his gnarled fingers as he opened one eye, peering up at him. "I do so hate to miss it, though."

Ben frowned down at him. "Miss what, Jubal?"

Jubal gave him a wan smile. "The rebuilding of the court, of course." He gestured to Reina with his chin. "And all that will transpire with yourself and young Reina here."

Ben shook his head. "It was only a dream, Jubal. Nothing more. The doors are destroyed now, anyway. So, it's done. I'm going home. And Reina is, too."

Reina shot him a look, but Ben didn't meet her gaze. He focused instead on watching the wound in Jubal's stomach seeping onto the floor. Jubal chuckled, a ragged, garbled sound. "If you say so, my boy. If you say so. We lay our best plans, and the Source laughs, as they say."

He grinned, then his lips fell. Ben could see he was growing weak. "Just promise me one thing."

Ben met Jubal's watery gaze. It seemed impossible to him that he was watching yet another familiar face fade from this world. He swallowed past a lump, his mind flipping rapidly through a series of similar scenarios, a collection of memories on which he'd rather not dwell. "What's that?" he asked him, forcing the words.

"Take my bones through the open door when you go."

Ben frowned down at Jubal. He wasn't at all sure what the old satyr meant. But Jubal often spoke in odd ways, so Ben didn't think much of it. He nodded. "I promise," he answered. Jubal nodded once.

"Good," he whispered.

As Ben and Reina watched, Jubal faded slowly and quietly away. Miraculously, his face appeared more peaceful in death than it had in life, and Ben wondered what his old friend might be seeing in the distant place that, for Jubal, had now come close. Ben imagined it was something far beyond anything he had ever known. He wondered if Jubal was greeting his family who had passed on before him, and Ben's own parents, in that space just past the one where the living dwelled. He was quite sure he was, and the thought of it warmed the space inside Ben that often felt lonesome and cold. Ben smiled softly as a quiet peace akin to the expression on Jubal's still face spread through his center.

The old satyr's palm had long gone slack, and Ben quietly slipped his hand from beneath it. Gently, he closed Jubal's eyes and whispered reverent words he had so long ago spoken—the ones he had said after he wept bitter tears at the loss of his parents. They were the words of his people, more sacred to him with each passing cycle.

"Let weary eyes now sleep, my friend.

And wake, with the Source, in Hereafter.

Release your grief, from this life, my friend.

And rest in eternity's rapture.

Through misty mountains you have gone,

To meet those gone before.

And someday soon, I'll greet you there,

Beyond the open door.

Leave the door unlatched for me,

So I can find my way.

And gather 'round to greet me there,

When I pass by that way."

Reina gripped his free hand. She gave it a small squeeze. Ben stood, and Reina helped him to lift Jubal carefully over his shoulder. Silently, he and Reina made their way out into the street. They picked their way through the rubble, following the trail of Jubal's blood. It spotted the scorched cobblestones in large red splotches, winding up the street towards the court doors—or what was left of them.

The stones of the foundation had been knocked from their places. They spilled out in a tumbled heap from the North Wall, and the doors lay beyond in a large pile of scorched pieces. Some of them were still in flames. Ben could barely make out the tip of the wing he had carved on the left door's surface. The rest of his carvings were completely charred.

It was clear by the mark who had done it. A large blue swath marked the ground of the hillside—its color rendered from the Banded Berry bushes that encircled the rogue mountain fairies' camp further west. "Marcus," Ben whispered.

He shook his head in disbelief, anger roiling in his chest at the sight of the banded mountain fairies symbol. That same symbol marked every banded fairy's left upper arm, a blue band of dark ink that signaled their allegiance to their leader—none other than Ben's brother, Marcus.

Ben and the others at the Timekeeper's Court hadn't been the only ones to survive the giants and the fires of the drake. Ben's brother and some others had survived, too. Together, Marcus and his faction of fairies had set up camp deep in the West Mountains. Ben had never been to Marcus's camp. He'd never had a reason to. Marcus and his lackeys had always kept to themselves. Until now.

Jubal had been right. He had stirred Marcus's anger by rebuilding the doors. It was obvious by this display that his brother was furious with him. Marcus had sent his men to give him a warning: Leave. Or else.

Reina appeared beside him, her hands slack and her face grim. "Who would do this?" she whispered.

Ben ground his teeth, watching as dark smoke rose from the ruined doors. "Marcus," he said flatly. He turned to her, hot anger and deep grief swimming in his gaze.

"It was my brother, Marcus."

CHAPTER 15

BEN

Ben laid Jubal's body down on the wide, flat stone at the back of his cave. Reina came behind him, covering Jubal's body with Ben's threadbare blanket. She pulled it up gently over the satyr's still face. Then she stood quietly beside Ben, allowing him a moment in his grief.

Jubal's sudden loss in the same place he had lost his parents, his home, and all that he had ever known brought back memories and feelings that Ben would have preferred stayed long buried. He stared hard at Jubal's still frame beneath the blanket, his nails biting little crescent shapes into his palms to stifle his tears.

Ben swallowed past a large lump. He couldn't believe Jubal

was really gone. So much wisdom went with him, so much joy.

He cleared his throat softly, causing Reina to turn. She smiled up at him quietly. Ben reached for her hand, when suddenly, her smile went slack. Her eyes rounded into large, green pools. She reached out one arm, focusing on something behind him. "Ben! Watch out!"

Ben started to duck, not sure which way to move, but realized it didn't matter. He had already been struck.

Something sharp burned in his right side, and he groaned as the sensation twisted with a sickening, squelching sound. He slid his eyes to Reina. Her face was all terror, focused on the burning spot in his side. Ben reached for her. "Rei," he mumbled.

The room went hazy as Ben fell.

"Ben! NO!" Reina shouted. Ben could hear her voice echo as his head knocked hard against the floor. Something warm and hot was spreading from the side of his head. It smelled like copper and rust. Reina's worried face hovered above him. Then, his eyes rolled back, and the world went silent.

Ben heard scuffling above his right ear. It grew louder as someone shouted, and he opened one eye to see a blurry image of Reina swinging a large, clay pot at someone's head. The someone was holding a spear, but he couldn't make out their features.

His side burned. He wanted to reach for it, but his head was aching so badly that he stayed still. The tip of the someone's spear glittered above him in the cave's dim light. The end of it was sticky and dark, and it occurred to Ben that he had been attacked, that the burning in his side had been caused by the spear's sharp blade.

Reina was dodging the blade above him now. He wanted to get up, to help her. He tried, but as soon as he lifted his head, his world went hazy. Reina swung the clay pot again, and his vision tunneled to a point just as she made contact with the side of his attacker's head. She shrieked as the clay pot shattered into pieces, and Ben closed his eyes as shards of sharp pottery rained down on him.

The next thing he knew, Reina was on her knees beside him, cradling his head in her hands, her face close. She was speaking, but her voice was muffled. He couldn't make out the words.

Ben opened his eyes. His lids felt heavy, but he moved over her, assessing for damage. There was blood along her right arm. "You're hurt," he croaked, frowning. His tongue felt thick, and he tried to swallow, but there was no moisture in his mouth.

Reina shook her head. "Never mind that now." She glanced behind her, where the body of his attacker lay limp on the cave floor. She turned back to him, her eyes desperate. "Ben, you've got to get up. I can't carry you, and he's going to wake up any moment." She tugged on his sleeve. "Come on, I'll help you."

Ben nodded. He held his breath, wincing as Reina helped him sit upright. His head throbbed, and the wound on his side burned sharply. The fabric of his shirt was sticking to the skin around it. He glanced down. Thick, dark blood radiated across his shirt from a jagged cut in his side. Ben sucked his teeth. It looked deep. Suddenly, he felt sick, and he turned his head, swallowing bile as Reina pulled a strip of linen from her one good sleeve. She wadded it into a tight ball, pressing it tightly to his wound.

Ben took over, trying not to feel the seep of his blood around the fabric of Reina's shirt. He held on to her with his free hand and stood on shaking legs, hissing as pain shot up from his side.

Reina glanced nervously behind them. The attacker moaned, rolling onto his back as Ben turned to look at him. "Come on, let's go," she said quickly. She urged Ben towards the cave's opening, but he didn't move. He stared down at his attacker in shock.

Ben could believe Marcus would destroy the doors. And he might even go as far as understanding his reasoning for it. His brother had long held bitterness over all they had endured, and even before Jubal had mentioned it, it had occurred to Ben that Marcus might not like his work.

But to attack his own brother? To try to kill him? He couldn't believe Marcus would stoop so low.

Instead of joining Ben at the Timekeeper's Court after the loss of their home, Marcus and a few others had retreated further into the West Mountains. Marcus ruled the camp there with an iron fist. Ben had heard rumors of his cruelty, but he had hoped they were simply that—rumors.

Ben had never truly believed them. But now? Now that he had experienced Marcus's violence firsthand? Ben believed the awful stories were true.

It had been said that anyone who dared cross Marcus would pay with their life. Apparently, Marcus thought Ben's work at the Court of Mountain Fairies was doing just that—crossing him. It was clear he was threatened, afraid of having his power as leader destroyed.

Ben was the firstborn, the heir to the throne of the Court of Mountain Fairies. It was possible that Marcus thought he was trying to restore the court and take what little power Marcus held as ruler of his camp. Of course, that wasn't what Ben was doing. He didn't care if his brother had his own camp, and he certainly wasn't trying to take any power from him. Ben had never cared about that. His work on the doors had been about keeping his hands busy and his mind off Reina. But Marcus didn't know that.

Reina tucked herself under his arm, supporting his weak frame as they moved. Much to Ben's relief, they managed to make it out of the cavern and onto Jade's back before Marcus awoke. Ben was in no shape to fight his brother. Marcus was naturally larger and stronger than him, and from what Ben could see, his brother had grown even more so in their cycles apart.

Ben was near fainting as Reina flung herself astride Jade behind him. His head throbbed, and he collapsed onto her feathered neck as Reina hooked one arm around his waist. She whistled low, and Jade lurched forward, lifting into the sky.

Ben groaned as the motion twisted the wound on his side. Something warm spattered onto his right thigh. He glanced down at it weakly. A dark red blotch had crept past the hem of his shirt. It was soaking the leg of his trousers.

Ben's vision spun, and he closed his eyes. A cool darkness crept around the edges of his mind. It threatened to overtake him. He hoped they would make it back to the Timekeeper's Court before it did.

He didn't remember most of the flight back home. He wove in and out of hazy consciousness as Jade undulated through the mountain peaks, catching snatches of Reina's whispered prayers that he assumed were for his benefit.

Her hand clung shakily around his waist, gripping to the dry edge of his shirt. Ben wished he could do more to help her support his weight. His arms felt like lead weights as he used the last bit of his strength to wrap them around Jade's neck. Maybe his weak grip on her feathers would help hold him upright.

Jade swooped low. The movement stretched his wound, causing a shard of slicing pain to rip through his side. Ben sucked in a sharp breath. Then his eyes rolled back, and the world went dark.

CHAPTER 16

REINA

Reina didn't bother stopping at the stable yard. Instead, she brought Jade down near the garden. Amelie burst through the great room doors just as Jade's talons touched the dirt. Her grey eyes were stormy round pools, and her cornsilk hair swished behind her as she jogged towards them. She frowned up at Ben's limp frame, then flicked her eyes to Reina.

"What happened to him?"

Reina slid off Jade's back, careful to keep Ben in his seat. She braced one hand on his low back. "We were attacked. Near the ruins of the Court of Mountain Fairies. It was another mountain fairy—Ben's brother."

Henri's stunned voice called from behind her. "Marcus?" Henri's dark, sharp eyes were wide as he scanned Ben's body. Johann was just behind him. The larger fairy flicked his eyes to Amelie, then focused on Benjamin with a solemn face.

Reina nodded. "Yes. Ben said it was him."

Henri scoffed, shaking his head. "Of course it was Marcus." He turned to Johann and jerked his chin, then the two braced Ben's shoulders and waist and lifted him from Jade's back.

The griffin cooed nervously as Ben's body passed her gaze. Reina patted her flank. "It's okay, girl," she said softly. "He'll be alright." Reina eyed Ben's body slung limply between Johann and Henri. She hoped she was right. "Be careful with him," she called.

Henri nodded, and then he and Johann disappeared through the great room doors.

Amelie put a hand over Reina's arm. "I'll take care of Jade," she said quietly. "You go." The gesture tugged at Reina's last bit of resolve, and a heavy lump formed in her throat. She pressed her lips together, holding back the tears that threatened to fall. Amelie gave her arm a squeeze, a knowing look in her eyes. "Go to him," she urged.

Reina nodded, then she wrapped Amelie in a tight hug. "Thank you," she murmured, her voice catching in her throat.

"Of course," said Amelie. "Now, go. They'll probably take him to his workshop."

Reina stopped by the kitchens on her way. Thanks to Ben's late grandmother, Ita, Tamarisk trees grew in the gardens of the

Timekeeper's Court. As the realm's former healer, Ita had used the healing properties of the trees' pink blossoms to treat ailments of body and mind all across the realm.

Reina pruned the trees herself these days, and the fresh blooms were usually hung above the stove in the kitchens on a string to dry. Later, they were placed in small jars in the cabinet beside it. The dried blooms were the ones Ben had used on her thumb, but Reina was looking for fresher blooms—the more potent ones. She found just such a supply above the stove, and she quickly brought down one end of the string to collect a handful of the fresh, pink flowers. Then she hurried to the workshop.

Johann and Henri had laid Ben on the cot in the corner. He was as white as the sheet, and a fine sheen of sweat had broken out on his forehead. Johann was arranging the sheet, and Henri was muttering under his breath as he cut away Ben's tattered and blood-stained shirt. He turned to glance at Reina as she approached.

"It was Marcus? You're sure?" Reina nodded as Henri's grim face stared back at her. He sighed. "I'm sure his spear was laced with Banded Berry poison. It's highly toxic to mountain fairies. Ita hated it. It causes terrible infections and heavy bleeding. She always had a hard time treating anything caused by Banded Berries, because its poison competes with the Tamarisk."

Gently, Henri lifted Ben's shirt from his wound. He sucked his teeth, knitting his brows. "Once, a few of the griffins fell sick. Ita tried everything she knew, but the griffins grew weaker every day. By the end, she had given them enough Tamarisk to heal a whole army. But it wasn't enough. She couldn't figure out what had caused it."

He peered up at Reina. "Finally, Ita had an idea. She searched the stable yard, looking for anything that might have caused the griffins' sickness. That day, she found a small bush growing near the mountainside—hidden behind the stable's right edge. None of us had ever noticed it before. She brought a bough around to us all, asking, but we had never even seen it. The berries were dark and small. They grew in clusters, and each one had a dark blue band down the middle."

"Ita knew what they were. She had seen them before. Banded Berries, she called them. Vicious things. She warned us away from them. Said they had killed fairies before." Henri shrugged. "We never figured out how the bush got into the yard. And in the end, the griffins didn't make it."

Gently, Henri and Johann rolled Ben onto his side. He groaned with the movement, his head limp on the pillow. Reina frowned down at the jagged wound on his side. It was already festering at the edges, and a fresh line of bright blood was running down Ben's midsection.

She glanced down at her knees. They were stained dark red. Sudden images of Jubal's blood pooling beneath her flashed into her mind, and she swallowed as panic rose in her throat. Jubal had been stabbed, too. He had died so quickly. She flicked her eyes to

Ben's pale face. If she didn't help him soon, Ben was going to pass as quickly as Jubal had.

Reina clutched the Tamarisk tightly in her palm as she searched the workshop. She needed a bowl or something like it to grind the flowers in. The shelves by the window were full of supplies, but then her eyes landed on her mug. It was sitting on the end, wrapped with a leather strap. She swiped it, tucking the Tamarisk blooms inside, and used the end of Ben's mallet to grind the blooms into a fine paste.

Quickly, she knelt by the cot. With shaking fingers, she swiped the paste across Ben's dark wound. Despite Henri's warnings otherwise, she prayed that the remedy would work. It had to. Because she just couldn't live in a world without Ben, even if she was about to be on the other side of it.

In a moment, Amelie appeared beside her with a fresh piece of linen cloth. Henri and Johann left quietly, and together, she and Amelie wrapped Ben's waist with the bandage. Then they rolled him gently onto his back.

The movement caused something to fall out of Ben's pocket, and Amelie grabbed it as Reina began tucking the covers tightly beneath Ben's chin. Amelie held the object out in front of Reina's eyes. "Here's your bracelet, Rei. Ben had it in his pocket for some reason."

Reina frowned at the bracelet dangling from Amelie's fingers in confusion. She flicked her eyes up to her. Amelie raised a brow. "What?"

Reina held up her wrist. Her bracelet was securely fastened there. "It's not mine," she said softly.

She glanced down at Ben, whose eyes were still closed. His breathing had evened out. That was a good sign. At least, she hoped it was.

Amelie held the bracelet closer to her face. "Well, whose is it then? It came out of Ben's pocket, and it sure looks like the one he made for you. Almost exactly like it, actually."

Reina studied the bracelet curiously. It didn't just look like her bracelet. It was an *exact* copy of the one Ben had made for her. The only difference was a slightly different clasp—a set of interlocking wings.

Reina's heart burned. She wondered whose it was. It couldn't be meant for her, or Ben would have given it to her along with the other one. Wouldn't he?

There was another possibility—one that made her stomach hurt. Her mind swirled as images of Ben smiling widely at a petite, dark-haired fairy over dinner flashed through her mind. Maybe the bracelet wasn't hers. Maybe it was Vic's. The idea made her want to vomit, but she tried to keep her voice casual. She shrugged nonchalantly. "Who knows? Ben must've made one for someone else."

Amelie studied the bracelet dubiously. "I doubt it. And anyway, if he did, then who? I certainly can't think of anyone."

Reina reached to smooth an imaginary wrinkle from Ben's blanket. Amelie's questions were starting to annoy her for some reason. "I have no idea, Amelie. Does it really matter?" Her voice had come out more sharply than she had meant it to. Amelie's grey eyes registered hurt, and Reina cringed. She hadn't meant to hurt her feelings.

Amelie raised one shoulder. "I guess not," she said softly.

Amelie turned her head, searching around the room. "Well, if it's not yours, then where should I put it?"

Reina held out her palm, not meeting Amelie's gaze. "I'll keep it until he wakes up," she said lightly. Amelie eyed her carefully as she dropped the bracelet into her hand, but Reina ignored her, fastening the new bracelet on her wrist beside hers. She tucked her hand across them, the cool gems of both flowers pressing into her palm.

"I'll see you later, okay?" Amelie said quietly.

Reina moved her hand to glance down at the identical set. "Okay," she said absently.

Though they looked exactly the same, the new bracelet felt foreign against her skin. She pressed her lips, watching its gems sparkle in the soft light. It probably felt that way because it didn't belong to her. Ben had made the bracelet for someone else. Reina vowed she would give it back to him just as soon as he was awake. Then he could give it to whoever he wanted.

The thought of someone else wearing the bracelet made her stomach twist into a hard knot. Reina hoped Ben would wait to give it away until she was gone. She knew it wasn't hers, but she didn't think she could bear to see it on someone else's wrist. Especially not Vic's. And especially not after what had happened between her and Ben in the kitchen in the Court of Mountain Fairies.

Outside, the sun was beginning to drop behind the mountains. It cast a golden glow inside the workshop, its light filtering gently across Ben's features. He moaned in his sleep, and Reina's heart squeezed.

Suddenly, she wanted to be close to him—as close as possible. Carefully, she slipped beside him on the narrow mattress. His shoulder had moved out from beneath the blanket, and she tucked it back over him, fighting the urge to trail her fingers up towards his chin.

Reina braced on her elbow, watching the waning light dance over Ben's lips. The memory of them on her own was still fresh in her mind. Instinctively, she leaned towards them.

She couldn't stop herself. Her fingers moved of their own accord, past the edge of the blanket to touch the sharp edge of his jaw, when suddenly his lips parted. "Reina," he mumbled. Reina's hand froze.

She started to sit upright, but Ben murmured a few more nonsensical words, and his right arm flung across her side, pinning her flat to the mattress. She waited, unmoving while his breathing leveled out. It only took a few moments.

Reina thought about getting up, but exhaustion was taking

over, and Ben's arm felt sort of nice. It felt good to hear him say her name in his sleep, even if he had made the bracelet for someone else. She curled onto her other side, closing her eyes.

The weight of Ben's arm and his soft, even breath on her hair were lulling her under. She would only stay a moment. Then she would get up and sit in the chair across the room.

Ben pulled her towards him.

Reina's eyes flew open. He was as close to her as he'd ever been, with only the thin blanket separating his chest from her back. His lips were resting on her hair, and she could feel his warm breath against the back of her neck. He mumbled in his sleep, and the whispers sent little zings down her spine. She shivered, and Ben's arm pulled her even closer.

Reina smiled. Even in his sleep, Ben was aware of her every move. They had always been like that. When she moved, he moved. She had always felt that Ben knew her better than she knew herself. That was why it would hurt so badly when she had to go back through the gate. She would be leaving the only person who had ever truly known her. Reina tucked herself into a small ball beneath Ben's arm. How was she supposed to survive without him?

A deep ache formed in her middle. Maybe it would've been better if she had never met Ben, better if she hadn't come to Caelium at all. At least then she wouldn't have to deal with all this hurt.

She sighed heavily against the lump in her throat. If she had just stayed in Monrovia, then she wouldn't have to go through this pain—the pain of losing Ben. Her heart squeezed, and she sniffled as a tear escaped down her cheek.

Ben stirred behind her, and she sniffed, wiping her chin. Reina glanced back at him, but his eyes weren't open. "Ben, I need to go," she whispered.

He shook his head imperceptibly, holding her tighter. "Stay," he mumbled. "Stay with me."

How could she refuse?

Deep contentment spread from her center as she settled back beside him. She closed her eyes, allowing Ben to hold her. She tried not to think about the fact that it was the first and only time he would.

Exhaustion threatened, but before she went to sleep, Reina pretended that this was her life. That she would stay in Caelium forever, with Ben, and he would hold her just like this. He hadn't made a bracelet for someone else or wrecked their last days together by staying away. She had no other life to lead in Monrovia. There was no betrothal, no Lord Malcom, no throne to occupy. There was just her and Ben. Nothing and no one else mattered. There was just the two of them on the cot in the corner of the workshop, and the words of the mountain fairy she loved.

Stay. Stay with me.

There was nothing Reina wanted to do more. And if things were different, she would have. She would have stayed with Ben forever.

CHAPTER 17

BEN

Something was tickling the tip of Ben's nose. He wrinkled it, sniffing, then, he brought his fingers up to scratch. The stretch of his arm pulled at the wound on his side, and he winced, remembering. In his sleep, he had almost forgotten the attack yesterday. The wound from Marcus's blade throbbed in time with his head, and carefully, he put his arm back down.

Ben frowned. His arm was resting across a warm lump. Wearily, he opened his eyes. He blinked in surprise. Reina's head was lying on the pillow beside him. Her mass of fiery curls was standing out in all directions. The end of one was what had tickled his nose.

Soft morning light filtered through the workshop windowpane, casting a warm glow on the side of Reina's face. The golden rays tangled with the tips of her hair, making it look like it was on fire. Ben reached out, gently grasping a small curl above her ear. It was as soft as the downy feathers on the underside of Jade's neck. Reina groaned, and Ben pulled his fingers away, suddenly self-conscious. Despite what had happened between them in the kitchen of the palace, he wasn't sure how to behave with her. Reina stretched, and he winced as he rolled onto his back, creating a little distance between their bodies on the close cot.

He watched as Reina pulled her arms over her head. She stretched long, curling the tips of her toes. Then, she sat up, scratching the side of her fiery head. She crossed her legs as she gazed out the workshop window, clearly in a daze. Then, suddenly remembering where she was, she flicked her eyes to him. "Morning," she said groggily. A tinge of uncertainty crossed her features, but she quickly masked it. "How are you feeling?"

Ben smiled. "Better, I think" he said quietly. His voice sounded like gravel. "My head aches, but it's not that bad. The side is pretty rough though."

Reina swiveled to face him. "Let me see it."

Carefully, Ben lifted his arm as Reina pulled the covers back from his bare torso. He expected the movement to cause a searing pain, but it seemed like it was a little easier this time.

Reina frowned at the bandage wrapped across his midsection. Ben glanced down at it. There was a dark patch of his blood staining the fabric. "Try to sit up on your elbow," she instructed. Ben obeyed, wincing as he pushed himself upright. The wound tugged and burned, but he ignored it, watching the morning light play across Reina's features in soft, scattered patterns. It was distracting in the best way. Ben didn't know how he hadn't noticed before how beautiful she was.

He continued to stare as she flicked her green eyes up to him. She arched a brow. "What?" she asked, swiping at her cheek. "Is there something on my face?"

Ben grinned. He shook his head. "No. It's nothing," he muttered.

He lowered his eyes to her mouth, and the heady urge to press them with his own washed over him in a wave. He leaned towards her, watching her lips part. He was almost to her when he felt her small hand press gently into the center of his chest.

She pulled back, staring hard at her lap. "Ben, no," she said quietly.

Ben blinked in surprise. After their kiss in the kitchen yesterday, he had thought of little else. The scene had replayed countless times in his sleep, and nothing would have pleased him more than to replay it while awake. He studied Reina's closed features, watching her flush then blanch. It was clear she didn't feel the same. He swallowed, grimacing as he sat up onto his palm. "I'm sorry, Rei. I didn't mean to..."

Reina shrugged, cutting him off. "It's okay," she muttered.

Without saying more, she scooted closer, focusing intently on unwinding the bandage from Ben's waist. When she finally pulled it free, she sat up on her knees, completely absorbed in assessing the wound. Ben flicked his eyes towards it. He'd sometimes gone with his grandmother Ita when she had cared for similar injuries. He hadn't seen his wound before, and he was certainly no expert, but it didn't look that bad.

Reina seemed to agree. As she studied it, her body visibly relaxed along with her features, and she smiled down at Ben, a clear expression of relief washing across her face. "It looks *so* much better," she gushed. She sat down cross-legged again. "I was worried. Henri said the Banded Berries have a strong poison. He said the Tamarisk might not work."

Ben nodded. He was relieved, too, but he couldn't focus on that right now. He was sure he was looking at her with a goofy grin, but the sunrise was playing beautiful tricks with her eyes. They were soft, green pools, their color amplified in the golden light. She dropped them as little patches of pink colored her cheeks, hiding behind her curtain of hair.

Ben hadn't meant to stare. Truly. It was only that he was mesmerized. He watched the play of light on her features as Reina reached to tuck her hair behind her ear.

Glittering lavender gems sparkled on her wrist. *Wait.* He flicked his eyes to them, his stomach dropping. There were two bracelets on it.

Ben's mind raced. He was sure she would have questions—questions he didn't know how to answer. How had she gotten the other bracelet? And how would he explain it?

He shifted through a series of explanations in his mind, but none of them felt right on his tongue. None of them were as fantastical as the truth, but he was sure she wouldn't believe it if he told her that the new bracelet had come from a dream world. That, in the dream, he had shoved the new bracelet into his pocket. That it had still been there when he woke up.

Too quickly, he sat upright, and his wound sent a sharp sunburst of pain radiating from beneath its frayed edge. Ben hissed. He squeezed his eyes shut and braced his back against the wall, working hard to pull ragged breaths in and out of his lungs. Reina touched his arm. "Ben? Are you okay?"

"Ouch," he said through gritted teeth. He opened one eye to see Reina's worried face hovering just in front of his own, and he relaxed, smiling at her.

She held his eyes, the patches of pink on her cheeks growing more vibrant by the moment, then she sat back onto her heels and dropped her eyes. Ben watched as she pulled the new bracelet off her wrist.

She held it out to him. "Here. This doesn't belong to me," she said flatly.

Ben flicked his eyes from the bracelet to her face. He studied her features, but Reina wouldn't meet his gaze. He frowned. She was chewing the inside of her cheek, and her right eyebrow had a funny arch. She was upset about the bracelet, but he wasn't exactly sure why.

"Rei, I can explain," he started, but she cut him off.

She shook her head sharply, causing the golden tips of her hair to shake. "It's fine," she said flatly. She held the bracelet out to Ben insistently. "I'm fine. Just…just take it."

Ben studied her face a moment more, then he opened his hand. He didn't know what to say. Wordlessly, Reina dropped the bracelet into it. She moved off the cot and faced the window, crossing her arms.

Ben watched her closely. Her face was pained, and she was still biting the inside of her cheek. He dropped his eyes to the lavender gems in his hand. He didn't know why the new bracelet had made her so upset. He flicked his eyes to her stiff posture. Maybe it was that she just didn't want it. But that didn't seem like all it was.

Regardless of why she was upset, he still needed to explain. He gripped the jewelry in his palm as he scooted himself towards the edge of the cot and placed his feet on the floor. Slowly, he stood, wincing as his head pounded and the wound on his side pulled.

He managed to make it to his feet without incident, but once he got there, he realized he had overestimated his strength. Reina was half turned towards the window, and he took a step towards her, reaching for her arm. "Rei, I…" but he didn't get another word out.

The room suddenly felt too hot. It started to spin, and the next thing Ben knew, he was staring up at a blurry-faced Reina from the floor. She put a cool hand to his forehead. "Ben?" she said worriedly, then more sharply. "Benjamin, open your eyes!"

Ben blinked back the blurred edges of his vision as Reina came into focus. He tried to sit up, but she forced him back to the floor. "You hit your head on the edge of the table. It's bleeding again."

Ben groaned. His head was throbbing.

Reina lifted onto her knees. He watched as she pulled her mug from the edge of the table. It was still half full of Tamarisk paste. She fished a clean bandage off the stack beside it, then bent over Ben's head, examining his new wound. Her fingers were careful, but Ben hissed as she hit a tender spot. She drew her hands away. "Sorry," she muttered. "It looks shallow. It should heal up fine." She met his gaze with her sharp green eyes. "But really, Ben. You've *got* to be more careful, okay?"

Ben nodded. "M'kay."

"Now be still," she commanded.

Ben grinned. He tried his best to lie still, watching as her brows knit together. She was so bossy. He kind of liked it.

Reina had just swiped some paste onto his head when Henri's upside-down figure appeared above him. Henri stared down at him with a goofy grin. "Ah, yes, prolonging the sick bed stay, are we, Benjamin?" Henri crossed his arms, peering curiously at Reina above Ben's head. She had moved to the wound on his side. Ben could feel her winding a fresh bandage over his waist.

Henri sighed, flicking his eyes back to Ben. "Not to worry. You can hide out in here as long as you like. It's not like there's a million things that need doing around here or anything." He sniffed.

"Johann and I will handle it." He grinned teasingly, then watched as Reina fastened the bandage, eyes sparkling. "Can't say as I blame you for wanting to stay. *Excellent* caregiver you've got there. Easy on the eyes and all."

Ben flicked his eyes to Reina. She shot Henri a warning look, and Ben grinned. His head was starting to feel less dizzy. He sat up onto his elbows, twisting to better see Henri. "Okay, Henri, that's enough," he said lightly. Henri chuckled. He bent to pick up something from the floor. "Hey, Reina, here's your bracelet."

Henri held the bracelet out in his palm. He watched as Ben and Reina froze, flicking his eyes between them in confusion. He frowned as his eyes slipped to Reina's wrist. Her own bracelet dangled there, its lavender gems glittering in the morning light.

Henri pulled the bracelet back slightly, a slow grin spreading across his face. "Oh, ah… Did I interrupt something, Ben?" he said teasingly. He raised his brows.

Ben's heart dropped. He knew what Henri was about to say. He slid his eyes to Reina's face, watching her frown in Henri's direction. It was clear she had no idea what Henri was talking about. Ben was glad.

"What are you talking about now, Henri?" she spat. She looked to Ben, whose cheeks were starting to redden. Neither Ben nor Henri answered, and Reina sat back, bracing her hands on her knees. She looked from Ben to Henri, narrowing her eyes. "Am I missing something here?"

Henri folded his arms as Ben sat upright. "You wanna tell her, Ben, or shall I?" he said with mock innocence. His grin was growing wider by the second.

Ben shot him a warning stare. "Just give it to me, Henri," he said flatly. He held out his hand, and Henri studied his face before dropping the bracelet into it.

"Okay. So, you wanna tell her yourself. I get it," he said in a sing-song voice. "I don't blame…"

"Enough, Henri!" Ben shouted. He glared hard at his friend, and Henri held up his palms in mock surrender. "Okay, okay. I'm going now. But before I do, let me just leave this here." Ben watched as he set a small glass jar on the workbench. "I remembered that Ita kept a small stash of this just in case the griffins ever got sick again. It's for the berry poison. It's all we have."

He backed towards the doorway, an irritating grin on his face. "As you were," he added.

Ben rolled his eyes. He wished he didn't have the blasted wound in his side. Then he could toss Henri out on his ear.

At last, Henri's annoying face slunk behind the door. Ben sighed, dropping his eyes to the bracelet in his palm. He turned it over and over, then slid it back into his pocket.

He could feel Reina staring at the side of his head, but he couldn't look at her right now. He waited while she wordlessly swiped Henri's small jar from the workbench. She sprinkled its contents on the wound beneath his bandage, then she set the empty jar back on the table.

She sat beside him again, peering questioningly. "What was he talking about?" she said quietly. Ben blew out a long breath. He leaned back onto his hands, staring hard out the window. Then he met her gaze. He might as well tell her now. Anyway, if he didn't, he was sure Henri would. And he didn't want that.

"We have a tradition in the West Mountains," he said slowly. He shrugged, dropping his eyes. "Well, the Court of Mountain Fairies did, at least." He slid his gaze back to her. Reina was staring at him blankly. He could tell she had no idea where he was going.

"What's the tradition?" she asked quietly. She was doing that thing she did with her eyebrow again. The one that showed him she was slightly irritated.

Ben wet his lips. His heart was hammering in his ears. He couldn't tell if his injuries were to blame or if it was the weight of his current conversation. Probably a little of both.

"When a male mountain fairy had…feelings for a female of the same, he would give her a gift." He flicked his eyes to the bracelet on Reina's wrist. She followed his gaze, then lifted her eyes to his face. Her features were unreadable, but her hands were clenched into fists, and she was chewing the inside of her cheek. Ben fumbled over his words. He wanted her to understand, but he wasn't sure he could explain it right. "What—what I mean is, we don't wear rings here, in the West Mountains. Not like the Mortals where you're from do." Reina had dropped her eyes to stare pointedly at the floor, as if the meaning of the bracelets was starting to dawn on her. He could tell it was making her uncomfortable.

Ben pressed on, hurrying to get his words out before he lost his nerve. He shifted his weight and sat slowly up on his knees, being careful of his wound as he scooted closer to her. He lowered his voice, the gravity of his words resting heavily in his own ears.

"Here, a single bracelet signifies the love of a friend. But a woman is considered betrothed when she wears a bracelet on each wrist." He waited, studying Reina's face.

She didn't meet his gaze. Her cheeks were flushed, and she looked like she might cry. Ben straightened onto one knee. It was now or never. He was going to do it. He was going to give her the other bracelet. "Reina, I…"

Suddenly, Reina scrambled to her feet. She dusted her knees, then tucked her hair behind her ears. "I've gotta go," she said quietly. Ben frowned up at her. His hand was holding out the bracelet. Her lips twitched as she slid her eyes to it, and she swallowed hard. She dropped her gaze. "Um, Amelie will be waiting for me." She jerked a thumb towards the courtyard. "Morning exercises."

She started towards the door, and Ben braced his hands on the edge of his workbench, hurrying to pull himself to his feet. His head swam slightly, but he ignored it, starting towards her. He couldn't let her go like this. "Reina, wait, I…"

She held up her palm. "You just rest today, okay? Amelie and I can handle the training, and Johann and Henri can handle all the rest." She shot him a half grin, but it didn't reach her eyes. Then she spun on her heel and was gone.

Ben stared after her, dumbfounded. He had been so close. So close to telling her the truth about the bracelet, about how he really felt. Clearly, she didn't want to hear it.

Ben ran a hand through his hair, blowing out a breath. His palm came away sticky with dried blood. His side and his right pant leg were caked with it, and he had sweated through the blanket several times during the night. He was in desperate need of a soak and change of clothes. He started for the stairs, ignoring his aching wounds as he trudged up them.

Somehow, he managed to bathe and change without passing out again. At last, he sank back into the soft pillows of his bed, allowing himself to relax. As he rested, he let his mind drift over the events of the past days. He had barely allowed himself to think about Marcus until now. Reina had filled his every thought. But Ben knew he would have to deal with his brother eventually.

Until yesterday, Marcus had kept to himself in his far corner of the West Mountains. Ben wondered how his brother had even known he was working in the valley. It was obvious one of Marcus's men had been patrolling near the court's ruins, or else he wouldn't have even known Ben was there.

Ben blinked hard at the ceiling, thinking. His brother had clearly been threatened by his efforts to restore the doors. That much was evident by the attack on Jubal and himself and the fact that the doors now lay in a charred heap outside the North Wall.

The reaction had been violent. Ben wondered what his brother might do if he followed through with his plans and attempted to restore the court to its former glory. Based on Marcus's actions so far, Ben knew it wouldn't be good. If his brother didn't kill him first, Ben was sure Marcus would raze any developments he made before they rose off the ground.

Ben frowned. The thought of the doors being torn again from their hinges infuriated him. And too, the days stretching end over end at the Timekeeper's Court without Reina gave him pause. He wasn't sure he wanted to stay here without her. Ideas and designs tumbled through his mind, and the more he thought about it, the more his plans took shape.

In his head, Ben could see the tumbled walls of the Court of Mountain Fairies restored to their full height and the doors once again opening freely to all who wished to enter. He would need to start there, with the walls and the doors. And he would need help—a lot of it, and lots of defenses against Marcus and his men. More ideas came one after the other, and before he knew it, Ben had crafted a plan to restore his home court.

The new bracelet lay where he had left it on his bedside table. Ben eyed it as he hauled himself to his feet. He had made his decision, once and for all. He wouldn't be staying in the Time-keeper's Court once Reina left. He was going home—to the Court of Mountain Fairies.

Reina was in the courtyard with the rest of the group. Amelie spied him first, and Reina swung her head towards him as he hobbled out the great room doors. Ben could see her frown from his distance. She turned to say something to Amelie, then she started towards him, marching. Ben sighed. She was going to be upset he was out of bed.

By the time she reached him, her eyes were round pools of green worry. "Ben, you should be in bed. You're not recovered yet!"

Ben waved her off. Despite his slow movements, he actually felt pretty good. "I'm fine, Rei," he said quietly, giving her arm a squeeze. "I need to talk to everyone, okay?"

Reina eyed his side dubiously, then scanned his face for signs of distress. When she didn't find any, she twitched her mouth, folding her arms. "Only for a little while, okay? Then straight back to bed."

She gave Ben a pointed look, and he sighed, grinning. "Okay."

Reina moved to Amelie's side. Ben watched as Amelie looped her arm through Reina's. She bent her golden head, whispering something in her ear. The rest of the Timekeepers were gathered behind them in a semi-circle. Ben put a hand on his hip and cut his eyes around the group. He inhaled, but before he could speak, Henri and Johann jogged through the arched opening of the courtyard wall. It was nearly time for lunch, and the two never missed. But it didn't matter why they were there. Ben wanted them to hear what he had to say, anyway. It concerned them, too, after all.

They stopped short, taking places beside Amelie and Reina just as Ben began to speak. Johann stood a little closer to Amelie than was necessary, and Ben thought he saw a faint patch of color tinting her cheeks as she smiled up at him.

"I appreciate you all giving me a moment of your day. I know you're all very busy with your training, and rightly so. After all we've endured at the hands of the Court of Orm, who we defeated, bless the Source…" Ben paused as the Timekeepers placed a fist to the left of their chest, and he joined them. They stood still, giving a moment of reverent silence and thanks for their victory. Ben nodded, signaling the moment's end. "It's appropriate that you would hone your individual skills to fulfill your duty to protect the known worlds, the Rotha-Am, the Royal family, and all created things." He paused, meeting each eye in the courtyard. "You are warriors, and I come to you today with a chance for you to use the skills you have perfected." Several Timekeepers turned to one another with grins.

Ben continued. "There is, and will always be, hatred and darkness in the known worlds, and it is our job to defend against it. That is why I am here to ask you if you would be willing to accompany me on a new mission, and, if it should come to it, to stand and fight." Ben waited, allowing the information to sink in.

Henri folded his arms. He leveled Ben with a hard gaze. "What kind of mission are we talking about?" He jabbed Johann's side. "We humble stable boys would like to know."

Ben grinned, flicking his eyes from Johann and back to Henri. They were anything but simple stable boys, and Ben knew it. They had fought bravely with the King's army to defeat Orm. "How does rebuilding the Court of Mountain Fairies sound?"

Henri's grin widened. He exchanged an excited glance with Johann. Then he turned back to Ben. "Marcus won't like it," he said seriously. Ben nodded, and Henri jerked his chin. "Which is exactly why we stable boys are in."

Ben chuckled. "I thought you might say that." He slid his eyes to the rest of the group.

"As for the rest of you, I'll leave it to each of you to decide what you might do. If you're weary of battle, I understand. No one will force you to fight. You can leave now, if you wish."

Ben waited, eyeing the group, but no one moved. "Alright, then." He nodded. "You all know that the mountain fairies' court was destroyed before your arrival by the Court of Orm. For many cycles since, it has lain in ruins. We considered it lost. But Time is marching true, and as the heir to the ruling seat, it falls to me to rebuild it." He gestured to Henri with his head. "As Henri said, my brother, Marcus, and his clan of banded mountain fairies will likely stand against us, along with whatever corruption they can muster. So, I need you, the Mortal Timekeepers, to stand guard against his attacks, and also to use any skills you have should their threats come to blows."

Several Timekeepers nodded, and most looked ready to fight at that very moment. Ben continued. "It will be a group effort, and not an easy one. In fact, I'll need more help than what this group can provide. I will need the Four Corners of Caelium to band with me on this task.

"I plan to ask King Ard-Mathan and his successor, Princess Evangeline Vasily, to petition the realm for help at the Castle Ball. It will take the strength of the whole realm to create a place of peace and harmony behind the open door of the Court of Mountain Fairies. And that is where I will begin again—with the doors."

Ben studied the group, assessing their reactions. There was simply no way he could accomplish this task alone. He would have to have their help for defense, even if the other courts banded together to help him. He couldn't do it without them.

"We will leave for the Court of Mountain Fairies the morning after the Castle Ball."

He flicked his eyes to each face in question. "So, who's with me?"

One by one, the Mortal Timekeepers stepped forward. Amelie, Henri, and Johann did, too. Last of all, Vic's small frame stepped silently up beside them.

Ben hadn't seen her come into the yard. Her dark brows were knit in a hard line. She wouldn't meet Ben's gaze, and she picked hard at her thumbnail with her forefinger. Ben could understand her hesitation. It was hard for him to go back there, too, after all that had happened.

All that was left was Reina. She stood alone behind the group, staring at the ground as she hugged her arms. Ben waited until she met his gaze. Shyly, she flicked her green eyes in his direction. He grinned, and she smiled back at him, but it didn't flood her face with light like it normally did. In fact, Ben thought it was the saddest smile he had ever seen her wear.

Then it hit him. The morning after the Castle Ball, Reina would be gone. Five days in Caelium. That's all he had left with her. Then she would pass back through the gate, and he would never see her again.

Chapter 18

REINA

The next four days passed in a blur. The Timekeeper's Court was in full preparation mode for the Castle Ball. Training for the Timekeepers had doubled, at Ben's instruction, and bundles of supplies and packs of dry goods littered the floor of the entry hall, ready for transport by griffin to the valley of the Court of Mountain Fairies.

Everyone was practically buzzing with excitement—everyone but Reina. She tucked herself behind her bedroom door and leaned against it with a sigh. With her heart so heavy, it was almost too much to bear. She needed a moment to herself. A moment to rest in silence.

A moment was all she got. She had no sooner plopped face down on her bed than a quick knock came from her door. Amelie's lithe figure appeared from behind it. Reina peeked up at her with one eye. Amelie was standing over her with her hands on her hips. She could tell by the look on her friend's face that she was about to make her stand upright, and again, Reina had no idea how she was going to do it. Among managing her own emotions, making sure things were taken care of at court for her absence, prepping for the ball, and helping get supplies together for the move to the Court of Mountain Fairies, not to mention worrying about her upcoming nuptials, or what her own court of Monrovia would look like upon her arrival, she was exhausted.

Amelie nudged the side of the mattress with her knee. "Reina, seriously, what are you doing? We've got to make sure your dress fits." A petite young woman with wavy, shoulder length brown hair appeared in the doorway behind her. Bea was holding Reina's dress for the ball high in her short arms to keep it from dragging on the floor.

Bea was a Timekeeper, like herself. Her special skill was Earth, which had always struck Reina as funny. Bea was so small, but when she brought her fist down on the ground, she made a crack even larger than Diego's.

Bea's bright smile flashed above the heavy fabric. "Hi, Reina!" she said cheerily. "I've just made the finishing touches to your gown. I hope you like it." She hung the long dress from the doorknob of the armoire and allowed its full skirt to trail out across the floor.

Reina gasped as she sat up onto one arm. In addition to cracking the ground with her fist, she wasn't at all sure Bea didn't have some other magical skill in the dress-making arena. Deep lavender satin fabric was cut in a strapless design, tight at the bust and then flowing outward in a gauzy skirt that fell just above the floor. Tiny green vines trailed up from the hem, and little purple five-pointed flower petals dotted each one, just like the flower on her bracelet.

Reina met Bea's expectant gaze. "Bea, you've outdone yourself," she said in awe.

Bea flashed another wide grin and clapped her hands softly together. "I'm so glad you like it." She turned to face Reina with a suddenly solemn expression. "I hope you'll accept it as your going away present."

Reina sat up and put a hand to her chest. "Of course. I would be honored."

Reina's exhaustion was momentarily forgotten as she stood before the floor-length mirror in her gown. She smoothed her hands along the fabric, enjoying the feel of it beneath her fingers. It was a perfect fit.

Amelie appeared beside her reflection. "Let's get you out of this gown, okay? Bea and I will pack it away with your other things." Reina nodded, and soon, her gown was gently folded into her overnight bag, ready for her journey to Leyth Castle. She and Ben were heading out later this evening. Arto and Lina had requested they come a night early so that the four of them could have dinner together. It had been ages since they had seen one another. Reina knew Ben was particularly excited to spend some time with Arto, who had been the Master of the Timekeeper's Court prior to his marriage to the King's daughter, Princess Evangeline Vasily. Reina just hoped Ben felt strong enough for the journey.

After dinner that evening, at which she did her best to avoid Ben's charged looks, Reina waited quietly by the stables for him to appear. Her overnight bag was perched at her feet, and she had chosen a simple, dark green travel dress in a light fabric for the ride. Soft slippers covered her feet. They were her favorite—a gift from Ben for her seventeenth Mortal birthday. The shoes were velvet, with woven designs. Glittering, golden fairy wings were stitched up the sides.

She studied one shoe as she leaned against the doorframe. Two entwining, golden circles, which she had always thought were rings, had been stitched onto the toe. Reina cocked her head. Now that she looked at them, it was possible that they could be bracelets.

Just then, Ben appeared from the courtyard archway. He held his small, leather overnight bag tucked beneath his arm, and his other hand was shoved into his pocket. He strode purposefully across the yard, then stopped a few feet in front of Reina.

It was the first time they had been alone since the workshop. Ben took in her frame from top to bottom, then he flicked his golden eyes back to her face. He grinned. "Hi," he said sheepishly.

It appeared he had just washed. The golden tips of his hair curled down over his ears and forehead. They glistened in the evening sunlight. He wore a loose, light linen shirt and dark blue riding pants, and he had even donned his shiny pair of brown riding boots, which Reina knew he had hardly ever worn.

Reina bit her cheek. "Hi," she said quietly, flicking her eyes away. Ben moved close, stooping to grab her bag in his other hand. Reina instinctively leaned towards him. He smelled like fresh soap and mountain air. She chided herself, pulling quickly away when she realized what she was doing. Being alone with him was going to be harder than she thought.

Ben moved slowly as he tucked her bag just inside the stable doors. He turned to face her, giving her his best grin. "Ready?" he said cheerfully.

Reina could tell his side was hurting. She flashed him a small smile. "Ready."

Reina helped him carry the dismantled crib and her bag through the stable and into the far yard. Cyrus was waiting there, and they strapped their supplies to the griffin's sides. When they were done, Ben held his hand out to her, and she took it, jumping astride. Then he tucked himself behind her, slipping his arm snugly around her waist.

Reina tried not to feel his closeness as she gripped Cyrus's feathers. Ben patted Cyrus's rump and whistled low, and then they were off, flying higher and higher until they were cresting the mountain peaks.

Reina had never been the most thrilled flyer. It was necessary, of course, and fun even, if she didn't think about how high they were off the ground. She was focused on her grip on Cyrus's feathers, trying to keep her eyes off said ground, when suddenly, Ben banked right.

Reina frowned over her shoulder. This wasn't the path to Leyth Castle. Ben was moving south, and the castle was nestled in the Haima Mountains in the northeast.

"Where are you going?" she asked.

Ben glanced down at her, then returned his eyes to look past the top of Cyrus's feathery head. "We've got a stop to make before we head to the castle."

Reina half turned to peer up at him. There was something in his expression that gave her pause. His golden eyes were shuttered. He was keeping something from her. "What aren't you telling me?"

Ben sighed. "I've been thinking." He twisted slightly in the seat, wincing as the movement pulled the wound on his side. "My wound isn't healing properly. It's the berry poison. It's so foul that the Tamarisk won't work properly. In a weaker host, the poison would've already done its job. I'd be with the Source by now."

Reina turned quickly to face forward in her seat. She couldn't even stand to think about that. She gripped her hands tighter into Cyrus's soft feathers. "Don't say that," she muttered. But she knew he was right. She'd changed his dressing just this morning, and she'd noticed the wound had a dark look. The deep parts had begun to fester again.

At first, whatever Henri had brought had made Ben's wound better. Reina had done her best to clean the wound and pack it tightly with fresh Tamarisk paste every day since. But they didn't have any more of Henri's remedy. Ben was strong and determined; anyone with less strength would've already succumbed.

She peered back at him. "So, where are we going then?"

Ben narrowed his eyes. "My grandmother always worried that she would encounter the Banded Berry poison again. So, she'd often taken up quests in search for a remedy. I can remember her leaving the Timekeeper's Court for long periods when I was younger. She always returned with a defeated look in her eye. Until one day, she didn't. I clearly remember the day she returned with a gleam and her satchel full of Sacred Thistle. She said she found it in the heart of the mountains. It's what Henri had in the bottle. I recognized it immediately."

Reina pressed her lips together. "How did she know it would work?"

Ben shook his head, smiling. "She didn't. But she took some Banded Berries with her to the spot where the Sacred Thistle grew. She said when she squeezed the berry juice onto them, the juice evaporated with a hiss, and the Sacred Thistle glowed with a soft light." He shrugged. "So, she took that as a sign from the Source that the Thistle would work."

"And did it?"

"Henri was affected by the poison in the stable yard at the same time as the griffins. It was before you came, many cycles ago. Henri was just a boy. He used to sleep with the griffins in the stalls."

Reina giggled. "He slept in the stalls?"

Ben grinned. "We couldn't stop him. Henri loves the griffins so much.

"Ita thought that he might've eaten some of the Banded Berries by mistake. Especially if he saw the griffins doing it. She asked him, but he couldn't remember. The poison had addled his memory. He recovered mostly with the Tamarisk. She was thankful he was alive, but the poison settled in his left hand. It withered. He went for cycles unable to use it."

Reina could remember Henri's near-perfect aim with his bow in the battle with the Court of Orm. She couldn't imagine him without the use of one hand. Ben continued. "Ita couldn't stand to see it. She wanted Henri to be well. There were times when his pain was so bad that he couldn't even ride. And Henri loves nothing so much as to ride a griffin. So, when she found the Sacred Thistle, she knew she had found the answer. Or she thought she had."

Reina peered up at Ben's jaw. "So, Ita gave him the Sacred Thistle, and his hand was well?"

Ben shook his head. "No. Instead, she tried it on herself first."

Reina's eyes went wide. "What, you mean she poisoned herself with the Banded Berries?"

Ben nodded, grinning at the memory. "She did. Then she used the Sacred Thistle to heal herself. Once she was certain it would work, she gave it to Henri. And, well, you can see his hand is as strong as it has ever been."

Reina faced forward. "So, we're going to get some Sacred Thistle?"

"Yes. Because with my attempts to rebuild the court, there's sure to be more encounters with Marcus and his mercenaries.

"But there's a part of the story I've left out."

Reina turned her chin. She frowned. "What?"

The muscle in Ben's jaw flexed. "The Sacred Thistle is guarded by the water horse and her master."

"What's a water horse?"

Ben pressed his lips together. "You'll see."

Cyrus touched down by a small stream in a high grove of evergreen trees. Dark moss blanketed the dirt along the stream's banks, and sheer, grey mountain peaks extended high into the clouds on all sides of them. The air around Reina was damp—a pungent mix of earth, wet rock, and trees.

Benjamin slid off Cyrus's back and held his hand up to her.

She blinked down at him, adjusting her eyes to the dim light as she hopped down to meet him. "How did Ita ever find this place?" she whispered. Except for the gurgling stream, the air hung heavy with silence, and she was hesitant to speak any louder.

Ben dropped her hand to sling an empty pack across his back. He belted a dagger to his side as he studied the close landscape around them. "I'm not sure," he said quietly. "I just know it took her many cycles. She showed me how to get here, just in case. Now, I'm glad she did. I would've never found it without her." He lifted his chin to the sky. "It's like she knew someday, we would need it."

Ben patted Cyrus's rump, causing the tall griffin to snort and turn back. Reina watched as Cyrus lifted into the air. He was flying back the way they'd flown in. The sight of it brought a chill to her bones. How did Ben expect them to get out of here? Or did he expect that they wouldn't?

"Ita knew my brother before, of course. She was his grand-mother, too." He shook his head. "Marcus was never…solid, I guess you could say. There was always an edge to him—a darkness that, for the most part, he kept contained. But after Orm rose to power and our home was destroyed, he went wild with rage. Arto tried to help him, but Marcus refused. We knew he'd gone deeper west, and we'd heard tales of how he held a band of fairies in his grip, but I'd never encountered his violence firsthand, until the other day." He put his hand gingerly over his side.

"Why did he attack you?" Reina asked quietly.

Ben shrugged. "Marcus has rejected everything he has ever known. He's chosen to go his own way, and he hates everything to do with the home we once knew. Me included." He shook his head. "I just didn't understand how much until he attacked me in Jubal's cave." He turned to Reina. "Once he finds out that I'm planning to rebuild the court, he will stop at nothing to prevent me from completing it. We've got to be ready, even if it means braving the water horse and her master."

Without saying more, Ben turned, disappearing beneath the low-hanging fronds of the trees beyond them. Reina stood frozen in place. What did he mean *brave* the water horse and her master? How dangerous were they? And *what* were they?

Reina shivered. She thought she'd already seen all the horrifying things Caelium had to offer. But apparently, she hadn't. Deep below her, in the heart of Caelium, there still lurked foul creatures she'd yet to meet.

She'd heard it explained best by Chaeronne. The centaur was King Ard-Mathan's general, and arguably among the wisest beings in Caelium. Last cycle, at the Queen's Mortal birthday celebration, he had spoken about the dark things that lurked in Caelium's deep. Reina had thought it a rather odd speech for a birthday party, but she supposed Chaeronne had to take his chance to impart wisdom whenever he was able. Because, as the Queen had said before his speech, "No one ever knows when the darkness might rear its ugly head. And we, those in the light, must be ready to cut it down."

Chaeronne had recited a story from memory, an excerpt from The Timekeeper's Tale. It was regarding the fall of Lionir, a being once known as the Master Timekeeper, who had later betrayed his own master, King Ard-Mathan, in a bitter bid for power after Lionir's wife's sudden death. Lionir's treachery had turned him into Orm, the foul, twisted, worm-like creature of Reina's memory. Orm had taken the throne, causing all the forces of darkness to be unleashed upon the known worlds. Thankfully, Orm was now defeated, and the King had resumed his rightful place of power.

As Chaeronne had explained, though darkness had almost always existed, the King's power kept the foul things created by evil in chains, bound inside the earth and unable to be truly free. But Orm's rise to power had weakened those chains, so when the Chasm opened at the Rotha-Am's—the Wheel of Time's—fall, a multitude of foul beasts sprang forth. It was only when Orm was slain that the Chasm closed, and the beasts that had escaped fell to ash like their master.

Though Orm had been defeated, deep in the heart of the earth, darkness still lingered. But only when those on the surface descended to meet it did they encounter such evil again. Reina had the sneaking suspicion that this was just the sort of thing she and Ben were about to do. Because a water horse and her master living deep inside the mountain seemed to fit the foul beasts of Chaeronne's description.

Reina shivered as a small breeze blew through the evergreens around her. She wasn't at all certain she was ready to meet such evil again. But it didn't appear she had a choice. Reluctantly, she moved through the low limbs after him.

Ben turned towards her halfway through the small grove and pressed something cool and metal into the palm of her hand. Reina peered down at it in the dim light. It was a slim dagger—the very one she had used in the battle with the Court of Orm. She'd kept it carefully stored away since the battle had ended, hidden in a small box on her nightstand. The sight of it brought a chill to the back of her neck. She'd only mentioned it to Ben once before, and the fact that he'd taken it upon himself to retrieve it for her without telling her that she would need it made a glint of anger turn inside her chest.

She glared up at him. "And what exactly will I be needing this for?" she spat.

Ben sighed. "Rei, listen, I'm sorry I didn't tell you ahead of time, okay? I should have, but I didn't." He wet his lips and tucked a hand over the hilt of the dagger on his side.

Reina folded her arms. She could feel him studying the side of her head, but she refused to look at him.

He blew a breath. "Okay. The truth is, I thought you wouldn't come. And I need you for this."

She slid her eyes to him, glaring. "So, you thought I would just leave you on your own? That I wouldn't come to help you with whatever"—she fluttered her hand—"*thing* is in there?" She huffed, brushing past him. "Obviously, you don't know me very well. *I'm* not the one who leaves their friends in the lurch to go off on their own. That would be you."

She marched ahead, only stopping when she reached a small opening in the sheer wall in front of them. Ben's low chuckle sounded from behind her. She could hear the soft crunch of his feet. She felt his warm breath on the back of her neck. Her heart ticked up a notch. He was standing much closer than was necessary, but she was enjoying his nearness too much to step away. He leaned over her shoulder, his voice low.

"Don't be mad, Reina. Please. I'm sorry. Truly."

She sighed and half turned to face him, dropping her arms. "I'm not mad that you didn't tell me. It's just…I just can't believe you'd think I wouldn't come with you if you had asked." She peered up at him, her face sincere. "You're my best friend, Ben. I'll always come to help you, no matter how dangerous the situation is."

Ben smiled down at her. He reached for her hand, lacing his fingers with hers. Reina flicked her eyes to their joined palms. The feeling of his touch was sending little zings up her arm.

"I know you would," he said quietly. "And you're my best friend, too."

CHAPTER 19

REINA

The path inside the mountain was narrow and stifling. Patches of purplish flora glowed at intervals, but Reina could barely see Ben's back in front of her face. The damp sides of the thin passage brushed slick against her upper arms, and she shivered, tucking her shoulders in tight.

As they wove deeper and deeper into the mountainside, the feel of the air began to shift. All light from the entrance faded, until the darkness pressed in on them from all sides. Scribbling scampers echoed from high in the rock, forcing images of creeping, crawling things into Reina's mind. She pushed them away, inhaling deeply against the push of the air's weight, fighting the panic that was rising in her chest.

Beneath her feet, the rocky path was slowly disintegrating, and a thick, squishing mire was taking its place. Her slippers grew increasingly hard to lift, until, suddenly, she found herself unable to move. She strained against the sucking muck holding her feet, but it was no use. She was stuck.

Panicking, she peered ahead. Ben was already moving out of sight. She tried to call to him, but her voice caught in her throat, a low, garbling sound emitting instead. Ben didn't hear her. She could hear his steps lifting and squishing beyond, and she blinked hard, focusing her eyes on the sound.

Just then, she caught a hint of the glint of his dagger, ready to move around a bend in the rock and out of sight. If she didn't hurry, she was going to be left alone in this narrow tunnel, with who knew what crawling above her. The skittering, crawling sounds around her intensified, and Reina's heart nearly beat out of her chest. Fear forced itself into her limbs, and she grit her teeth and pulled hard on her leg, a *thwock* reverberating off the walls with her shoe's release. She blew out her breath as relief flooded her, and gingerly, she stepped forward onto solid ground, pulling her other shoe out behind her.

Ben's wide-eyed gaze met her around the corner. He had turned back once he realized she wasn't directly behind him, and his face had a sheer look of panic that did nothing for Reina's mental state. He flicked his eyes over her frame, assessing her for damage.

She frowned up at him, her anxiety allowing quick anger to escape. "What?" she whispered accusingly. "Why are you looking at me like that?"

Ben stepped towards her, his hand finding her palm. "It's nothing. I just thought…" He shook his head and reached his free hand to lift his dagger. "Never mind. Just stay close. The lower we descend beneath the surface, the more darkness we will encounter. We can't be too careful."

Reina nodded, swallowing against a lump in her throat. She wished he would've told her sooner where they were going. As it was, she didn't feel prepared to meet whatever "darkness" Ben was talking about. Maybe if he'd said something before, she wouldn't feel so sick to her stomach right now.

Ben held tightly to her hand as the passage began to descend sharply downward. Soon, he was forced to release it, and they were crouching sideways, bracing their hands against the wall on the steep descent. Reina's shoes slipped on the loose rocks, and she gripped the sides of the slick walls with both hands, her fingernails ripping against sharp stones as she fought to keep from losing her grip.

In moments, the air shifted again, and an ethereal, disembodied whispering began to scamper past her ears. Reina shook her head, closing out the sounds. She was sure they were part of the "darkness." Her heart hammered in her ears, but she had no choice but to go forward. There was no way she could climb back up.

Instead, she focused on the soft padding sound of her slippered feet and the feeling of the hard stone beneath her fingers.

Just then, she heard Ben's feet slip. He made a small grunt as his back hit the steep path ahead of her with a sharp thud, and his fingers made scraping sounds against the wall as he began to slide.

"Ben!" Reina shouted, a bit too loudly. The whispers backed away from the sound of her voice, then slowly returned, filling her ears with their dark gloom.

Ben's slide stopped a short distance below her. She heard him hop down into the cavern beneath, a dull, glowing light illuminating his bare feet. He peered up at her and lifted his arms. "Let go, and I'll catch you," he whispered up to her.

Reina bit her lip. The disembodied whispers of the narrow passage were clanging loudly against the inside of her ears. She certainly didn't want to stay with them, but the idea of dropping down to Ben made her stomach lurch.

Without thinking more about it, she closed her eyes and released her hands, letting her bottom slide on the loose rocks beneath her. At first, she kept her seat. Then the pathway dropped out entirely, and she was falling through the open air. She pressed her lips to stifle her shriek, landing on Ben's chest with a hard thud.

He grunted with the impact, falling backward to roll down a small bank. Reina held tight as they tumbled, and Ben whipped his hand protectively behind her head. He cradled her to his chest until, at last, they were still.

Reina was lying flat on her back, and all of Ben's weight was pressing down on her. She couldn't speak, couldn't breathe. Her mouth opened and closed like a fish out of water, and she gripped the front of Ben's shirt, blinking up at him. He pushed himself backward, peering worriedly down into her face. "Reina?" He shook her gently and raised his voice. "Reina, breathe!" he shouted. She tried to obey, but her chest was paralyzed. No air would go into or out of her lungs.

Ben scrambled onto his knees, panic creasing his features. He lifted Reina onto his lap, then he held her chin, peering deeply into her eyes. "Breathe" he murmured. "You've got to breathe, Reina."

All at once, her spasmed chest opened, and she sucked in a breath, wheezing. She collapsed forward onto Ben's chest, tears welling into her eyes. "There you go," he whispered. "That's it. Nice, easy breaths." He cradled the back of her head, rubbing soothing strokes over her hair as she pulled ragged breaths into and out of her chest.

Finally, she sat upright, swallowing. "It's ok. I'm alright," she croaked, answering his worried expression. "Really, Ben. I'm fine."

Ben frowned as he pushed a wayward curl behind her ear. "You're sure?" he said uncertainly.

Reina nodded. "I'm sure." She squeezed his arm, then rolled off his lap.

Ben pushed off the ground, then held his hand down to her. She took it, brushing dirt and debris from the back of her skirt as she stood. She turned, facing the cavernous room.

They had come to a wide underground lake. By the distance they had descended, Reina guessed it to be well below the surface. The top of the lake was still and calm, and the water glowed with a soft, white light that illuminated the high dome of the cavern overhead. Long, fingerlike projections descended from the cavern's ceiling, as if they were reaching for something they could never quite grasp—a treasure just below the water's surface.

A narrow strip of flat rock extended in a crescent shape around the edge of the water, dropping off midway to the other side to meld with the sheer, slick rock of the cavernous dome. Ben moved to the edge of it. He held his dagger warily aloft and followed the crescent shape with his eyes, landing on the point where it disappeared into the walls. Then he lifted his head, studying the dome of the cavern for some hidden passage. He turned to Reina. "There's no way around it. We'll have to swim through," he said gruffly.

Reina searched the water's surface dubiously. She flicked her eyes to him. "Swim it?" she asked uncertainly. Ben turned his eyes to the surface, then back to Reina.

He shrugged. "There's no other way through that I can see."

Reina chewed the inside of her cheek. She scanned the cavern carefully for some small opening, but there wasn't one. She peered down at the surface of the glowing water. "What kind of things are in there?" she whispered.

Ben shook his head. "I'm not sure. I've never been here before. Ita only took me to the opening outside." He shrugged. "All I know are the stories that she told me. I'm just following her directions, hoping for the best."

Reina frowned at him. She was irritated he didn't know more. "Well, you'd better tell me the stories then, so I know what to expect."

Ben crossed his arms. "It's not a lot of information, really. Ita was very vague." He shook his head slowly back and forth. "It was almost like she couldn't remember." He frowned. "And the more she talked about it, the more nervous she became. So, I couldn't ever get her to say very much. We'll just have to go with what little she told me."

Reina huffed, sticking out one foot. The whispers from their descent still tingled in the back of her head, and the prickle of fear was threatening to rise in her chest again. She was ready to move on from this place as quickly as possible. She frowned. "Whatever information you've got, I probably need to know it, Ben." she said hotly.

A thin smile passed quickly over his face. She could tell he was amused at her irritation, and it made her even angrier. Her fingers flared to flame. "I'm *serious*, Ben!" she shouted.

Her voice reverberated off the walls, and Ben spun towards her, holding up his hands. "*Shhh!* Reina, be *quiet!*" he whispered loudly. He scanned the surface of the water with his eyes, then turned back towards her.

Reina flicked her eyes to the water, quenching the fire in her fingertips.

Ben sighed. "The first thing you should know is we need to be *quiet*. The quieter we are, the better, okay?"

Reina nodded. She studied the lake's surface over Ben's shoulder, but she wasn't quite sure what she was looking for. He turned to face it, the muscle in his jaw flexing. "Beyond that, I only know that there is a water horse and a master. And that the Sacred Thistle lies beyond them."

Ben stepped one foot gingerly into the edge of the pool. He waited, then brought the other foot to meet it. He looked down, wiggling his toes, then grinned back at Reina.

"It's nice. The water feels nice. Come on." He held out his hand to her. She bent to remove her slippers, then gripped his palm as she stepped over the edge. Ben was right. The water was soft and smooth, with just enough heat to feel refreshing and comfortable at the same time. She smiled up at him. "It *is* nice," she said quietly.

Ben nudged her arm. "See?"

Reina giggled, but abruptly, the sound caught in her throat. A tinny, choking sound took its place. She gasped, panic rising as she clutched at her neck. No air was going into or out of her lungs. She felt just as she had a moment ago, when she'd hit the ground on her back, stopping her breath. Her throat squeezed tighter, and she winced. She felt as if a long, clawed hand was holding it shut with all its might.

Ben sloshed towards her, his eyes wide. He shook her shoulders. "Reina?" he shouted, not caring about the volume of his voice.

But she didn't meet his gaze. Instead, she was focused on a spot just past his shoulders, towards the middle of the pool, and what she saw there had her terrified.

CHAPTER 20

BEN

Ben turned slowly to look over his shoulder. There, standing in the middle of the lake, was a beautiful young woman. Long, dark hair skimmed the surface of the water at her waist, and she had bright, iridescent eyes. Ben squinted at them. They were much like Kai's, his merrow friend from the Southern Sea, but there was something…*off* about them.

The tips of her ears were pointed, and she had high cheekbones and full lips framed by a perfect, oval face. Her skin was so pale it was almost translucent, and small, shimmering scales lined the edge of her temple. To Ben, she looked nearly like any other merrow woman. But when she opened her mouth to smile at them, it was full of glistening, sharp teeth.

Her right hand was held in front of her, partially fisted, towards Reina's neck. Her nails were sharp and long, dark at the bases. She released her grip on the air, and Reina fell forward on her hands and knees, into the water. She coughed and sputtered, spitting dark, grey water from her throat.

The strange merrow woman grinned wider, a dark, ominous expression, devoid of joy. Her voice made a rasping hiss through her sharp teeth. "There is no laughter in the loch, my dear," she said. "Only whispers of the darkness that has been done." She chuckled low. "And the darkness that will be."

She stepped towards them, her movement making no ripples on the surface of the water. "The memories of my visitors haunt me, but they have no escape." She shrugged one pale shoulder, her dark eyes glimmering at the unseen voices hovering at the high ceiling. "They're all I have now."

Ben had the distinct feeling that he should run. Lift Reina from the water and go back the way they had come, up and out of the mountain. He glanced back at the path and bent to grip Reina's upper arm, ready to haul her over his shoulder. But then he remembered: The path was too steep. They'd had to fall the last bit of it, and he knew they'd never make it up and out again. Their only way out was through.

He turned back to the merrow woman and wondered if their journey had been worth their efforts. Was the Sacred Thistle worth risking Reina's life in this horrid place? He looked down at her still heaving body. He wasn't sure now if it was.

The merrow woman narrowed her eyes, as if she could read his thoughts. "You've come for the Sacred Thistle," she rasped.

Ben nodded, helping Reina to her feet. "Yes," he said. His anxiety had made him speak more loudly than he'd anticipated, and his voice bounced back to him from the walls, causing the merrow woman to shrink. The whispers shrank, too. She covered her ears until his voice dissipated on the rocks. Ben studied her quizzically, trying to make sense of the merrow's odd behavior.

The woman glared up at him. "If you wish to behold the Sacred Thistle, you must speak *softly* in this place," she spat. "Else, you risk disturbing the water horse. And if she is set free, I cannot control what happens to you after. The water horse has a mind of her own, you see. She has less"—she flicked her eyes greedily up and down Ben's frame—"control."

The merrow woman held out her palm, drawing an orb of water from the pool below. She lifted a small amulet from her neck and dropped two drops of dark liquid into the orb floating in her hand. She flicked her eyes to Ben. "I grow lonely, you see." She shook her head, furrowing her winged brows. "She never meant to hurt anyone…the water horse, I mean." She moved closer to Ben, holding out her clawed hand. The orb had taken on a delicious fragrance that was vaguely familiar to him.

The merrow's eyes grew sorrowful. "Everyone leaves. They

never stay. They come for the Sacred Thistle, but never for me." A dark tear trickled down her left cheek. "She only means to keep you here…the water horse, that is. She only wants your company." She cocked her head to the side, pleading. "But she grows hungry, and there isn't much to eat here in the loch. There's only one way to keep you, or at least, that's what she tells me." She shook her head sorrowfully. "And I can't deny her what she asks. After all, I grow hungry, too."

A tingle of fear was growing at the base of Ben's neck. He looped his fingers through Reina's hand and squeezed. He was beginning to understand why his grandmother had been nervous to talk about this place—and why she couldn't remember. The fragrance of the orb had pricked his mind. It had carried him back several cycles, to the Timekeeper's Court, when his grandmother had tended to Henri.

The pain in Henri's hand had been so severe that his grandmother had used a sweet Elixir to make him forget. It was the Elixir of Oblivion—used to weaken the mind and body, and for the purposes of the water horse, to make one's memories pass more readily out of one's head.

The merrow woman gazed down at the dark orb floating on her palm. Her fingernails curved around it like sharp talons. Silently, she slid her eyes to Ben's hand wound in Reina's and back up again. "Only one of you may come," she hissed. She lifted her orb higher. "And you must drink. To forget."

Ben tightened his grip on Reina's palm, pulling her closer.

"I won't go without her," he said loudly.

The merrow woman shrank back, hissing. "*Quiet*, I said," she rasped.

Ben stood silent. "Alright," he said, more quietly. "But like I said, I won't go without her."

The merrow woman's dark gaze studied their entwined hands curiously. Within the last few moments, her eyes had become opaque, even to the edges. She flicked them up to Ben, her pale lips showing all her sharp teeth. "Then you must choose. Either you wish to possess the Sacred Thistle, or you do not. There is no other way."

Ben glanced down at Reina. Her fingernails were digging into his upper arm, but she was glaring right back into the eyes of the merrow woman. "I'll stay," she said flatly.

Reina turned her gaze, peering up at him seriously. "It's okay, Ben. Really. I'll wait for you here."

Ben frowned down at her. He studied her eyes, reading her expression. "You're sure?"

She nodded again, more emphatically. "I'm sure."

Ben pulled her into his chest. He brought his lips to her ear. "I'll come back for you, I promise," he whispered. He pulled back to gaze into her eyes. They were wide green pools, and he wished he could dive into them instead of diving with the awful merrow woman into the loch. He took both of her hands. "Promise me you'll wait for me here, okay?" He peered into her gaze, willing her to obey him.

Reina smiled a tight smile, squeezing his hands. "Okay," she whispered. "I promise."

Ben had no faith that Reina would keep her word, but that didn't keep him from hoping she would. Reluctantly, he stepped away, moving cautiously towards the merrow woman. She grinned wickedly at him behind her outstretched palm, and Ben fought the urge to shudder. Her smile was wide and terrifying. "Drink, my dear. Drink and forget," she rasped.

Ben could see no way around it. He would have to drink the Elixir. He'd never tasted it before, but he'd heard horrible stories—namely from Reina, who'd been given the Elixir each evening without her knowledge for many Mortal years before she passed through the gate into Caelium. She had not known who had given it to her, but she had said that the Elixir made her forget. It made her weak and vulnerable. Now, she believed it was to stop her from ever coming to Caelium. Ben frowned. Weak and vulnerable—not the best state to be in with the strange merrow woman.

Ben eyed the dark orb floating in the strange merrow's palm. It was a dangerous potion, to be sure. But she seemed bent that he was to drink it if he was going to follow her. Ben gripped his palms at his sides. He had to have the Sacred Thistle. His recent incident with Marcus had renewed in himself his grandmother's worry that the Banded Berry poison was likely to be a problem in the future. Besides, he wasn't completely recovered. He needed the Sacred Thistle to heal his own wound.

He reached out his hand, and the merrow woman passed the fragrant orb into it. Ben stared down at it, bracing his nerves. But as he gazed into its liquid surface, he found himself drawn towards it, and soon, he was lifting it to his lips.

The taste of it was indescribable on his tongue. It was sweet and tangy—delicious by any account. Ben could see how some had become obsessed with its flavor, craving more of it before the last of their drink was gone.

He downed the last drop and wiped his chin with the back of his sleeve. Already, the back of his head felt fuzzy, and he could feel the tendrils of the Elixir weaving themselves through the edges of his mind. The merrow woman grinned. "Follow me," she hissed, backing into the water. She continued that way until every bit of her body was submerged except the bridge of her nose and her glistening eyes.

Ben turned to give Reina a last glance. "I'll come back for you," he said, slurring.

She nodded, her delicate brows pulled low. "Be careful," she whispered.

Ben nodded. He turned towards the waiting merrow and took two steps, stumbling. He had no idea how he was expected to be careful in this state. His arms felt weak and heavy, and he could barely lift his feet. He was growing tired. So tired. He wished he could lie down and sleep for a while.

At last, he could no longer hold his weight. His knees gave way, and he pitched forward, falling face first into the luminous water. Reina's piercing scream reverberated off the cavern walls behind him. "Ben!"

Ben blinked below the surface. The merrow woman was coming towards him, her dark hair floating behind her in twisting tendrils. He blinked. It was the merrow woman, wasn't it? He frowned, squinting. Her head and hair looked much the same, but from behind, her body was changing into a most horrifying shape. Ben tried to make sense of it as she grasped him with her clawed hands and tucked him to her side.

Ben cringed. Her body had a sickly, slick feeling, like the slippery silkweed that wrapped around his legs when he waded in the lake near the Timekeeper's Court. He could feel her powerful muscles propelling them deeper and deeper below the surface. He blinked through his haze, his addled mind trying to make sense of what he was seeing. But he wasn't at all sure that the Elixir wasn't affecting his vision.

The merrow woman's body was not what he'd been expecting. He'd seen Kai and several other merrows change into their sea forms. But this was not that. No, this was something else entirely.

Two large, feathery fins had sprouted from her back. They looked like wide wings, and the Merrow woman flapped them broadly, propelling them down below the surface. And her tail. It wasn't that of a normal Merrow—it was twinned. Ben knew

Merrow tails to be quite beautiful—even Kai's. This one was large, dark, and twisted.

Down and down the merrow woman swam. Ben was losing breath—or at least, he thought he was. He couldn't be sure. His head was so fuzzy that he was having trouble thinking. He worked to focus, hoping he would still have strength and mind when they reached land to make it out of the loch with the Sacred Thistle.

His chest was burning from lost air. Ben opened his mouth, ready to take on water. Somewhere in the back of his mind, he knew he was about to die, but strangely, he wasn't worried about it.

Just then, the twisted merrow began to rise. Ben gasped as they broke the surface, pulling in a gulp of dry air. The merrow pushed him out onto the hard earth, and he rolled, coughing and gagging as the thick, foul smell of rotting flesh sunk down into his chest.

Ben blinked in the dim light. Just in front of him, the half-eaten corpse of a small deer crawled with worms and creeping things. Its one eye bulged, the other, an empty socket peering out at him. Ben felt sorry for the poor creature. He wondered how it had come to be in the loch.

His stomach turned, and he sat up, retching. The merrow woman hissed a laugh from behind him. "Sorry," she rasped. "But even we water horses have to eat."

Ben wiped his mouth with his sleeve, peering at the twisted merrow. She braced her pale arms on the edge of the pool, her body submerged to her chest. Her wing-like fins swished at her sides, and her two tails treaded the water in unison.

Ben remembered the seahorses Kai had warned him to stay away from on the shore of the Southern Sea. From a distance, they looked like any ordinary horses, but when they came too close, the pull of their stormy, grey eyes caused you to climb onto their back and be pulled to your watery grave. The Court of the Sea used them as guardians, preventing unwanted entry to their court.

He studied the creature in front of him quizzically. She certainly wasn't a seahorse. And she wasn't quite a merrow, either. No, she was something altogether different—something twisted, dangerous, and dark.

"*You're* the water horse?" Ben asked incredulously.

The merrow grinned wide. "And her master," she added, dark eyes gleaming. She gestured to her twin tails with one clawed hand. Ben noticed she'd also developed two ragged blades of fins on the underside of her forearm. "I'm two-in-one—a shapeshifter, you see. Your mate's scream caused the water horse's release. It was too loud, you understand." She frowned delicately. "The screaming frightens her…the water horse, I mean."

The water horse sighed, studying the room around her with her opaque eyes. "I once roamed where I wished, before I was…this. And for some time after, too—at least while the throne held its former occupant. But since Master Orm's defeat, I'm locked in this watery tomb." She glanced at the half-eaten deer. "With only these measly snacks that wander in on occasion. They satisfy my hunger—and hers—but their memories are muddled at best." She eyed Ben's head curiously. "Nothing like *your* memories, I'd imagine."

She clapped her hands together gleefully. "But no matter. You're here now. And you'll keep me company. Won't you?" She eyed Ben with a gaze something akin to pleading.

Ben's vision was starting to blur, and he blinked to clear it. He glanced down at his legs, which lay limply beneath him. He was sure he couldn't walk. The water horse pointed to the corner opposite him. "There is what you seek," she rasped.

Slowly, Ben swung his head. On the wall, a cluster of Sacred Thistles grew in a wide, starburst pattern. Their centers held tiny, three-pointed, white petals. Water dripped onto them from the high ceiling, then fell to the pool below, illuminating it with a glowing, white light.

Ben lifted shakily onto his hands and knees. If he could just get the Thistle, maybe the water horse would carry him back to Reina. Then they could be on their way.

He dragged himself slowly across the stone floor, somehow managing to make it to the wall before he lost his strength. He collapsed as he grasped the Thistle closest to him and pulled, lifting its hair-like roots from their place at the base of the wall. He placed it in the small pack at his side, reaching his arm to gather another and another until the bag was full. Then he dropped his arm, his chest heaving.

Ben braced himself against the cavern wall, trying to catch his breath. Even the small exertion of picking the Thistles had completely exhausted him. His head spun, and he could feel himself sinking into a deep sleep. He tried to fight it, but there was simply no use. The Elixir was too powerful. There was no way he would ever make it back to Reina. Not like this.

Just before his eyes closed, he could see the horrid water horse moving towards him in the water. Her eyes were completely black, and she wore a hideous grin on her porcelain face. Ben would've scrambled backward, but he was too weak to move. He lay helplessly against the wall as she reached for him, her clawed fingers pulling his body close to the pool's edge.

"Yesss, my dear. I'm so glad you have come to keep me company," she hissed. She opened her jaw, baring her sharp, pointed teeth. "Now, this won't hurt a bit. The Elixir is working, you see, and soon, you'll be asleep. You won't remember it. I promise."

For a moment, a trace of odd sorrow passed her expression. She looked as if she might cry. She petted Ben's hair with her long fingers, turning her head to the side. "I do wish you could stay with me, my dear. I get so few visitors, and I *do* so enjoy the company." She wet her thin lips. "But at least I will have your memories." She swallowed greedily. "And I am so very hungry. It's been so long since a mountain fairy passed this way." She frowned. "The last one escaped."

Ben braced himself. There was nothing he could do. He was too weak from the Elixir to even lift his arms. Distantly, his mind drifted to Reina waiting above him. He wished he could tell her to run, to climb back up the path. But he couldn't. And anyway, he wasn't sure she could lift herself back up to the path they had come from.

Wearily, he closed his eyes. Even though it had brought his demise, he was thankful for the Elixir to ease him into sleep. He hoped his death would be quick.

His eyes drifted open once more, and he glimpsed the water horse as she lifted her clawed fingers towards his ear. She inhaled deeply. And then she began to pull.

Ben could feel a fuzzy, numb feeling spreading from the spot where her fingers were focused. It wandered inside his head, and his mind felt as if it had been pricked by a sharp needle, then drawn out in a long, slow strand towards the terrible woman's palm. A shallow, light sensation began to take the place of the heaviness of his thoughts, and he relaxed, allowing the Elixir's effects and the water horse's pull to empty his mind.

Just then, he heard a faint, watery sound in front of him. He closed his eyes as peace spread through his thoughts. This was it. This would be his end. Soon, he would be with the Source. He would be with his mother. With Jubal, and Ita, and all the rest.

A sharp, slicing sound cut the air. A shallow gurgling noise followed, and then…nothing. The pull of the water horse was gone. Ben opened his eyes to groggy slits.

The merrow woman's dark hair lay partially covering her face.

Her head was at a wrong angle, and her arms lay limply over the edge of the pool. Dark, red blood spilled out from a deep gash on her neck, and her glistening eyes stared flatly beyond him.

Ben lifted his head with great effort. The merrow's terrible, twisted body was gone. In its place, a delicate, rose-colored tail remained. Long, iridescent tendrils fluttered from the end of it. The pallor of her skin had dissipated, and Ben thought to himself that she had, at one time, been quite beautiful.

Ben's addled mind somehow came to a realization: It was only her alliance with Orm that had made her twisted and dark. What lay before him was her true form—her true identity. She had only returned to it in death.

Ben frowned down at her weakly. His fear of the water horse was gone. He felt nothing for the merrow before him but pity.

It was a shame she had sacrificed herself this way. She had given herself over to Orm, and for what? Ben was sure Orm had made her illustrious promises if she served his foul side, promises of serving herself as her own master. And she had. She was the master of the water horse.

Ben studied her limp frame. But had she truly been the water horse's master? Ben thought not. No, the water horse had been hers. Instead of ruling herself, she had been a prisoner in a life of lonely darkness in a cell of her own making.

Within moments of her passing, a faint, shallow whispering began to curl around the walls of the cavern. The whispers grew louder and louder, lifting high into the domed ceiling as they swirled about the room. "Where is the opening?" they murmured. "Show us the way."

Ben blinked up at them. *Memories*, he realized. The memories of her victims. The water horse had collected them to keep her company. There were so many voices—so many bodies she had sacrificed for her hunger's desire.

At once, a purplish-blue light began to glow from the dome of the cavern. It spread across the stone surface like a winding, glowing vine, twisting and curling its long fingers towards the walls. Some of the projections dissipated, while the ones in the center continued their path, curving and twisting down the far wall. As Ben watched, the glowing vines wound themselves into a tall arch, whose tips reached down to the floor. Its shape looked much like a door.

The whispers chattered excitedly. They swirled faster, collecting themselves before the door. Then, their voices seeped beyond, and they passed straight through the stone.

Ben winced, lifting his hand to the space above his ear. The pinprick had started on the side of his head again. It felt like it had with the water horse's fingers.

A sickening, funneling feeling began. His own memories trickled back through his ear, audible whispers filling the hole that the water horse had created. Ben's stomach turned as the phantom needle was drawn away. He turned, retching what Elixir was left in his stomach.

Reina stood above him, her dark red hair dripping water on the stone. She knelt, wiping the edge of her small dagger on the front of her skirt. "Ben? Are you alright?" She tucked her cool hand to Ben's forehead. He could barely see her outline.

"Yes," he mumbled. But he wasn't sure that he was.

Reina stood, searching the cavern wall where the glowing arch had appeared. "This has to be the way out," she said. She walked along the wall, careful to avoid the half-eaten deer's carcass, running her hand across the stone. Three quarters of the way across, where the arch had appeared, she paused, her hand finding a small dip in the stone inside of it. She gripped the edge with both hands and braced her feet, pulling with all her might. To Ben's amazement, the stone began to shift, and a hidden door slid open.

CHAPTER 21

REINA

Reina's chest heaved as she rested against the damp rock wall of the narrow tunnel. She peered ahead. There was barely any light in the pass, and there was no way to tell if she was moving in the right direction. But they'd had no choice. This was their only way out.

Ben had lost consciousness back in the cavern after she sliced the awful merrow woman's throat. Reina had been dragging him by his ankles ever since. The muscles in her shoulders and back ached, but she was afraid to rest too long. What if something even worse than the merrow woman was lurking down here?

She lifted Ben's feet, pulling him on. The tunnel had banked upward several paces back. She worried about dragging him, but the ground here was soft. It couldn't cause too much damage. Heavy, glowing moss flanked a narrow stream, which wound down the tunnel's center. She peered back at him, checking his face in the dim light. He was still out.

She crested a hill, and the tunnel turned down again. Reina sighed. It seemed like she'd been dragging him forever. Or maybe it had only been a few moments. She wasn't sure, but Ben felt heavier by the moment. Sweat was pouring into her eyes, and her back and legs burned from all the pulling. She paused again, trying and failing to catch her breath. She couldn't go on much longer.

Up ahead, a glinting sliver of light from the left wall played gently on the surface of the stream. Reina blinked up at it. Were her eyes playing tricks on her? She narrowed them, focusing. No, that was definitely a light shining from an opening in the rock. She took a deep breath and lifted Ben's feet again, dragging him on.

At last, she reached the light source. It sliced a wide, glowing beam through a large gap in the rock wall, the interior of which was obscured by a wall of falling water. With her last bit of strength, she pulled Ben's limp frame through the base of it. She emerged on the other side, blinking in surprise as she swiped water from her eyes.

She laughed incredulously. They were in the alcove of the library—in the Timekeeper's Court. Reina had known the passages behind the fall in the library led to the underground river, but she would have never guessed the path they had taken from the water horse's lair would have led them here.

As quickly as she could, she pulled Ben from the shallow stream to dry ground. She settled him on the mossy floor and hurried out the library doors and towards the kitchens. She was certain there would still be some Tamarisk hanging above the stove.

Sure enough, fresh blossoms hung above a set of boiling pots on the stove top. The steam lifted to their pink petals, which were already drying out in the heat. Reina plucked a handful of them, along with a mortar and pestle, and raced back towards the library.

Ben still lay where she left him, sleeping soundly. Quietly, she knelt to his side. She hurried to grind the Tamarisk with Sacred Thistle, then she gathered some water from the pool and lifted the mixture past his lips. She tucked his chin to help him swallow. Then she waited, watching.

Several moments passed before Ben began to stir, and then he panicked. He shot up from the floor in a dash and pulled his dagger, blinking as he crouched in a defensive position.

Reina scuffled backward as he turned in a wide circle, watching him blink in confusion. She ducked behind a small chair, staring out at him with wide, green eyes. Ben's own eyes found her, and instantly, he relaxed. He dropped his dagger, moving towards her with his hands in an outstretched plea.

"I'm sorry. I thought…" He collapsed on the chair in a heap, running a hand through his hair. "The water horse. Or the merrow woman…" He waved his hand. "Whatever she was. I thought she was here."

Reina moved to face him, shaking her head. "No. She's gone. For good."

She crossed her arms, hugging herself as she dropped her eyes. The fear and relief of what they had just come through was suddenly overwhelming to her. Her lower lip trembled, and she sucked in a breath.

Ben stood, wrapping her close to his chest. "It's okay," he whispered. "We're safe now."

Reina pulled back slightly, eyes welling. "I thought you were dead when I saw you lying against the wall. Your eyes were closed and…and that *horrid* woman was doing something strange to your head." Her voice caught in her throat. "I thought I'd lost you," she said, trembling. "She was going to kill you. Eat you. Make you one of those awful, whispering voices."

Ben buried his nose on the top of her head. He nuzzled her hair, kissing her crown. "You'll never lose me, Reina. Not ever. Not for anything. Not even in death."

CHAPTER 22

REINA

Reina scratched Cyrus's feathered chin as Ben made sure their bags and the crib were secured. He turned to her, offering his hand as she swung astride. She grinned from her high seat on the griffin's back, thinking how glad Lina would be to see Cyrus again. Cyrus had become Lina's griffin almost as soon as she had come to the Timekeeper's Court. They had been through a lot together, even the battle with the Court of Orm.

Cyrus was the fastest griffin in the fleet, and before long, the three of them touched down near the stables behind Leyth Castle in the Haima Mountains. Reina slipped off his back as Ben and the stable hand unloaded their goods. She stared up at the high walls of the glittering castle, struck again by the beauty of this place which had once been so desolate in the foul hands of Orm.

Sheer mountain peaks rose on all sides, and the Rotha-Am hovered just above the rear castle walls, turning Time with its wheel within a wheel. Its light bathed the landscape beneath a soft, blue glow. Reina watched it turn steadily just above the castle's back spires. She remembered the dark cycles when it had not moved as it did now. The memory of the battle on the plain, where so many had lost their lives in what had eventually been the Court of Orm's defeat, played behind her eyes. Reina had fought bravely alongside the King's army, which had included beings from the four corners of Caelium and Timekeepers from her own Mortal Realm.

She had been struck by their sudden victory, brought on by the bravery of Princess Lina, who had fired an arrow forged from the Great Clock through Orm's chest. The rightful King then reclaimed the throne, and the Rotha-Am had been restored, thus saving Time, and with it, all created things.

Reina could feel her Amloga glowing with the memory—the place in her left chest—a piece of Time placed there by the Source. It mirrored the harmony of the Rotha-Am and enabled communion with the Source. She placed her hand on top of it just as Ben appeared beside her.

He stood in reverent silence, and Reina knew he was remembering the battle and victory, the same as she. But for Ben, it was different. He had lost his home and his family at the hands of Orm, and Reina knew his memory of those dark days was colored with much grief. She felt that grief emanating from his being, and she reached out her hand, slipping it around his upper arm.

She was glad he planned to rebuild the Court of Mountain Fairies, but it made her sad that she wouldn't be here to see it. Ben turned to her, his face a mix of joy and sorrow. He reached his opposite hand to cover hers on his arm, giving it a squeeze. His face said more than his words ever could, and Reina smiled up at him as he gazed down at her.

"Let's go see Arto and Lina, okay?" he murmured.

Reina nodded. "Okay."

As they moved towards the castle steps, Reina thought about how glad she was that they had come. Being at the battleground and revisiting those memories had somehow brought closure to her heart. And it would be good to say goodbye to Arto and Lina before she went back through the gate.

Above all, the extra moments alone with Ben were a gift. She was enjoying their time together, and she tried her best to push the idea that he had made a special bracelet for someone else—most likely Vic—from her mind. She didn't want to waste what precious moments she had left with him thinking about that.

Arto met them halfway up the front steps. His long, lithe frame jogged towards them, and he grinned broadly at both before pulling Ben into a bear hug. "Ah, Benjamin. So good to see you, my friend." Arto pulled back, studying Ben's face. "How are things at the Timekeeper's Court?"

Ben smiled. "Everything is in order, Master Arto."

Arto chuckled heartily. "My days as Master of the Timekeeper's Court are long past me, but I remember them fondly." His face suddenly went solemn as he squeezed Ben's upper arm. "And I miss Ita daily. She was as much a grandmother to me as she was to you."

Ben nodded. "She was. I miss her, too."

Arto clapped Ben's shoulder before he turned to Reina. "Always good to see you, Reina." He cut his eyes to Ben mischievously. "Doing your best to keep Benjamin here in line, I trust?"

Reina chuckled. "I do my best, but he causes so much trouble, it's hard to keep up." Ben shot her a look, and she wrinkled her nose at him playfully.

Arto clapped his hands in front of him. "Alright, let's get you two settled. Lina will be dying to see you. I'm sorry she couldn't meet you here, but it's hard for her to get around these days, what with the pregnancy and all. She'll see you both at dinner, though."

Inside the castle, Arto led Ben and Reina past the large, throne room doors at the back of the entry hall. There, he turned right, moving into a bright hallway with an arched, stone ceiling. Colorful panes of glass lined the walls from floor to ceiling, and the evening sun sparkled through them, with golden light casting intricate, glittering patterns across the floor.

Reina studied the iridescent hall in awe, watching the colorful patterns dance in the sunlight. She had never actually been inside Leyth Castle, but she already felt that this corridor would be her favorite. There was no way another could rival its beauty.

Soon, however, she was proven wrong. The hall opened at its end to an enormous, circular gathering area. Light stone rose in columns to the soaring roof, and dark red carpet lined the floor, a gilded, swirling design covering its plush surface. Reina craned her neck to see the high ceiling. The entirety of its vault was made of the same intricate, colored glass as the hall, albeit on a much larger scale. The picture of a golden lion roared in its center.

Reina followed Arto until she was standing in the center of the room. She craned her neck, watching the light dancing through the high panes like pockets of sky spilling through the branches of trees. It was mesmerizing. Images of flowers and giant oaks surrounded the lion, their glittering tones casting a kaleidoscope of ever-changing shapes on the walls and the floor.

Several arched hallways led away from the central room. Arto moved ahead, taking the second from the left. Reina and Benjamin followed behind him, climbing a tall, spiral staircase to a second hallway above. Arto moved to the end of the hall, where two dark, wooden doors were situated across from another. He pulled open the door on his left, peering at Reina.

"Reina, this will be your room. Ben will be just across the hall. Your things should already be inside." He backed down the hallway. "I'm going to check on Lina. If you need anything, we are in the farthest hall to the right. Dinner will be served in the gathering hall—that's the circular one in the center—at sunset. It will just be us four. The King and Queen have gone to the North Forest at the urging of the Four Winds. See you then."

Ben waved and Reina nodded. "See you there," she called. Arto shot her a grin, then turned to jog back down the stairs.

Reina could feel Ben's eyes on her before she even looked. They were in the hall outside their rooms, where they had planned to meet. She had pinned her hair high on her head and chosen a dark green column dress for dinner. It was sleeveless with an open back, and its collar came high on her throat. Bea had cut the dress rather close. Reina was conscious of the fabric clinging to her curves. She wondered what Ben would think of it.

Nervously, she slid her eyes in his direction. Ben's golden curls had been smoothed behind his pointed ears, and he had shaved his stubble close. He wore a trim, dark suit and matching leather shoes. Reina had never seen him look better.

Ben continued to stare, and she shuffled her weight, her cheeks pinking under his gaze. He shot her a lopsided grin, and her stomach did a flip. That smile was doing nothing for her nerves.

"What?" she said, struggling to keep irritation from her voice.

Ben shook his head, still grinning. "Nothing. I just think you're probably the most beautiful woman I've ever met."

Reina blushed deeper, a smile creeping over her lips despite herself. He was being ridiculous. She pursed her lips. "Then you haven't met many women."

Ben shrugged. "I don't need to. I already know I've met the most beautiful one of all." Reina dropped her eyes, secretly pleased. Nerves and excitement jostled for position as Ben moved across the hall. He extended his arm, and Reina looped her hand shyly beneath it, the feel of him sending little thrills through her fingers.

The gathering hall was even more breathtaking in darkness than it had been in the light. A thousand candles glittered from a long table at the room's center and from sconces all along the wall. Their light was reflected against the ceiling's glass, making it look like a blanket of colorful stars. Arto was standing at the far end of the table, and Lina sat in the chair to his left. She grinned and tried to get up upon their approach.

Reina bowed to her quickly, then waved for her to take her seat. Lina's belly bulged beneath her pale dress. She was heavily pregnant. In fact, she looked like she could have the baby at any moment. "Please, don't stand," Reina pleaded.

Lina nodded, then gripped Arto's palm with one hand and reached back to brace herself against the arm of her seat. She eased herself back down onto the cushion with a huff, rubbing her rounded belly. "Whew," she said, chuckling.

Arto had moved behind her chair. He was arranging a second

cushion at her back. Lina shook her head, grinning. She shot Reina a look. "He fusses over me a little too much. But I love it." She tipped her lips up to him, and Arto leaned over her seat, planting a quick kiss.

Reina blushed at their exchange. Being in Arto and Lina's presence always made her feel like she was intruding on an intimate moment, especially when they kissed each other like that. Arto gazed at Lina a moment longer before he pulled away. He looked as if he were just remembering Ben and Reina's presence as he gestured to the two seats on his right. Grinning, he shook his head. "I'm sorry, I've forgotten myself. Please, do sit down."

Reina took her seat, and, in moments, two servants appeared at her side. One filled her glass, while the other filled her plate.

Arto took his own seat at the head of the table. He grasped Lina's hand, smiling over at Ben and Reina. "So, tell me, what's new in the West Mountains?"

Ben swallowed a bite of bread. "Everything."

Arto nodded. "Like what?"

Ben took a sip of tea from his fluted glass, then sat back in his chair. "Well, for one, I saw Marcus."

Arto's dark, almond eyes bulged. "What? When?" He shook his head, looking to Lina and back again. "I thought he kept mostly to himself. At least, that's what our patrols tell us."

Ben dipped his chin. "You've been keeping tabs on him then."

Arto nodded seriously. "Of course. We had heard that he was

somewhat of a…a brutal leader, but since he hasn't lately caused much trouble, we've left him alone."

Ben nodded. It was true. Marcus and his clan hardly ever ventured from their far corner in the west. "Yes, the banded fairies don't often cross their bush line. That is, unless Marcus feels threatened." He folded his arms, frowning. "I must've threatened him with my recent activity."

"And what's that?" asked Arto. He templed his fingers, resting his elbows on the table as he peered at Ben intently.

Ben continued. "I had a dream. And a gift from the Eiks. It was a clutch of lumber, dispatched by Willow from a fallen Eik in the Grove. In my dream, I rebuilt the doors to the Court of Mountain Fairies," Ben trailed off, glancing quickly in Reina's direction. "Among other things," he muttered.

Arto tilted his head thoughtfully. "So, you followed the Source's instructions from your dream and rebuilt the doors in the waking hours."

Ben nodded. "Exactly." He frowned. "Except, it didn't quite go as planned. Marcus attacked Jubal, the mountain satyr. He killed him on sight, and he destroyed the doors. They're burned to ash outside the ruins now." Ben glanced back at Reina. "When Reina and I moved Jubal's body into his cave, Marcus attacked me from behind. He aimed to kill me, I think. Or at least incapacitate me." He glanced again at Reina, and she smiled a small smile as he reached to clutch her hand beneath the table. "If Reina hadn't been there, I wouldn't have made it. Marcus would've killed me, too."

Lina sat listening with her arms wrapped protectively across her rounded abdomen. She frowned worriedly at Arto as Ben completed his speech. Then she turned her eyes to Ben and Reina.

"This wicked violence cannot be tolerated. My father will not stand for it. If it pleases you, we can intervene. You only have to say the word."

Ben nodded. "And I thank you for that. But what I really need is help—defenses and aid." He sat straighter in his chair. "The more I think about it, the more I feel that the doors were only the beginning. They were only my first commission." He gazed down at the table thoughtfully, then lifted his eyes to Arto and Lina.

"I believe that my dream led me back to my home court, but the doors were just the start. My real purpose is to restore the court in full. You both know the Court of Mountain Fairies is my home. It's my heritage. I'm the heir to the ruling seat, and its restoration falls to me." He shook his head. "It won't be an easy task, and it will take all the help I can get."

Arto lifted his chin. "Marcus won't like it. He'll be ready to attack. He's already demonstrated he'll kill, if it comes to it."

Ben nodded. "It will be dangerous. I'll need defenses, some of which we have available at the Timekeeper's Court. The Mortal Timekeepers have been training since they fought in the battle with the King's army. But even with them, I still need more support. I believe we can accomplish the task if the courts band together.

And, too, the work will go more swiftly if we have many hands."

"Then it's settled," Lina said decidedly. "We will send out a decree at the Castle Ball tomorrow night asking for aid. Many will come for you. I am sure of it."

She smiled across the table at Reina. "Meanwhile, you have a lovely counterpart, who I'm sure is more than willing to help you."

"Yes," Arto interjected. He eyed Reina's wrist pointedly. "Reina, I can't help but notice you wear a bracelet. A sign of close friendship among the fae, is it not?" Reina nodded as Arto slid his eyes to Ben mischievously. "And might a matching one for the other wrist be in order soon, Benjamin?"

Reina could feel Ben stiffen in the chair beside her. She wished she could disappear beneath the table. Or sink into the floor. Anything but sitting here, thinking of what she didn't have.

She flushed as Arto flicked his eyes between the two of them, and quickly, she lifted her glass, hiding behind the rim. She sipped long, avoiding the questioning stares of their hosts. Arto couldn't have known that Ben had made a bracelet for someone else. But still, his words cut her deeply, even if they were by accident.

Ben fumbled with his own glass. "I, ah…" He lifted it, taking a hurried sip, then set it back down onto the table. Reina couldn't stand it any longer. She couldn't bear to let him say what she was sure he was going to say. He wasn't going to give her the other bracelet. He had made it for someone else, and that was that. She squeezed her eyes shut, then opened them, the words tumbling out of her mouth before Ben could say more.

"I'm going home," she said quickly. Her voice sounded high and tight in her own ears. "To the Mortal Realm. The throne of Monrovia waits for me there. As well as my betrothed."

For a moment, the room was totally silent. Ben dropped his eyes. He stared at his lap as Arto cleared his throat, but it was Lina who spoke first. She reached her hand across the table to grasp Reina's palm. She gave it a squeeze.

"And what an honor to have you as their leader, Reina. The brave woman who was first through the main gate." Reina smiled at her. She was grateful Lina had broken the tense moment.

Lina flicked her eyes to Ben, kindness shining in her blue gaze. "And a great loss to all of us here in Caelium."

Beside her, she felt Ben shuffle in his seat. Her heart burned that he hadn't given an answer to Arto's question. It would have been better if he had just told him the truth, that he had crafted another bracelet to give to Vic once she was gone. It would have hurt to hear it, but maybe it would be good, too. Maybe if she heard it from his own lips, it wouldn't sting as badly.

Reina picked at her plate for the rest of the meal. She slid her eyes to Ben's. To her amazement, he hadn't eaten much either. Usually, he would've been on his second helping by now.

At last, dinner was over. Reina stood, glad to be released from Ben's presence. Across the table, Arto helped Lina lift heavily from her seat. Reina watched them go, Arto lovingly supporting her low back as they walked towards their rooms. He whispered something in Lina's ear, and she giggled, throwing her head back. Her long blonde hair streamed down to her waist, and Reina thought she had never seen anything so wonderful as the two of them together.

Ben snapped her out of her reverie by clearing his throat behind her shoulder. "I, um, I'm going to the nursery in a little while if you want to come. To get the crib ready." He moved beside her, stuffing a hand into his pocket. Reina crossed her arms. After what had happened at dinner, she just didn't feel like being around him. It was too hard. She twisted her lips. "I don't know. I'm just tired, you know? I think I'll get to bed."

Ben nodded quickly. He shrugged, frowning as he looked away. "Oh, yeah, of course." He started to back away from her. "I'll, um, I'll see you tomorrow, then?"

Reina nodded. "Okay."

Later that night, as she lay tossing and turning, Reina wondered what Ben might be doing. More than once, she got up to go to the nursery, but she never made it past her door. She had questions, mostly about the bracelet and who he would give it to. She knew she had no right to ask. She had no claim on Ben, and it was his business who he spent his time with once she was gone. It was none of her business who he chose as a close friend—or who he chose to be more. Besides, she was betrothed. That was as good as married—in Monrovia, anyway.

She flipped onto her stomach, burying her face into the pillow. One more day in Caelium, and then it would all be over. In some ways, it would be a relief. Once she was away, once she didn't feel the pull of Ben's presence on her every moment, maybe she would feel better.

Maybe once she was married, she would even be able to let go of this life, to let go of Ben. She prayed it would be so, because the Source knew, she couldn't take this torment much longer.

CHAPTER 23

REINA

Reina was surprised when her eyes opened to the midday sun streaming through her window. She had slept longer than she meant to, and she hated that she'd wasted half the day. When she had told Ben she was tired, she only half meant it. But it seemed like her body had taken the words to heart. Sighing, she stretched long, raising her arms above her head.

A knock sounded on her door, and she sat up groggily. "Be right there," she called, yawning. Flinging on her robe, she padded to the door. She opened it to find Ben, wild-eyed, on the other side.

"Reina, come quick. Lina's having the baby. Arto asked me to come get you. He said Lina needs your help."

Reina blinked in surprise. She tucked a hand to her chest. "*Me?* Why me? I've never even *seen* a baby be born, let alone helped with a delivery."

Ben tugged at her arm. "Just come on, okay?"

He pulled Reina, stumbling, out into the hallway, and together, they hurried towards the gathering hall. Preparations were already being made there for the Castle Ball. A large dance floor had been erected in the center of the room and long rows of tables had been set up along the far walls for food and drinks. Wide streams of sparkling gold fabric hung from the high ceiling in draping rows. They cascaded down the stone walls to meet the carpet beneath.

Reina could hear Lina's groans before they reached her door. Her grey wolf, Remus, was perched outside in the hallway, his green eyes trained sharply on the door. Ben held it open, and Remus bounded inside. Reina cast Ben one last furtive look, then, she took a deep breath and stepped in behind him.

Remus moved to sit near Arto, who was pacing worriedly at the end of the bed. He stopped when he saw Reina, relief washing his features. Reina wondered at his look. If Arto thought she had any idea what to do, then he was going to be sorely mistaken. Arto ran a hand through his hair, gesturing silently for her to go to Lina. Queen Astrid and another elegant, lovely woman with dark auburn hair and large eyes were at the far bedside. Although she had never met her, Reina was almost certain she was the realm's healer, Elysia.

Reina sank down beside the bed as Lina reached for her palm. Sweat beaded on Lina's brow, and the healer dabbed it with a cool cloth. The woman smiled at her, and Reina was struck again by her beauty.

"Reina, this is our healer, Lady Elysia, from the Southern Sea," said Queen Astrid. "Elysia, meet Reina, from the West Mountains."

Reina nodded to the lovely woman. "Nice to meet you," she said softly.

"Likewise," said the woman. Her voice was like velvet in Reina's ears.

Lina was struck with another pain, and she ground her teeth and lifted her head off the pillow. "Let's give a push now, Lina," said Elysia encouragingly. Lina nodded, then took a deep breath. She lifted her head once more, her face turning dark red with the effort. At last, she relaxed onto the pillow, and Queen Astrid dabbed her face with the cloth. Elysia checked beneath the sheet that was draped over Lina's knees. "And once more now, Lina. That's it, strong now!"

A peal of musical laughter rang out from Elysia's lips, just as a sharp cry emanated from beneath the sheet. She lifted the baby up in her arms. "Say hello to your daughter, Evangeline!" cried Elysia.

Lina collapsed back onto the pillow as Elysia laid the baby onto her chest. Soon, the baby nursed, and Lina stroked her tiny cheek with her thumb, murmuring softly into her tiny ear. Arto moved to the side of the bed, pure joy on his face at the sight of his daughter. He put a palm protectively over the baby's back, and he and Lina shared a kiss above her tiny head.

Reina couldn't stop the tears from flowing at the sight of them. It was one of the most beautiful things she had ever witnessed. Lina turned towards her, smiling brightly.

"We have a request," she said softly. Reina nodded. She had no idea what it could be and was baffled that she had been invited to attend the Royal birth to begin with. Lina continued.

"We would like to name her after you, if you will allow it."

Reina blinked at Lina in surprise. She didn't know what to say. Lina reached for her hand. "We can think of no better namesake than the brave Mortal Timekeeper who was the first through the gate. So, we would like to call her Rayna."

Reina gazed down in awe at the sweet, tiny bundle, who was snuggled against her mother's chest. She pressed her lips together, stifling more tears as she looked to Arto and Lina. "It would be my great honor," she said softly, her eyes glistening.

Lina squeezed her palm once more. "Thank you. We know you will be a brave ruler, wherever you are, Mortal Realm or otherwise. And we hope our daughter will be as brave and as strong as you, one day. We send our best with you as you pass back through the gate.

Reina's heart was full as she readied herself for the Castle Ball. It pleased her to know that the Royal family thought so much of her that they had named their little daughter after her. It was a great honor, and that, along with their well-wishes, had somewhat soothed the fact that she would soon be leaving.

She smoothed her lavender gown across her stomach as she stood in front of the full-length mirror, studying her appearance. She had wound her hair into a half-up knot, allowing some golden-red curls to slip out and frame her face. The green vines on the skirt brought out the color of her eyes, and the lavender fabric complemented her creamy skin, which shimmered delicately in the evening candlelight. For jewelry, all she wore was the bracelet Ben had given her. The lavender petals of the flower at its center matched her dress perfectly.

Reina grinned. She felt lovely. She hoped Ben would think so, too. Because this was her last night with him, and she wanted it to be perfect.

CHAPTER 24

BEN

Ben shuffled nervously in the hallway outside Reina's room. He tugged at the collar of his dinner shirt. It was too tight. Reina was moving behind her door. Ben straightened his jacket and smoothed his hair. Then he stuffed his hand into his pocket, ensuring the bracelet was there for the millionth time.

He had already decided. Tonight was the night. He was going to tell Reina how he felt about her, and he was finally going to give her the other bracelet.

Ben knew he shouldn't. There were several reasons why it was a bad idea, one of which was the fact that she would resent him forever if he kept her from her throne. But he couldn't help himself. He loved her too much not to tell her the truth.

There was no way he could forget the thousands of times he had caught her eye or shared a private joke. He couldn't forget his dream or their kiss in the kitchen at the Court of Mountain Fairies. All those moments had led up to this, even if he hadn't known it at the time. Reina meant everything to him. He knew it now. Without a doubt, Reina was his one true love.

Just last night, he had dreamed again of her hands covered in cake batter, two bracelets gleaming in the sun on the counter behind her. When she kissed him, it felt as real as it had before. Only this time, she didn't go through the gate. Instead, the image shifted, and every memory he had with her played before his eyes.

The last one wasn't a memory. It was new. Reina's belly was rounded and large. She floated in the pool at the waterfall, her fiery hair drifting above her in a long stream. Ben dove in after her. She wrapped her arms around his neck, bringing her lips close to his ear. "I'll stay," she whispered. "I'll stay with you."

In Ben's mind, it was final. There was no one else for him, and there never would be. There was only Reina. And he had to tell her before it was too late.

Ben gathered himself as he rapped lightly on her door. Then he stepped back, waiting. He'd gone to the gardens earlier, while she was attending the birth. To his amazement, he had found a patch of Mountain Aster tucked in the back left corner. He twirled one delicate flower between his fingers thoughtfully as Reina pulled her door wide.

Ben couldn't speak. He had thought she was at her most beautiful last night, but he'd been wrong. This version of Reina was by far the most beautiful he had ever seen.

She had enhanced her lashes with some substance. They fluttered lightly above her green eyes, which sparkled like two deep pools. Her lips were the perfect shade of pink, and Ben stared at them for longer than he should have, causing an identical shade to spring onto her cheeks.

"Reina, I," he stumbled over his words. "I, ah… You look beautiful," he croaked.

He wanted to move towards her, to crush her in his arms, to beg her to never leave. But it wasn't the right moment. They hadn't even been to the dance floor yet. He would wait. Tell her after. When they were alone.

Reina blushed a darker shade, her lashes sweeping to the floor. "Thank you," she said quietly. She flicked her eyes up to him, twisting her mouth slightly. You look pretty good yourself."

Ben grinned. "Thanks." He held the flower out to her. "This is for you."

Reina raised her brows in surprise as she took it from him. "My favorite," she said, smiling brightly. Their fingers brushed lightly in the exchange, and a tingling jolt ran up Ben's forearm.

He pulled it behind his back, flexing his palm. He wondered if Reina had felt it too.

Reina tucked the flower behind her ear, its sharp contrast to her hair making her even more becoming. As if that were even possible. Ben had thought it wasn't, but the petals' delicate shade pulled the warmth in her cheeks, and he nearly lost his breath. Remembering himself at the last moment, he extended his arm, and she took it, her small hand burning through the fabric of his suit jacket.

Ben sipped at his punch absently. Henri was to his left. He was chattering on about some situation with the griffins, but Ben couldn't hear him. He set his cup on the high table, his face partially hidden behind a large centerpiece. His eyes were carefully trained beyond it, on the lovely woman swirling around the dance floor.

Reina spun, the gauzy lavender skirt of her dress floating out behind her. Henri was still chattering. Ben nodded vaguely at his words, but in truth, he wasn't sure what he was nodding about. Finally, Henri gave up and moved on to another table, leaving Ben alone with his thoughts. Not surprisingly, they were completely consumed with Reina.

Ben knew he should mingle. After all, every court leader in the realm was present at the Castle Ball tonight. These were the people he was calling on to help him rebuild his home court. He really needed their help, and he knew he should try to recruit a bit, but he didn't want to waste one moment. He couldn't bear to be without his eyes on her.

The King had already dispatched the decree, which had been blessed by the Four Winds and thus sent out from the Eiks to each court in Caelium. But it was up to each court ruler to decide if they would help with the West Mountains endeavor. It wouldn't be easy or safe, and Ben worried that the realm hadn't lain long enough in peace to consider joining another battle, especially not one that wouldn't directly affect their own courts.

He flicked his eyes to the platform on his right, where King Ard-Mathan and Queen Astrid sat on two high-backed seats. Arto was on their left, speaking with the centaur called Chaeronne from the east. Ronne wore the blue sash signifying his role as the general of the King's army. He was a fearsome figure, his muscular frame dwarfing even Arto's tall body in size. His wife Maria stood to her husband's left, listening intently. Her long, dark hair was woven into a thick braid down her back, and her bay flanks had been carefully painted with festive, swirling designs.

Just then, Arto turned and motioned him over. Ben nodded, adjusting his jacket as he moved in their direction. He stopped before the King and Queen, bowing deeply with his fist over his left chest.

"Your Majesties, I wanted to thank you for your support of our West Mountains endeavors. We few remaining mountain fairies have long been without our home, and it is my deepest hope that soon, it will be restored."

The King and Queen had both worn their most festive attire. Queen Astrid wore a narrow column of sparkling blue, while the King had donned a thick cloak of dark blue over his dinner jacket. The Queen smiled down at Ben kindly, eyes that matched Lina's crinkling at the edges. But it was the King who spoke. His gilded crown rested lightly on his sandy hair, his sharp blue eyes peering deeply at Ben below. "You are most welcome, Benjamin. It brings us great joy to see you honor your legacy. And it is our hope that the Four Corners of Caelium will come to your aid." Ben bowed again, then turned to Arto and Ronne.

Arto put an arm around his shoulder. "Ben, this is Chaeronne, general of the King's army, and my great friend. Ronne, meet another great friend of mine. This is Benjamin: Heir to the ruling seat of the Court of Mountain Fairies."

Ben was quietly stunned at the use of his title. He hadn't heard it used in many cycles. It caused his throat to tighten with memories, but he swallowed past it, smiling tightly.

Ronne tucked a fist over his left chest, which was crisscrossed with battle scars.

"The Court of Warriors greets you, Benjamin. We in the east have received the King's decree. Our warriors grow restless in this time of peace, and we are more than willing to come to your aid. You will find us in your West Mountains home as soon as you have need of us."

Ben didn't know what to say. He blinked in surprise as Arto squeezed his shoulder. He'd never dreamed the Court of Warriors, the court of the very general of the King's army, would come to help him. He nodded up at Ronne's sharp features. "Thank you," he murmured. He was so overwhelmed, it was all he could manage.

Ronne and Maria moved to stand by the King and Queen, and Arto crossed his arms as he and Ben turned towards the dance floor. Swirling couples crowded there in the center of the room. Ben searched the group, catching a moment of Reina's bright red hair among the fray. But then someone whirled in front of her, and she was gone.

Ben grinned as he watched his friend Kai swirling his selkie mate. He dipped Elysia until her dark auburn curls skimmed the floor, and she giggled before lifting her chin to plant a kiss on his lips.

Arto nudged Ben's arm. "That could be you and Reina, you know."

Ben turned his head. He kept his face neutral, but his chest was burning with Arto's words. "What do you mean?" he asked innocently.

Arto nodded his head towards Kai and Elysia, who were now coming in their direction. "You know what I mean," he said quietly.

He did, but he chose to ignore it. Ben couldn't allow his heart to hope more than he already was.

Kai was already wrapping his arms around Ben's shoulders. Ben grinned, hugging him back. It had been too long since he had seen Kai.

"Ah, Benjamin, my friend. It's so good to see you." Kai's long, silver hair was pulled into a fishtail braid which trailed below the collar of his dark suit and down his back. He pulled away to eye Ben's frame with his glittering blue eyes, grinning broadly.

Ben smiled. He knew what Kai was thinking. He had gained quite a bit of muscle since he'd last seen him.

Kai raised his brows. "There's more of you than I remember, Ben. Must be the West Mountains air."

Ben chuckled, nudging Kai's large bicep with his elbow. He puffed out his chest. "This only happens to us land-dwellers," he teased. "You water hoppers wouldn't understand." He squinted at Kai's shoulders, as if they were too small to see. In truth, he and Kai were almost the same size, but there was no way he'd let Kai know that.

Kai laughed, then looped his arm across Elysia's shoulders. "What do you think about this, my love? Should I take up land-dwelling full time?"

Elysia rolled her eyes. "Keep me out of your childish squabbles, boys. I've got bigger fish to catch." With that, she planted a kiss on Kai's cheek. Then, she lifted his arm from her shoulders and moved towards the far end of the room.

Lina was sitting there on a low settee, baby Rayna nestled in her lap. Ben watched as Elysia grinned down at the small bundle.

She held out her arms as she settled onto the settee beside Lina, who promptly laid the new baby into them.

Kai watched her, a sideways grin on his face. "When should we expect your announcement?" Arto asked from behind his shoulder.

Kai swung his head, his face still held the goofy grin. "What announcement?"

Arto jerked his head towards the settee, where both women were cooing over the baby. "When will you and Elysia have one of your own?"

Kai hesitated, turning to look at Elysia again. "Soon, I hope. Seamus and Ena already have three, and Elysia grows more restless without one each day." He paused for a moment, pulled into some distant reverie, then he turned back to Ben and Arto, grinning.

"Anyway, I have another announcement." He eyed Ben with his sharp eyes. "We received the decree. The Court of the Sea will come to your aid."

Ben let out a breath. "Thank you, Kai. It means more than you know."

Kai nodded. "It's not an unfamiliar sensation for many in our clan to be separated from our home, and we wouldn't wish such a thing on anyone, especially not a friend." He patted Ben's shoulder, then nodded to both men before moving across the floor towards his mate.

He knelt at Elysia's feet, bracing a hand behind her back and lifting the other to stroke the top of the baby's dark, downy head.

Ben watched as Kai lifted his eyes to Elysia. She grinned down at him, their look so full of love that it made Ben's heart ache.

"Two courts down, Ben," Arto said quietly. He folded his arms, his eyes scanning the dance floor. "You're unlikely to hear from the dryads." Ben flicked his eyes to the far corner, where Willow stood silent. She looked enormously out of place, hugging her wooden shoulders. A group of merrow women had formed tightly about her. They chattered animatedly, and she smiled politely, but it looked as if she would like nothing more than to jump out the window and escape back to her North Forest home.

Dryads were known to be quite shy, especially outside of their Grove. It was where they preferred to stay, guarding the Eiks, the messengers of the Four Winds. Arto inclined his head, watching Willow. "Mostly, they will come and go as they please. It's more likely they will give you supplies and encouragement, but don't expect much else."

Ben nodded. He knew Arto was right.

Arto studied the room a moment more, then rested his eyes on Lina. He clapped Ben on the back. "Alright, mission accomplished with the decree, yes?"

Ben nodded. "Yes." He turned to Arto. "Thank you, my friend." Arto grinned broadly, causing the wide scar on his neck to pull at the edge—a mark of his victory with the Court of Orm.

Just then, Reina stepped off the far end of the dance floor. She turned, moving swiftly towards the center hallway. Ben stiffened.

She was headed out to the terrace. It was now or never.

Arto leaned close. "Go get her," he whispered. He started to stride away, then called over his shoulder. "See you tomorrow, okay?"

Ben barely acknowledged him. All he could think about was Reina's lavender skirt slipping further down the hallway.

A large, second ballroom joined the hallway with the back terrace. The room was quiet, barely lit by a few wall sconces. Ben could hear shuffles and giggles as he moved across the floor to the terrace doors, where couples hid in the shadows of the unused room for a moment out of sight. At the far wall, gauzy curtains billowed inward from the open doors on the night breeze. Ben moved past them, allowing his eyes to adjust to the dim starlight.

Reina stood alone at the end of the long portico, the blue light of the Rotha-Am illuminating her back from where it hovered just beyond. She was facing away from him, her arms braced on the stone balustrade.

Ben stuffed his hand into his pocket. The gems of the bracelet were cool against his palm. He tucked it around them, his heart thumping in his ears as he moved towards her. The sound was so loud, he wondered if she would be able to hear it in the quiet evening air.

He was almost to her, her soft, cinnamon curls diffused gold in the bluish light. Ben was ready, more than ready to tell her that he wanted her to stay. He opened his mouth to do it but stopped short when he heard her sniffle. She tucked her chin, swiping at her eyes. "Reina?" he murmured.

She turned slowly to face him, bracing her palms on each side of the stone behind her. "What is it, Ben?" she asked, too cheerfully. Her voice sounded tight to his ears, but her eyes betrayed her like they always did.

Ben frowned, moving closer to her, studying her face in the dim light. He searched her green eyes. "Reina, I have to tell you something. It's something I've been meaning to tell you for a long time."

He gripped the bracelet, ready to lift it from his pocket. He would get down on his knees. He would beg her if he had to. And if she accepted the bracelet, he would put it on her other wrist. They would be betrothed.

Reina sniffed. She jerked her head sharply back and forth. "It's fine, Ben. Really. I don't need to hear it, okay?" She dropped her eyes as she crossed her arms, chewing on the inside of her cheek.

Ben blinked at her in confusion. She wouldn't meet his gaze. "Reina, please. You're about to leave, and I have to tell you that I don't…" She held out her palm, cutting him off.

"I can't do this, Ben," she said shakily. "*We* can't do this." She sniffed. Tears were brimming in her eyes, which were sharp with pain. Angrily, she swiped at them again. "Please. Just don't do this, okay? I've got to go home. Everyone in Monrovia is counting on me, just like everyone here is counting on you." She sighed. "We both have jobs to do. Big ones. We can't let allow ourselves to get in each other's way." She paused to collect herself, looking up at the starlit sky. She twisted her mouth.

"I think it's best that I leave tonight, from Leyth Castle. That's what I was trying to do when I left the ball."

Ben blinked at her as realization settled in. "You mean…you were going to leave without saying *goodbye*?"

Reina shrugged one shoulder. "We've said goodbye in a thousand ways over the last few days, and I've already said good-bye to Amelie, and Henri and Johann and the others." She just stared at him, and Ben shook his head, tucking a frustrated hand to his chest.

"What about *me*?" He scoffed. "You thought I would be fine if you just…just *left* without telling me?" He shook his head, pain searing his chest. "And with the idea that I might not ever see you again?" He ran a hand through his hair, disbelief tingling down his spine. He was hurt, so hurt that she would even consider it.

Reina lifted her chin, her voice carefully controlled. "I thought you would be upset, but that you would get over it. You have other…" She trailed off as she dropped her eyes, picking at her skirt. She swallowed. "It might've been easier. For me, for both of us, if I had just left."

Ben ground his teeth. "Well, I wouldn't have. I wouldn't get over it, Reina. Not now, not ever!"

He closed the distance between them in one step and tucked his arm around her back, only pausing to memorize her face before dipping his lips to her own. His kiss was insistent. Determined. Desperate.

At first, Reina resisted, but then her body molded against him, and she brought her hands to wind into his hair. Ben held her tightly, every bit of him screaming for her to *Stay, stay, stay.*

When he finally pulled away, he was trembling, and he tucked his free hand into his pocket, intent on making her his mate, once and for all. There was no one else, not in this world or any other, that could ever compare to the woman in his arms right now. There was no one for him but Reina.

He started to lift the bracelet as Reina wet her lips. "Ben, I've got to go," she whispered.

His hand halted inside his pocket. He frowned, his heart squeezing. "Reina, no. Please stay," he pleaded.

She studied his face, bringing one hand to trace the edge of his jaw. She planted another small kiss on his lips, then gently, she pushed him away. "I've got to go, Ben," she choked out. Her voice was barely a whisper. "I'll miss you. More than I can say."

She started to move past him, and Ben's heart lurched after her. He fell to his knees. "No, Reina, please."

But she had already opened a gate in front of her, and she didn't look back before she stepped through.

CHAPTER 25

BEN

After Reina had gone, Ben headed straight to the castle stables. He threw himself across Cyrus's back and flew to the Court of Mountain Fairies as fast as he could. Once there, he sent Cyrus home. Then, he set to work on the Western Wall. All night, he set stones on top of stones until his upper body throbbed and his fingers blistered open and bled.

He almost wished Marcus would come. Even death would have been a sweet relief to the pain he was feeling. But he didn't. So now, Ben was lying flat on his back against the scorched earth, his body throbbing while the mid-morning sun was sending its blinding light to the back of his aching skull.

He blinked against it as he sat up groggily, trying to swallow past the dusty taste that had permanently adhered itself to his tongue. He tried to stand, and every muscle in his body screamed against the motion. It felt like he was ripping the flesh from his bones. *Good.* Maybe if he had enough physical pain, the other pain wouldn't hurt so much.

"Care for some water?" Kai's voice grated against Ben's ears, and he winced as his friend strode towards him from the southernmost part of the tumbled wall. He stopped when he got close, doing a double take. Ben was sure he looked a wreck. Since he had come straight from Leyth Castle, he hadn't bothered to change, and he'd soaked through his clothes with sweat several times during the night.

He had tossed his suit jacket and his shoes somewhere up the hillside. His white dinner shirt was stained with streaks of dirt and blood, and there was a big rip in one sleeve. He glanced down. His pants didn't look much better. Both knees were caked with dirt, and the bottom hem had unraveled on the left side.

Kai's piercing blue eyes peered into Ben's face. "Rough night?" he asked.

Ben glared up at him, watching a broad grin spread across Kai's face. Ben scratched his head. "You could say that," he croaked. The words felt like sand against his throat.

Kai nodded. Wordlessly, he cupped his palms in front of his body. Ben felt a faint breeze as a ball of water materialized into Kai's hands from the air around him. It collected itself above Kai's palms, hovering. He held it out to Ben. "Sorry, but I didn't bring a glass."

Ben tipped Kai's hands, drinking every last drop. He wiped his chin with the back of his palm. "T'sokay," he mumbled.

Ben stood with effort. He turned to the wall and began to stack stones where he had left off before he passed out sometime in the night. Kai watched him curiously as he strained. The large stones felt heavier than they had last evening, and Ben struggled to haul them into position. He ground his teeth, grunting as he laid one at chest height.

"Where's Reina?" Kai asked.

Ben paused for a moment, resting on the stone he had just laid, then he turned to lift another stone. "Gone," he said flatly. He grunted as he swung it towards the wall. "She left last night. Back to her home in Monrovia." Ben fumbled the stone in his arms, and Kai reached out to steady it.

He helped him place it on top of the others, then turned to face Ben. He narrowed his sharp eyes. "Why? I thought she was happy here. As a matter of fact, I thought you two might…"

"No," Ben said, cutting him off. "We didn't. We…aren't. She's already betrothed. She's due to be married any day. Then, she and her husband will take the Monrovian throne."

Kai frowned as Ben lifted another stone. He helped him carry it to the wall. "I see." He waited thoughtfully as Ben caught his breath, then started in again. "Did you try to—"

Ben shook his head sharply. "Kai, no offense, but I don't really want to talk about it, okay?"

Kai nodded, frowning. "Okay. But if you change your mind…"

"Thanks," Ben said quietly. He flashed Kai a quick smile, and Kai grinned in return.

At last, Ben sat heavily on the nearest tumbled stone. He was wiped out. No food, and barely any water. Kai crouched next to him as he swiped the sweat from his brow. He changed the subject. "We've brought some materials from the Selkie Isles mines," he said. "Going to put them to use on the Southern Wall. Most of the stones there were decimated. We didn't have a lot to work with."

Ben lifted his chin wearily. "That sounds great. Thank you."

Kai dipped his own. "Also, we were planning to set up sentries from the Force and Guard at vulnerable points along the wall. That is, if you agree."

Ben frowned. "I agree. We need all the defenses we can get. They can work in shifts with the Mortal Timekeepers and the centaurs. One group will work on the walls while the other two stand guard and patrol. Then they will rotate."

He gazed further west, past Jubal's cave, where a narrow pass was hidden between two sheer mountains. "It may be wise to patrol the pass. That's where Marcus's men will come if he attacks. And I'm sure he will."

Kai nodded. "Agreed. I'll tell the others. They're already here." He eyed Ben's appearance once more. "In the meantime, take a break. You look like you've worked all night."

Ben grinned. "I agree with that idea, too," he said tiredly.

Ben stood weakly, watching as his friend moved away. Kai was right. He was on the verge of exhaustion. His hand trembled against the stone wall, braced there in case his knees buckled. There was no way he could let himself get this tired again. Especially not with the chance of an attack. Right now, he was the only one manning the Western Wall, and in his current state, he was too easy a target.

As he rounded the corner to the North Wall, Maria met him, along with her twins. The young centaurs were nearly full grown. One was bay like his mother, and the other had the greyish swirls of hair on his flanks like his father, Ronne. They gripped tightly to their spears, their keen, dark eyes darting out from their curtains of long, black hair, searching the countryside for danger. The young centaurs held their chests up proudly, and Ben noticed they wore the leather vests of a warrior, though they hadn't yet seen any battle. Ben had no doubt they would charge, and if need be, hunt down an invader. Courage was just a part of the centaur's blood.

Maria smiled kindly at him, adjusting the basket against her hip. She lifted the lid, and a sweet aroma wafted from inside of it. She handed Ben a warm bundle of parchment. "Eat and rest," her smooth voice said quietly. "There are others who will take over your work. You have done more than your fair share for this day."

Ben accepted the wrapped parchment gratefully, along with a small jug of water. "Thank you, Maria. Tell the others that we will meet at dusk at the Southern Wall." Maria nodded. Then, she and the twins moved past him to round the corner.

Once he was past his doors, Ben collapsed against the chaise in the large back bedroom. His legs hung uncomfortably over the end of the seat, and it occurred to him again that he needed to build a bed. He sighed. With Reina gone, he didn't feel like it. The chaise would just have to do.

He pulled the ragged blanket under his chin, Maria's parchment lying forgotten on the small table behind him. He closed his eyes. He was too tired to eat, anyway.

Dreams were Ben's only relief from his torment. And if he'd had a choice, he would have lived there. All through the night, it was Reina he held in his arms. She wore a bracelet on each wrist, and she was his. Forever. He nearly always knew he was dreaming, but he didn't care. And he wondered if somewhere, on the other side of the gate, Reina was dreaming of him, too.

CHAPTER 26
REINA

Reina stared blankly at her reflection in the floor-length mirror. It seemed unbelievable to her that she was back in Monrovia again. When she'd first felt the pull of her Amloga leading her to the forest clearing behind Lina's cottage, she'd been certain she was on a journey from which she'd never return. Yet, here she was.

At first, she'd felt out of place in her new realm, and she had often longed for a familiar sight or smell to remind her of home. But now, after so long in Caelium, she wasn't sure she still felt the same. In fact, she knew she didn't. She felt just the opposite. Caelium felt more like home now than Monrovia did.

Already, she'd been back in Monrovia for weeks. Things should've felt more normal now, shouldn't they? But they didn't. She still felt out of place. Here she was, surrounded by all the things she used to know. They were familiar, but they just didn't feel like *hers* anymore.

A soft knock sounded on her doorframe, and then Lydia's small, dark head peeked around the corner. Reina smiled expectantly at her through the mirror's reflection. "My Lady, your sister is waiting in the drawing room." Reina nodded at Lydia's reflection, and then her maid was gone, the door shutting soundly behind her.

Reina took one last look at herself in the mirror. Her own face stared back at her, slightly hollow-eyed, with a tinge of sadness hovering at her edges. She took a deep breath and raised the corners of her mouth, attempting to banish any hint of negativity from her reflection. But it was no use. Her smile looked flat. Anyway, it didn't matter how she looked. She knew Cecilia would still be able to tell there was something wrong. Her sister was a master at reading her feelings, almost as good as…as Ben. One slip of her voice, one hesitation. That was all it took. Cecilia could tell, every time.

The fever had taken Reina's father and mother when she was just 7 years of age, and Cecilia, then 5, had made a very narrow escape. She hadn't survived unscathed. Reina could still remember her small body lying in the bassinet, wracked with fever. She had never cried outright, but the memory of her mewls and the sores that had covered her was enough to make Reina weep if she thought about it for too long. Later, they had discovered that Cecilia was unable to walk. And to make matters worse, the fever had taken her eyesight.

Reina thought about the Tamarisk in Caelium. She wondered—if her sister had been given access to such a remedy, would it have prevented her from the pain and hardship her illness had caused? But there was no use in thinking such things. Cecilia was permanently bound to her rolling chair, and she would never again have the ability to enjoy the look of a morning sunrise or the gardens in bloom in spring. The thought made Reina's heart ache.

When she really thought about it, she had to admit that Cecilia was the main reason she had returned to Monrovia. Reina wondered at how the court had fared so well in her absence. With Cecilia at the helm, she had expected to return to a kingdom in chaos. But that wasn't the way of things at all. In fact, it appeared that peace and prosperity reigned. The flourishing Court of Monrovia and Cecilia's calm and confident manner made Reina question whether her assumptions about her sister's abilities had been wrong after all.

It didn't hurt that Cecilia had the unwavering support of Reina's betrothed, Lord Malcom. He never seemed to stray far from Cecilia's right hand. In truth, Reina had not seen one without the other in weeks, including at council meetings and court hearings, where she had watched in awe as her sister alternately wielded an iron fist or a gentle hand, according to what the situation required.

Though the council had appointed a regent when they were children, Reina had begun to lead under the regent's guidance when she turned fifteen. That was short-lived, because soon, she had felt the pull to leave Monrovia. Cecilia had assumed the ruling role in her absence, with the promise that Reina would return from her "world travels" when she was eighteen.

To Reina's extreme amazement, no one had questioned her leaving. And to this day, no one knew where she had truly gone. A miracle of the Source, she was sure. She preferred to leave it that way, allowing the court, her sister, and her betrothed to believe she had needed time away before she returned to the demanding role and her rightful place on the throne.

Reina stepped into the drawing room, just as Lord Malcom was standing upright. Cecilia was seated in front of him on a low settee, facing the windows. The afternoon sun shone golden light sideways through the large panes in front of them. Cecilia was bent over a book, her long, fair hair partially covering her face. Her fingers flying over the raised bumps on the page.

Reina shut the door, and both of their heads turned in synchrony. She started across the carpet, watching as Cecilia lifted a slim hand to Lord Malcom's arm. Cecilia's wide smile let Reina know she recognized her footfalls. "Reina, come see," Cecilia's lilting voice called. "Malcom has brought me the most wonderful gift. It's a selection of fairytales about a girl who travels to a distant land. She falls in love with a fairy there and has all manner of adventures."

Reina gave Malcom a small smile as she sat down on the settee beside her sister. Her heart gave a little squeeze, both at Malcom's sweet gesture and the truth of her sister's words. For all they knew, Reina could've written the story about her own adventures. "How kind of him," Reina replied.

Reina watched as Lord Malcom's dark eyes flicked towards her. He smiled politely, and she dipped her chin in thanks. She was grateful Cecilia had been gifted such a kind protector during her absence. She made a positive note in his favor: *Kind.*

Lord Malcom was of noble stock, the son of the great Lord Anders from the neighboring Court of Almatto. Reina and Cecilia had known him since they were children. He'd spent a lot of time at the Monrovian court, and as such, he had become a familiar fixture to them both. Reina studied his slim figure. Malcom was tall, well built, and though he wouldn't be thought of as traditionally handsome, he had a kind face and strong features. She watched as his gaze drifted to Cecilia, and it occurred to her that her betrothed could've been much worse. Too, Malcom had been selected for her by her parents before their deaths. And that had to count for something, didn't it? Reina put another positive note in his favorable column.

She turned to her sister, watching as Cecilia brushed her hand lovingly over the last page before closing the thick book. She turned towards Reina, her crystal eyes alight with excitement. "Are you ready?" Cecilia asked her.

Reina's eyes were focused on the book in Cecilia's lap. She was busy daydreaming about the story—both the one Cecilia had been reading and her own travels to Caelium. She wondered how much the fairytale mirrored her own adventures, and she was tempted to ask Cecilia more about it.

She hadn't learned the system of raised dots that her sister used, and from what Reina had seen, there were no printed letters on the pages above them in her book. That was likely a good thing. The story would only serve to make her think of Caelium anyway. Not to mention those she'd left behind there. Reina just didn't think her heart could take that on the eve of her wedding day.

She moved her eyes to Cecilia's face, watching as her sister's fair brows raised expectantly. "What did you say?" Reina said absently.

Cecilia giggled, a musical sound. She gave Reina's forearm a squeeze. "Tomorrow! Are you ready for tomorrow?" Reina didn't answer, and Cecilia playfully swatted her arm. "Your *wedding*, silly. And the coronation. They're tomorrow." She shook her long blonde curls, draping one loose, thick lock behind her slim shoulder. "You haven't forgotten, have you?"

Reina could feel the heat of Malcom's steady gaze. It caused a flush to bloom on her chest, but she smiled lightly, being careful not to look at him. Malcom was a good man, and he wasn't unattractive. Reina just didn't want to think too heavily about the fact that she was going to marry him tomorrow. She just wasn't ready. She wasn't sure she would ever be.

Cecilia's delicate brows wrinkled as Reina squirmed in her seat. "Yes. I'm ready," she said, too quickly. Her voice sounded clipped in her own ears. She knew her sister had caught it.

Cecilia narrowed her eyes before she extended her opposite hand. Lord Malcom swiftly grasped it. "Malcom has been so kind to me during your absence. He's never been far from my side. Isn't that right, Malcom?"

Malcom smiled down at her, his perfectly groomed face alight. "It's been my honor."

Cecilia grinned. "And kind, too, don't you think, Reina?" She lifted her chin at Reina expectantly.

Reina nodded, not looking at him. "Yes." She could feel Lord Malcom watching her curiously, but she didn't look at him.

Cecilia squeezed her shoulders up by her ears, grinning broadly. She pulled Malcom's hand towards Reina, then lifted Reina's own hand to touch it. Reina felt Malcom's strong fingers wrap around her palm, and she swallowed convulsively, hoping her face appeared serene.

Malcom's smooth hand felt nothing like Ben's. Reina tried not to think about the difference. She flicked her eyes to his palm. There were no calluses from woodworking, no wood stain around the nails. And, worst of all, she felt nothing. Absolutely nothing, at his touch.

Cecilia placed her own slender hand on top of their joined ones. She took a deep breath.

"I wish you both a lifetime of happiness," she said softly. Her voice held a tinge of emotion that seemed out of place with her words. It sounded watery to Reina's ears, and she flicked her eyes quickly to Cecilia's face.

Cecilia's eyes stared at the air between herself and Lord Malcom, and she wore a funny expression, one that Reina had not seen before. Her eyes were glistening with unshed tears. Cecilia sniffed. "There could be no greater joy for me than for the two people I love most in this world to be joined to one another for all eternity." She turned her head to Reina, a hint of desperation in her face. "Take care of him. Please, Reina."

Reina frowned at her. She didn't understand why her sister was so upset. She nodded, reaching her free hand to give her sister's arm a squeeze. "Of course, I will," she said softly. Cecilia nodded once, then turned her chin lightly to Lord Malcom.

"Malcom, please call Felix to take me to my rooms. I'm tired, and I think I'd like to lie down now."

Lord Malcom pulled his hand from Reina's. He shook his head. "I can do that. No need to call Felix." Without saying more, he moved towards her, bending expertly to brace her in his arms. He was ready to pick her up, but Cecilia stopped him with a light hand on his shoulder.

She shook her head swiftly, looking past Malcom's face. "No, Malcom. You take Reina to the gardens. You two should spend some time together before tomorrow. Felix can take me this time."

Malcom paused, frowning down at her. Reina thought Cecilia's smile was flat, but she nodded encouragingly. "Really. It's okay. Felix can do it."

Malcom pulled his arms away, stepping back uncertainly. He looked like he didn't know what to do with his hands. He stared down at them, then lifted one to smooth his already tightly combed hair. "Alright. If you're sure?"

Cecilia lifted her chin. "I'm sure."

Slowly, Malcom moved to the corner of the room. He tugged once on the long-braided cord, and, in moments, Felix appeared— a short, stocky man with burly forearms and shaggy brown hair. Wordlessly, Felix moved to the front of the settee and bent to lift Cecilia. She wrapped her arms around his neck as Felix moved silently towards the door. Cecilia called over his shoulder. "I'll see you tomorrow, Reina."

Reina nodded, even though Cecilia couldn't see. "Tomorrow," she said, too brightly.

Lord Malcom was still standing by the cord in the corner. His hands were knotted in front of his waist, and he was staring after Felix and Cecilia with an odd look. Reina watched him quietly from the settee. The room was silent in the wake of their exit, and she was acutely aware of his tall frame standing to her left.

Suddenly, he turned his eyes to her, meeting her shy gaze. When he realized she'd been staring at him, he looked away quickly, crossing his arms.

Reina did the same. Her hands felt tingly, and she searched her immediate area for something to busy them. Cecilia's book was still lying on the settee beside her, and she quickly swiped it. She pretended to examine the cover, then turned to the first page, studiously running her fingers across the raised dots.

In a moment, Malcom came to sit beside her. He was close. He smelled like cinnamon mixed with some other sharp spice. It was nice. Reina made another positive mental note in his favor: *Smells nice.*

He rubbed his palms against the knees of his dark pants and cleared his throat, the sound reverberating against the marble flooring. Reina didn't look at him. She hoped he didn't ask her what she was reading. Outside of the title, she had absolutely no idea what the raised dots said.

Malcom angled his body towards her. "Enjoying your book?" he said gruffly.

Reina bit her lip. She nodded.

"What's it about?"

Drat. "I, erm, it's a...it's a fairytale." Malcom nodded. He didn't push it, even though Reina knew he knew she couldn't read it. She was glad. She made another mental note: *Understanding.*

"Want to take a walk in the gardens?" he asked, uncertainty lacing his voice. Reina snapped her book shut. A walk would do her good. Anything was better than having to sit with Malcom so close to her side. She felt like she was about to jump out of her own skin.

Reina had forgotten how lovely the gardens were. Of course, they were nothing compared to the gardens at the Timekeeper's Court, but she tried not to think too much about that. It was dusk, and the subtle warmth of the sun rested lightly on her shoulders. There was a light breeze, and the quiet hum of summer nestled around her like a warm cocoon. She wrapped her arms around herself and sighed.

Malcom turned to her slightly. "Cold?"

Reina shook her head. *Pays attention.* Another merit for her betrothed.

They walked on in silence, the light crunch of the pebbled path beneath their feet the only sound. Reina reached to brush a bough of hanging flowers as they moved beneath a large trellis. The trellis was enclosed in vines. They twisted heavily across the wooden frame, dimming the light beneath it. She and Cecilia had often played under the trellis as children. Reina grinned at the memory. It had made the perfect hideout from their maids.

The thick vines were in full bloom. Heavy boughs of light lavender petals hung from the ceiling of the trellis like a fragrant canopy. Reina peered up at them. Their color was striking. They were almost as lovely as the Mountain Aster—almost.

Malcom stuffed his hands into his pockets. "Let's stop here for a while." A low stone bench was positioned behind them, and he sat on it. He smiled kindly at Reina and patted the seat beside him. The diffused light played against his sharp jaw, and he ran a hand through his dark hair, then leaned to rest his forearms on his knees.

Reina cocked her head. In this light, she could see why the female courtiers always fawned over him. While not exactly handsome, Malcom had a certain draw. She made another tick in the positive column: *Attractive.*

Reina sat beside him. She fidgeted with her bracelet, whose gems nearly matched the petals above her head. Malcom flicked his eyes to her fingers. "A gift?" he asked quietly.

Reina's hand froze. She dropped her eyes to the bracelet, nodding. "For my birthday."

Silently, Malcom reached for her arm, lifting her wrist to study the bracelet in the waning light. In a moment, he let her wrist go, again resting his forearms on his knees. He peered thoughtfully at his feet. "Who was it from?"

Reina's heart skipped. She swallowed, fumbling her words. "It was from a…a friend," she said, hedging. She hoped he wouldn't ask her more. As it was, her heart was squeezing, and tears were welling in her eyes.

Malcom leaned back against the trellis beam. He sighed. "A male friend, was it?" He peered at her sideways, and Reina reddened. She nodded slowly, covering her bracelet with her palm. Why was he so curious about it? And why did she suddenly feel so self-conscious?

Malcom was silent for a moment. He stared beyond the hanging vines, then he angled his body towards her, staring gently at the side of her face. Reina peeked over at him. The kindness in his face was almost more than she could take. He nudged her with his knee, and she dropped her eyes.

"Reina, you've been away a long time. I don't expect that you wouldn't have developed…feelings for someone else." He shrugged. "It's normal. It would be that way for anybody." He paused, waiting until Reina looked up at him. He gave a small smile. "But you and I have a duty to fulfill."

Reina stared at her lap, chewing on the inside of her cheek. She knew he was right, but she could hardly bear to hear it. Malcom continued. "It's bigger than you and me, or any…feelings we might have." Malcom swallowed, hesitating.

He reached to place a hand on her arm. "I'll make you a promise," he said quietly. "I promise to let go of the past. Mine and yours. I promise to show up tomorrow and the day after that, and I won't stop showing up. I'll be there. Every day. Okay?" He looked at her expectantly, and she made another mental note in his favor. *Loyal.*

Reina studied him out of the corner of her eye. Malcom was better than she deserved. but she couldn't say the same of the reverse. He was *too* good for her, especially in her current state. Malcom deserved someone who could give their whole heart to him, not someone like her—someone who's heart was tethered by a long string…a string which refused to snap, no matter how far she traveled. Even if she traveled to another world.

He was too kind, too good, to be treated with disrespect. And if there had been any other way, she would have told him the truth. She would have stood up right then and there and refused to marry him. But he was right. Their duty to the realm was bigger than them both.

There was no other way. She had to marry him tomorrow. She had to forget. Forget Caelium…forget Ben…forget all of it.

So, as he lifted his trembling hand to her chin and lowered his face to her own, Reina closed her eyes and leaned into his kiss. His lips weren't Ben's, but they were warm and persistent. And they almost did make her forget.

Almost.

CHAPTER 27
BEN

Ben and Arto worked tirelessly on the Western Wall. Many evenings, they worked past nightfall, while the Force and Guard stood watch in the darkness. Nothing escaped the merrows' and selkies' keen, glittering gazes, which were so used to the dark depths of the sea.

Tonight was one such night. Two merrows were stationed to Ben's right and left. Two more were beyond him, patrolling at staggered lengths near the mountain pass.

The centaurs had completed the Eastern Wall yesterday. Not surprising, as their strong, able bodies were made for such work. Chaeronne had brought along wagons, too, which enabled the group to work faster than the others. Like the Court of the Sea, they had hauled in their own materials from their home court in the far east.

Swirling sandstone blocks in deep oranges, tans, and browns thus built their section of the wall. Each stone had been carefully etched so that when they fit together, their design at first appeared like a great, winding river, but when Ben squinted, it became a thousand running horses.

After, the Court of Warriors had set to work on the North Wall. At the rate they were working, Ben expected it would be complete by tomorrow or the day after.

True to Arto's words, Willow and the others remained absent from the West Mountains. Instead, the centaurs had used their wagons to haul load upon load of fresh timber from the North Forest, which Willow had left waiting for them at the Forest Door. It was more lumber than Ben could possibly have imagined, and his heart squeezed, thinking of how many of the dryads' beloved North Forest trees had been sacrificed to bring such a bounty.

Ben had instructed the centaurs to bring the lumber inside the walls. When they finished hauling it in, he had been sure there was more than enough to rebuild each and every dwelling that had been there before, and some besides.

The Southern Wall had been completed this morning, set with deep stones mined from the Selkie Isles. They glittered brightly, even in the moonlight. Ben had been down to examine it earlier. His mouth had gone slack as he stared at the new wall in awe.

A colorful mosaic stared back at him. It shimmered and changed hues in the sunlight. Its top reminded him of crested waves, while the stones beneath it waved like high grasses and shifting schools of fish. A golden door was pictured in the center of the wall—an image of the door to the Court of the Sea. Gilded roses entwined with Water Thistles, the symbol of the Court of the Sea, shimmered along its border.

When their wall was complete, the selkies and merrows had transferred all their efforts into defense. They were vigilant and tireless, but to Ben's relief, no attacks had come thus far. He hoped it stayed that way. Ben hated putting anyone in danger, least of all the kind friends who had come to his aid.

At last, he and Kai set the final stone at head height onto the Western Wall. Ben's hair hung in limp strands, plastered to his neck and forehead. He wiped it with the back of his forearm, which was equally as slick with sweat. Even though the sun had long set, the air was still quite warm, and Ben had long since removed his shirt.

He sat heavily on the ground, and Kai collapsed beside him. His friend pulled some water from the air and deposited it into a set of clay cups they had recovered from Jubal's cave. The chill left behind from the water Kai had pulled felt good on Ben's skin. He accepted his cup and drank deeply, savoring the sweet taste of the water sifted from the mountain air. It had an earthy flavor, mixed with a hint of leftover sunshine.

Kai sipped from his own cup. He never seemed too thirsty, despite their hard work. Ben wondered if it was because he was permanently water-logged from his sea-dwelling lifestyle. Kai patted Ben's shoulder with his free hand.

"A good day's work, my friend. Fish Wall to the south, Horse Wall to the east, and Forest Wall at the north are all complete." He eyed Ben from the corner of his gaze, his eyes shimmering in the moons' light. "And what will you call the Western Wall?"

Ben leaned his head back against the stones. They were still warm from the day's hot sun. He smiled. "I think I'll keep the Western Wall name. It's what it was called before, and it's the only wall made entirely of the original limestone." He flicked his eyes down, rolling his cup thoughtfully in his palms.

"Its stones hold the memories of the court, the good and the bad. It's where my people used to come so long ago, to send messages to the Source, ones of grief and sorrow and ones of joy." He shrugged, his mind on the distant past. "Of course, the messages were all lost to the fires of the drake."

Ben folded his arms, thinking of the small scrap of parchment he had found in the kitchens of the palace. He had scrawled a quick message on it—one full of his grief. Then he had carried it to the Western Wall.

Emotions from his past and present had rolled over him as he tucked the message securely between two stones. It wasn't lost on him that the action was so like what he and Reina used to do when they left messages for one another, tucked inside the stones behind the waterfall. Ben hadn't realized at the time that he had been mimicking the Western Wall practice from his childhood, but now that fact seemed very plain. Pain and joy in equal measure swirled in his belly, and his throat closed around a lump. He had lost so much. And now he had lost her, too.

The next few days were a flurry of activity. With the walls done and so many hands to the task, the dwellings inside the court walls were quick work. Before Ben knew it, the new structures were complete. The palace he had saved for last, but soon, it was restored, too.

Ben had even given himself the luxury of a bed and some basic furniture. Though, he wasn't quite sure why. It was only him living in the palace, after all, and he didn't really care if he had furniture or not.

Now that the work was done, Arto had gone back to Leyth Castle to be with Lina and…the new baby. Ben still couldn't bring himself to say her name. Most of the centaurs had returned to the east, save Maria and Ronne's twins, who remained for defensive purposes. The Mortal Timekeepers and Force and Guard remained, too. They provided armed patrols throughout the day and night. Ben worried about them, but he worried even more about when they would be gone. Marcus and the rest of the banded mountain fairy clan had been strangely silent throughout their work, and Ben had to admit, it made him nervous. He knew something was coming. There was no way Marcus would let the restored court stand.

Kai stood across the makeshift workbench Ben had built by the open space between the Western and Forest Walls. Once again, Ben was rebuilding the doors. He had etched the carvings the same as before, and he had even found the iron handles in the rubble. He eyed them where they lay on the end of the bench, their glittering, glass wings shimmering in the sunlight.

Kai knelt to the nearly completed door and squinted one eye. He smoothed his hand across the wood, grinning broadly. Kai had been "helping" him, but Ben had been forced to undo much of his friend's work over the course of the morning. Woodworking was not Kai's gifting, that was for sure.

Kai stood, knocking his knuckles against the door. "I built this one, right? I mean, mostly?"

Ben's lips twitched, and he half turned to hide his smile. "Um, yep…with a little help."

Kai chuckled low, shaking his head. "Elysia's not going to believe it." He put his hands on his hips. "Can't wait to tell her."

Ben returned his smile. "When are you going home to see her? I'm sure she misses you."

Kai nodded. "She's been staying with Lina and the baby, but when Arto gets there, I'm sure she will head home. I guess I'll meet her there." He frowned, eyeing Ben. "Are you sure you are okay for me to go?"

Ben nodded, shrugging lightly. "Sure. Things are wrapping up here, and you can't stay in the West Mountains forever." He eyed the iridescent scales along Kai's temple. "Besides, I think you're starting to dry out."

Kai smirked. "That's not how merrows work, but very funny."

Ben laughed. "Just saying."

With the centaur twins' help, Ben and Kai hauled the giant doors into place. Ben fit them with the iron handles, then Kai pushed the left door shut. Ben left his door open just a crack. Kai frowned over at it. "You're not going to close it?"

Ben shifted his feet. "No." He flicked his eyes to Kai, watching as his friend's glittering blue eyes narrowed. Ben sighed, running a hand through his hair. It was kind of hard to explain. "Fair warning, it's kind of a long story."

Kai nodded. "Let's hear it, then."

"Well, we have a custom here in the Court of Mountain Fairies," he started. He shrugged. "Well, really, it's more of a tradition. It comes from the Histories."

Kai folded his arms. "Go on," he prodded.

"Once, long ago, just after the foundations of the known worlds were fashioned, when the earth had risen, and the seas had sunk into their low places. The valley, here at the Court of Mountain Fairies, was covered in water. The first mountain fairy stood on the hillside overlooking the valley, which was then a still lake. He wondered to himself why he had been created, and why the Source had brought him to the valley in the first place. There was nothing there to speak of, except the water that filled the valley to the brim. Many days passed much the same, with the lone mountain fairy gazing out over the surface of the water.

"At last, loneliness overwhelmed him, and he considered leaving the place entirely. He sat on the hillside for many more days, contemplating this, until he collapsed in exhaustion. He fell into a deep sleep, and when he awoke, the water had drained away, and the valley was covered with Lavender Mountain Aster.

"The first mountain fairy blinked down in amazement. He sat up, studying the flowers carpeting the valley below. All of a sudden, a funny wavering in the air caught his attention in the valley's northwest corner. He peered down at it, confused by the strange movement, until at last, curiosity got the best of him. The fairy moved down the hillside to get a better look.

"When he arrived there, a set of large doors appeared in the midst of the wavering, in the very spot we are standing right now. And the right door was standing open.

"The first mountain fairy was beyond curiosity now. He was compelled—drawn to the open door by some strange expectance inside his being, and his hand moved of its own will to pull the door wider. There, on the other side, lay the most beautiful fae, asleep in the tall grasses. Lavender Mountain Aster grew about her in a ring, and when he knelt to greet her, she opened her eyes. They were as green as the grass that waved about her, and when she smiled up at him, he was immediately taken with her. The new fae sat up, and tipped her chin, lifting her face to kiss him. As their lips met, an eternal bond formed between the two, because, you see, mountain fairies mate for life. When the bond is formed, it can never be broken.

"The moment they kissed, their bond was sealed, and a set of perfect, crystalline wings sprouted from her back—a symbol that she had found her mate. The first mountain fairy was surprised to find that their bond had caused him to sprout wings, too. It was the love that brought on the wings. The bond between them, which would tether one fae to the other for all eternity. The wings were just the evidence.

"The first mountain fairy was overcome with joy at his new companion, and he fashioned her two bracelets from the Mountain Aster blooms to express his love. It is why, to this day, our mates wear a bracelet on each wrist on their mating day and all the days after. And it is why, we leave the court door open—so that love might have the chance to meet us on the other side."

Kai leaned against the left door thoughtfully. "Wings, huh." He searched the air about Ben's shoulders playfully, then shrugged. "I'm not seeing any wings, Benjamin." He sniffed and stared out into the distance with narrowed eyes. "Seems a little fantastical to me."

Ben laughed and rolled his eyes. "Of course. Says the man who sprouts a tail when he hits the water."

Kai slung his head back in a roaring laugh. "Hah! Okay, then. What happened to the wings? Why don't you have any?"

Ben shrugged. "They used to be common. Almost every mountain fairy had them. I mean, once they bonded with their mate, anyway. But now, they're extremely rare." He flattened his lips. "As rare as the mountain fairies themselves. Except for Henri, Johann, myself, and Vic, and whatever small band Marcus keeps hidden deeper west, there aren't many possibilities for wings." He folded his arms. "Mountain fairies and their wings are almost non-existent, since Orm took the throne and the near destruction of the Rotha-Am. Even though the known worlds have recovered, the elusive wings have yet to make their reappearance. But then again, not one of us has taken the bond, either."

Kai nodded sagely. He pressed his lips, suppressing a smile. "So, Ben, who are you leaving the door open for?"

Ben shot him a surprised look, then dropped his eyes. He had been thinking about the wings, and he hadn't been expecting that question. He shrugged his shoulder lightly, feigning innocence. "Only the Source knows."

But Ben knew. He would always leave the door open for Reina. Even though he knew he had lost her.

CHAPTER 28

REINA

Reina's trembling fingers tucked a wayward curl back in place beneath her sparkling tiara. She couldn't have been more nervous. Her wedding and the subsequent coronation ceremonies were today, and the entire realm would be in attendance. Everyone she had ever known in her Mortal life would soon bear witness to what should have been the best day of her life. She should have been thrilled. So, why did she feel so awful about it?

She peered at her hollow-eyed reflection. It was just nerves. Everyone was nervous on the day of their wedding, weren't they? Of course, they were.

Reina didn't turn as Cecilia's chair moved past her door frame.

She could hear the wooden wheels creaking across the floor as Lydia fussed with the back of her hair. It still amazed Reina that her sister could move so expertly through the palace alone. But Cecilia had long since memorized the countless corridors and rooms of their home, so it shouldn't have come as a surprise.

Lydia's small, dark brows were knit together in concentration as her hands expertly arranged the last coil. Then she stood back, smiling at her creation. "All done, My Lady," she said, quietly folding her hands. Reina studied her hair—an intricate mass of twisted, curling knots at her crown. She smiled at Lydia through the glass. "Thank you, Lydia. It's lovely. Truly." She tried to make her eyes match her words, but when she peered into her own gaze, her reflection looked flat. Lydia curtsied once, then her tiny, dark frame slipped out the open doorway.

Cecilia appeared in the mirror beside her. She didn't speak, and Reina tucked her arms across her bodice. Her fingertips traced the embroidered fabric at her waist as Cecilia cleared her throat. She peered to the left of the glass expectantly. "Reina?"

Reina couldn't look at her. She was afraid if she did, she would burst into tears. Cecilia waited, ever patient. Reina could just make out her long, blonde hair from the corner of her gaze. Cecilia sighed, then pushed her chair backward. "Come sit with me by the window."

Reina chewed on the inside of her cheek. The last thing she needed was to have a heart-to-heart with her sister right now. She could barely keep it together, and she was sure Cecilia would unravel the tight hold she had on her fraying nerves. She sighed and dropped her arms, then moved across the floor.

Cecilia's eyes were closed when Reina sat on the chair across from her, a small table between them, already laid for tea. She had spent many mornings here with her sister, before she had gone to Caelium. Every morning, in fact. They had discussed everything here, from court business to their favorite books to their quarrels with friends and boys that had caught their interest. It touched Reina that her sister had remembered their daily routine. Cecilia's slender hand reached for the tea pot, and she slid her hand around Reina's cup, while expertly pouring the tea to just the right level from the brim. Then she set the pot down in its place and added a dollop of fresh cream and two sugars, just as Reina liked.

Reina grinned over at her sister, who was now busy filling her own cup. There seemed to be nothing Cecilia couldn't do. Cecilia took a sip from her own cup and relaxed back into her chair. She closed her eyes, the morning sun playing across her eyelids.

Cecilia was so beautiful. Her light brows were perfectly arched, and her nose was slender and sloping, stopping at just the right distance from her wide, full lips. Even her eyes, though they couldn't be used for their original purpose, served her beauty. Since losing sight, they had taken on a lovely crystalline shade that shimmered like stars, complementing her milky complexion. Cecilia had chosen a very becoming silver dress to match them today, and it followed the slim curves of her body in soft lines.

At last, Cecilia was done with her sunning, and she opened her eyes. She set her teacup back onto its saucer and folded her hands, a clear sign she was ready to get down to business. She peered across the table towards Reina, her expression serious. "Alright, enough of this, Reina. I'm your sister. I can tell something is obviously wrong with you, and you're going to tell me what it is. Right now."

Reina blinked, startled by her sister's pointed words. She couldn't remember ever hearing Cecilia speak to her with such authority or conviction. Commanding the Court of Monrovia in her absence had surely given her practice, and Reina was beginning to see how the court had prospered with such a leader at the helm. Cecilia arched one light brow. "Well?"

Reina grinned. She shook her head. "It's just nerves. Nothing more."

Cecilia blinked at the open air. She twisted her lips slightly. Reina could tell she didn't believe her. "You're certain?" she said, pressing.

Reina nodded. "Yes," he said softly. Her voice sounded hollow in her own ears. How could she tell Cecilia about everything she had experienced, about all she had lost? About Ben and the Time-keeper's Court and the Court of Mountain Fairies?

Her throat tightened. It was too much. If she opened the flood gates now, she would surely drown.

Cecilia pressed on. "There's nothing about..."—she fluttered her hand in the air—"whoever gave you this bracelet that you're not telling me?"

Reina frowned as she fumbled with stones of the flower on her wrist. "Who told you about my bracelet?"

Cecilia grinned. "I felt it on your wrist yesterday in the drawing room. When I grabbed your arm? So, tell me. Who gave it to you?"

Reina wet her lips. She couldn't tell her. There was just too much to say. It didn't matter now, anyway. She was marrying Lord Malcom and taking the Monrovian throne. This was her place. It wasn't in Caelium anymore, and it wasn't with Ben in the West Mountains. Her heart sank at the thought, but she was determined to get used to it.

She picked absently at her bracelet's lavender gems, searching for words. Then, her fingers paused. She glanced down, her brows raising.

There was a little gap in the flower petals on the right side. Reina wondered how she hadn't noticed it before. Curious, she hooked her nail under its edge, and to her surprise, there was a small click. Then, the petals popped open. She gasped.

"What?" Cecilia said quickly. She knit her brows. "Reina, what? Did you hurt yourself?"

Reina couldn't answer. She was in shock, staring in disbelief at the locket on her wrist. A tiny roll of parchment was tucked inside of it. "It's a locket," she murmured.

"What?" said Cecilia.

Reina lifted her head to her sister. "My bracelet. It's a locket."

Cecilia wheeled her chair swiftly around the small table and pulled up near Reina's side. "Let me see," she said quickly. She held out her fingertips, and Reina put her wrist beneath it.

Cecilia's nimble fingers explored the stone flower's face, which was lifted on a tiny metal hinge. She moved them to the locket's base beneath it, quickly landing on the rolled parchment inside. Reina watched her sister's expression as Cecilia raised her brows. "There's a message," she said quietly. Cecilia reverently lifted the tiny roll from its place, turning it over and over in her fingers. Then, she held the tiny scroll out to Reina.

"Read it." she commanded. Reina didn't move, and Cecilia stared hard at the air just to Reina's left. "Now, if you please," she said, raising her voice slightly. Reina wanted to chuckle at her sister's demanding words. And she would have if her voice wasn't caught in her throat. Cecilia was so unlike the quiet, shy sister she remembered. With a shaking hand, she slipped the parchment from her sister's fingers.

It was funny how such a tiny thing could bring about so many memories. The parchment was no larger than her fingerbreadth, yet flashes of the rock wall behind the waterfall and little notes left in the garden, and the library, and the stable yard played in her mind. She used to think that Ben had her routine memorized, and maybe he had. But she knew him, too. And she had left just as many messages as he. Her heart squeezed as she unfurled the tiny message. She missed him more than she could say.

Her sister sighed loudly as Reina silently scanned the words. "Reina," she said pointedly. "I can't *see*, remember? You have to read it aloud."

Reina would've smiled, but her lips were trembling too hard. Ben's small scrawl blurred under her gaze, and a tear dropped onto the paper, blurring the last word. But it didn't matter. She knew it by heart, anyway.

One afternoon, long ago, Ben had told her a story. She thought nothing of it at the time. But now, her mind gripped his every word. It was about the first mountain fairy ever created by the Source. She closed her eyes, remembering.

Ben had said that the Court of Mountain Fairies had a tradition. He'd read it to her as they sat in the library. Reina had tucked her knees to her chest in the seat across from him in the alcove, while Ben recited from the large tome called the Histories. It held all the stories of Caelium, right from the very beginning, and it was still being written to this very day.

From what she could recall, the story said that when a mountain fairy found his mate, he would give her two bracelets, signifying his love. The first mountain fairy had fashioned his mate a bracelet for each wrist from the Lavender Mountain Aster that sprang around the doors where he had found her, so the latter mountain fairies had followed suit. But the next part of the story was what made her heart sing and break in equal measure.

The first mountain fairy had found his mate beyond the open door that appeared in the valley below him. So, now, if a mountain fairy found his mate, he would send her a message to meet him at the doors of the court.

That evening, he would leave a small crevice open in the court door for her. And if she returned his love, she would lie down behind it. The mountain fairy would wait all night outside the court door, and in the morning, he would pull it wide. This gave his mate all night to be certain she was ready to take the bond. The next morning, if he found his love lying there, he would give her two bracelets, much like the single one Reina now wore on her wrist. Then, they would take the bond. And the bond was eternal. It could never be broken, no matter the circumstance.

Reina only had one bracelet. Ben had given it to her on her eighteenth Mortal birthday, as a symbol of their friendship, or so he had said. Reina had believed him. He'd said it was commonplace for his people to exchange such a gift between close friends. He'd made her think he'd meant nothing more of it. But his message now made her think something different.

"Reina! Tell me! What does it say?"

Reina swallowed past the lump in her throat. Her voice wavered as she recited Ben's words.

"It says, *I'll leave the door open for you.*"

CHAPTER 29

BEN

Ben had only just fallen asleep when the acrid smell of smoke curled around his nostrils. Somewhere in the distance, he could hear the terrible roar of the drake. Closer, a more familiar scream tingled the small hairs along his spine. It sounded like his mother, and it was in this very room. Ben shot up in bed, his eyes drawn to the center of the bedroom, where his mother's small frame was dissolving into ash in a mass of flames. Ben threw back his coverlet.

"Mother!" he screamed. But it was too late.

She was already gone.

Ben's body was wracked with sobs, and he woke to find that his covers were soaked through with cold sweat. The sound of his mother's voice screaming from the flames still echoed in his ears, and he sat up on the side of his mattress and braced his elbows on his knees. He ran his fingers through his damp hair and sighed. He was still shivering. And terrified.

Somewhere deeper west, a roar not unlike the one he had heard in his dream echoed down his hallway. Ben stilled, lifting his ear to the sound. But the hallway was silent. He didn't hear it again. He shook his head. His mind was playing tricks on him. Easy to do that when you were alone in the dark.

Outside, he could just make out a thin pinkish-yellow line hovering over the horizon. He slid his feet to the floor and stretched his arms over his head. Might as well get up. He wasn't going to be able to go back to sleep now, anyway. He padded across the floor, being careful not to look at the spot where his mother had disintegrated during the night. He swallowed a sour taste. For some reason, the scent of burning flesh clung to the inside of his nose.

He moved to the kitchen and fumbled through the cabinets for a dish and cup, thankful again for Amelie's kind gesture. She had brought load after load of goods to the palace from the many rooms at the Timekeeper's Court. Even the pantry was completely stocked. Ben had protested, but Amelie had insisted.

After a while, her deliveries had begun to come daily, and soon, Ben suspected she was checking up on him. There was something about the look in her large grey eyes that made him think she was worried. Sometimes, she would even give his shoulder a squeeze. Amelie never actually said she was worried about him, but Ben could tell.

She chatted endlessly with him about the Timekeeper's Court—who was doing what and how wonderfully they were all faring. Henri and Vic had been spending a lot of time together, which, to Ben, was surprising. Henri had never been very close to anyone but Johann and the griffins.

Vic hadn't yet visited the Court of Mountain Fairies, but Ben wasn't very surprised. He was sure, like himself, that their home court brought back too many hard memories. It was easier to stay away. Besides that, Amelie seemed to be keeping her busy with tasks at the Timekeeper's Court, and she'd been helping Henri with the griffins while Johann came and went, so it was no wonder.

Ben set a kettle to heat, then cut a thick piece of bread from a fat loaf. He slathered it with jam, then leaned against the island as he ate, letting his mind wander—a dangerous pastime when one had memories he needed to forget. He stared across to the opposite counter. Reina's bracelets had been right there, and she'd been right in front of him. He shook his head, forcing himself back to the topic of Amelie.

Johann often came with her, whether he really needed to or not. It seemed that his friend was rather taken with Amelie, and it seemed like Amelie was fond of him, too. Ben had seen him studying her long blonde hair more than once with a look that was all too familiar—a look that made Amelie blush. She looked at Johann sort of the way that Rei…Ben cut himself off. *No.* He couldn't think about that.

Sighing, he set the rest of his breakfast on the countertop, uneaten. He folded his arms. What he really needed was to get out of this kitchen. He pushed off the counter and made his way to the library in his bedroom. Maybe he could read for a while. He scanned the shelves, stocked full of books from friends across the realm, but nothing caught his gaze.

Frustrated, he plopped onto the chaise and rested one foot over the top, thinking. Everyone had gone home. There was no one to talk to. Not that it really bothered him. In fact, he was glad for the quiet after so much flurry of activity.

He pressed his lips. But the house was *too* quiet. Eerily so. It made him dwell on his dream from the night before, among… other things.

He stood quickly and strode towards the great hall. He had expected Amelie to come already. She had gotten into the habit of visiting him in the early morning, which Ben expected was to catch him off his guard. That way, she could really get a good look at his emotional state. Ben frowned. He understood her reasoning, but who was ever really in a great mood in the early mornings?

He peered out the front window. It didn't look like Amelie was going to make it this morning. He could wait for her, or maybe he would go for a swim. The water might help to clear his head.

Ben headed out, moving swiftly down the cobblestone street. The restored dwellings loomed on his left and right. Silent, empty shells. Ben peered inside one as he passed. The interior was dark. Solitary. He was beginning to understand the first mountain fairy's loneliness.

At the court doors, Ben hesitated. He hated to leave the place unattended. He was the only one here right now, and he didn't know how many men Marcus had at his disposal. But it wasn't likely he could stop an attack by himself, anyway.

He looked behind him, past the street to the silent dwellings beyond. Clusters of dark windows stared back at him vacantly, and Ben wondered to himself if it would always be just him, here, alone in his court. Despite his solitary nature, the thought struck him with a profound pang of loneliness. He again felt a deep kinship with the first mountain fairy.

Like his ancestor, Ben wondered why the Source would have brought him to such a desolate place, especially when it held for him so many dark memories. Some of them, like his mother's death, had driven a spike so deep into his chest that he wondered if he would ever pull it free. His Amloga Flame ached and burned, and he pressed his hand flat over it, wincing.

Just as a precaution, he lifted an axe he had hidden just inside the door. He strapped it to his side, then stepped over the threshold. He had decided to head to the waterfall, but he wasn't at all certain it would do him any good. Ben thought of Reina's long hair floating above her in the water and frowned. Most likely, it would make him feel worse. He couldn't escape her, no matter how hard he tried. Reina was everywhere he looked.

His thoughts drifted to her bracelet–the gift he had given her for her birthday. Amidst the flurry of the Royal birth at Leyth Castle, he'd managed to sneak into Reina's rooms unde-tected and slip a secret message inside of the lavender locket's petals. By now, she had probably found it. Ben wondered what her reaction had been.

He sighed. It didn't really matter, did it? It didn't matter what she had thought about him declaring his love for her. Reina was gone, and, no matter how much he wished she had stayed, she hadn't. Worse, she was probably wed to her betrothed, by now. The thought made Ben feel sick, but there wasn't a single thing he could do about it.

CHAPTER 30
REINA

Cecilia's crystal eyes glittered. "Ben." She nodded. "It's a good name." Reina peeked over at her from the corner of her eye. It was strange to hear Ben's name coming out of Cecilia's mouth.

She had tried to tell her everything. Well, *mostly* everything. She'd left some parts out—the rather gruesome and fantastical parts, like how the man she loved was a mountain fairy, or how she'd stepped through a magical gate into another realm. She'd also conveniently omitted the fact that she'd fought alongside centaurs, dryads, merrows, and other beings in the battle to save Time itself.

Her own identity as a Mortal Timekeeper would also remain hidden. Her sister didn't need to know all of that. Anyway, Reina wasn't at all sure Cecilia would believe it. Besides, what did it really matter? It wasn't like she would be going back there, anyway.

"And you love him?"

Reina's head snapped upright. "What?"

Cecilia's gaze was direct. "Ben. Do you love him? It's obvious he loves you. He wouldn't have gone to all this trouble with the message in the bracelet if he didn't."

Reina dropped her eyes to the small parchment between her fingers. "No, I suppose not," she murmured.

Cecilia frowned. "You *don't* love him, then?"

Reina chewed the inside of her cheek. She shook her head slowly back and forth. "No," she whispered. It wouldn't come out louder than that. She shook her head harder, frustrated. "I mean… that's not what I meant." Her hands were shaking, and the small paper crinkled with her movement. She took a deep breath. "I can see that he loves me. I mean, *now* I can. I wasn't sure before."

Cecilia leaned towards her slightly. She placed a hand on her arm. "Of course, you can. But how do *you* feel?"

Reina waited. Her heart was hammering in her ears, and thick tears threatened to spill down onto her cheeks. Her voice caught in her throat. "I…" She swallowed, then crumpled the small paper in her fingers. "It doesn't matter."

Reina sniffed hard as she pulled her arm from beneath her sister's hand. She stuffed the tiny message back into its place inside the locket and closed the lid. Then she stood up, smoothing her wedding gown. "Come on, we're going to be late. Lord Malcom is waiting."

She didn't wait for Cecilia to answer. Instead, she turned on her heel and moved out the door with purposed steps. There was no point in saying more about it. So, Ben loved her. So what?

She hurried down the corridor and slipped around the corner, backing into a quiet, dimly lit sitting room. It was one that was hardly ever used. Reina knew she would be alone.

She pushed the door closed behind her and sank down on the floor in front of it, allowing her emotions to wash over her unchecked. Her hands were shaking as she opened the lid of the locket once more. She pulled the crumpled paper free.

As she studied Ben's words, her chest caved in on itself. Pain moved over her in waves, and she traced her finger across Ben's script as her sister's question floated through her mind. *Do you love him?*

Reina carefully folded the paper and tucked it back inside its hiding place again. Of course, she loved him. How could she not? He was her Ben, and he had been her whole life since she'd passed through the gate.

She took a deep breath and swiped the tears from her cheeks. But that was then, and in a few moments, she would marry Lord Malcom and take the Monrovian throne. That was more important than her or Ben's feelings…wasn't it?

She stood on shaking legs and turned to face the door, plastering a pleasant smile on her face. Lord Malcom and her people were waiting, and she couldn't afford to put this off any longer. She had to move forward. And it had to be now.

Reina peered into the sanctuary below from the high window of her bridal suite. The chapel, with its soaring, grey stone arches and glittering, stained glass windows, was as lovely as she had ever seen it—and fuller, too. Every seat in the house was filled, and the people chatted amongst themselves in excited tones. Up front, the large pipe organ began to play, and her heart trilled in her throat. She flicked her eyes to Ben's bracelet. It was time.

Lord Malcom entered from a side door next to the platform, a pleasant expression tacked on his kind face. He wore a slim cut, black suit and white shirt, and a small flower was pinned to his lapel. It matched the ones in Reina's bouquet. She glanced down at it, a realization suddenly dawning on her. The flowers in her bouquet were lavender aster.

Reina stepped shakily down the winding staircase. Her sister was poised at the sanctuary doors, ready to move through. Cecilia's sharp ears heard the last step creak, and she turned her face, flashing Reina a small smile. It disappeared behind the doors as Felix wheeled her inside.

Reina moved to the back door's small window, watching her sister's procession in amazement. The people clearly adored her. They murmured excitedly amongst themselves at her appearance, and each row Cecilia approached stood. They bowed deeply as the wheels of her chair made their way up the aisle.

Her sister, for her part, seemed to take it all in stride. She often paused on her way forward to grasp a hand or murmur recognition or thanks, and she inclined her head to each row in such a regal fashion that Reina was quite in awe of her.

But that was not all.

What really struck Reina was Lord Malcom. Reina watched him from the edge of the doorway, while he watched her sister. In fact, he couldn't seem to take his eyes off Cecilia. Malcom gripped his hands at his waist as Cecilia moved towards him, a rapid play of emotions moving across his features.

Momentary awe gripped him, but he swiftly adjusted his posture, molding his face into a placid expression.

At last, her sister came to meet him. He bent towards her, and Reina watched as Cecilia whispered something into his ear. Malcom's face contorted briefly as he took her hand. He lifted it to his lips, brushing a gentle kiss on top of it. Reina frowned. Though he kept a careful smile, there was a hint of sadness in his kind eyes. She knew the look. It was the same one she was sure was mirrored in her own face.

Reina's heart squeezed as Malcom's stricken face watched her sister move past him. The pang of his loss was clearly acute, and it was in that moment that Reina realized. In fact, she didn't know how she hadn't seen it before.

Every moment from the past weeks played in her mind. Every look, every touch. It was as clear as day. Lord Malcom loved her sister, and she was almost certain that Cecilia loved him, too.

Just then, the pipe organ began playing a familiar tune. It was Reina's cue. Lord Malcom pulled his gaze away from Cecilia, who had taken her post on the opposite side of the platform. Reina moved inside the doorway. Lord Malcom flashed her a grin, but it didn't meet his eyes. She smiled back at him, then squared her shoulders, and moved forward.

Reina's thoughts swirled as she moved down the aisle. Clearly, Lord Malcom loved her sister, and so did the people. The Monrovian Court was in excellent shape. It was better than it had ever been, even when Reina was at the helm. She wasn't sure they even needed her anymore. So, what was she doing? Why was she going through with this?

She stopped beside Lord Malcom, and he blinked down at her, then flicked his eyes over her shoulder. Reina followed his gaze. Cecilia sat placidly behind them in her seat. No one would have noticed her distress. But Reina did. Cecilia's brows were pulled too high, and her mouth was a small line.

Just then, a loud *whoosh*, and the sound of tearing metal sounded in the vestibule. The organ came to a screeching halt as shouting and frightened cries peppered the crowd. Reina jumped as the back doors of the sanctuary blew open.

Amelie's hurried frame came bursting through them. Mur-

murs of confusion and shock trickled through the pews as she started up the aisle. Her grey eyes flicked from left to right, then rested on Reina. "I'm sorry to intrude," she said loudly. "But I need to speak with the bride. Urgently."

Reina stared at her friend in shock. She lifted her eyes to Malcom. He gave her a small nod, clearly uncertain. Reina moved away from him to meet Amelie in the middle of the aisle. Amelie's eyes were wild, desperate. Reina frowned. "Amelie, what are you doing here?"

Amelie grasped her hands. She shook her head. "Reina, I was late," she said breathlessly. "I—I had been going to check on him every day, but today, I was late. Please, there's no time to explain. We must leave. Immediately."

Panic rose in Reina's chest as she studied Amelie's expression, and a feeling of dread descended squarely onto her shoulders. She lowered her voice. "Amelie, what's happened?"

Amelie studied her feet, then lifted her eyes to meet Reina's worried gaze.

"It's Ben. He's missing."

CHAPTER 31

BEN

Ben hadn't seen Vic for weeks. Now, here she was. She grinned and raised her hand in a wave as her lithe figure moved down the hillside. She adjusted the basket at her waist as she stopped in front of him. "Hi, Ben," she said cheerily.

"Vic," he said, nodding. Ben scanned the hillside behind her. "Where's Henri?"

Vic shrugged. "Just me, I'm afraid. He and Johann are in the stables."

Ben nodded, casting his gaze towards the east. His swim would have to wait.

He turned back to Vic. "So, what brings you here? I wasn't

expecting to see you. I mean, I know how hard it is to be back here." He shrugged. "It's even hard for…" Ben trailed off.

Vic was peering over his shoulder with a pained expression. He watched her eyes, following them to the court doors. He turned back to face her. "Do want to see inside? It's much the same as you remember, but it's different, too."

Vic flicked her gaze to the mountain pass beyond them. "Yes," she said quickly. She bit her lip. "I mean…Yes, I'd like to see it."

Ben walked ahead as they made their way down the first cob-blestone street. Towards the end of the lane, he realized Vic was no longer following him. He spun, searching around the vacant dwellings. He just caught sight of her dark head as it moved between two buildings on his left.

Ben started after her, following her silent figure down a narrow alley to the street beyond. There, she made a right and stopped in front of the last dwelling on the left. It was a low structure of wood and stone tucked beneath a narrow staircase, which led to more housing above. She stood there, unmoving, as Ben came to stand behind her.

"This is my house," Vic whispered. "Or, or it was…before." Ben looked beyond her to the squat, stone dwelling. It had clearly been rebuilt by the Court of Warriors. Swirling gold and deep rust-colored stones dotted the façade. He moved to Vic's side, peering at her pained profile. "It still is, you know." She peeked up at him. There were tears in her upturned eyes. Ben smiled. "The house. It's still yours. You're welcome to move into it anytime." He shrugged as he looked up and down the lane at the vacant structures. "It's just me here, anyway." Then more quietly. "Plenty of space for *at least* one more, but I don't think we can handle more than that." He shook his head in mock distaste. "Too crowded."

Vic giggled, then pursed her lips. "Well, in that case, do you want to come in?" She lifted the basket from her arm. "I've got food." She raised her dark brows.

Ben grinned. "Sure."

It was late afternoon by the time Ben and Vic were done talking. Ben hadn't realized how lonely he'd been, and he was ashamed to know he had led most of the conversation. It wasn't like him, but he couldn't help it. He'd been lonelier lately than he cared to admit.

He stopped at the court doors and held one wide, allowing Vic to step through. She glanced furtively at the mountain pass to their left, then turned to face him, her eyes alight. "I had a great time today, Ben," she said quietly.

Ben smiled at her. He'd had a good time, too. Vic was open and easy to talk to. It had made the day pass quickly. "Me too."

She twisted her lips, studying the court doors. "I'm glad I came."

Ben nodded. "I'm glad too." He stepped outside to meet her.

"Walk me up the hillside?" she asked. "Henri saddled Jade for me. She's waiting there."

Ben nodded. "Sure."

Vic had just turned to walk up the hillside when Ben heard a sharp whistle by his ear. Vic fell flat, but before he could see why, a sharp pain pierced above his left shoulder blade. Ben grunted as the searing pain spread through to his chest. He dropped his eyes to the spot. The tip of a dark arrow was sticking out from his skin, its end covered with Banded Berry poison.

Vic was already standing again. Ben frowned up at her as he fell to his knees. It was strange. Vic hadn't screamed. In fact, she didn't seem shocked at all that Ben had just been shot.

Ben's vision began to swirl. He fell forward, Vic bracing his shoulders with her hands. Her face was pained as she stared down into his eyes. "I'm so sorry, Ben," she said softly. "I had no choice."

Ben's head bounced against a tall mountain fairy's back. He'd originally been commanded to walk, but when it was clear the berry poison was taking over, he'd been thrown over the shoulder of the largest of Marcus's mercenaries. He closed his eyes. His temples ached with all the bouncing. He wished it would stop. It felt like they had been walking forever.

Sometime later, he opened his eyes to slits. They were still moving through the dark mountain pass. Ben had no idea the pass was so long, but then again, he'd never been much further than the Western Wall of the Court of Mountain Fairies. There had never been reason to. His whole world had been east of that wall, and later, it had been in the Timekeeper's Court. Now that he thought about it, he realized that something about the ominous looking pass had disturbed him. He'd instinctually stayed away from it.

The air was cooler here. Damp and chilled. The rock walls had a heavy feeling that cloaked Ben like a stifling coverlet. Every step his large captor took, the light seemed to diffuse further and further, until all but bright colors were drained from the small party. Even in his addled state, Ben could feel something sinister lingering in the encroaching darkness.

Vic's small, bare feet were just visible on the hard ground behind him. His shoulder throbbed, and he shut his eyes against the pain, grimacing. What had possessed her to betray him like that? Ben searched his muddled mind for an answer.

He thought back on her sudden appearance at the Timekeeper's Court. Everyone had liked her immensely, and despite Reina's misgivings about her, even he had eventually come around. It hadn't occurred to him that she might be working with Marcus, and he certainly wouldn't have expected her to do what she had just done.

Ben felt the air widen slightly as the pass fell away to the land beyond. His captor set him onto his feet, and Ben blinked at his surroundings, attempting to get his bearings. He had never seen anything like it.

A giant, warbling darkness surrounded the banded mountain fairies' hideout, and the very air pressed against his shoulders like a heavy cloak. The hair on the back of his neck stood on end, and he braced himself to run, but from what, he didn't know. His captor pushed him from behind with the blunt end of his spear, and Ben grimaced as the arrow that still protruded from his back was clipped by the edge of it. He took a reluctant step.

There was no mistaking it. Evil was afoot in Marcus's camp. The only thing Ben had ever seen or felt that came close to it was on the battlefield with the King's army in the fight against the Court of Orm. Though he knew that evil of all kinds still lingered in the dark places of Caelium, he had never expected to feel such an oppressive presence like that again. And what was even more disturbing was that his own brother was at the helm of it.

The door to Marcus's camp was constructed of twisted, thorny vines that curled and curved around one another in a tangled web. They spread high above him, and wide, in an oblong shape. They were Banded Berry bushes, like the one that had been at the back of the stables. But these were huge in size. They encircled the camp in an oval ring.

Their poison was now coursing through Ben's veins from the arrow that had pierced his skin. Soon, the fever would set in, and Ben didn't know how long he would last after that. Before, Reina had been there, and she'd quickly come to his aid with the Tamarisk. And Henri, too, with the Sacred Thistle. But out here, Ben was sure there was none of either to be found.

Large, sharp thorns scraped Ben's arms as his captor pushed him through the doorway. As he stepped beyond the twisted vines, the acrid scent of burned flesh hit Ben's face like a hard wall. It conjured all manner of images in his mind, not the least of which was his recent dream of his mother. He halted his breath, hoping to push the images away, but the poison had weakened him, and in moments, he had to suck in again, the harsh scent bringing bile to his throat.

There was no movement inside the camp walls, no visible signs of life, though countless small huts of the same twisted vines were scattered at intervals. Ben studied the huts curiously. Were all these dwellings for mountain fairies? Surely not. He thought only a few had escaped to the west with his brother. Ben could hardly believe it. There were too many to number.

He'd been under the impression that his clan had been almost entirely wiped out. But now he wondered if his assumptions were true. Ben knew there were ways to hide the truth, even in Caelium. Wherever evil persisted, it could always be done. And his brother's camp was definitely one of those places. Apparently, Marcus had hidden the numbers of survivors well.

The camp was a dark world all to itself, and Ben could see now why the air here was cooler and stifling. Thick, dark clouds swirled above the jagged, towering mountains, which encircled the camp in a tight ring. Only fractions of sunlight were able to pierce the ground below.

If Ben hadn't known better, he would've thought they had left the West Mountains. No bright grasses carpeted the dry ground, and the area was completely devoid of flowers or trees. No moss hung in the craggy cliffs, and there were no animals of any sort. The landscape lay silent, depressed.

A piercing scream bit the back of Ben's head, and he swung to find Vic on her hands and knees near the thorny wall of the fortress. She was sobbing. Ben's heart dropped to his feet as he followed her gaze. He could see now where the smell of burning flesh had come from.

Before her, mounted on the thorny wall, was a male mountain fairy. Or what was left of him. His features were almost completely charred, and his left arm was devoid of flesh on the forearm and hand. His shirt had melted into the skin of his shoulders. It hung in ribbons at his waist, as if ripped by an animal. And before him, on the ground, lay a perfect pair of iridescent wings. Ben could tell they had been removed prior to his burning. There wasn't a spot on them, save the bloody nubs where they had been severed from his back.

Vic reached a shaking hand forward and brushed the tip of one of them, her body wracked by wails and sobs. A member of the group pulled hard on the back of her dress, and the collar dipped low, exposing two jagged, purplish scars across her shoulder blades—right where her wings used to be.

Between the sight of Vic prostrate before the burned fairy and the Banded Berry poison, Ben's knees were starting to waver. He knew he wouldn't be able to stand upright for much longer. His captor nudged his side, and they gave way, so he found himself hauled onto the fairy's large shoulder again. Vic was similarly slung across another shoulder behind him, and she kicked and wailed against the tall fairy's back until he shouted for her to be silent. Then all Ben could hear were her stifled moans. He wondered who the burned fairy had been.

His vision was starting to blur as they moved into a dark cave on the opposite side of camp. Momentarily, he was stood upright, and the arrow was yanked from his back before he was flung unceremoniously to the cold, damp stone floor. He pressed his cheek against it weakly as blood poured from his wound, wetting the back of his shirt.

Just then, someone gripped him by the hair, and he was forced to his knees. His mouth was dry, and little prickles of chill radiated down his arms. *The fever*. It wouldn't be long now. The thought of his imminent death vaguely troubled him, but it didn't really matter. He'd lost Reina, so why should he care?

Honesty comes easier when one is close to death. Problems that once loomed large cease to matter, and one is able to see their desires for what they truly are with sudden clarity.

Ben saw his desires with clarity now. He didn't want to live without her. In fact, death would be a welcome escape. The sooner he could go, the better.

The poison was gaining strength. Ben could no longer feel his legs, and his eyes were shuttered to pinpoints of dim light. He closed his eyes as he felt himself lurch forward.

He was falling…weightless. A weightlessness not unlike floating in a wide, still pool. But there was no water here. There was only cool, white silence. It bathed Ben in a peaceful light, and he allowed his body to relax into it. He could feel that he was drifting. To where, he didn't know, but he was certain he would arrive there any moment…

He was suddenly choking, and in the silent light, he lifted his neck, gasping for air. His throat was tightening, and he lifted his hands to it, flailing his legs in the weightless limbo. Then the bottom fell out, and Ben was suddenly thrust back onto the cold, stone floor of the cave.

Someone was gripping his neck, while another held his shoulders. They were forcing some strong, bitter liquid down his throat. He sputtered and coughed, thrashing against his captors. At last, they released him, and he rolled onto his hands and knees, coughing and retching violently.

A deep voice from his right spoke eerily from the darkness. "Bitter Elm, to counteract the poison." Marcus's tall frame stepped into the dim light. "Brother," he said flatly. He smiled, but no kindness touched his eyes. They were dark and void. Not at all like Ben remembered them.

He stepped towards Ben. "We have no Tamarisk here, you see. It is forbidden. We have…other ways of doing things. And Bitter Elm's roots do the same as the Tamarisk, or nearly."

Ben didn't answer. Truth be told, he couldn't speak. The concoction had scalded his throat so badly that he wasn't sure he would have a voice for a while.

Marcus stepped past Ben's quavering frame. He folded his arms, moving around Vic's crumpled figure in a wide circle, like a wild animal would stalk its prey. "You'll have seen Nual, yes?"

Marcus's eyes flashed a wicked black, but Vic didn't meet his gaze. Tears streaked silently down her cheeks, and she sniffed. "You promised me," she whispered.

Marcus gave a mirthless laugh. "Ah, yes, I did." He stopped in front of her. "But you broke the rules, and you both knew the consequences."

Vic lifted onto her knees. She glanced quickly at Ben then looked away. "But you said if I brought him here, you would have mercy. You said Nual could live!"

Marcus stared at her thoughtfully. "Yes, but you see, I couldn't allow that in the end." He folded his arms behind his back. "It wouldn't be fair if I had shown mercy in this case now, would it?" He shook his head, tsking. "No. I don't think so. There must be order. I couldn't allow it."

Vic scrambled to her feet. "But I did what you asked!" she shouted.

Before Ben could process what was happening, Marcus took one lunging step towards her. He swung the back of his hand heavily through the air, landing it squarely on the side of Vic's jaw. She recoiled from the blow, and blood spattered from her lips as she fell hard onto the ground. Her small body lay lifeless, and for a few moments, Ben thought she might be dead, but then she began to groan and stir. She brought a shaking hand to the side of her face, where a blue-black mound was already forming along her jaw.

Marcus spun on his heel and slowly moved past Ben towards an eerie throne that was seated just at the edge of the darkness. Ben hadn't noticed it before, and his stomach turned at the sight. It was made entirely of charred bones, and the shorn wings of so many Fairies hung behind it, like trophies on the wall. Marcus sat on the throne, bracing his right hand on top of the rounded dome of a darkened skull. He leveled Vic with his gaze. "And now, we must decide what is to be done with you."

Vic frowned up at him from her place on the floor. "I don't care what you do with me anymore," she murmured.

A dark grin formed on Marcus's lips. He leaned forward, resting his elbows on his knees. "Is that so?" He turned to look up at the gruesome collection on the wall behind him. The large captor who had carried Ben was pinning Nual's bloody wings to a small open spot. A small spatter of dark blood dripped onto the floor below them. He turned back to her, and Vic raised her chin. Her lips trembled, but her eyes were direct. Marcus rested his elbows on the arms of his seat and brought his hands to temple in front of his nose. He cut his eyes to Benjamin, then back to Vic. Ben frowned. He could see an idea forming in his brother's gaze, and whatever it was, it couldn't be good.

Suddenly, Marcus stood. A smug grin rested squarely above his chin. He moved towards Ben and Vic and began pacing slowly back and forth.

He stopped in front of Ben, tilting his dark head. "A challenge, perhaps, for you, Ben?"

Ben glared at him. The spot on his shoulder throbbed, and the effects of the poison hadn't completely worn off. He still felt weak, and his thoughts were still hazy. Marcus grinned down at him. "If you fail to comply, Vic will be forced to take your place. Would you care to hear the terms?"

Ben glanced at Vic. Her face was a mask of pure horror. She shook her head at him. "No. Say 'No,'" she mouthed.

Ben turned back to Marcus. "I accept," he croaked.

Marcus chuckled low. "Good. Very good." He began to pace back and forth again. "Like I mentioned before, we have a certain way of doing things here. Those that…displease me, require the proper punishment." He gestured to the wings behind him. "Take these, for example. We don't hold here with the *old* traditions. No nonsense like waiting behind an open door for one's mate, you see. If someone is found to be behaving in such a manner, well…poor Nual is a good example." He glanced at Vic, who stared pointedly at the floor.

Marcus sighed thoughtfully, halting his steps. "In fact, I have already dispatched my men to dispose of those fine doors you continue to foolishly build." He flicked his eyes to Ben, who glared at him. Marcus smiled. "The rest of the court will follow after. That much is settled." He tapped his foot in thought. "But you see, here I find myself in an interesting predicament." He drummed his fingers against the back of his hand. "Normally, I would just throw poor Vic into the Dragon's Well. But she has already been of such use to me in acquiring Ben, here, for an audience, even if she has failed me in the past." Vic bit her lip as Marcus flicked his eyes to Ben, then back to her. "She tried once before to aid me, when she secreted the Banded Berry bush seeds into the stable yard."

He shook his head. "They were meant for you, Ben. But all that it succeeded in doing was killing a few griffins and maiming another mountain fairy who worked in the yard." He wrinkled his dark brow. "I almost sent her to her death for that particular infraction. But she appears to have redeemed herself this time. So, I don't think that will do. Not at all."

He strode slowly towards Ben, stopping just before his knees. "No, I've got a better idea. Instead, let's allow Benjamin to take your place. And if he survives it, I will allow Vic to survive, too." He raised one finger. "With one contingency." He flicked his eyes to Ben, and they flashed dark with excitement.

"If you survive the drake, then you will have Vic as your mate. You and she will take the bond. *My* bond. The one I give to you. It is the way things are done here. Similar to the bond you know, the bond I give cannot be broken. Once it is done, it cannot be undone—even in death."

Silent tears dripped from Vic's chin as Marcus brought his face close to Ben's nose. "Let this be a warning: if you survive, *brother*," he hissed, "and you refuse this betrothal condition, then I will hunt down your *other* mate, and she will follow you into the Dragon's Well. Do I make myself clear?"

Ben frowned up at him. His mind swirled at Marcus's biting words. "My mate? What do you mean?" Marcus moved back to his throne. He sat, leaning towards Ben, an evil grin on his lips. "I've installed my spies in the valley of the Timekeeper's Court, Benjamin. Foolishly, your *mate* has returned through the gate." He chuckled mirthlessly. "She believes she can rescue you."

Ben blinked at Marcus blankly. He couldn't mean what Ben thought he did. Surely not.

"It's Reina, my dear brother. She is here."

CHAPTER 32

REINA

Reina's hands shook as she fumbled to open the box on her nightstand. She pulled off the lid, tossing it aside as she lifted her dagger. Its sharp blade glinted in the sunlight, and she slipped it into the waist of her dress. *Her dress*—she was still wearing her wedding dress.

Amelie's blonde head appeared in the doorway as Reina slung her pack over her shoulder. She looked up expectantly. "I've sent a message to the roots of the Eiks," said Amelie. "With the Court of Mountain Fairies unoccupied, there's sure to be an attack. And we will need help if we are to rescue Benjamin."

She moved to Reina's side, grasping both of her hands. "Henri is frantic." She frowned. "It seems Vic is missing, too. Henri hasn't been able to find her since this morning. He thinks she may have gone to meet Ben at the Court of Mountain Fairies, that they were both intercepted by Marcus's scouts." She shook her head. "I don't understand why they would want to take her, too."

Reina's heart squeezed at the thought of Vic visiting Ben alone at the new court. Images of them both in the kitchens of the palace swirled in her mind, and she swallowed hard, pushing the thoughts away. She wondered if Vic wore the other bracelet now, too. Ben's letter in the locket of her bracelet was at odds with that thought, but still, it was possible. For all she knew, Ben had already given Vic two bracelets.

Reina snapped her eyes shut, pinching her brow. That was enough of that. She needed to focus on the problem at hand: saving Ben—and Vic—from whatever horrors Marcus might be inflicting on them. She had already seen firsthand the lengths Marcus would go to maintain his power when he had attacked Ben in Jubal's cave. He was vicious, and she had no doubt that he had ideas to destroy both Ben and all the good work he had done to the Court of Mountain Fairies.

Henri had already gotten four griffins ready for flight by the time she and Amelie reached the stables. His usually jovial face was grim as he greeted them in the yard, his bow and quiver slung across his back. He shook his head. "I should have gone with her. I should have..." He cut off, his voice cracking.

Amelie put her hand on his shoulder. "It's not your fault, Henri. Vic made the decision to go alone. There's nothing you could have done."

Henri nodded. "I know, but still. It's just..." He shook his head. "I just hope they're all right—both of them."

Johann appeared behind him, two long blades tucked across his back. He handed two more to Amelie, and she tucked the blades crisscross over her shoulders like he had done. Reina knew her friend had developed more skills than just swords since coming to Caelium. The Mortal Timekeepers had always known that evil persisted in the deep, dark places of the known worlds. Because of it, they had honed their individual strengths in elemental control for use when needed.

Amelie's skill was Winds. Reina had often watched her sit in silence and solitude in the courtyard of the Timekeeper's Court, waiting for a small breeze. As soon as it lifted the tips of her hair, she would open herself up to it, allowing the Wind to course through her body as it picked up speed, until a swirling vortex whipped around and through her. She had described it to Reina as a relinquishing of oneself—a surrender that was so complete, she would almost become lost inside it. She thus became a conduit for the Four Winds to use her as they willed.

Reina knew what Amelie meant about giving up control. Her skillset was Fire. A good fit, or so Ben had said, for her fiery personality and flaming hair. Her Fire skill required a sense of surrender, too. Just in a different way. Her biggest hurdle had always been controlling herself, controlling the fire already within her. The Fire skill seemed to respond best if she submitted herself to the Source. Only then would she have the control she needed to direct the flame.

The others had already gone ahead with the rest of the griffin fleet. Winds, Earths, Waters, and Fires rode in twos and threes, just as they'd done three cycles ago in the battle with the Court of Orm. Their skills hadn't been used outside the courtyard in the long cycles since, and Reina wondered how the Timekeepers would fare once they reached the banded mountain fairies' lair. She prayed to the Source they would have success.

As she moved toward Cyrus and jumped astride, Reina felt much the same as she had the first time she had ridden towards the battlefield. She had hoped she would never have to journey this way again, and her heart was burdened that she was again required to fight the evil that lurked in the shadows. But there was no other way. She had already lost Ben once. She wasn't going to do it again.

It was as clear to her now as it had ever been. Reina loved Ben, heart and soul. There was no one else for her, and there never would be. She had to save him—or else she would die, too.

Reina was certain that if Ben left the court door open, she would lie down behind it. In the morning, he would swing the door wide. Then the cord of their bond would snap into place. They would be forever one. An eternal match—with Ben sprouting wings to prove it.

CHAPTER 33

BEN

Water dripped from above him, dampening his head. Ben hugged his arms across his chest. He was freezing. In the far corner, Vic huddled against the wall. Her back was to him, and she shivered, sobbing quietly. Iron bars marked the exit of their tiny hole, which was somewhere below Marcus's makeshift throne room. Beyond them, Ben could hear the quiet, despondent moans of hopeless suffering.

Vic sighed heavily, glancing at him over her shoulder. She sniffed and wiped her nose with the back of her arm. "I truly am sorry, Ben," she whispered. "Marcus wouldn't let me return without you. He promised Nual would live if I brought you to him." She shook her head. "And I *had* to get back here." Her tears started anew. "I should have known. Marcus has never kept any of his promises. Not from the very beginning."

Ben didn't answer. His mind was consumed with thoughts of Reina. Where was she now? Why had she come back here? Surely it wasn't to rescue him like Marcus had suggested.

He thought she would be married by now. That she would be ruling her Mortal kingdom from the Monrovian throne. Apparently not.

Marcus had threatened to kill her if Ben didn't take whatever twisted form of the bond he had created. Marcus said it was eternal, like the bond Ben knew. If Ben took it, he would never be with Reina. Even if she had returned for him. Instead, he'd be bound to a mate he didn't love, and that bond would never break.

Ben spoke softly into the dim light. "Why would Marcus do this? Why would he force us together? I mean, assuming I even survive the Dragon's Well?"

Vic turned, her back resting against the damp wall. She bit her lip, thinking. "Out here with Marcus, true love is forbidden." She shrugged softly. "It's a force all to its own, love is. And it can't be contained, no matter how one feels about it." She glanced over at Ben. "That's why Marcus forbids it. That's why he forces us together in a bond of his own making. It's why he takes our wings, if we choose true love. It's why he forces our mates into the Dragon's Well." She shook her head slowly back and forth. "Marcus won't allow what he can't control."

She paused, studying Ben's face. "It's why he's bent on destroying your court doors, twice over. And it's why he worked hand in hand with the Court of Orm to destroy the Court of Mountain Fairies in the first place."

Ben's mind reeled with memories. He knew what Vic was saying was true, but he'd tried to forget it. Their own mother and father had died in the drake's fiery breath. The fact that Marcus had a hand in that was unthinkable.

Vic sat upright. "I want you to know that we didn't know, before we came here, what Marcus had done. He masqueraded as a kind master at first. And for a time, he was one. We all thought we were coming to a better life, and I think even Marcus, in his own twisted way, thought he was bringing us to one. When Time was restored, he ruled for a long while with grace and honor, and we all thought by following him, we had made the right choice.

"He filled in the Dragon's Well, cutting the drake off from the surface. But somewhere deep inside, he harbored a darkness that refused to be contained, and soon, he ordered the Well dug out again." She hung her head. "Since, he's only grown worse. It's as if the darkness seeps from the Dragon's Well, infecting his mind and everything else in its proximity. None of us are fully immune. You stay long enough, you open yourself up to it, and you will become like him." She flicked her eyes to Ben.

"It was by chance that I saw my mistakes. Marcus didn't realize that by sending me out to the Timekeeper's Court, my mind would be cleansed of the evil he harbors." She rested the side of her head on the wall. "The longer you stay away, the clearer things become, or so it's been in my case" She flicked her eyes to Ben, then looked away. "It makes me truly sorry for what I've done, both with the griffins and Henri all those cycles ago, and now, by bringing you here." She frowned. "But Marcus threatened me. And true love persists in the face of all evil. He knew that. He knew I would do whatever it took... for Nual and for..." She trailed off, swallowing convulsively. "He used it to my disadvantage, like he's done with so many others. And now, he's doing it with you and Reina." Her lower lip began to tremble.

Ben flexed his palms. He thought about all those wings, hung like prizes behind his brother's grotesque throne. They were a banner of true love and true love lost—a dark reminder of the true bond that was made at the open door.

In a sense, Ben felt that his own wings had been clipped. Even though he and Reina hadn't truly taken the bond, he still felt like they had. In his heart, he was bound to her forever.

Though he'd not sprouted wings only to have them removed, he knew what it felt like to have love severed, cut down with no hope to recover. It was a sickening feeling, like the swift fall of an ancient Eik, with the axe leaving only a stump in its place.

It was hopeless. How would he ever reach her again? Even if he survived the Dragon's Well, he'd be forced into a bond with Vic. And if Ben refused that bond, Reina would die. Those were Marcus's terms. And Ben believed him.

He worried about what Reina might think. Would she believe that he'd been forced to bond with Vic? Or would she think it was a choice he had made—a bond of his own making?

Ben hung his head. He didn't know which was worse: dying in the Dragon's Well and never seeing Reina again, or surviving and having to face her at the surface. If he lived, Reina would be forced to bear witness to his bond with Vic. And then he would be forced to watch Marcus destroy her.

Too, there was the Court of Mountain Fairies. If Marcus hadn't already destroyed it, he would soon. So, what was the point of it all, anyway? What was the point of his dreams and Willow's gift and Jubal's death? What was the point of his love for Reina or rebuilding the court of his heritage? Ben scanned his small cell. There didn't seem to be a point. Because here he was, facing his death, with no one and nothing to show for it.

The longer he thought about it, the deeper Ben sunk into despair, a creeping darkness curling itself around the edges of his heart. He should've never come back to the valley of the Court of Mountain Fairies. He should've just stayed at the Timekeeper's Court. Then he wouldn't be in this mess. Reina would still be safely in Monrovia. He would've still lost her, yes, but at least she wouldn't be dead. And maybe he wouldn't be dead, either.

He thought of Kai and Arto, Chaeronne, Maria, the twins, and all the Mortal Timekeepers. They would likely come to his defense. He wondered how many of them would be cut down as they fought to defend the Court of Mountain Fairies. Too many to count, that was certain. And after they had already faced so much loss, only three cycles ago. The thought of it made bile rise in Ben's throat. This was all his fault. Every bit of it.

Just then, the large fairy who had lugged him through the pass appeared beyond the bars. He was carrying a small torch, and he lifted it to eye level as he peered through the iron grates. A smaller fairy with one lame foot shuffled down the corridor behind him. A large, iron ring which held several keys was fastened to his neck. He was much older than the larger fairy. Grey hairs had begun to sprout in front of his pointed ears, and the top of his rounded head was bare. He was very thin and had a long, hooked nose and very few teeth.

Slowly, the shorter Fairy sorted through the keys hanging on his neck until he lifted one in his gnarled fingers. He dragged his useless foot along the floor towards the lock. A sickening *clink* sounded as the key turned in place.

The sound felt to Ben's ears like water overflowing the rim of a cup. There was no more space. No time to think. Nowhere to run. Nowhere to hide. He was going into the Dragon's Well. Panic rose in his chest, and his stomach squeezed, threatening to spill its contents onto the stone floor.

Vic scrambled up from the floor and pressed herself flat, her fingernails digging into the damp stone wall. She glared daggers at the taller fae as he reached for her arm.

"Don't do this, Jin," she whispered. But the tall fae narrowed his golden eyes and gripped her hard by the upper arm, jerking her forward. Vic yelped and began thrashing at the fairy's tall head with her free fist. He dodged her attempts as he twisted her arm behind her back. In response, she kicked hard at his shin, succeeding in ramming his knee with her small foot. Jin grunted, then hauled Vic over his shoulder, frowning. He held her by the back of her knees as she thrashed against his back, screaming. He paused in the hallway, looking at her head behind his shoulder.

"Quiet," he said sternly. "Unless you want me to throw you in with the drake, too."

Vic paused her blows in midair, then let her fists drop, sobbing defeatedly as Jin moved down the hallway.

Ben watched them go, uncertain of what he was to do. It seemed Jin had forgotten him. The smaller, older fae still stood holding the door open. His dark, beady eyes rested on Ben, then he jerked his head in the direction the tall fae had gone.

Ben blinked at him blankly. No one was going to drag him or throw him over their shoulder? He was just supposed to walk himself to the Well?

Ben stood slowly, leaning heavily against the wall. He tested his legs. The berry poison seemed mostly gone. They only shook a little bit. He moved to the iron grates, gripping the cool metal with his palm, bracing himself for what was to come. Silently, he moved past the short fairy and turned into the dim corridor.

He'd been blindfolded on the way in, but now, he was free to look around him. The fact that he was allowed to see troubled him a little bit. That meant that no one expected him to survive what he was about to do.

Slowly, he moved down the long, dark passage. The short fae shuffled along quietly behind him, his keys jingling from their place around his neck. His lame foot scuffed against the floor. Water dripped onto Ben's head from the rolled stone ceiling above them as he passed countless iron grates on his left and right. Behind them, quiet moans and sad whispers drifted out of the darkness to his ears.

Suddenly, the bars to his left shook. Gnarled fingers with long, dirty nails gripped the grates, and an elder fairy woman's face appeared in between them. Her grey hair was twisted into knots beneath a stained kerchief, and one eye was covered with a thick patch of fabric that was wound around her head. Ben flicked his eyes to her then moved to go past, but she reached out her hand, staying his arm.

"They have forgotten us," she whispered. "They have forgotten us all."

Her words chilled Ben to the bone. He nodded politely then shifted slightly out of the woman's cold grasp. "Don't forget us," she called after him. "Please."

Ben turned, flicking his eyes to the short fairy behind him. He had a curious look on his face. Sorrow pulled at the edges of his features, marked with so much suffering. "Please," the short fae added. His voice had a gravelly quality, as if it was seldom used.

Ben flicked his eyes to the elder woman behind the bars. He nodded once, then turned away, continuing down the corridor. He didn't stop again. The woman's words had pricked a place deep inside of him, a sadness that mingled with his fear and threatened to overwhelm. He didn't want to linger with that feeling, especially not in this horrid place. He had to keep his wits if he wanted to survive the Dragon's Well.

In front of him, the dungeon hall forked. One path went upward towards the light, and the other was hewn deeper beneath the stone of the corridor. Though small torches were set at intervals along the walls, a darkness permeated the pathway that made Ben pull up short. Beyond it, he could hear threads of excited chatter and winding chants. They drifted inside his head with a sickening dread, and he braced himself against the opening of the dark path, his feet stopping of their own will.

In his mind, he was right back to the day the drake had destroyed the Court of Mountain Fairies. Visions of the large, black dragon swooping low over the stone structures of his West Mountains home filled the space behind his eyes, and he couldn't move himself forward.

He had been playing just outside the Western Wall—he and Johann and Henri. They had made a game of waiting until some of the more interesting residents appeared to tuck their rolled parchments inside the wall. The three would wait until their backs were turned, at which time they would sneak behind them and collect the messages, reading them swiftly before secreting them back into their places between the stones. The game, reading the people's private words to the Source, brought shame to Ben's face when he thought of it now. But at least it had saved them from the drake.

He could still hear the dragon's horrible shriek as it swooped beyond the dark mountain pass. Its shadow had momentarily blocked the sun as it passed over their heads, and Ben could still feel the terror-stricken fear bubbling up in his stomach at the sight.

The worst had been the screams. Horrible, terrible screams as the dragon emptied its fiery breath over the valley. Some people had scattered, but so many had been consumed along with the court.

Ben, Henri, and Johann had hidden above, in a cleft of rocks, watching in horror as everything they had ever known went up in flames. From his perch, Ben could see that the drake had a rider, someone guiding the beast over the valley, directing it to consume each corner of the court. His heart had sunk as the drake flew past their hiding place, and a band of fae rebels poured out of the pass. Their arm bore a large blue swath of color. His brother Marcus had been among them. And he'd been the one to take down the doors.

Marcus hadn't been wearing a shirt. The wings that had sprouted on his back the previous summer had been shorn at their roots. The wounds where they had been gaped just beneath his shoulder blades. He'd wielded an axe, chopping the high doors into pieces.

Marcus hadn't always been this way. Ben could remember a time when his brother had been kind and generous. Even Vic had recognized it—a fragment of the fae he once was, peeking out from the monster he had become.

After Marcus had lost Rose, he'd changed completely. He'd left the court and hadn't returned. The day it was destroyed was the first time Ben had seen him in a full cycle.

Rose had been Marcus's mate. Ben had attended their bonding ceremony. He'd remembered how Rose had wound her dark red hair into a long braid, decorated with Lavender Mountain Aster. It reminded Ben of Reina's long locks.

Their parents had warned Marcus against taking the bond with her, but Marcus wouldn't listen. For all her faults, Rose had been a great beauty. Marcus had been in love at first sight.

Shortly after their bonding, she'd been killed. It was after Orm had taken power. She'd been in Meallta, where she worked for the Court of Orm. Rose was selling her body from her perch in her second story window. She was to collect the unwitting souls and deliver them to the evil ruler, at which time, he sacrificed them at the Rotha-Am—the Wheel of Time. He was using their Amloga—their Flame of Time—to power the wheel, causing it to turn at his own pace and his own direction. His goal had been to stop Time completely, thereby destroying the known worlds and assuming all power as his own, but he'd been destroyed in the process, by a half-Mortal princess. Evangeline or Lina Vasily.

At some point, Rose had gotten greedy. After she discovered that she could fetch a higher price, she had begun sacrificing her customers on her own. Ben had heard that the dark forces used them in a process of reanimation, trading the Amloga from one soul into the body of another, creating a corrupted version of the victim's original self—dark servants to the evil abounding under Orm's foul hand.

Word had travelled back to the Court of Mountain Fairies that someone had seen a fairy with long, red hair have her wings shorn while the giants held her fast. They said she'd been taken, sent as a sacrifice herself to the Rotha-Am for her treachery against the dark ruler.

Rose had been the first, but many others had followed her footsteps, lured into greed by their harsh occupation. And by the end, nearly all the fae women in Meallta had met the same fate.

After her death, Marcus's heart had gone black. In a sick twist, he'd come to serve the Court of Orm himself. He'd helped to dig the Dragon's Well, unearthing the evil that had been buried in the deep places of Caelium after Orm's defeat. And when the time had come, it had been Marcus who had unleashed that evil on the valley of the Court of Mountain Fairies.

Ben's back was beginning to sweat, despite the cool temperature. The short fae behind him gave him a nudge, and he stepped forward, the smell of dark mold and stale air lifting to his nose. The sound of chants roared loudly as he neared the end of the tunnel. His heart sped in his ears. In a moment, he'd be in the Dragon's Well, and he didn't know if he'd ever come out of it.

The last thought he had before he stepped out of the dark hallway was of Reina. Where was she now? Ben hoped she'd stay away. He didn't want her to see it. Any of it. But he knew her. He knew she would come.

CHAPTER 34

REINA

The pass was too narrow for Cyrus to fly through. Reina could see that, even from her high perch. She touched down on the hillside above the Court of Mountain Fairies and led Cyrus to a small grove of trees. Below her, the valley was a flurry of activity. Selkies and merrows, centaur warriors, and Mortal Timekeepers stood at intervals along the walls. Johann and Henri were armed at the doors. They didn't move, scanning the pass for movement. Arto and Kai moved up and down the hillside, on patrol, while Chaeronne rode swiftly down the ranks. He carried a fearsome spear, and swirls of war paint covered his sides. His two sons flanked closely behind him, equally dressed and armed.

The Mortal Timekeepers held no weapons, save their open hands at their sides. Reina knew they were trained in hand-to-hand combat, and some had swords at their backs, but their elemental skill sets were a better service to the group than traditional weapons would be. They needed open hands to use their skills—their power gifted from the Source. Not ones with armed with wood and iron.

Just then, a scuffle broke out along the Western Wall. Reina watched in horror as a large mountain fairy with a dark blue stripe across his face sprang from the tall grasses. He yelled a battle cry, then swiped the legs of a petite selkie woman from under her with his spear. He leered over her, plunging his blade through her chest.

What happened next was in slow motion. Banded mountain fairies appeared from all sides. They scaled down trees, moved from behind rocks, and streamed out of the pass in droves. Some carried torches and others bows or spears, which Reina knew were laced with the berry poison. Chaeronne and his sons rode out to meet them, flanked by a band of centaur warriors, while those against the walls braced for attack. Blades clashed as five banded fairies set fire to the hillside with their torches. The high grasses and flowers immediately caught, and soon, a thick ring of fire was blazing around the northern wall. It curled dangerously close to the edge, then swiftly moved past it, heading south.

Reina turned to Amelie, who'd just touched down on the ground behind her. Amelie slid down, and Reina handed her the bag of Sacred Thistle she and Ben had collected from the water horse's chamber.

"You're going to need this. It's Sacred Thistle—the only truly effective remedy against the Banded Berry poison. Their weapons are armed with it, and it can kill swiftly if it's not reversed."

Amelie took the bag, nodding. She pulled Reina into a swift embrace. "Be safe, and bring them home," she whispered.

Reina waited until Amelie had positioned herself at a safe distance. Below them, swords clanged, and daggers squished into flesh. Several Mortal Timekeepers and Merrow Forces were working to put out the fire on the ridge. They drew water into their palms from the surrounding air, tossing it onto the blaze. But it was no use. The fire was spreading faster than they could contain it.

A Timekeeper named Jenae stepped out before the blaze. She knelt to the dirt, placing her palms flat against the ground. Then she closed her eyes. Several others joined her, and a gentle tremble began in the ground beneath them. Several centaurs surrounded the group, holding off the banded fairy warriors, while Amelie moved from her place to stand above them on the hillside. She took a deep breath and closed her eyes, then held out her palms. At once, a gentle suction pulled at the air around Reina, and the tips of Amelie's hair began to lift. A small breeze tugged at the hem of Reina's skirt, and soon, she was bracing her stance against the full force of the Four Winds.

The heavy gale swirled around the hillside, until Amelie was lifted into the air. The Winds swirled about her in a funnel, twisting her hair above her head and billowing her skirts. She remained still, silent, as the Winds collected themselves on her palms. Then she returned to the ground, and her eyes opened.

She pressed out with her right hand, and the Winds unfurled off it like a long cord. They wrapped themselves around the ankles of a banded fae warrior who was about to slit a Selkie Guard's throat. Amelie retracted her hand, and the fae attacker fell to his knees, allowing the selkie to spring upright and plunge his spear into the center of the fae's chest.

Amelie's left hand shot outward, and a group of three fairies who had pinned a centaur warrior against the northern wall were smacked flat to the earth. They didn't stand, and instead were trampled under hooves, while a group of merrows finished them with their spears.

Jenae and the Mortal Timekeepers were still kneeling on the ground, which was now vibrating as far up the hillside as Reina's feet. The rumbling grew, and she stumbled and stepped backward, holding on to the trunk of a small tree. The fire still blazed below her, now completely encircling the court. It was at least as tall as her head and whipped down the ridge by the western wall to meet the southern corner. She could barely make out the battle beyond the flames.

At just that moment, the earth beneath the Mortal Timekeepers hands began to crack—a jagged line forming in the dirt. They stepped back from it quickly as a gush of water sprang up. It flowed out from the crack like a fountain, pooling at the Timekeepers' feet.

Immediately, selkies and merrows surrounded it. The Time-keepers stepped away, save the Waters, as the sea dwellers lifted their hands in unison towards the fountain. The water responded immediately, rising above and beyond them like a wide wall. More and more selkies and merrows joined the group, extending the wall of water into a semi-circle around the court. Centaurs and Time-keepers guarded their rear as they continued to raise the water into a wide dome above the court walls. It rose and rose, until it peaked in the center of the court. Then, it continued its path, until the entire valley was encased in a protective dome. Once the court was covered, the fountain stopped, and the Earths knelt again to the crack, stitching the ground to cover it.

Reina flicked her eyes to the pass. No more fairies seemed to be coming out of it. Now was her chance. She had to get to Ben before it was too late.

Reina walked for what seemed like an eternity. The air inside the pass was thick and dark, like a heavy weight, and she had to pull hard to get breath into her lungs. Her heart was beating so hard and fast, she was soon exhausted. She paused, gasping as she held her side.

She trudged ahead, and soon, the walls narrowed. Panic rose in her throat as she imagined the dark rock squeezing her flat from each side. She closed her eyes, forcing herself to breathe in and out, pressing her hands against both sides of the dark, damp stone. The pass narrowed until it scraped her shoulders. Her heart hammered in her ears, and she moved forward mechanically, one foot, then the other.

She continued this way for a long while, until at last the rock began to widen. She opened her eyes. Up ahead, she could see the pass open, and a massive, ominous, bramble of thick, wooded vines which spread out beyond it. Her chest relaxed slightly. She had made it. And somewhere past the warbling darkness and tangled, wooden vines, she would find him.

CHAPTER 35

BEN

Ben emerged from the dark passage to step inside a high dome of dark rock. In the middle of the large cavern was a wide, yawning pit. Row after row of bench seats scaled the walls, and Ben craned his neck, following them as they rose high above towards the rounded ceiling. Cheers, jeers, and taunts were hurled in his direction from the seats, buzzing inside his ears. Ben studied the arena in awe. It was completely full—of mountain fairies.

For so long, he'd thought he and his friends at the Timekeeper's Court were some of the last ones left, besides the few that had followed Marcus further west. He'd never known so many of his clan had survived. Yet here they were. Countless fae men, women, and children were all gathered to see his doom. Their faces were gaunt and haunted, full of hunger, pain, and something he keenly recognized. Fear.

Jin was standing across the room, Vic tightly held at his side. He grinned across the pitch at Ben, gesturing to the wide pit at its center. Then he tossed his torch past the edge. Ben watched the torch tumble down, down, down, until the flame was a pinpoint prick in the darkness. Then, the flame blinked out.

Marcus appeared on a high, stone platform midway across the arena. Jin dragged Vic in front of it, then pushed her to her knees. Another guard gripped Ben by his upper arm and moved him roughly towards her. He stopped a short distance from Vic's back. Ben watched Marcus grin down at her from a high seat as two scantily dressed fae women draped their arms across his shoulders. Ben could see the scars on one of the women's backs, the space where her wings had been shorn. She met his gaze, and something like desperation passed in her eyes before she looked quickly away from him.

Marcus held up one hand, and immediately, the crowd grew silent.

"A surprise for you, Vic," Marcus crooned. He gestured to his left, where two guards escorted a small, slight woman from the shadows onto the platform. She was dirty and thin in her threadbare dress, and she blinked against the light of the arena as if she'd been kept long in the darkness. Her hair was short and dark, much like Vic's, and her eyes were a startling shade of violet.

"Tanis!" Vic screamed.

Tanis blinked below her, searching for the scream's owner. She locked eyes with Vic. "Mother!"

Ben stared blankly up at the young woman, then he slid his eyes to Vic's back. Vic had a daughter? Vic crumpled towards the dirt, sobbing loudly in front of him. She gazed up at her daughter, whose eyes had begun to fill.

"Why did you not stay hidden?" Vic called. "Why?" She fell forward onto her arms, moaning uncontrollably.

Tanis gazed down at her mother, pain gripping her face as tears streamed down her cheeks. The guard holding her arm jerked her roughly to the edge of the platform. Then he gave her a hard shove. Tanis screamed as she fell towards the dirt. Her arms were bound behind her back, and she had nothing to break her fall. She hit the ground in front of Vic with a sickening crack, then rolled onto her back, her face a mask of pain.

Ben winced as she rolled. The bone in her right shoulder was obviously out of place, a sunken dip at the meeting of her arm and chest. She moaned as Vic shuffled towards her on her knees. She bent towards her, and Tanis spoke softly through her sobs.

"I'm sorry, Mother. I tried. But then I heard you were returning, and then Father…" She trailed off, shaking her head. "I tried to find you…before he…" She swallowed hard, a pale sheen of sweat blanketing her forehead. She flicked her eyes to the guard above her. "But they caught me in the pass."

Marcus stepped towards the edge of the platform above them. He folded his arms behind his back, grinning down at Vic and Tanis. Ben could tell by the look in his eye that he wouldn't like what his brother was about to say next, and he sent a silent prayer to the Source that they wouldn't be the words he was imagining.

"What an interesting development," his brother began. "Young Tanis, alive. And to think I didn't even know of her existence." He shook his head, chuckling mirthlessly. He directed his gaze in Tanis's direction.

"How is it that I have passed eighteen cycles of your young life and not known you even existed? It was unbelievable enough that your parents hid their wings, bound beneath their dress to escape my notice." He shook his head and made a *tsk* sound beneath his breath, scanning Tanis's thin frame. "*Quite* unfortunate. Especially for your father, Nual. But nothing hidden lasts for too long." He began to pace above them, moving slowly. Ben could see the feral look in his eyes.

"I'm sorry, indeed, that it has come to this. But I'm afraid I have no other choice. The rules are the rules." He stopped, facing the small fae women below him. He raised his voice, addressing the crowd.

"As punishment for her parents' disobedience, Tanis will meet her doom—in the Dragon's Well!"

A roaring cry lifted from the seats above them, as seemingly every fairy in the dome agreed with their master's sentence. They stomped their feet on the hard rock, and a deafening rumble vibrated beneath Ben's feet.

"*NO!*" Vic cried. "Send *me*, instead! Send me! Please!" She collapsed forward onto her forearms, bowing to the platform. Marcus gazed down at her in contempt. He cocked his head to the side.

"I'm afraid that would be bending my rules. And we can't have that, now, can we?"

The guard nearest Tanis lifted her roughly from the ground, and Vic scrambled after her, scratching at the guard's bare feet. She fumbled over her quick words. "Please, I beg you," she pleaded. "She's innocent!"

But the guard ignored her. Tanis leaned towards her mother's hand as he dragged her away, sobbing. "It's alright, Mother. I'll be alright," she called.

Ben watched helplessly as Tanis was dragged towards the wide pit in the room's center. She had set her face like flint, but he knew she was terrified. His mind raced. Maybe he could help her escape the dragon, if he could survive himself.

Just then, Vic broke free of her captors' bonds. Tanis was approaching the edge of the pit. The crowd's chants were a deafening roar. Vic hurled herself forward, twisting left and right to evade the grasps of more guards. She managed to reach the edge of the yawning abyss.

She turned to Tanis, smiling as she lifted her hand to her daughter's cheek. Then, without a word, she stepped backward over the rim. Tanis screamed as her mother slipped out of sight. And suddenly, the crowd went silent, the sacrifice of a mother for her daughter resonating in ripples through the high rows.

CHAPTER 36

REINA

Reina could hear the roar of a distant crowd. She moved swiftly in the roar's direction, then paused, staring ahead in the dim light. She appeared to be in some sort of makeshift throne room. She crept inside, her dagger drawn as she carefully assessed her surroundings. No one was present. Not even one guard.

In front of her, a large seat made entirely of charred bones sat on a platform, and behind it, a gruesome wall of iridescent wings was hammered to the stone. One pair near the base still dripped fresh blood onto the floor beneath it. Reina stood slack. She studied the sickening throne and the wall behind it as a lump formed in her throat. So many wings. So much death.

To her left, a long, dark tunnel had been hewn out of the rock. Torches were placed at intervals along the walls. From beyond it, the roar of a crowd again reached her ears. Silently, Reina crept down the tunnel to meet it.

Reina hovered at the tunnel's far end, where the stone widened into a high, arched dome. She tucked herself flat against the wall and peered around the edge. The place was crawling with guards. Above her, the crowd stood to its feet, roaring cheers and chants, louder than anything she had ever experienced. She peered up at them in amazement.

A thousand fae faces were focused on the base of a raised platform on the far side of the dome, where a slight, dark-haired woman was kneeling over another fae who looked much like her. *Vic.* And someone else. Her relative, maybe? Reina blinked, focusing.

Near the women, a taller, male fairy with golden curls stood between two guards. Her heart dropped to her feet as he adjusted his weight. She would have known him anywhere. "Ben," she whispered.

Just then, the guards escorted the younger, dark-haired fairy towards a large pit in the center of the room. Reina frowned. She appeared to be hurt. Her face was a mask of pain as the guard jerked on her arm, which hung at an odd angle from her thin shoulder.

Vic screamed as the smaller fae was led to the edge of the pit. She wrenched her arm free of her guards, dodging forward as more guards swiped for her. She paused at the edge of the pit to touch the younger fairy's face, then she stepped backward, falling headlong into the dark pit as the crowd fell silent.

Reina gasped as she disappeared below the ledge, causing a guard to whip his head in her direction. He narrowed his eyes, scanning the edge of the tunnel. Reina tucked herself flatter against the wall, holding her breath until he turned away.

Across the room, Marcus stood on a high, stone platform. He watched Vic's display without emotion, his arms clasped behind his back. Then he waited in the silence of the crowd, studying Ben thoughtfully on the ground beneath him. The muscle in his jaw flexed.

"It appears I will need to make…an adjustment to our agreement, Benjamin," he announced flatly. "Vic will never survive the drake, so if you make it out alive, you will take the bond with her daughter, Tanis, instead."

Reina's eyes flicked to Ben. Her mind was running so fast, she couldn't understand what Marcus meant. Had Ben agreed to marry Vic before she'd flung herself into the pit? Had she agreed also?

"And remember," Marcus added, "If you manage to make it out of the Dragon's Well alive, and you refuse to follow this agreement, then both you and Tanis will die, and your mate, Reina Argynon, will also meet her doom."

Reina's arms went cold, and her heart dropped into her stomach. Her mind was numb, and she flicked her eyes quickly around the arena. Did Marcus know she was here? Or did he know she was back in Caelium? Her head spun. How did he know?

Ben's guards jerked him hard towards the gaping pit, but he didn't fight them. Reina watched him from her hiding spot as he shuffled forward. She wanted to scream at him to fight back, but she knew it wouldn't do him any good. Marcus clearly wanted him dead, or at least under his control. If he didn't go into the pit, then she was sure Marcus would kill him where he stood.

She swallowed convulsively, her mind swirling. This bond Marcus mentioned couldn't have been something Ben had chosen. Could it? Was Ben and Vic's planned bond one of true love? Reina pressed her lips. She thought not. It would have to be something more sinister—something of Marcus's own design. There could only be one reason Marcus would want Ben to bond with Tanis. And before, with Vic. Marcus wanted Ben under his control.

Reina hugged her arms to her chest, watching Ben move towards the gaping hole. She hoped she was right. She hoped the bond with Vic wasn't something Ben had chosen, but she couldn't be certain. Reina swallowed as Ben stepped to the Well's edge. But none of that would matter if he didn't survive.

Ben said no words as his feet approached the rim of the pit. He was facing her, and she had the sudden urge to leap from her hiding place and cause a distraction, so Ben could get away. Instead, she moved to the center of the tunnel's edge, allowing the light from the dome to illuminate her frame. She wanted Ben to see her. She wanted to look into his face. It might be the last time she ever had the chance.

Four fae guards immediately turned in her direction, but still, she didn't move. She could see the moment Ben's face registered her appearance. His cheeks went slack, and he mouthed her name, but she couldn't hear him say it over the roar of the crowd. The audience had stood to their feet, stomping the stone until the whole of the dome vibrated with their movement.

The last thing she saw before the guards gripped her by the arms was his lips mouthing, "I love you."

"I love you, too!" she shouted. But she knew her voice wasn't loud enough. It disappeared into the crowd's deafening roar. The guard to his left pushed roughly at his back.

Then he was gone.

CHAPTER 37

BEN

Ben had never experienced a free fall in darkness, and it wasn't something he ever wanted to experience again. His stomach was somewhere up by the pit's rim, while his body hurdled backward in the ever-lengthening tunnel, with no knowledge of what was beneath him. For all he knew, the drake was waiting at the bottom, and he'd be torched before he even reached the base.

The top of the pit was a small circle of light above him now. He held his breath and tucked his knees, awaiting impact. But a hard landing never came. Instead, he splashed heavily into dark water, swirling and spinning end over end in a heavy current.

The water was pulling him under. He sucked a breath just

before he lost the surface. He pulled hard and kicked, fighting the swirl. But the current was too strong. He was sucked lower and lower, his chest burning from lack of air.

At last, he dropped from beneath the swirling water, landing feetfirst on a bed of soft sand. He looked up. Above him, the vortex of water swirled and foamed, but his body rested in a pocket of dry air. He sucked it down greedily, even if it did taste stale and dark.

Suddenly, the ground beneath him began to tremble. He was sinking, the sand shifting below him to envelop his body in its grip. Ben sucked down one more gulp of air before his head went under. Sand and silt pressed in on him from all sides, filling his ears and nostrils. Below, he could feel his feet were free, and he kicked hard, hoping to quicken his descent. It worked, and soon, the rest of his body dropped into another air pocket. But this one was much wider.

Ben's back landed on soft earth, and he rolled to his feet, spitting silt and swiping sand from his nose and ears. Water dripped on his head through the sand ceiling above him, and he could hear the trickle of a shallow stream behind. Glowing, purplish-blue flora blanketed the walls, and Ben blinked in the dim light, focusing. The cavern was enormous—dragon-sized. But there was no dragon to be seen.

Three small tunnels were set in the base of the wide wall to his right. Ben moved towards them cautiously. He reached to his back, then to his side, then dropped his arms. His stomach sank. He had no weapons. His axe had fallen from his waist after he'd been shot with the arrow on the hillside, and he hadn't thought to take his dagger. He'd not known he'd need it for a swim at the waterfall.

He peered up, thinking of the drag of the current in the well above him. "Some swim," he muttered. It was quite different than the one he'd planned this morning.

This morning seemed a lifetime ago now, deep beneath the ground in the Dragon's Well. In some ways, Ben guessed it was. After all, when he emerged from this horrible pit, he'd be bonded to Tanis, and none of their lives would ever be the same. He was sure, too, that by now, the Court of Mountain Fairies had been destroyed. His heart ached at the thought, and it ached equally that the dome full of fearful mountain fairies above him would never see it.

Inevitably, his heartache brought him back to Reina. He thought of her standing in the tunnel, watching him be thrown to his death. He wondered what had happened to her. He hoped Marcus held was holding up his end of the bargain. He hoped he was waiting for Ben to emerge from the Well and take his bond with Tanis. He hoped Reina wasn't already dead.

Suddenly, the ground beneath him began to shift, and he squatted low, bracing against it. The moving earth shivered and shook, and for a moment, Ben thought the ground was cracking. He braced himself to fall further beneath it. But then he was lifted up.

Fragments of dirt, sand, and rock tumbled from the space around him, and it was then Ben realized—he was on top of the dragon's back, being lifted towards the rippling sand-ceiling. He fumbled with his hands as his heart caught in his throat, searching for something to hold. The dragon shook his leathery skin, causing more rock and dust to fling from his shoulders and revealing raised, dark spines fanning out in front of Ben. Just as his feet began to slip, he leapt towards one, hooking it with one hand. He grunted loudly as his body swung, holding tight as the giant drake lifted one clawed foot to step forward.

Quickly, Ben clamped his lips shut. He hadn't meant to make any noise. But it was too late. The dragon had already lifted his head. He sniffed at the air, blowing hot smoke from his nostrils. A low grumbling started in the dragon's throat, and to Ben's shock, he spoke.

"Who dares disturb my slumber?" he growled deeply. He lifted his nose higher in the air, narrowing his large golden eyes at the ground beneath him. "Hmmm, you might as well reveal yourself." He blew another puff of smoke. "I can smell you." He flicked his eyes about the cavern. "Both of you."

Ben's palm was beginning to sweat. His fingers were slipping from the dragon's slick spine, and he hurled his other hand upward, just catching the edge of it. His foot kicked the tender spot just above the dragon's flank with his motion, and he winced as the beast turned his head towards him.

The dragon grinned in Ben's direction, showing two rows of sharp, white teeth. They were as long as Ben's body, and they gleamed in the dim cavern light. "Ahhh, here's one of my intruders." He sniffed at the air. "A young, horrid little thing." He pulled his lips wider. "But you do smell delicious." Ben frowned at the dragon's profile. "Tell me," the dragon continued, "what did you do to be sent into my Well?"

"I did nothing," Ben snapped.

The dragon chuckled low in his broad chest, a rumbling, fearful sound. "Ah, but it cannot be so. Everyone who comes down to meet me has done one thing or another. Even one as young as you." He appraised Ben's hanging body. "But you're not the youngest I have seen. I've eaten one that had yet to pass her sixteenth cycle." He licked his teeth with his forked tongue. "But that made her no less delicious."

A tiny motion in the middle tunnel to their right drew Ben's eyes, and immediately, he regretted looking. Because the dragon whipped his head in Vic's direction, just before the slight fae succeeded in tucking herself back inside the doorway. "Ah! Another horrid, young thing!" the dragon said cheerfully. "A delightful surprise, indeed." He took another heavy step towards Vic's tunnel, and she glared out at him.

The dragon dipped his nose, blowing her short, dark hair off her forehead with his hot breath. "You have a scent reminiscent of my last victim. Nual, I believe was his name?" Vic didn't answer.

She folded her arms and stuck out her chin. Ben had to admit, for all her treachery, she was nothing if not brave.

The dragon curled his long tail around his back legs and shuffled his wide wings, causing a puff of dust to rise into Ben's face. He coughed and sputtered in the haze as the dragon continued. "I was instructed not to kill the fae, you see. Simply"—he lifted one sharp claw in Vic's direction—"maim him." He turned his clawed foot towards his face, clicking two long, dark claws together thoughtfully. "I assume he died later? And then you were sent here?"

Vic fisted her palms. "What happened to Nual is none of your business," she spat. "And if you plan to kill me, then let's get on with it."

The dragon laughed out loud, a booming noise that shook the ground. "Hah! A *brave* one, I see. Well, then. As you wish."

His chest began to glow bright orange beneath his leathered scales, and the heat of it lifted to Ben's face. The spike he had been gripping suddenly became too hot to hold, and he was forced to release it, dropping hard to the ground behind the dragon's right forefoot.

Just as he hit the earth, a loud whirring sound began in the dragon's throat. Ben flicked his eyes to Vic. Her gaze was steady, right on the dragon's face. The orange glow tracked from his chest to his throat, and Ben knew she only had moments before she was covered in flames.

"Watch out!" he shouted. But it was too late. The drake was already spewing a stream of fire, straight in Vic's direction.

Ben watched as she tucked herself flat against the wall of the small tunnel, her back to the drake. When the stream of fire finally stopped, a cloud of smoke hazed over the opening, and he peeked from behind the dragon's wide foot, searching for her. A tiny flicker of flame persisted in the mouth of the tunnel. He heard her screams before he saw her body. Then the smoke cleared.

The back of Vic's dress was on fire. Orange-gold flames licked up the fabric, and she tore at it with her arms, screaming. The tips of the hot fire reached her hair, and she shook her head frantically, then ran from the mouth of the tunnel. She zig-zagged left and right, hysterical from the pain. The dragon tracked her motions with his large head, and before Ben could register, the orange glow had started again. Vic ran furiously to her left, where a wide, gaping slit in the rock perched high above her in the stone wall. Ben peered over at it. It looked like a blind gap in the rock. Deep darkness leached from its interior, and he couldn't see anything past its surface. Its opening was much too high for a small fairy to reach.

As he watched Vic's path, the orange glow in the drake's belly intensified, and Ben crouched low beneath him as the heat from his internal blaze threatened to burn the top of his head. "Vic! Run!" he shouted.

Then the whirring rumble started, and fire spewed from his giant throat.

Vic had reached the far wall by this time. She scratched and leaped at its flat surface, but she was too small, and the gap in the stone was too high. Ben thought about running to her. If he put her on his shoulders, she might've been able to make it to the gap. But his thought came too late. This time, the blaze engulfed her, and the dragon didn't halt his breath until her shrieks were silent.

Ben shrank from her awful cries. The only mercy was that they ended quickly. He stared at her crumpled body lying at the base of the wall. Smoke lifted from what was left of her clothing, and he turned his face as the scent of charred flesh and burned hair lifted to his nose.

The dragon moved towards her, his heavy footfalls shaking the earth. He lifted her limp body gingerly between two claws, then he dropped her into his mouth and swallowed her in one gulp. Ben stood behind, watching in horror. He couldn't believe it. Vic was gone.

When he considered her actions now, Ben thought he understood. She had been protecting Nual, yes. But she'd had even more at stake than any of them knew. Vic had been protecting someone other than her mate by obeying Marcus's commands. She'd been protecting her daughter.

Ben was sure when Vic had told him she had to get back to the banded mountain fairies' camp, she had meant it for Tanis. He thought of her stepping backward over the edge of the pit, the way she'd lovingly touched Tanis's face. Vic had been a mother, and a mother's love had no bounds. Ben could see that now. There was nothing Vic wouldn't have done to protect her daughter from Marcus's gaze, even if it meant planting banded berries in the Timekeeper's Court or bringing Ben to be thrown into the Dragon's Well.

The dragon swung his head, peering behind him where Ben crouched low to the ground. He grinned and chuffed a puff of smoke. "One horrid, little thing down, and one to go," he hissed. The orange glow began in his belly, and Ben could see from the look in his golden eyes that he planned to burn him where he stood. He looked swiftly to his left and right. There was nowhere to go, nowhere to hide, save the three small openings at the end of the room.

The drake took one step towards him, and Ben shot off across the cavern, headed for the furthest tunnel on the left. He could hear the footfalls of the dragon pounding the earth behind him. He ran with all his might, just reaching the opening before the dragon spewed his fiery breath.

Flames licked the back of Ben's shirt, and he leaped, making for the back end of the shallow tunnel. As he jumped, his foot hung on something beneath him, and he pitched forward, falling headlong into the dirt. He flipped swiftly, scrambling to press his back against the cool stone of the back wall. He closed his eyes and let the cold stone seep into his skin. The dragon's breath had only singed him, but it stung all the same.

Ben searched the ground in the middle of the tunnel for what had tripped him, and he was horrified to see the dried, white bones of a lower leg and foot lying at a warped angle. He followed the leg to where it connected to a bony torso, and then a skull. Two more skeletons just like it lay against the side of the tunnel to his right. Fragments of charred clothing clung to their frames, and between the closest two, something slight and metallic glimmered in the dim tunnel light. Ben flicked his eyes to the opening. He could hear the dragon moving outside, but he couldn't see him yet. Silently, he scooted to the right and reached between the two bony arms of the tunnel's former occupants. He could barely see the item for which he was reaching, as it was buried in a charred pile of soot. But then a cool metal blade slicked past his fingers, and he closed his palm around the hilt of the sword.

He crouched in the back of the tunnel, waiting, until a large golden eye lowered itself to the tunnel's opening. It narrowed as the dragon caught sight of Ben. "There's no use hiding, horrid, little thing," he crooned. "The faster we end this, the better. Then I can go back to sleep."

Ben didn't wait. He sprang to his feet and ran headlong towards the eye with the blade of his sword. The eye widened as he closed in, and his blade squished as it sank into its diamond-shaped center with satisfying accuracy.

The dragon roared and pulled backward, but Ben didn't let go. He allowed himself to be lifted by the sword's hilt into the air. The dragon swung his head left and right, bellowing, but still, Ben hung on. His heavy feet staggered towards the wall where Vic's body had lain.

Ben peered behind him as the dragon careened towards the wall. If he didn't move fast, he would be crushed under its weight. He had only a moment to decide. The dark gap in the rock loomed before his eyes. He swung his feet backward and leapt into it, just as the dragon made impact.

Ben rolled forward as the dragon bellowed in anger behind him, then he spun, watching. The dragon lifted his clawed fingers and pulled the sword from his eye, causing black blood to spurt from beneath it. He roared in fury. The orange glow began to lift from his throat, and a whirring sound breached the gap's opening.

Ben sprang onto all fours and scurried backward, narrowly avoiding the drake's hot blaze. The gap was momentarily illuminated by his fiery breath, and Ben could see that the rock angled sharply upward at a short distance in front of him. He dug his nails into the stone, pulling himself forward until he reached it. Then, he hooked his hand on a slim ledge of stone above him and began to climb.

CHAPTER 38

REINA

Water dripped from above Reina's head. She lifted her face to it, allowing it to fall into her mouth. She was so thirsty. She'd asked for a drink, but the guard who had brought her to the small, dark cell had ignored her, and the short fae with the lame foot and the keys had just peered at her sorrowfully. The floor was cold beneath the fabric of her wedding dress, and she shivered, hugging herself with her arms.

Reina laid her head back against the wall. Inevitably, she thought of Ben. Her heart sank as she remembered his expression as he fell past the edge of the pit. *I love you,* he had said. She wondered if the drake had already killed him. She hoped he would escape.

Just then, the short fae and a tall guard appeared at her door. The short fae fumbled through the keys around his neck and lifted one to the lock. It clinked, and her door swung inward. The tall guard jerked his chin, and Reina stood to her feet. Her knees shook and her hand trembled as she braced herself against the wall. She was sure she was headed into the pit behind Ben.

She shuffled slowly out into the dark corridor as the guard pulled her arms roughly behind her back and secured them with a thick leather strap. There could be only three things that would warrant her being brought out of her cell. Either Ben was dead, and Marcus had decided to kill her, *or* Ben had survived but refused to take the bond with Tanis, and she would be killed, *or* Ben had survived and was about to accept the bond with Tanis. If so, she was sure Marcus would want her to witness it. Then, she'd only *wish* that she were dead.

The dark, dungeon corridor stretched out endlessly before her, and her vision began to haze. She glanced down at her wedding dress, now ripped and dirt stained. Could it have been only this morning that she was in the Mortal Realm, on her wedding day? It seemed impossible. Now, she was headed to face Marcus, to face her death. And even worse, to face the fact that she would be separated from Ben. Forever.

CHAPTER 39

BEN

Ben's muscles burned as he pulled himself higher and higher up the steep wall. He reached up again for the next ledge, but his foot slipped at the last moment, and he was left dangling by one arm. He ground his teeth and lifted his other hand to meet it, fighting for grip with his toes. Somewhere above him, he could hear voices…laughter. He frowned.

"Hey!" he shouted. "Down here!"

At once, a thick rope was thrown over, and he gripped it in his palms, pulling himself up the rest of the way. At last, he reached the edge, and he pulled up to his elbows, panting. Above him on the other side, two fae guards stared down at him.

"Welcome back," one said darkly. "The first to make it out this cycle, right, Jin?"

The guard who had carried Ben into the camp and pushed him into the pit stared down at him, grinning darkly.

"Yep. Lucky him."

CHAPTER 40

REINA

The throne room was ablaze with torches. They illuminated the dark cave from every wall and hung in a large, cascading cluster of light, like a makeshift chandelier, from the center of the ceiling. Reina flicked her gaze about the room. Tanis's small frame stood waiting before the throne. A tall guard held tightly to her shoulder. Reina could see she'd been dressed for the occasion, though which occasion, she wasn't sure. A dark formal dress, almost black, hung limply from her thin shoulders, and her wrists were fettered with iron chains.

Just then, the guard who had pushed Ben into the pit appeared from the shadows beyond the throne. Reina searched his face frantically, and soon, Ben appeared behind him. Her heart leapt in relief. She scanned his soot-stained body for injury. He was moving normally, and besides a dark spatter across his face and shirt, there were no signs of blood. He didn't appear to be hurt. He flicked his eyes up, searching the room as Jin and the other guard brought him before the throne. He caught sight of her, just as Jin hauled him to stand beside Tanis. She smiled tightly at him, and he returned the gesture, his face a swirl of relief and sorrow.

Marcus stood from the throne, clasping his hands in front of his waist. Reina could see he was wearing his best dress—a thick crown made from the Banded Berry vines and a dark leather cloak that hung past his knees.

"It seems you've survived the drake, after all, Benjamin. How delightful," Marcus crooned. "Though the girl's mother wasn't as lucky." He gestured to Tanis, who stood silent, staring at the floor. "Now, all we've left is the rest of our bargain."

He flicked his fingers quickly towards Reina's guard, and she was hauled roughly to stand in the center of the room, just behind Ben and Tanis. The guard held the blade of his spear to her throat as Ben swung his head to her. "Don't touch her!" he shouted.

Another guard hit him behind the knees with the blunt of his spear, and Ben crumpled to the floor. His golden eyes were full of grief as he stared up at her.

"I'm sorry, Rei" he murmured. "I'm so sorry."

Reina pressed her lips, swallowing against the sharp blade. She blinked once to let him know she'd understood.

The bond ceremony took only moments. It was uneventful, and flat at best. Both Ben and Tanis kneeled before Marcus. He bid them both to hold out their palms, and in turn, he sliced a shallow gash in the center of each with his sword. Then he joined their hands and spoke a few words with his sword held high.

"The bond of blood is now unbroken. Let what we have joined this day be everlasting, and if one should so break it, let it be to their death."

The blade was, at once, removed from Reina's neck, and she swallowed hard, blinking at the side of Ben's face. He never looked at her, and instead, focused his eyes on Tanis, whose hands he still held. Tanis never raised her eyes, and tears dripped off her cheeks to the floor. Reina peered desperately at Ben's profile. She willed him to look at her. But he didn't.

He smiled as Tanis raised her eyes to his face. The corners of Tanis's trembling lips smiled back at him, and Reina's heart sank. She blinked at them both in confusion. Was there something to Marcus's bond? Was it more than just some false bond of his own making? Had Ben and Tanis chosen this? Maybe they had. Otherwise, why were they looking at each other like that?

Reina's stomach turned as she watched Ben gaze into the small fae's startling lavender eyes. She wished Amelie had never come for her. If she hadn't, she'd have never come back to Caelium. She would have never had to see Ben holding hands with his new mate, smiling like she was the only one for him in the known worlds. Her guard pulled on her arm, and gratefully, she dropped her eyes.

She didn't look back at them as she was hauled outside. She couldn't. Her heart couldn't take it anymore.

Chapter 41

BEN

Ben's heart ached as Reina was dragged outside. He could see from his peripheral gaze that she was staring at him, but there was nothing he could do. He couldn't look at her, couldn't give Marcus any reason to believe that the bond he had imposed on him and Tanis was anything but rock solid. He whispered to Tanis under his breath, causing her to raise her eyes. "Smile," he whispered through his teeth. She lifted her eyes and managed a quick grin. Then her face fell, and she was crying again. "Tanis, you've got to stop, okay?" he murmured.

She nodded, swiping the tears from her cheek with her forearm. "'Kay," she muttered. "I'll try."

Soon, the throne room began emptying, and he and Tanis were escorted outside. Ben scanned the landscape for Reina, but he could see no sign of her.

Jin held up a small key before Ben's eyes. Ben blinked at it. "What's this?" he asked him.

Jin jerked his head to Tanis's wrists. "The shackles. You can keep them or not. Marcus doesn't care now that the bond is done."

Ben glared at Jin as he swiped the key. "I think not," he said flatly. He turned to Tanis and shoved the key into the locks, freeing her wrists. She lifted them to her chest and rubbed the red spots where the metal had pinched.

Jin stepped towards her, holding a finger in her face. "But if you try to run, they go back on again," he hissed. She frowned up at him with her violet eyes, then nodded. "Good," Jin spat. "Now, go."

He pushed Tanis forward, and Ben lunged to catch her fall. He grasped her arm just before her hands smacked the hard dirt, and she quickly pulled herself upright, glaring at Jin's grin behind her.

"Come on," she muttered to Ben. "I'll show you where we're staying."

They walked for a long time, weaving in and out of the small huts made of twisted vines. Shadowed faces of fae men, women, and children hovered in the doorways, and Ben couldn't help but notice their looks of despair. Tanis moved past them, towards countless other dwellings, and Ben was shocked again at the sheer number of mountain fairies who had escaped the fire of the drake.

They stopped at a small hut near the edge of the fortress wall, and Tanis moved towards the door. She turned to him. "This was my mother's home," she said quietly. "Now, it will be ours."

Ben stepped through the threshold, peering about him. A small bedroll lay in the far corner and a cooking pot rested over a fire pit in the middle of the room. Tanis knelt to it and twisted her palm, igniting the flames.

Ben looked to her in surprise. "You are a Timekeeper," he murmured.

Tanis tucked her short hair behind one pointed ear. "Yes. My father was, also. And his father before him." Ben studied her as she stirred the contents of the pot.

She stood, smoothing her dress as she moved to the back of the small room. There, a small, thin rug sat beneath a single chair. She moved the chair to the side, her lavender eyes scanning the doorway. She lifted the rug's corner. A latched wooden door with an iron ring was hidden beneath it. She slid her eyes to Ben.

"This is where I was hidden, away from Marcus and his prying eyes. I'm most comfortable down here, so it's where I'll sleep, if you don't mind."

Ben nodded mutely, and she gave him a small smile. He didn't know what to think. Then, without another word, she lifted the latch of the door and disappeared behind it.

Ben tossed and turned on the bedroll all night. He was worried about Reina, where she was, if she was okay. He knew he'd hurt her at the bonding ceremony. Tomorrow, he'd have to find a way to get to her somehow. Tanis would be fine in his absence. He was sure of it. She was good at hiding. She'd done it her entire life. No one would ever think to look for her under the floor. She could stay there until he returned.

After he apologized to Reina… Well, Ben didn't know what would happen after that. He crossed his arms over his chest, thinking. He supposed he would live out his days here. With Tanis.

Ben frowned, blinking into the darkness. That didn't suit.

He thought of the countless faces, full of fear, that had looked down on him from the arena, of the wretched woman and the short fae with the lame foot in the dungeons, of all the wings pinned to Marcus's sickening wall. No. That didn't suit at all.

When he returned, he was going to do more than simply accept his fate. Much more. He was going to find a way to free his people. He was going to bring them all back with him to the Court of Mountain Fairie, no matter what.

CHAPTER 42
REINA

Reina hit the ground with a hard thump. The guard had dropped her outside the pass, then turned wordlessly to go. All the way out, she had thought he was going to kill her. But instead, he just left her here. Alone. She rolled onto her back and stared up at the sky, allowing herself to catch her breath.

Ben had taken the bond with Tanis. If it was anything like the bond she knew, it was unbreakable. Eternal. Reina's very center ached at the thought. The feeling radiated down her arms, and she squeezed her palms tightly.

There was nothing for it. There was nothing she could do. But at least Ben was alive. And, for now, so was she.

A lump formed in her throat, tears stinging her eyes. Maybe Ben didn't want saving. After the ceremony, he'd smiled down at Tanis like he actually loved her—like their bond was true. Reina closed her eyes. She'd just have to accept it. Ben was gone.

She rolled to her feet, trudging in the direction of the Court of Mountain Fairies. She hoped it was still there. When she'd last seen it, it had been covered in a dome of water, and a ring of fire had encircled the court with thick flames. She moved silently through the pass until she came to the grove of trees beyond. Suddenly, someone sprang out from behind her, holding a blade to her throat. She held up her hands, blinking.

The blade relaxed.

"Ah, it's just you," came a familiar voice from behind her.

Reina blew out her breath. "Henri," she said quietly.

Henri moved in front of her. "How is he?" he asked.

Reina bit her cheek. "He's alive." She dropped her eyes. "And he's taken a bond."

The muscle in Henri's jaw flexed. "And Vic?"

Reina lifted her head, her eyes sorrowful. "She's gone, Henri, I'm so sorry."

Henri hung his head for a moment. "She wasn't who we thought she was, was she?" he said quietly.

Reina shook her head again. "No, she wasn't. But she has a daughter. Her name is Tanis."

Henri lifted his eyes, scanning the pass behind her. "Tanis," he said thoughtfully.

Reina pushed the door to the great hall closed behind her. There was too much activity outside. Too many questions.

To her amazement, the court was still standing, with not even a scorch at its edges. Most of the Force and Guard from the Court of the Sea were still there, along with Arto, Chaeronne and his sons. But Reina didn't want to see anyone.

She slid down the doorway, landing hard on the ground. Tears gathered in her gaze as she glanced at the floor beside her. Jubal's blood stain had once marred the spot, but now, the dark wood had been scrubbed clean.

She put her hand to the spot, suddenly remembering her and Ben's promise to him. She wiped her eyes. Tomorrow, she'd retrieve Jubal's bones where they rested at the back of his cave. She'd carry them through the open court doors and place them at the Northwest Corner, in a place of honor.

CHAPTER 43

BEN

Morning came slowly, but it came all the same. Just after sunrise, Tanis appeared from the door in the floor and wordlessly began stoking the fire. Ben sat up on the bedroll.

"Good morning," he said quietly.

She flicked her eyes to him. "Good morning."

Ben studied her profile. "How would you like to get out of here?" he whispered.

She lifted her violet eyes, and a tiny smile touched the corners of her lips. "Only if they all come with us," she said quietly.

Ben smiled. "I wouldn't have it any other way."

Within moments, he and Tanis had crafted a plan. Tanis's hole in the floor beneath the rug was more than just a hole. There was a hidden passage beneath it that led to the mountain pass. Ben would sneak away and alert Reina and those in the Court of Mountain Fairies of what was coming. While there, he'd retrieve his weapons and some help, and then he'd return to the fortress to kill Marcus and his guards, thereby freeing himself, Tanis, and all the rest. And he wouldn't forget those in the dungeons.

Tanis, meanwhile, would serve as a distraction. Jin had been set outside their dwelling as a guard. Ben had noticed a gleam in Jin's eye when he pointed his finger in Tanis's face. He could tell the tall fae was taken with her. Tanis had her mother's beauty, and Ben was sure she could beguile him while he was gone. It would give Ben plenty of time to do what he needed to do and to return to the camp undetected.

Tanis nodded as she lifted herself from beside the small fire. She moved to the doorframe, leaning softly against it. "Good morning, Jin," she said sweetly. Sneaking quietly from the bedroll, Ben could hear the smile in Jin's voice. *Good.* His suspicions had been right. Silently, he moved the rug and lifted the iron handle on Tanis's room. Then, he slipped inside and out of sight.

Chapter 44

REINA

Jubal's bones were still covered by the threadbare blanket, right where she and Ben had left him. Henri had helped her carry a long box up the hill for them, but he'd left when she'd asked. Reina felt like she needed to do this alone. After all, it was she and Ben that Jubal had asked.

It was sort of morbid, what he'd asked of them—carrying his bones into the restored court. Reina had thought she would be squeamish about it, but the act felt so sacred that she found she had no problem doing it. She knelt beside him and touched one curled horn sticking up above the blanket's edge. "You're going home, Jubal," she said quietly.

Just as she started to lift the blanket, someone cleared their throat behind her, and she turned abruptly, holding her dagger to the intruder's throat. Ben's face stared down at her, grinning. His golden eyes danced in the morning light, and there was a thick stubble growing on the turn of his chin. It did funny things to her stomach, and she dropped her blade along with her eyes, suddenly embarrassed. "What are you doing here?" she whispered.

Ben knelt beside her, smiling quietly. "What, you think I'd leave you to Jubal's bones all by yourself? Not a chance." He brushed past her and lifted Jubal's small frame, blanket and all, and laid them reverently into the box. He closed the lid, then turned to face her.

Reina wouldn't meet his gaze. She couldn't. He knelt beside her, lifting her chin with his rough palm, but she kept her eyes carefully averted. "Rei, are you going to look at me?" he asked her.

She tucked her lips. Already, a large lump was forming in her throat. If he didn't stop, she was going to cry.

"I wanted to ask you," he said quietly. "Why did you come back here?"

She flicked her eyes to his face, and her anger inexplicably flared. Didn't he know by now that she would come? She raised her voice. "To rescue you, you idiot!"

Ben blinked at her in shock, then broke into an easy laugh. He pulled her into a hug, pressing her to his chest. "Of course, you did." He pushed gently away, holding her at arm's length. "Any other reasons?" he asked, eyes gleaming.

She dropped her eyes, looking away from him. "You know why," she muttered.

He pulled her chin back to face him. "Yes," he said quietly. "I do."

He lowered his face to hers, and before Reina could stop him, he was kissing her. And despite herself, she was returning his kiss. *Ben.* Unable to help herself, she wrapped her arms around his neck, pressing him to her as his hands swept around her back.

Suddenly, her eyes popped open, and she pulled her arms away. She pushed her hands hard against Ben's chest, backing towards the wall. He stared after her, confusion creasing his features.

She shook her head. "No, Ben. We can't," she whispered. "Your bond. You took a bond with Tanis."

Ben sighed. He ran a hand through his hair, giving her his lopsided grin. "You think that matters?" he said quietly. "You think what happened in Marcus's fake throne room was real? That the stupid bond he made us take held any truth?"

Reina folded her arms. She shrugged. "From what I could see in your smile, it looked pretty real."

He stepped towards her and pulled her arms apart, taking her hands as he peered deeply into her eyes. "Well, it wasn't, Reina. It wasn't real at all. It wasn't a *true* bond. Not one of my choosing. Not one of true love." He stepped closer, dipping his head. "I *had* to fake it. To pretend. To keep you safe."

He gripped her chin, rubbing her jaw with his thumb. "What

we have is real. You and I. The only *true* bond I have is with you."
He paused, studying her face. "You feel it, too, don't you?"

Reina smiled quietly. "Yes," she murmured. "I feel it."

After Jubal's bones were safely stored at the Northwest Corner of the Western Wall, Ben and Reina went to find the rest of the group. They gathered at the corner, just outside the doors. Kai, Chaeronne, Arto, the Timekeepers, and all the rest listened intently as Ben outlined their plan.

Ben had decided. They were going to free the mountain fairies. All of them.

CHAPTER 45
TANIS

Tanis leaned heavily against the doorframe of her dwelling. She inclined her body towards Jin, watching his eyes as she lifted a medallion hanging around his neck. "What's this?" she asked him playfully. Jin grinned down at her, then flicked his eyes to his chest and back up again. "It's nothing, just something Marcus issues to his guards."

Tanis leaned her head thoughtfully. "Can I wear it?"

Jin nodded. Grinning, he pulled the necklace over his head and placed it around her neck. She giggled, batting her lashes as she grasped his arm.

Suddenly, Jin frowned. Tanis froze as he stepped forward and swept his eyes around their dwelling. She stepped into the doorway nervously. The edge of the rug was flipped back. She had forgotten to lower it over her door. She backed away as Jin narrowed his eyes. He stalked towards her, his spear aimed at her throat. Its tip tapped hard against the medallion.

"Where is he?" he ground out. "Where is Ben?"

Tanis swallowed nervously. "He's gone."

CHAPTER 46
BEN

Ben moved silently through the pass. He ignored the heavy weight of the air and the sinister feeling that gripped him across his chest. Soon, it would all be over. The pass would open, and he would be back in Marcus's dark fortress again.

Kai moved just behind him, his spear aloft, his sharp merrow eyes flicking in all directions. Reina and the others had stayed in the valley to defend the court. Only he, Kai, and a few other members of the Force and Guard had come this way.

They were almost free of the pass's tight walls, when suddenly, Kai grunted from behind him. Ben swung his blade, narrowly missing the blurred figure that had dropped onto Kai's shoulders.

He swung again as the fae brought a blade tightly to Kai's throat. Before the fae could move, Ben brought his dagger up through the fae's back. A sharp grunt bit the heavy air, and then Kai tossed the attacker from his shoulders, leaving a limp figure lying between them on the ground. Ben's breath was coming hard and fast. He flicked his eyes to Kai.

"They know," he whispered. "They know we're coming."

CHAPTER 47
REINA

Back at the Court of Mountain Fairies, Reina stood motionless before the doors. Henri stood to her left, and Johann was just beyond them. Suddenly, a blurred figure moved inside the tree line, just to the left of the pass. Reina crouched low.

"Henri, did you see that?" she whispered.

"I saw it." He lifted his bow, aiming at the spot, but before he could release, three mountain fairies, whose faces were marked with a dark blue band, sprang from the tall grasses. They leapt onto Johann's back, and Henri released his arrow, hitting one of them squarely in the side of his neck. He fell to the earth as Reina twisted her palms, igniting a ball of fire over each hand. She kept her eyes trained on the other fae, who were battling against a selkie and merrow at the base of the Western Wall.

"They know Ben's coming," she shouted. Henri loaded another arrow as Reina tossed a ball of fire towards the closest fae's head. He dodged it and began charging towards her. Henri released his second arrow, lodging it in the fae's broad chest.

Three more banded fairies moved out of the pass, charging towards them with their spears. A wall of water pushed up from a group of merrows to the right of the fae. It doused them in a large wave, dropping them to the earth.

Reina frowned. "I need to get to him," she shouted, tossing her second fireball. The flame hit its mark, igniting the hem of one fae's dark shirt.

Henri released a third arrow. "Go!" he said, gritting his teeth. "Go save them!"

CHAPTER 48

BEN

Ben slashed with his left hand, then his right. His arms burned, and sweat poured into his eyes. Bodies of banded fae warriors littered the ground around him, and he stepped across the large one he'd just felled, heading towards the throne room. Behind him, Kai swung hard with his spear while the rest created a giant wall of water that threw their opponents off their feet.

The inside of Marcus's throne room was dark and quiet—too quiet. At the back of the room, Ben could see Marcus sitting calmly on his throne of bones, turning a long dagger over and over in his palms. He flicked his eyes to Ben.

"Ah, Benjamin. So good of you to rejoin us." He balanced the blade of the dagger on his first two fingers. "And what brings you to see me this fine day?"

Ben glared at the dagger in his brother's palm. It looked about the right size and shape for the wound he'd inflicted on Ben's side that day. He frowned up at him.

"Marcus, this has gone on long enough. I'm here to give you two choices. Either you release the clan, or you die. Today." Marcus chuckled under his breath. He stood lazily, bouncing the hilt of the dagger to his palm. "I don't think that's how it's gonna go," he said, grinning. He took a lunging step towards Ben, and with it, he flung the dagger, sending it whizzing by Ben's ear. Ben smiled as the dagger missed, then he crouched into a defensive position and raised his own dagger high. Marcus pulled a sword from his side as he descended to the floor, then the two lunged.

Metal clanked against metal as Ben and Marcus swung violently at each other's heads.

Ben ground his teeth. "You don't have to do this, Marcus," he shouted. "You can let go. Turn away from this darkness! Come with me. Come home!"

Marcus swung hard at Ben's side, and Ben spun out of the line of the sword's path. The tip of the blade ripped the fabric of his already tattered shirt. Marcus frowned. "Never," he said flatly. Ben lunged forward, sparring until Marcus was backed into the hall. He continued pressing his brother until they emerged inside the wide dome beyond it.

Marcus swung left and right, narrowly missing Ben's neck. Ben held him off, clanking his shorter weapon against the long sword as he moved steadily forward.

He flicked his eyes beyond Marcus's shoulder. The edge of the pit was just beyond them.

Suddenly, Marcus side-stepped and spun, putting Ben between himself and the wide well in the earth. He lunged forward, pressing the tip of his sword against Ben's throat as he backed him to the pit's edge.

Ben raised his chin, fighting for balance against the edge of the blade and the edge of the earth below. Marcus grinned down the length of the sword. There was no light left in his eyes.

"I'll never give in. This is my home now."

Ben searched his brother's face. There was nothing but darkness there. Ben knew in that moment that his brother was gone. Marcus was Marcus no longer. Only a twisted version remained. There was no hope of seeing Marcus to redemption.

With his last bit of strength, he swung his dagger up to the sword. It knocked the tip from his throat, and Ben ducked, spinning away from the pit's edge, putting his brother between him and the pit. Marcus swung hard. Ben missed the block, and the tip of it slashed across his upper stomach. He jumped backward with the sting, reflexively swinging his dagger and knocking the blade from his brother's hand.

Marcus was off balance from the move, and he stumbled, his

feet unsteady at the pit's wide edge. Ben made eye contact just as his brother slipped.

"Marcus!" Ben shouted. But it was too late.

His brother glanced up at him, just before his body dropped below the ledge. Marcus's expression hadn't changed. His eyes were as dark as the well below him.

Marcus had become darkness itself.

Ben shut his eyes, falling to his knees in exhaustion. He imagined the drake burning Marcus to ash under the ground beneath him, and he shuddered. He wouldn't wish that on anyone. Not even someone as horrible as Marcus.

Ben buried his head in his hands. As much as he knew there was no choice, he still grieved that his brother was truly gone.

Silence echoed in the stillness before him, until a shrill scream pierced the air at his back. Ben's eyes snapped open.

Reina.

CHAPTER 49

REINA

Reina flicked her eyes from side to side. The throne room was empty. She stalked further in, blinking against the dim light.

Outside, there had been no movement. When she'd arrived, Kai and the others had been sitting on the ground, heaving and covered in sweat. Dead fae guards littered the ground around them, and the people were still hidden in their houses, too fearful to investigate.

A single, long dagger was lying on the floor of the throne room, and she bent to retrieve it, turning it over and over in her palm. Her heart chilled at the design. It was the same one Marcus had used when he'd tried to kill Ben. A dark line, like ink, gleamed at its sharp edge. Banded Berry poison.

Beyond the darkness of the far hall, she heard a shout. It sounded like it was coming from the dome. She gripped the dagger in her palm and stood, heading towards it.

Just then, she heard a slight noise behind her. A sharp burn pierced her back. She gasped, looking down at her midsection. A gleaming blade poked through the bodice of her wedding dress. It was sticking through her upper stomach, the blade's edge dark with berry poison. Reflexively, she reached for it. But just as suddenly, it was gone.

A sharp sound bit her ears as she fell to the earth. It could have been her screaming, but she wasn't sure. All she remembered was seeing Jin's hard face leaning over her as she lay flat on the ground. "He should've killed you when he had the chance," he hissed. "But I always have to do Marcus's dirty work."

Hot, red blood was pooling on the stone floor beneath her, and she could feel her life draining out with it. With her last bit of strength, she gripped her small dagger hard in her palm, and swung it sideways, lodging it in the side of Jin's throat. It sank deeply. Immediately, Jin's eyes went flat, and he fell to the floor beside her.

CHAPTER 50

BEN

Ben held his middle as he jogged back up the hallway. Blood seeped between his fingers from Marcus's sword wound, and already, his head was growing fuzzy. He knew it was the Banded Berry poison from the blade.

Ahead, he could see Jin's body lying limply on the floor of the throne room. And just beyond him, a tangled mass of red hair lay in a pool of dark blood. He frowned at the familiar frame. "Reina," he whispered. Then louder, "Reina!"

He increased his pace, rushing to her side and pulling Jin's body backward from where it lay on her arm. He knelt to her, putting his hands to the sides of her pale face. Her green eyes fluttered open. "Ben?" she murmured.

He smiled, relief washing over him in a wave. "Yes. It's me, Reina. It's Ben." He brought his face low, kissing her lips. They were cool to the touch.

The pool of her blood continued to widen below him, wetting his knees. He searched her torso for its source. Finding it, he pulled his shirt free and wadded it into a ball, pressing hard on the spot. Reina flicked her weak gaze to the gash on his abdomen. A wide stream of blood poured from it, mixing his blood with her own on the floor. She reached a limp hand towards it. "You're hurt, too," she rasped.

Ben shook his head. "It doesn't matter now," he said quietly.

Ben could feel the flow of life trickling out with his own blood. The poison from the blade was coursing through him, and his arms were growing numb. He couldn't think clearly. He glanced down at his torso, wincing. The wound was deeper than he'd realized. It was bleeding heavily.

He searched the floor beneath Reina as the pool of her own blood widened. He frowned. His efforts weren't slowing the flow, and she was growing more pale by the moment. Or maybe it was his blood he was seeing there.

At last, his hands grew too weak. He released them from her wound. He couldn't hold them there any longer. In fact, he couldn't feel his arms. All he wanted was to lie down and sleep. But Reina, she needed him. His mind swirled, his vision going double. He blinked. Maybe he could rest a bit first. Reina would be alright.

Wearily, he laid himself beside her on the stone. She turned her head to him, and a weak smile formed on her pale face. Weakly, Ben brushed the hair from her eyes.

"I love you, Ben," she whispered. "I always have."

He nodded, a lump forming in his throat. He struggled to speak around it. "I know. I love you, too," he said quietly.

A spark of light lit her eyes at his words, then it faded just as fast. She struggled to speak. "If you leave the door open for me, if you wait for me, outside of it, I'll lie down all night behind it." She swallowed, her voice thinning. "And in the morning, I'll still be there, waiting for you."

Ben smiled. His heart swelled. "I've always left the door open for you, Reina. Even before the doors of the court were rebuilt, the door of my heart was always open to you."

Her eyes fluttered. Ben could tell she was having a hard time keeping them open. She smiled softly. "So, we're agreed, then?" she whispered.

Ben nodded, kissing her cheek. "We're agreed."

She smiled a tiny smile. "Good. Then kiss me, and we'll take the bond. Forever."

Ben pulled her close, cradling her in his arms. He reached a shaking hand into his pocket, pulling out the other bracelet from where he'd kept it all this time. Then he lowered his lips to her own. He kissed her long and deep, realizing with bittersweetness that his lips were the same temperature as hers now.

As he kissed her, a funny feeling started at the back of his shoulders. A sweet burning, a warm light. It felt good. Right. True.

Henri and Johann appeared above them. From the corner of Ben's gaze, he could see their lips moving, but he couldn't hear their voices. Ben didn't try to hear them. It didn't matter what they were saying now.

All his focus was on Reina's perfect face. She was still and quiet now—at peace. And soon, Ben would be, too. He closed his eyes. He could feel himself fading fast. And he knew when he awoke, she'd be right there, waiting.

CHAPTER 51

BEN

Ben was in free fall again. Or…was he was swimming? If he was being honest, he really wasn't sure. He kicked with his legs, and smooth water sluiced past his ankles. So, it was swimming, then.

But how was he in water? He flicked through his last memories, searching for an answer, but he couldn't come up with one. The last thing he remembered was lying in Marcus's throne room with Reina, watching as she faded from his life. He squinted in the open water, remembering. He'd been fading, too.

Suddenly, he had the terrifying notion that he was back in the Dragon's Well, and he flailed in the darkness, trying to avoid the current. He pulled hard with his arms, hoping he was headed to the surface, then he paused, testing the water's weight. Ben frowned. There was no dreadful current, no panic in his system. So, that couldn't be right.

He allowed himself to float a moment in the water's peaceful silence. No, this felt different than the Well had. In fact, it felt completely different. It felt wonderful. He let his arms relax and fluttered his feet as he rose.

Above him, glimmering light glittered along the water's surface. The light danced down towards him, creating iridescent patterns on his face. Ben lifted his arm, reaching for the long prisms. He opened and closed his palm, watching the light play across his hand. It was mesmerizing.

As he opened it again, the prisms of light collected themselves into one glowing, silver strand. He grasped it, pulling up on its long, winding path to the surface. As he climbed, the air in his chest grew thin. But he didn't panic. Instead, he let his legs relax and reached hand over hand to continue ascending on the long stream of light.

At last, his hands broke the surface, and the light scattered, dissipating into the trees. Ben looked down. He was suddenly standing in a shallow pool. Smooth pebbles squished between his toes, and a dappled, golden light shone down through the giant, overhanging oak trees' branches, creating iridescent, dancing patterns on the wide pool's surface. He looked to his left and right, realizing his pool was connected to a wide river. It twisted over wide stones with a gentle current as it wound beyond him to disappear behind the grey mountains.

Ben eyed the mountains fondly. They looked somewhat like his West Mountains home, but they were different, too. As he studied the landscape, somewhere in the back of his mind, a vague familiarity of his surroundings began to bubble to the surface. A warm, homey feeling grew in his belly. A nostalgia. A peace. He was certain he had been here before.

A gentle breeze lifted the tips of his hair, and then a soft Wind whispered through the treetops. It glided past Ben's ears, creating the sensation of tinkling laughter all around him.

Across the water, a pair of Weeping Willows began to sway. Ben watched them, mesmerized, as the Wind drifted through their long branches. He had the distinct feeling that the trees were dancing and—was that music? Ethereal melodies drifted with the laughter in the Winds, and he peered closer between the Willows as their branches began to part.

There, in their midst, was a large set of doors. Ben blinked at them. They weren't like the ones in the Court of Mountain Fairies. No, these doors were quite different. Ben moved towards the opposite bank, enjoying the gentle current swirling around his ankles. He stepped onto dry ground, and moved past the willows, drawn to the doors by a curious force he could not explain.

The Willows' branches closed behind him like a quiet cocoon. Inside, the soft melody grew louder. It was surrounding Ben now—a thousand ethereal voices swirling about him. They seemed to be coming from every tree in the forest.

The wide doors rose quite high above Ben's head. He lifted his hand, trailing the winding engravings on their gleaming surface. He'd seen these doors somewhere before…but where?

And then, it dawned on him. They were just like the doors to the throne room at Leyth Castle. An identical set. He examined them further, raising his brows in surprise. The right door was open, just a slit. Without thinking further, Ben pulled it wide.

There, in a bed of wild Mountain Aster, lay Reina. She was sleeping, and the air around her wavered and quivered—much like a gate. In fact, the whole surface of the doorway quivered in the muted forest light. He placed his hand flat against the wavering air, and a thrill coursed up his arm and into his chest. It ignited his Amloga Flame, and Ben gasped as his left chest glowed brightly through his white shirt.

The light flowed out from his Amloga. It coursed through his arms, running up to his head and down through his legs until his entire body glowed with the white light. Last, it curled around his back, illuminating his newly acquired iridescent wings all the way to their tips. The feeling was one of unspeakable joy. A fullness. Right and true.

He stepped through.

Ben blinked at the quick change in his surroundings. He was back at the palace, in the Court of Mountain Fairies. He studied the grand hall. It looked exactly the same as before. There were the high-backed seats, the tapestries and carpets, the windows—all of it. He moved further inside.

"Reina?" he called.

Her voice lifted from a back room. "In the kitchen!" she replied. Ben grinned.

Her back was facing the doorway, and he leaned against the jam, studying her figure. She hummed as she worked, and her hair was piled on top of her head, held away from her face by a wide, green band. Some little pieces had escaped their bonds, and she wiped them back with her forearm. As quietly as he could, he moved towards her, then tucked his arms around her waist. He buried his nose in the crook of her neck, inhaling. She smelled of cake batter. "What are you making?" he asked her.

Reina lifted the spoon, then turned her body to face him and wrapped one arm around the back of his neck. She tipped her chin. "I'm making a cake—for my Mortal birthday," she said happily.

Ben nodded mutely. He had only vaguely understood her. He was too absorbed in the movement of her mouth to catch what she was saying.

He frowned down at her. "How old are you again?"

She grinned, pointing the spoon at him. "It doesn't really matter now, does it? Not when you have forever." She popped the spoon in her mouth, then licked her lips. "Mmm, it's good. Want a taste?"

"Yes," he whispered, lowering his lips. "I would."

He touched her lips with his own, and all of the troubles of his old life were forgotten. This life was something new. Something enduring. This was him and Reina, forever. And for Ben, that would always be enough.

Reluctantly, Ben pulled himself backward. "I just remembered something."

Reina frowned. "What?"

Ben sighed and tucked a loose curl behind Reina's ear. "Jubal's bones. I wonder if they're still here."

Reina grinned. "I've already checked."

Ben frowned. "What do you mean?"

Reina smiled. "I checked for Jubal's bones when I first arrived." She shrugged. "They're not here."

Ben blinked. "What? How?"

Reina grinned up at him and popped another kiss onto his mouth. "There aren't any bones where we now live, Benjamin. Only bodies—healed and whole." She smiled lightly, excitement lighting her eyes. "Jubal's healed body is already here."

Ben raised his brows. "He is?"

Reina giggled. "Of course, silly. He lives in the Northwest Corner with the rest of his family."

Ben braced his hands on the countertop behind her, and Reina giggled again at his shocked expression. She set down her spoon and wiped her hands on a small towel.

Behind them, on the countertop, two identical bracelets lay side by side. She slid one on to each wrist, then placed both arms back around Ben's neck. She lifted her face, studying his eyes.

"They're all here, Ben. Your mother, your father, Ita, everyone who was lost to Marcus, to Orm—all of them. In fact, everyone is waiting for us. They're all so excited to see you. They've been waiting for so long."

The cake batter was left abandoned as Ben and Reina hurried from the palace. Daylight was gone, and scores of hanging lanterns crisscrossed the air above them in the cobblestone street. Light, gentle melodies wafted between the warm buildings to their left and right, and a brilliant, starry sky unlike any Ben had ever witnessed peeked down at them between the lights. Ahead, Ben could see the gentle sway of couples as they danced. Every face held joy and delight, and everywhere, there were wings.

Jubal swirled with a slight, satyr woman, but he was younger now. His movements were smooth, and his face was unmarred by grief. He caught sight of Ben and grinned over his mate's small head. "Ah, Benjamin, at last you have come." He moved to pull

Ben into a full embrace, then he stepped back, studying Ben's eyes.

Ben frowned down at him. "Your bones, Jubal. I brought them, like you said. I didn't forget."

Jubal flipped his hand. "Ah, leave the bones to fall to dust! They were old and worn out, anyway. I've no need for them any longer." He spun in a circle, dancing a small jig. Ben chuckled at his spry movements. "Besides," Jubal said wryly, wiggling his brows, "I've got a new set."

Past Jubal's shoulder, a small, dark fairy woman was waiting. Like the others, she was younger than Ben remembered. He moved past Jubal in haste and broke into a run as his mother held out her arms.

"Benjamin," she breathed, as he crushed her with a hug. "It has been so long."

His father stepped beside her, bracing his rough hand across Ben's back. "My son," he said, his voice gravel. Ben wrapped his free arm around him as his mother pulled backward, placing her small hands on each side of Ben's face.

"And yet, it feels as if no Time has passed." She shrugged. "But that is the nature of the Hereafter. Time holds no bonds for us, once we have passed beyond it."

Ben's grandmother Ita appeared by his mother. Her voice was caught by her joy as she pulled him down to hug her small frame, and he chuckled despite himself. Playfully, he tugged on the edge of her hair. Her hazel eyes were the same, but dark golden tendrils peeked out at him from under her kerchief. Ben was amazed. He had never seen Ita without her grey hair.

She kissed his cheek. "Welcome, Benjamin," she breathed. "I've missed you."

He hugged her once more, squeezing his eyes shut against happy tears. "I've missed you, too, Ita," he breathed. She smiled.

His mother took his hands, her eyes gleaming. She pointed at the lanterns over her head. "Every day here is the Festival of Light. The open door in the valley was only a foretaste of what has come. The love of the first mountain fairy for his mate and the love you and Reina and many others have shared on the other side is here, perfected, as are all things. And it is the Great Wish of the Source that all beings pass through the open door to the Hereafter, where, for us all, the Source has redeemed all things.

"In the former life, all Caelium rejoices. For there, the Court of Mountain Fairies is restored to its former glory, twice over. Marcus's dark fortress has been destroyed, and with it, the great Dragon's Well has been filled in. Those whom Marcus held captive have been made free, both above the ground and below, and the Western Wall brims with messages of good will and messages of peace to the Source."

Relief washed over Ben, but then he frowned. A thought had just occurred to him. "Who will rule the restored court?" he asked her.

His mother smiled, but it was Ita who answered. "It will be you, Benjamin. You and your Reina."

Ben frowned. "But…how? We're here now. Why would we return?"

His grandmother smiled patiently. "It is the will of the Source. Nothing in all creation can stop the fulfillment of that great desire. In mercy, Amelie was allowed to make it to you with the Sacred Thistle just in time. You have been allowed past the open door into the Hereafter, but you cannot stay. It is not time yet, you see. The Source has more work for you to do."

Ben took her hands. "But I'm not sure I want to return," he said quietly. "Everything is so perfect here. And you are all with me. There is a chance if I go back, the darkness will come to us again. We will have to fight to keep the light."

His grandmother reached above her, grasping a hanging lantern. She held it to eye level. "The light is within you, Ben. And it always will be. True, you will have struggles in the former life. But the darkness will always be overcome. For the flame within you is strong and mighty. It burns with the very power of the Source." She placed a hand to Ben's cheek. "And besides, we will see you again when your work is done. You and your Reina will dwell with us here in the end."

Later that evening, Ben danced with Reina in the streets, just as Jubal had said he would. And after, they stood with all the rest, each holding a lantern in their palms. They whispered words to the flame inside it. Words of true love for each other. Words given to them by the Source.

Ben thought of all that had come to pass. A flood of memories swept over him, and with them came a clarity he had never known. For the first time, he truly understood the depth of the open door in the valley of the Court of Mountain Fairies. He thought of the first mountain fairy and his mate, of the bond they had shared there, and of his own bond he'd experienced with Reina—one of true, eternal love.

He knew what his mother meant. The open door in his West Mountains home was but a shadow of things to come. Though his bond with Reina was true—a real, endless bond of great love, he had experienced, now, an even greater love than the one they shared. And this one lay just past the open door of the Hereafter.

He remembered the feeling he'd had when he had touched the wavering space at the door's glimmering surface. Light had filled his frame, and love had coursed through him in the light's gentle wake. It was a love unmatched, a love unspeakable and full to bursting. It was love complete.

Ben knew now: It was the love of the Source. That love flowed through his being still, all the way to the tips of his iridescent wings.

As a gate appeared in front of them, Ben grasped Reina's hand. "Are you ready?" he whispered.

Reina smiled up at him. She was more beautiful than he had ever seen her. "I'm ready," she whispered back. "Let's go home."

With his family and Jubal looking proudly on, Ben and Reina stepped through the gate's wavering surface. Instantly, they were back home in Caelium, at the Court of Mountain Fairies. And though he had left the Hereafter, Ben knew, without any reservation—he was forever changed by the open door he had stepped through.

ABOUT THE AUTHOR

Charlemayne Reeves has been writing stories since she can remember. She comes from a family of storytellers, so it's kind of in her blood. Charlemayne is a Christian wife and mom, who enjoys telling epic tales of truth and light. She holds a master's degree from Belmont University and enjoyed a long career in healthcare prior to becoming a writer. Since, she has retreated to the hills of Tennessee with her husband, two children, and their beloved cat, Captain Meow.